I0719981

The Insufferable Mr. Fletcher

A NOVEL

LINDO FORBES

NAPART INC.

The Insufferable Mr. Fletcher

Copyright © 2023 by Lindo Forbes

All rights reserved.

No part of this publication may be reproduced, distributed, or transmitted in any form or by any means, including photocopying, recording, or other electronic or mechanical methods, without the prior written permission of the publisher except in the case of brief quotation embodied in critical articles and reviews.

The story, all names, characters, and incidents portrayed in this production are fictitious. No identification with actual persons (living or deceased), places, buildings, and products is intended or should be inferred.

EBOOK ISBN: 979-8-2231553-5-5

PAPERBACK ISBN: 978-1-7381463-0-7

Book Cover by Zandra Murray, Zandragon Designs.

First edition 2023

Also by Lindo Forbes

The Indomitable Mr. Temple – Leigh and Quincy
The Inscrutable Mr. Yang – Claudia and Ian

Contents

Dedication · IX

Chapter 1 · 1

Chapter 2 · 9

Chapter 3 · 20

Chapter 4 · 29

Chapter 5 · 41

Chapter 6 · 57

Chapter 7 · 70

Chapter 8 · 85

Chapter 9 · 101

Chapter 10 · 122

Chapter 11 · 134

Chapter 12 · 148

Chapter 13 — 156

Chapter 14 — 162

Chapter 15 — 167

Chapter 16 — 190

Chapter 17 — 202

Chapter 18 — 217

Chapter 19 — 229

Chapter 20 — 243

Chapter 21 — 260

Chapter 22 — 278

Chapter 23 — 285

Chapter 24 — 293

Chapter 25 — 302

Chapter 26 — 312

Chapter 27 — 328

Chapter 28 — 333

Chapter 29 — 345

Author's Note — 364

Junior's Bookshelf — 366

Acknowledgements — 367

About the Author — 370

To those who shake tables against injustice in all it's forms, remain ungovernable.

Chapter 1

"**I** NEED A HARD body with a firm hand and light touch to help deliver paradise. Preferably two. Three would be magical." Junior Sano burst into the construction break room on the set of *Elysian*, now shooting its fourth season in Toronto. "Any takers?"

Twenty pairs of eyes long used to her antics bounced between Junior and the head carpenter, waiting for the punchline. They'd come to expect nothing less from the 5'10, bronze-skinned, Afro-Latina stunner.

"I've involved myself in the big delivery. You're not going to make me wait for someone to come downstairs when you're right here, are you?" Junior batted her lashes in comical exaggeration. It wouldn't be the last time she acted outside her jurisdiction as the design tracker which is why no one wasted their breath pointing it out. "There's a gourmet coffee cart and pastry table being set up."

The producers had arranged for a treat to celebrate the successful car stunt. Fans of the popular science-fantasy opera had come to expect one big episode each season and this pulled all the stops. The crew had rehearsed, blocked, and storyboarded for weeks. Yesterday they filmed the hero car escaping through the side of a dilapidated building while the chase car tumbled into a fiery wreck.

Now the treats were here and Junior couldn't wait to see what bounty would be delivered.

The head carpenter nodded at some of the assembled workers, who followed Junior outside into the warm May sun. Since the warren of trailers and cube vans parked out back, this side of the studio lot was slightly less congested but no less trafficked. Crew members, delivery drivers, and couriers were in and out of this entrance all day.

Their office was located in a five-storey brick building, an abandoned warehouse retrofit for studio space, in the Port Lands. The ground floor had seven cavernous, high ceilinged rooms of various sizes that had been converted to sound stages. A freight elevator separated the row of loading bays used as lock-up storage at the back of the building. There were three floors with the same layout: long hallways with offices on either side converging on the central reception area where the production office operated.

The fourth floor was currently unoccupied and the third floor was home to one of their sister shows, currently between seasons, about a ragtag group of tween misfits getting into hijinks. *Elysian*, the show Junior worked on, was on the second floor.

Having worked in the building, on the show, for almost five years there wasn't a stairwell, alcove, or service elevator she didn't recognize. Her fellow technicians, coming and going from project to project, brought the same transient familiarity she imagined one got from summer camp. And the sheer chaos of trying to put together thirteen episodes of television never failed to excite her.

Junior flashed Leigh a familiar hand gesture as she watched her friend pull into a short-term parking space. Leigh returned the gesture with an indulgent tolerance born over fifteen years of friendship. People were always asking if they were sisters and while Junior refrained from commenting on the laziness of the assumption–being Black was their only 'resemblance'–she instead announced, to the decade-her-senior Leigh's amusement, "I'm the eldest!"

Stepping out of her car and giving her glasses a quick polish with the edge of her shirt, Leigh came around the back of her car to the trunk.

"Friends, this is Leigh Bridger, proprietress of Peach's Books and Bakeshop. And this," Junior gave a lusty sigh, slumped on Leigh for effect, and indicated the tightly packed pale pink boxes in the flipped open hatchback, "is paradise."

Leigh shook her head, likely at Junior's familiar straddling of friendly flirt and femme fatale. Extending her hand as Junior straightened, Leigh gave each person a quick shake. "Hi, nice to meet you."

Leigh stacked four boxes in each set of arms, and the final two in Junior's.

"Dios mío, these are heavy!" Junior oophed.

"Mini pound cakes. It's in the title." Leigh shut her trunk and wrestled a tote bag from the passenger seat.

Making their way through the maze of long and winding hallways to the atrium outside of Studio B, Leigh quickly spread a tablecloth from her tote on the folding table and gestured for the helpers to unburden themselves. "Thanks for your assistance! I appreciate it."

"Look at them. This isn't the first time they've provided satisfaction by the mouthful," she teased Leigh under her breath. Junior winked at the woman she knew erupted into furious blushes at the slightest provocation.

"I thought you swore off co-workers?" Leigh asked once the laborers were out of earshot. She laid out the framed business card and matching bronze serving sets from her tote.

Junior had already lifted the lid off one of the boxes and popped a pastry in her gob. Around a mostly chewed butter tart, she confirmed, "A little flirting never hurt nobody."

Built like a modern-day pin-up girl, Junior had a smile that would tempt the holy. Except for the three days a month when her reflection showed a too-wide mouth, weirdly large eyes and a paltry bosom leading to an insurmountable ass on top of thunderous thighs, she wielded her smile like a weapon.

Junior flipped the lid on another box and popped a mini cupcake straight in her face. "Will they set-up now?" Leigh asked.

"Later. The executive producer wants to give a speech first." Junior rolled her eyes and as bland and dry as ever added, "Shocking, I know. It's so unlike our intrepid leader to want to preen and glory hog."

"Throw a tarp or something on the table until you guys are ready so it's safe from prying eyes and rogue nibblers." Leigh swatted Junior's hand away from another box.

Unaffected, Junior beamed "This is going to be a hit! Thanks for delivering."

"Thanks for the business!" Leigh handed over an envelope with her invoice.

Junior sent a quick text then linked arms with Leigh and led her back to her car, gossiping the whole way.

Giving her a final squeeze, Junior watched Leigh back out of the parking lot and called out, "I'll drop your gear off on my way home tonight."

At Leigh's wave, Junior made her way back inside to her office, certain the invoices and purchase orders on her desk had mutated in her absence. What was it about a disorganized inbox that inspired people to pile more crap on top?!

"All visitors are supposed to have a pass." Davis Fletcher appeared out of nowhere. Junior's head, at constant odds with her hormones, doused the spark of attraction at the sight of the disturbingly good-looking yet profoundly annoying know-it-all.

And what a sight he was: a soft tan sweater over a white button-down shirt pushed up to his forearms with a forest green tie and beautifully fit charcoal slacks indicating he worked out enough to be fit and strong but, thankfully, not all 'roidy muscles. Junior often wondered what it would take to get him to submit to jeans and a hoodie like everyone else. Even his thick, dark hair was combed meticulously off his forehead as though it too had received the memo about the sins of casual dress.

Every time Junior spoke with Davis, she was reminded of the saying about never meeting your heroes—an expression she vehemently believed should also apply to handsome strangers in the workplace.

At the beginning of this season, she'd seen the new guy around but hadn't had a reason to get close. She'd done enough inconspicuous leering to know he was an assistant, which meant they wouldn't have much opportunity to cross paths because, though she was a part of accounting she worked primarily with production design and had no business in the executive suites. At first, Junior wasn't even sure they worked on the same show. It wouldn't have made a difference because she didn't need to know much more about him than she already did.

She'd noticed he was particularly self-contained for a workplace as boisterous and casual as a production office. His tightly leashed reserve made her wonder if he maintained control in all circumstances or if he might let his freak flag fly given the right motivation. But those were idle musings. He could have a wife and six kids or be a toxic incel nice guy—though why would God make a man that handsome if he wasn't gonna bone?—and it would all amount to the same harmless work crush. Junior liked knowing he was in the building. The threat of running into him at any time kept her lip gloss fresh.

Unfortunately for Junior, it turned out that Davis Fletcher, the New Guy, was a grade-A dipshit.

Her first exposure to his brand of all-encompassing pedantry came three weeks after she'd first laid eyes on him. He'd been sent to Production as the trusted right hand of studio head Olivia Young, with the nonsense glamour title of associate co-producer. It took exactly one meeting to ruin her perfectly constructed illusion.

"Junior!" Marin, the line producer, had been standing beside him and had called out as Junior headed toward her office. "Have you met Junior Sano, our production design tracker?"

As she'd made her way over, Junior saw the telltale twitch of his brows and took a fortifying breath. *Here we go.*

"You're Jaime Sano, Jr.?" His expression warred with his voice to most accurately convey his disbelief. "I'm sorry, I expected Jaime to be a man."

This train is never late.

Her smile had been bright and welcoming. "Yes, I am a source of much confusion. It's pronounced Jaime."

He'd looked at her blankly.

"My name? You said *JAY-me*—it's pronounced *Hi-may*, soft J like jalapeño. It's a lot, I know. You can call me Junior. Everyone does."

"Can girls even be Juniors? I mean, strictly speaking?" He'd taken her outstretched hand and shaken it limply before immediately smoothing his tie.

Junior'd caught the motion. Had he wiped off her touch? *Strike Two.*

"They can. Women, too." Her smile had dimmed. It wasn't like Junior hadn't endured some version of this very inquisition any time she introduced herself. Her father, in a profound but not unprecedented act of egomania, named her after himself despite her very much being a daughter. Her mother, delirious from thirty-six hours of complicated labor, was just happy the baby was out. Healthy, yes, but mainly out. The forms were submitted while Yesenia recovered from the aforementioned torturous labor and the rest was history.

Not that it truly mattered. Aside from the one especially torturous semester in middle school when the mouth breathers tried to make 'Hymen' happen, and the few family members who still called her 'Hammer', everyone called her Junior.

"Of course," Davis had amended. "I didn't mean—uh ... It's nice to meet you, Junior. I'm Davis Fletcher."

"Junior holds all of Design together expertly," Marin had praised. "I don't know how you manage it, Junior, I'm just glad you do."

"I see the cheques are still clearing," Junior had joked to Marin. Turning to Davis she'd said, "And you're Olivia's assistant, right? Welcome to the circus!"

"Actually, I'm more like her eyes and ears." He'd somehow managed to simultaneously sneer down his nose and avoid eye contact with her. *Strike three, Dickface.*

"Eyes and Ears. Got it," Junior had said, all attempts at warmth vanished.

After that first encounter, her initial attraction to the tall, medium-built man with dark hair, dark eyes, and cheekbones sharp enough to sculpt marble was relegated to the crawlspace of her mind. It joined hot yoga, learning Russian, and palazzo pants as things she'd attempted and quickly abandoned, never to be spoken of again.

If she'd worried that she'd drawn the wrong conclusions, seeing him in action with their colleagues had reinforced her position. He was exactly the type of man who dropped you mid-conversation if someone 'more important' crossed his eye line and had, on multiple occasions, inserted himself in a group only to steer the conversation to himself. He also unironically Actually'd anyone about any subject at all.

Life was too short to deal with that type of fuckery.

Since she didn't frequent the schmoozy executive suites dominated by the pack of Fratty HetBros that included their executive producer, Junior was blessedly spared the pleasure of Davis' direct attention. She answered the rare work-related questions he asked and otherwise gave him a wide berth.

Shaking off the memory, she smoothed her features into a serene blankness. "She isn't a visitor, Eyes and Ears, she's a vendor." Junior waved the envelope for emphasis.

"Most people don't embrace the vendors," he pressed.

"I'm not most people." Junior refused to answer the question she knew he was asking. "Besides, she brought cake. That type of contribution should be rewarded."

Davis kept pace with her to the stairwell leading up to the production office. "And that's all it took for you to lead her arm-in-arm through the stages? Snacks?" His whole body seemed to be frowning.

"Yup! Haven't you heard? I am surprisingly easy!" Without giving him a backward glance Junior hustled up the steps, leaving him alone with his stern reproval.

Chapter 2

DAVIS EXITED THE EXECUTIVE producer's office, pulled the door closed behind him, and took a moment to recalibrate. He'd expected Eli Gorman to be more malleable after the successful car stunt and yesterday's grandstanding at the elaborate pastry table but, instead, the executive producer was giving him the same old runaround. Davis closed his eyes and inhaled deeply.

"Oh, Lord. What now?" Davis opened his eyes to see the showrunner making her way toward him.

Davis exhaled. "Same as always. Eli's making me dance for his entertainment. You going in there?"

"Nope, I was looking for you."

Quinn Nelson was quick-witted, easy with a smile and, now, Davis' partner and champion in this potentially new phase of his career. She and Olivia had a close working relationship at Fifty-Four Media and, because of Davis' position as Olivia's right hand, they'd got to know each other fairly well. It didn't take long for Davis to realize the 48-year-old, auburn-haired white woman's brilliant mind worked at a higher frequency than most mere mortals.

There wasn't a story idea she couldn't improve or a plot hole she couldn't fill. At the end of the first season, when their lead actor checked into court-mandated rehab, Quinn had the sorceress separate the character's soul from his body–thereby freeing production to recast the role. Season two had their hero desperately searching for her true love whose soul was trapped in the body of the sorceress who'd doomed them in the beginning. In season three, the hero fought her attraction to the man she loved while he wore the face of her mortal enemy, creating a fan frenzy. Suddenly the intense but reliable hetero pairing became a pansexual allegory that saw the fan base double.

And now, the final episode of season four, she'd helped Davis workshop his seedling idea into a solid enough concept to launch a spin-off series. Everything rested on this episode which made Eli's current power play harder to swallow.

"We'll be starting prep on Block 7 next week. Are you ready?" Her smile held a bolstering undertone of encouragement.

"I gave Eli a budget outline weeks ago and I'm still waiting for his notes. Not to mention he hasn't given me any guidance on what I'm supposed to do in the cost report meeting for this episode. I'm not ornamental–this is my episode!" Noting Quinn's smirk, he amended, "Our episode." They'd arrived at his office and Quinn plopped herself on the couch.

"No, it's yours," She reassured him, "But you're getting worked up prematurely. First of all, this episode's costs won't reflect on you. Second, our controller and her team are–" Quinn put her fingers to her lips and made a loud kiss.

Olivia had made her intention clear. Davis was to use this opportunity to learn all the nuances of creating episodic television. "But what if it gets picked up? I'm going to have to know this stuff and I don't even know what I don't know! Eli is supposed to be showing me, but he's been dicking me around..."

"Fucking Eli." Quinn sighed. "I can show you the basics but honestly, you just have to jump into the deep end. Keeping your head above water comes with practice."

"And budgeting?"

"I'm the ideas, Fletcher. Numbers are not my bag." Quinn sat up and he saw the exact moment the lightbulb went on over her head, "But you know who can help? Junior!"

"Junior Sano?" His head swam causing him to sway in his seat a little. Davis had a chronic case of foot-in-mouth-itis when it came to Junior. No matter how hard he tried to talk to her like a normal person, he could count on one hand the number of successful interactions he'd had with the woman. "I... I don't think..." Davis couldn't even get the words out.

"She's a doll. She'll be happy to help! I'll ask her to touch base so you two can coordinate your schedules. Don't worry, Fletcher. We'll get you taken care of!" Quinn smiled and headed back to her office.

Davis stood outside in the small communal area ignominiously called The Butt Lounge, trying to order his thoughts. After Quinn's suggestion that he get help from Junior, Davis had read the same page of script for an hour before deciding to get some fresh air. On the one hand, Eli was throwing his weight around by being his classic obstructionist self. There was absolutely nothing new there. On the other hand, there was information Davis wanted and his options for getting it were limited. It was quite probable that being forced to help him would be the final nail in the 'getting close to Junior' coffin. Was it a price he was willing to pay?

As if he'd conjured her, Junior stepped through the door and the familiar spike of adrenaline flooded his system.

Davis would never forget the first time he'd seen her. She'd stood at the top of the stairs, laughing with someone he couldn't see. When she'd turned to make her way down, her laughter still echoing in the stairwell and her smile still lit on her face, he'd gasped. Davis had seen beautiful people before. You don't spend six years working at a television studio and not have your fair share of encounters with actors and celebrities. Yet Junior Sano had stolen his breath and then skipped merrily past him down the stairs.

She was no less breathtaking today than she was all those months ago. Davis still had to bolster himself to speak with her, to hope she'd stay and chat instead of subtly, yet deliberately, leaving the room whenever he approached. And now here she was, the sun burnishing her rich, warm brown skin making it seem like she glowed.

Her curly hair, usually pulled into a tight bun under a Girl Power baseball hat, was gathered haphazardly atop her head. And her rendition of the Canadian Tuxedo highlighted every dip and curve of her body. She was built to hold, every swell and rise of her a perfect handful for squeezing and gripping, for sinking into.

Davis watched as Junior wandered to the curb where the rattle of a diesel engine punctured the relative quiet of the moment.

She bowed her head slightly to a courier as he approached. "As-Salam-Alaikum."

"Wa-Alaikum-Salaam." He returned the gesture. "How lucky–the only delivery I have is for you, Junior."

While signing for a package she chatted in a mix of English and Arabic. She seemed to know a lot about him, asking after his wife and daughter. When Junior smiled her smile at the man, Davis felt its effervescence tickle his skin. He'd been favored with that smile from her exactly once. One time before she banished him from her sphere and all their subsequent interactions went to seed.

The list of things he'd buy, steal, sell, or trade to go back to that day and make it so she never stopped smiling at him was endless.

She waved goodbye while reaching into her back pocket for her phone before noticing Davis. Nodding at him, the most acknowledgement he ever got from her, she settled on the bench as her phone rang.

"No, Dad, I have not accepted Jesus Christ as my Lord and personal Savior. Mom said I don't have to!"

Davis heard her father's laughter through the phone. He watched as her eyes darted to his before she curled herself in the opposite direction and lowered her voice to quietly continue her conversation. After a few more minutes, her voice rose again as she attempted to end the call.

"Todavía estoy en el trabajo," she explained. "I'll call you back. Sí. Yes. Yes! Sí, después! Okay, ciao!"

Facing Davis, she waved her phone. "My Dad. He rambles."

"Trying to get you to mosque?"

"Huh?"

"Friday prayers?" Davis was confused by Junior's confusion.

"Uhhh? Oh! I'm Catholic. Kinda. Essentially. Though converting to Islam would only add to my grandmother's list of my failures. No, I take that back. She'd be thrilled if I participated in any religion. To her, it's all a gateway back to the Pope." Junior shook her head, seemingly biting back any additional conversation.

"Sorry–I just... I heard you with the courier and I thought..."

"Ah. I know roughly nine Arabic words. You heard me use four of them."

Davis knew that wasn't strictly true. He'd heard the ease with which she switched between languages. But he'd already stepped in it by making assumptions about her faith, desperate to engage her on any subject at all–as if he didn't know Christian Arabs exist–so he focused on not making things worse.

The common factor in their most successful interactions was Davis' trap staying shut, which is what he'd do now. Less talking equaled less problems.

He considered her again. Davis would bet all the money he had, and a lot of money he didn't, that Junior didn't know the courier outside of work. He'd wager she'd fostered the relationship a delivery at a time, an involuntary muscle brightening the man's day, without conscious effort.

"What, I can't be friendly to the man? Whose name is Yusef, by the way." Defensiveness crept into her voice.

Damnit. Too little talking with too much looking. "Not at all." He tried to appear cool and unaffected. "It's surprising."

"To watch someone make chit-chat?"

Chit chat. To her, it was a simple matter of small talk. He pushed himself off the wall, a small feeling of vindication thrumming through him. "To watch someone make a connection." She had no idea what it was like to be offered such easy acceptance as a matter of course. She had no idea how greedy he was to have hers. He moved toward the doors to return inside. "I'll see you up there."

Junior tipped her head slightly in acknowledgement without further comment. Davis figured this would be the last of their zero-sum engagements. Once she spoke with Quinn, he was certain things would get drastically worse.

***

"And then Walter told the painters the blue *he chose* was 'too cold' and asked them to 'warm it up a bit'." Junior was filling Sandrine in on the production designer's latest drama. "The man is a menace!"

"So now what?" Sandrine, the controller and Junior's direct supervisor, laughed at her dramatic retelling.

"A warm blue is basically purple so I asked him if he specified to the painters whether the color he wanted was closer to mauve or lavender. He called me a Philistine and swept out of my office," Junior shrugged. "I guess we'll see."

"There you are!" Quinn turned abruptly into Sandrine's office. "Did you get my text?"

"It was clear to me someone stole your phone, so I ignored it," Junior answered reasonably. How on Earth was she supposed to take a request like that seriously?

Quinn gave her a mockery of a smile. "Har har."

Sandrine choked on her cucumber basil water and demanded, "Donne-moi le!" Junior pulled up the text in question and placed her phone in Sandrine's outstretched hand who read in her French tinged accent, "'Can you take a look at Fletcher's budget? Eli's giving him the runaround and he's freaking out. Thanks!' Kissy face kissy face."

"The kissy faces really sell it!" Junior agreed. "Why would you subject me to surplus Fletcher? Don't I suffer enough?"

"Wait, we're still doing that?" Quinn asked Sandrine. "Surely by now, he's paid his debt to society for his egregious behavior."

"Yes, well… it was a very limp handshake," Sandrine answered drily.

Junior's two friends, who were also her supervisors, enjoyed a chuckle at her expense. They were sympathetic to her initial outrage but, due to their roles and maturity levels, were incapable of holding on to the grievance with the same fervor.

"I'm glad this amuses you." Junior glared. "Might I remind you I am the design tracker? Which means I track production design-related costs."

Marin had been encouraging, if a little skeptical when Junior started to take on more responsibility in the middle of season two. Part of it was the money that would come with her increased responsibility. Another part of it was the collapsing of three jobs into one but, in the end, it worked out perfectly. Junior knew this opportunity was rare and very specific to the environment of this show.

"What I don't do is attend production meetings or fraternize with Fletchers, yet somehow my week will be chock full of both!" Junior had known it was a bad omen that she'd run into Davis two days in a row. There wasn't enough handsome on the planet to make putting up with him worth it. "And now you want to add even more Fletcher?"

"Okay, well, I didn't know about the Walter thing when I bragged about how amazing you are and how happy you'd be to help out a friend. Sorry." Quinn apologized without a hint of remorse.

"You're the friend in this scenario?" Junior snarked.

"One of the very best."

"Hmph," Junior rolled her eyes. "Today's actions call that claim into question."

"I know you're busy, even without the Walter of it all. Fletcher doesn't need you to teach him how to budget, he wants feedback on the mock-up he's already created. You can do the whole thing without speaking to him if you want!"

Now there was an idea. *Looking* at Davis was always a delight. It was the speaking to him she could do without.

Quinn took Junior's hand in hers. "I feel for the guy. If this works, he'll have created an entire property from a throwaway line in season two. Do you know how incredible that is? And Eli's stringing him along when all he wants is to know if he's on the right track."

Junior had done her best to keep her interactions with Davis down to what was strictly necessary to do her job. A huge part of her success had everything to do with the fact their roles required very little exposure to each other. However, hearing that Eli somehow didn't want Davis to have this information... "I will do this for you, Quinn Nelson." She pulled out her phone to email Davis.

"And a little bit to stick it to Eli?" Sandrine teased.

"The unintended side-effect doesn't hurt," Junior admitted. If Davis succeeding thwarted Eli even slightly, it would be worth her increased exposure to the insufferable pedant.

"Thanks, friend." Quinn wrapped her arms around Junior's neck and placed a noisy lip smack on her cheek. "I owe you one."

Junior snapped a picture of Quinn kissing her reluctant face. "This is for when I come to collect," she threatened playfully.

"I'll be ready!" Quinn called over her shoulder as she hustled out of Sandrine's office.

Junior pinched the bridge of her nose and let out a dramatic sigh, "I cannot believe the two of you."

Sandrine, completely lacking in contrition, answered, "What was I supposed to say to the production designer? No?"

"Yes!"

"Walter made it clear that he'd rather reschedule than proceed without you. There was no arguing with him."

Junior gasped with realization. "This is revenge for saying book Kavinsky is a terrible boyfriend and Lara Jean deserved better, isn't it?"

"No." Sandrine's hazel eyes sparked petulantly. Her pout and the effortless chic of her golden bob enhanced her innate Frenchness.

"No, Lara Jean didn't deserve better? Because John Ambrose McLaren was right there!" Junior challenged.

"No, this is not about your hot takes. This could be good. If it goes forward, Davis will be promoted and there'll be an opening at Fifty-Four."

"To be Olivia's assistant?" Junior wrinkled her nose.

"Don't say it like that—"

Junior continued grumbling as though Sandrine hadn't spoken at all. "To make her coffee, follow her around with green drinks, and maintain her calendar?"

"First, Davis makes her coffee because Davis makes coffee. Have you seen him? It's like a chemistry experiment! And he follows her around with green drinks so she'll ingest something other than coffee and pinot. Neither act is a requirement of the job," Sandrine reasoned. "And second, there are worse things than being on Olivia Young's radar."

Olivia Young was founder and CEO of the studio, Fifty-Four Media—a highbrow play on 'LIV'. She started as a segment producer for the local affiliate TV station before branching out to lifestyle shows, then children's programming, and now scripted television. For many people, working on a Fifty-Four Media production was a badge of honor.

"I would love to consider the benefits of your thoughtful suggestion, but I'm going to be too busy with meetings all week." She pouted, checking her phone. "Which means increased exposure to Fletcher's Actually-ing. I want you to know it might be my undoing."

"You're being melodramatic." When the accusation left Junior unmoved, Sandrine added, "I know Davis is...intense."

"Overbearing," Junior corrected.

"Focused," Sandrine amended. "But he knows his shit and has Olivia's ear. Play nice."

"Me?" Junior reared with her hand on her chest. "I always play nice. If I put a letter opener through his trachea, it'll be on you."

Junior's threats had been known to border on criminal conspiracy and only got wilder the more worked up she became.

"Please do not put your letter opener in any part of anybody." Sandrine returned to her seat and shooed Junior away with a gentle flick of her wrist.

"Killjoy." Junior stuck out her tongue and flounced from the room.

Chapter 3

JUNIOR SPENT THE FOLLOWING three days moving things around to accommodate her new role as Walter Buchanan's human calculator. Despite the inconvenience, she was flattered her impact was so appreciated. Junior worked hard at what she did and though she understood, fundamentally, every single member of the crew was replaceable, it felt good to think maybe her loss might be felt a little more than others.

Junior collapsed onto one of the oversized, plush velvet armchairs in AJ's office. AJ was multitasking with her usual aplomb and held a finger up to let Junior know she'd be done soon enough. There were issues with cast travel and equipment, and AJ was using the office phone to deal with one while she remained on hold on her cell phone for the other—which was a fairly typical occurrence for the production coordinator.

She hung up the office phone with a "Blergh!" letting the frustrated noise whoosh out of her body.

"What time did you start today? Wanna go for a drink later?" Junior leaned over to offer AJ her bag of Starburst.

"Yes! Does 8:30 work?" AJ poked around, plucking out all the yellow candies.

"It does!"

She and AJ had started in the film industry at the same time but didn't meet until they both worked on a kid's game show seven years ago. They'd been inseparable ever since.

"What are we drinking to?"

"Me? Not doing murders despite my increased Dickface exposure."

"I like it." AJ nodded. "Noella dumped all this shit in my inbox because she forgot she needed insurance certificates for the location tomorrow, fake smiling her apology while reminding me she needs them within the hour. I will also be drinking to not doing murders."

"Ugh. I can't stand her." Junior's lip curled. The location manager, a yoga blonde who only pretended to downplay her family's wealth, brought a spectacular level of entitlement everywhere she went.

"What do you think of these?" AJ pointed at a pair of rose gold Adidas with a glitter toe cap on her monitor.

Junior got up to lean over AJ's desk. "You hated the last pair of Adidas you got. You said they were so uncomfortable you'd rather walk barefoot through a gas station toilet than wear them again."

"Okay, but what do you think? Cute, right?"

"Definitely," Junior agreed. They both froze when the hold music from her cell phone paused, but it was only so a different Muzak playlist could start. "How long have you been on hold?"

"Almost two hours."

"Seriously?"

She nodded with a closed-lipped smile that let Junior know exactly how annoyed she was about it. AJ stood up from her chair and raised her desk to the standing position, which made Junior laugh because AJ was 5'5" straight from the chiropractor. All other times, she was a robust 5'4". With thick, dark lashes framing her chocolate brown eyes and a light dusting of freckles, AJ was the picture of sweetness and light. The middle child of Trinidadian immigrants of Chinese and Indian descent, Adrienne Ramcharan had an unwavering love for all things sparkly and a possible gambling problem. Though if you asked her, she'd point out Serena Williams didn't have a tennis problem nor did Sandra Oh have an awesomeness problem and continue making her preposterous bets.

"Did you see? Your grandmother is a meme again!" AJ laughed delightedly. "Was there some sort of awards show retrospective or something?"

Junior's maternal grandmother, Paolina Garza, was a renowned Latin American beauty queen turned actor. She had small but memorable parts in many films, but her most notable role was as the femme fatale in the wildly popular telenovela, *Corazón de Vidrio.*

Every couple of months, her grandmother was meme'd strutting out of a room or slamming a door or arching her brow deviously. It didn't bother Junior–her grandmother had died long before she was born–but she tried her best to keep it from her mother who wouldn't understand.

"Too bad her estate doesn't get paid every time someone plays a video of her on social media. I'd never have to work again!" Junior laughed.

"You don't have to work now," AJ challenged. She was one of the few people at the office who knew the truth. People usually got so weird about money, especially when it was tied to a modicum of fame, that Junior preferred to keep the details to herself as much as possible.

"I do!"

"Yeah, right." AJ narrowed her eyes. While writing up a purchase order, she changed the subject. "Do you know what Kelly said to me last night?"

"Unless it was something along the lines of 'I've mastered the art of breathing through my eyeballs so go ahead and get comfortable here on my face,' I don't want to know." Junior sniffed dismissively as she always did when the conversation arrived at AJ's wet blanket of a boyfriend.

For a person covered neck to ankle in tattoos, he was the boringest human Junior had ever met. AJ so rarely dated men, less often than Junior dated women, that Junior was convinced she simply didn't know any better. She'd made AJ assure her on multiple occasions that he was at least good at routinely curling her toes because she honestly couldn't understand the allure otherwise.

"That's what guys mean, right? Sit *on* their face and not hover?"

"Yes? The fact you don't know that is reason enough to ditch the dead weight," Junior insisted.

Ignoring her friend, AJ continued, "He said we should start eating for fuel only. What do I do with that?"

"Was the bong bubbling at the time?"

"I wish." AJ rolled her eyes and popped another Starburst in her mouth.

"He's already so boring and now you can't even enjoy your food? How can you stand it? Please tell me he's a good kisser. I can forgive a lot for a great kiss."

"You are such a sucker for that grade school action," AJ teased.

"I really am!" Junior acknowledged. "Remember Ashley? Talk about a gold-star kisser."

"The one you broke up with because they wanted to book a trip to Marseille?"

"Six months out! Who does that?" Junior screwed up her face as she sank further into the armchair. "They said it shouldn't be such a problem to 'plan for the future'. I couldn't listen to them complain anymore."

"At least they hadn't spent any money. Unlike poor Bianca," AJ commiserated.

"That woman had no one to blame but herself. And besides, I reimbursed all her costs." Junior and Bianca had met in Florianopolis, both looking for the distraction of Mardi Gras without the chaos of Rio de Janeiro or São Paolo. Junior had extended her stay twice, for a total of four extra weeks. Bianca, reading more into the flight changes than intended, surprised Junior with her own ticket to Toronto at the end of their month together. Few conversations in Junior's life had been more awkward. "What I'm saying is, with the right kiss, I'm sure I could be convinced to only eat for fuel. Something tells me Kelly lacks the range."

"He's not as bad as all that," AJ assured her.

"For your sake, I hope you're right."

A voice rang over the intercom announcing the start of the concept meeting in ten minutes.

"Ugh. I gotta go. Wish me luck."

"There'll be booze later. Keep reminding yourself of that!" AJ said on an encouraging note.

Junior had planned on getting to the boardroom early so she could choose her seat strategically. Unfortunately, the gang was already there, thwarting Junior's attempt to be inconspicuous. And, of course, the only seat available was beside Davis goddamned Fletcher.

Perfect.

She muttered a quick 'thanks' when Davis slid his chair over to give Junior more space and did her best to pay him no further attention.

The first AD, after making sure all the attendees were present, began the meeting. He and Quinn went through the story and the way this episode would tie into the overall mythology of the series.

If she cared, she might wonder why Davis seemed so antsy. He was more tightly wound than usual, which was saying something. His eyes kept darting her way and every time he shifted in his seat, Junior caught the faint scent of baby powder. Weird. She would have pegged him as a 'gun metal' or 'jaguar semen' type. Another shift in his seat knocked their knees together.

Was he always this skittish? Thank God she'd taken Quinn's advice to work on his budget electronically.

Being this close to Davis was distracting. He constantly traced his lips with his thumb and let his tongue find it as it rested on the corner of his mouth, sometimes grazing his teeth along the joint—it was all she could to keep from imagining how it would feel on the inside of her wrist, on her hip, on her jaw.

Finally losing her patience with his restrained fidgeting, she turned her bag of Starburst toward him in silent offering, hoping he'd settle down if his mouth had something to do. Hoping it would curb her inappropriate thoughts of offering her body as something his mouth could do.

Whether it was in response to being offered candy or being caught zoning out, Davis' horrified head shake helped extinguish her sudden awareness of his lips and hands and tongue. Junior returned to her notes, not needing or wanting the knowledge of his possible oral fixation, while she prayed with the zeal of a fanatic that none of those thoughts could be read on her face.

Davis cleared his throat and proceeded to lead the meeting. His normally pinched voice was smooth and inviting, and his rigid posture loosened slightly. The whole thing startled Junior since, usually, they both quietly observed during the concept meetings.

"The important thing to remember is that this is an adjacent story, not a prequel or an origin tale. This is an ancient order which has tipped the scales throughout history. Our sorceress is one of their number, but we don't know where she lands in the hierarchy, as it were. We're getting a look at the true players of this game," Davis explained.

"We're going for timeless markers of power. The clothes and jewelry should be decadent but not gaudy. The aesthetic is aloof refinement," Quinn added.

"While we're using this episode as a possible springboard to another series, it is still very much part of our larger story. All we're doing is zooming out a little. We're not suddenly making *The Golden Girls*, as fun as that might be." Getting the tittering of laughter he'd clearly been after further lowered his shoulders from their place at his ears. This moment must have been the source of his nerves. He'd stressed for nothing as far as Junior could tell.

Quinn closed out the meeting with a reminder about what they were aiming for with this episode. As Junior gathered her things, Davis leaned into her space to ask, "Were you able to follow that?"

"Pardon?"

"The finale. Do you understand what's supposed to happen?" He clarified.

Knowing she could be called to speak to Walter's grand ambitions at any moment, Junior had read this script more carefully than usual. She knew the episode forward and backward. Davis needn't worry his pretty little blockhead about her. "This is your first *Elysian* finale, Eyes and Ears, not mine. Rest assured; I know what's happening."

Leaving him and his confused eyebrows in their seat, Junior escaped the boardroom with the rest of the crew.

"Junior, lass," the production designer caught up to her in the hallway, "I need you in the props meeting later today. The Twins will need more leeway for this episode."

"Walter, we have a perfectly good thing going," Junior reminded him in front of her office door. "I go to the concept meetings, and then all the other meetings happen without me. I receive everyone's broad strokes of what it will cost and–ta-da!–I finesse a workable budget for you to completely ignore."

"I dinnae!" The objection burst out of him.

She had no idea how many times they'd had a version of this conversation but she'd wager it was closer to a hundred than not. "You do. Every episode."

"Bah!" he dismissed the scold. "You have to sit through the meetings with me and come on survey–"

"Survey?" Junior blurted. Being trapped on a bus with the various department heads as they traveled from location to location was an absolute deal breaker.

"Come on survey," Walter continued, "because I need you to work your magic in real-time. A lot is riding on this." He gave her his winningest smile and pushed her door open.

Stepping into her office, Junior turned on him. "For the millionth time, Walter, I don't work for you!"

"If there were any justice," he muttered. Walter believed anything that made him look good was a tool in his arsenal, available at his disposal. And Junior always, always made Walter look good.

"You impossible man!" She searched the ceiling for patience.

Walter's reputation for extravagant sets and crushing attention to detail was well known. Also well-known were the raging clashes he routinely got into when anyone attempted to stifle his creative visions. Somehow, he worked surprisingly well with Junior, considering they were both hot-headed and prone to dramatic outbursts.

The difference was Junior's ability to speak to Walter's ego without losing sight of the objective. She got Walter what he wanted without ever loosening the reins. Junior was sure at least part of her continued job security was directly tied to her ability to keep Walter at peace. "What time is the props meeting?" she relented in exasperation.

"See, lass? Ye cannae deny a Highlander!" Walter crowed.

"All the brogue in the world will not get me on survey, Walter!" she called at his retreating form.

"You and Walter at it again?" AJ's second assistant Hodan teased her from the doorway.

"One day I will put my hands around his neck," Junior grumbled.

"We've got a pool on who makes the first move," Hodan joked. The young Somali woman's soft, shoulder-length curls bounced lightly around her brown, heart-shaped face.

"You don't!" Junior gasped, aghast.

"We don't," Hodan said unconvincingly as she dropped a small stack of paperwork in Junior's inbox, "But if we *did*, the current book is three-to-one."

Junior rolled her eyes and huffed "AJ!" as Hodan giggled her way down the hall.

Chapter 4

ON HIS WAY TO the boardroom for the props meeting, Davis noticed Junior in a serious discussion with the head carpenter, Remington, the set decorator, and the rigging best boy, Ali, in the main production office. Remington and Ali were part of Junior's inner circle. He'd seen them goofing around and bantering playfully all over the building so often that the serious conferring made Davis double-take.

"What do you mean the set dressers have to install a carpet on Saturday? I know for a fact that stage has a painted floor." Junior's voice carried across the room as she looked between the three men for an answer.

"Walter saw an area rug somewhere last weekend and had to have it. The only day available for install is Saturday," Remington explained, "But us carps are scheduled in there to get ahead of the painters."

"And we're in there with the new grid. I'm not interested in any noise about the fancy floor." Ali added.

Davis watched as Junior rubbed her temples. "How big is the rug?" She looked upward, probably doing some quick calculations based on their answers, and sighed heavily. "What you're telling me is, with the furniture, lights, and equipment, the work on the painted floor was for nothing."

Ali put his hands up to block further questioning. "What I'm telling you is we're going to be in there rigging so everyone best have a hardhat."

They continued back and forth, listing the conflicts with Junior seeming to keep track of it all in her head. The amount of information she could recall, the math she could do on the spot, was staggering. He could watch her work all day. He'd love nothing more than to massage her neck and bring her refreshments and smooth the furrow between her brows.

"What did Walter do now?" Jamal Denton sidled up to Davis, startling him out of his reverie.

"Do?" Davis bumped the assistant props master's fist in greeting. He quite liked the merry mischief-maker. They'd always got along and lately Jamal had been making more of an effort to include him in extra-curricular gatherings, though Davis tried not to read too much into the gesture.

"That is Junior's homicide face," he laughed. "And since Remy's over there, Walter is most definitely the cause."

Davis didn't realize that look specifically signaled homicidal thoughts. He'd seen her wrangle it into neutrality before speaking to him once or twice. She'd given him a version of it this morning when he'd asked her to gauge his performance at the concept meeting. Unfortunately, his tone and eye contact gave his words unintended meaning and he'd, once again, botched an encounter with Junior. "Actually, the unlawful taking of human life makes it murder face, not homicide face."

Jamal grinned as he and Davis entered the boardroom, "That's between Junior and Walter."

The props meeting began once Junior joined them from her parley in the bullpen. "Sorry!" She hustled into the boardroom, giving Walter a speaking glance, as she took a seat.

Imani and Jamal, collectively known as The Twins, were Nova Scotian first cousins born fifteen days apart. They had matching honey-brown complexions, stocky builds, and amber eyes. Their organic yin and yang personalities shone through in their work, making them one of the best props departments in Toronto.

Imani asked specific, pointed questions about the size and scope of things: is it a functional walking stick or a stylish affectation? Will the keys unlock things other than doors? Does the pendant hold anything or is it just a looking glass? Are the goblets ceremonial or simply ancient?

Davis always assumed the more subdued and serious-minded Imani was the driving force behind their success since Jamal was a notorious class clown. Sure, he was a hard worker and extremely personable but Davis hadn't experienced the other skills Jamal brought to the table.

He asked big, abstract questions about story and continuity: do the Mothers move in and out of time or through it linearly? Have they always had power or did they seize it at some point? Do they interact with the world outside? Is the castle their only residence? Davis furiously scribbled notes while Jamal asked his questions.

Davis spoke to what he could and deferred to Quinn when he couldn't. Walter used a shorthand with The Twins borne of many successful seasons together while Junior translated his words into practicalities. They made it through some follow-up questions and when The Twins were satisfied, they stood up.

Jamal said, "Aight, cool."

Imani said, "Thanks!" They nodded and left.

A shell-shocked Davis turned to Quinn and said, "Wow."

"I know." She smiled. "Wait until you see what they come back with. It will blow your mind."

"Without fail," Walter agreed, answering his phone.

"I have the final notes on your budget," Junior said to Davis while glaring at Walter.

It took Davis a moment to realize she'd spoken to him. "Pardon? Oh! Great, thanks."

"Do you mind coming to my office to get it?" Junior kept her eyes on Walter, "I need to deal with him before he disappears."

Sometime last season, Walter had insisted that Junior's desk be moved from the accounting department to an office across from his. Davis thought maybe, based on the scorn she was currently levelling at him, the move was a miscalculation on Walter's part.

"Sure. No problem." Davis made a calculation of his own. If she was busy being annoyed with Walter, maybe she'd be too distracted to get annoyed by him. "Is now good?"

"Yeah." She nodded, gathering her things.

As they walked to her office, Davis rehashed the email she'd sent him last Friday: *Quinn mentioned you wanted some feedback. Send me your budget and I'll take a look. jr*. Sixteen perfectly professional words that Davis combed through, randomly placing emphasis in an attempt to infer hidden meaning.

The subsequent emails were no help as they were equally brief. Whether she was sending spreadsheets for staffing or equipment, providing helpful questions to focus his planning, or pointing out his blind spots, Junior's messages were quick and concise. It was the most successful continuous interaction he'd had with her and he'd only had to relinquish speaking directly to her to achieve it.

Now he sat in her office trying to seem calm while tension knotted his guts. What was the right tone to strike here? Appreciative, obviously. Could he swing casual? Probably not. If only he knew how Quinn had obtained Junior's help. Did she have to force her? Did Junior resent having to help him? He didn't realize Quinn and Junior were friends. How much had Quinn told her? How much had she told Quinn?

He looked at the super-sized calendar taking up the entirety of the back and side wall. The color-coded notes indicated everything from episode number to shooting location. The highly intricate system told her, at a glance, exactly what was scheduled for the various departments under production design.

In fact, aside from the three Funko Pop figurines, a City of Scarborough banner, and a poster of a Canadian flag emerging from a Panamanian flag behind her, her office was surprisingly bereft of personal touches. There was nothing to distract her from the information she needed to do her job.

"I, uh… thanks for your help with this, Junior. I know how busy you are. I really appreciate it."

There. Simple and to the point.

"Uh-huh."

What did *that* mean? "I…"

"Gimme a sec," she placed a document embellished with colorful tags and sticky notes on the desk in front of him, "I'll be right back."

Up and out of her office before Davis could respond, Junior stalked over to Walter.

"Walter," Junior's tone was deceptively polite. "Do I seem like a woman who enjoys games?" Before Walter could answer, she continued, "Because you seem to believe we are playing a game. I told my boss, Sandrine, the *controller*, all the costs for that set were in because you assured me all the costs for that set were in!"

Davis was in awe of her audacity.

"Ah, the carpet." Walter clued into his transgression.

"Yes, Walter, the carpet. The carpet for which I have no purchase order. The carpet you've bought to cover the floor with a custom hand-painted design!"

"I know what I said, lass, and I'm sorry for it."

"You're 'sorry for it'? Why do I bother monitoring what goes on in this department? I could've sat outside reading about the dashing sea captain and the reclusive genius racing to complete the first worldwide telegraphic network in 1870s China and it would've made the same difference!" Junior's foot stomp straddled whiny petulance and ballsy insolence.

They were all flailing limbs and broad gestures and heated arguing. Davis was flabbergasted. No one spoke to the production designer that way. No one. Her role was clerical—she wielded no authority over production design and was owed no explanations over the decisions made therein.

In all the talk about their clashes, Davis assumed Junior bravely held her own during Walter's infamous rages. Having never witnessed one in person, Davis hadn't imagined her brazenly storming up to the man and berating him! This was Junior's third season as design tracker. How had this gone on so long?

The sound of Walter's booming laugh snapped Davis back to attention. The man's eyes shone with the satisfaction of meeting a respected rival on the battlefield. Whatever part of the argument Davis missed, Walter was eating it up. "I promise, lass, it's truly finished now."

Junior tilted her face away with a huff.

"Oh, now." Walter put himself in her sightline, "Come see for yourself. It's a beauty!"

Her scolding demeanor vanished, "I can't now but I'll stop by later and take a look."

Davis couldn't figure out their dynamic at all.

"Aye, then you'll be wanting to know where I found it and how you can get yer hands on one!" he teased her retreating form.

"Being born at the top of a country is not a personality, Walter!" she shot over her shoulder as she returned to her office. She grumbled to herself, "If I have to hear about the Highland way one more time."

Davis chuckled. "Northerners live a hardscrabble life. It marks us."

"You're from Scotland?"

"No, Northern Ontario."

"Yeah? Quinn must love having the backup." Junior rifled through her desk drawer, "She's constantly making fun of me for being such a city kid."

"You're from here?"

"Scarborough born and bred." Junior looked past him to the office window to get her bearings. Thumbing eastward she said, "I grew up six subway stops and a bus ride that way.

Davis hesitated for a moment, unsure how far to continue the banter. "Quinn's from Levack. That's practically the equator compared to where I'm from. I grew up in a small town outside of Red Lake in the Kenora region."

He had her attention now. "Really? The furthest north I've been is Thunder Bay."

He grinned his approval. "I went to university in Thunder Bay. My hometown's about a seven-hour drive north from there."

"Seriously?"

"Yup." Davis always enjoyed imparting this bit of trivia, "Fun fact: if you drove the same distance from Red Lake to Toronto going south, you'd end up close to Orlando, Florida."

Junior's dropped jaw was the perfect reaction. "Okay. You can have 'being born at the top of a country' as a personality. Walter cannot."

Davis laughed at her declaration. "I promise not to lord it over him."

"You should. He needs humbling." She rolled her eyes. "Walter made one of the writers cry in Block 2 because he told Walter 'urn' wasn't interchangeable with 'vase' in the script. You seem to be the only one capable of any humbling."

"A) I'm sure other people do. Marin must, for example. I'm just the only one who's so loud about it and 2) you'll notice I didn't tell him he couldn't have the area rug, only that he messed with my numbers."

Davis conceded the point. "So now what?"

"Now nothing," Junior shrugged. "I sorted the conflict with the riggers and the dressers, accounted for the cost, and since the fancy rug's price tag doesn't tip him outside the budget I padded for this very reason, we're good."

She was a puzzle he'd never have enough pieces to solve. Speaking to her was always like this—her answers we so unexpected, so intriguing, each one spawned five more questions.

He had to tread carefully. "Isn't 'sorting conflict' outside of your purview?"

"It is," she agreed, "but no one likes the art director so they come to me because I'm good at problem-solving and like telling people what to do."

Davis had grossly underestimated Junior's influence over production design. "So, all of that with Walter was for show?"

"No." She frowned. "Walter needs to be told when he's crossed a line. My work—*my time*—has value and I won't allow him to disregard it unchallenged."

Davis nodded his understanding.

"Besides," Junior continued with a cheeky wink, "Walter likes a bit of roughhousing."

He had no idea what to say in response to that. Work. *Bring it back to work*, he reminded himself. Davis raised the annotated budget. "Thanks again for all your help."

"I hardly did anything. It was in pretty good shape when I got it."

"Yeah? That's reassuring." He allowed himself a moment to bask in the praise.

"Oh, let me show you one quick end around." She gestured for him to stand beside her and look at her monitor. "Think of it as a failsafe."

Junior proceeded to explain how this particular spreadsheet was best used to flag redundancies. This close to her, Davis was taken with the steady, rhythmic throb of her pulse on the elegant line of her neck and the teeny freckle beside the dainty diamond earring she wore. The bubblegum on her breath clashed with the sweet-but-smoky fragrance of her skin. Or was it her hair?

Davis was listening to her, he was. But a considerable amount of his concentration was required to keep himself from running his nose along her jaw to investigate the source of her scent.

"Do you have any questions?"

"I, um…" Davis hesitated. He made fool enough of himself without the added pressure of having Junior watch him read. Straightening, he returned to safety on the other side of her desk. "If it's alright with you, I'll look at it later and follow up if I have any questions?"

"Whatever works," she nodded.

He made his way back to his office where he had a scant half-hour to relish this interaction with Junior before regaining his composure for the next meeting.

***

The rest of the week played out similarly with Quinn and Davis working together to guide the vision of the episode. Blessedly, Junior did not have to attend any of the technical meetings or anything to do with effects, so she was able to retreat to her office and stay on top of her work in the snatched moments leading up to the production meeting.

It was, by design, a way more tedious affair–a page by page, line by line reading of the script that was open for every person's input. And somehow, between Davis and the first AD, the meeting stayed loose and upbeat instead of the slog Junior always understood it to be.

She took this opportunity to observe her surroundings. Junior was struck, again, by Davis' ability to lead. He was confident, open to ideas, and very well prepared. He held the room with an assertiveness that still allowed for debate. What she had always taken as nitpicking was, in reality, deep attention to detail. His constant repetition seemed more like an attempt at providing clarity and intention not, as she'd perceived it, condescension.

Yes, she still found him exacting and overbearing. But in the context of work? It was interesting to watch the things Davis noticed.

As the meeting wrapped up, she looked around the boardroom and wondered why this determined Davis hadn't stuffed the other irritating Davis in a locker. Perhaps he was participating in a study to discern the exact amount of annoying required to outweigh overall hotness. She supposed society's loss would be science's gain.

They were going to camera on the season's final episode on Monday and Junior made it through prep unscathed.

May wonders never cease.

"Hey, Junior?" Davis maneuvered his way through the departing bodies.

Maybe she spoke too soon. Though she had to admit, his approach didn't faze her–she felt fairly inoculated against Davis' general...Davis-ness. "What's up?"

"I, uh... I meant to ask before–what you said to Walter about creating a telegraph network in 1870s China... Is that a real book?"

"It is."

"I think I'd enjoy something like that. Maybe, when you're finished, you can let me know what you think and I could check it out?" The words spilled out of him.

"It was very satisfying. I've moved on to a hard-as-nails bounty hunter and the gorgeous spitfire he rescues from a vigilante mob in 1884 Wyoming," she explained dramatically. "Do you read romance? Because the telegraph book you're asking about is a historical romance novel."

"Historical romance." He sounded out the seemingly foreign words. "That's what you read?"

"Mostly."

Davis tilted his head in contemplation. "What makes it historical? Would, say, the 1980s be considered historical?"

"That's what you took from what I said?"

"My sister is obsessed with a present-day series about reluctant and runaway royals. Since you specified historical romance, it made me wonder about the distinction."

Junior gave it a bit of thought before answering, "I level out somewhere after the steam age but before the automobile. The emphasis on etiquette and firm rules for interactions between the sexes and classes really amps up the longing and yearning. I'm a fool for that stuff." The warm, open expression on her face slammed shut at the sound Davis made. He could try to deny it but Junior heard the snort of disbelief that triggered his current coughing fit.

What would he know about wishing against all logic and reason for circumstances to be different? He couldn't imagine desperately rattling against the cage of society's limitations. Davis could mock all he wanted, she wouldn't let him diminish the joy she found in those stories. "Anyway, we're done here, right?"

It wasn't a question.

Junior left the boardroom without waiting for Davis to get his breathing back under control.

Chapter 5

"THAT WOMAN WAS FLIRTING with you."

"Who was?" Davis looked into a pair of pitying eyes. He was at Betty's with Jamal and Remington, enjoying the rare early finish on a Friday. With the final episode starting on Monday, everyone was in a celebratory mood.

"For real?" Jamal answered in disbelief.

"Here we go," Remington sighed.

Davis shrugged. "For real, what? She was just being friendly."

"Stop. Stop, stop, stop!" Jamal held up his hand. "When I said 'come link up with the mandem for a beer' you should've disclosed your lack of game."

Davis was still trying to find the balance between professional and personal. He'd never been great at toeing that line and hoped he was reading this properly. This invite definitely seemed personal which is why he'd agreed to join them. He took Jamal's mockery as confirmation.

"It's not that I lack game, whatever that is–" Davis started.

"Whatever that is?" Jamal choked on his water.

"You don't know he has no game," Remington said, giving Jamal's back a firm slap. "What we witnessed was a lack of awareness."

"We're unwinding over a couple of beers. I don't need 'awareness'."

Remington took in the way Jamal's hand clutched his chest, his face twisted in horror, and chided Davis, "You're not helping."

"I suppose you have 'game'?" Davis' voice was a mix of incredulity and mild annoyance.

"I'm a 35-year-old, six-foot Filipino with a job, a house, and a full head of hair. I don't even need all the game I got. I'm on every Lola's radar from here to Sacramento." Remington Shaw, the embodiment of the lyric 'I'm a lover, not a fighter, but I'll crack your teeth', preened.

Davis gave an amused shake of his head. "Duly noted."

"Evenin', lads!" AJ saluted as she and Hodan pulled the neighboring table over and settled in.

Davis wasn't especially surprised to see the production coordinator and her second assistant here. Betty's was a favorite among industry folks. It was common to run into colleagues trading stories and gossip about other shows. Them sitting at this table, however...

"Did Junior bail?" Remington asked.

"She saw Ali at the bar and stopped to chat." Hodan gestured vaguely to the front door.

Davis looked over and saw them. With slowly dawning horror, Davis realized that he was out for drinks with Junior's inner circle and that she would, at some point, join them. There was very little hope of this ending well for him.

"Yo, Davis, you're a good-looking dude. Tell me you know that," Jamal demanded.

"I guess..." Davis managed.

"Oh man, that wasn't even modesty." Hodan pointed out, hanging her purse on the back of her chair. "You're going to break Jamal."

"I'm concerned about your specific interest in my physical appearance," Davis said warily.

"He's like an apex predator but for hotness," AJ explained, re-wrapping her hair in its topknot. "He immediately finds it and gravitates towards it."

"I don't think your analogy is accurate," Davis muttered.

"And for good reason. There's strength in numbers!" Jamal talked over Davis with zero shame at his shallowness.

"It's more of a simile," Remington countered Davis' assertion before asking, "Is it a choice? Like those celibate dudes chasing enlightenment?"

Jamal's gasp was sharp and pained.

"I date. I've dated," Davis defended himself. He didn't date a lot and it hadn't been recent, but his was a far cry from celibacy. His work was the priority and Davis didn't mind focusing on that.

"Then I need to know!" Jamal demanded. "She was cute and definitely interested."

AJ scanned the room. "Who?"

"Patio. Pink sundress." Remy tilted his head toward the bombshell in question.

"Maybe he's in a relationship," Hodan offered.

Davis didn't answer. He was too focused on escape. Would texting his sister to call him in ten minutes be worth answering her barrage of questions? Debatable. Assuming she even received the message in a timely fashion.

The server arrived with a tray of ice water. "Can I get you all anything to drink?"

Just like the entirety of their conversation, Davis noticed, the ordering of drinks was an overlapping, onslaught of words. Miraculously the server took it all in stride. He wasn't faring nearly as well.

"Great. I'll be right back!"

"So, because you're in a relationship," Jamal looked Davis up and down after their server left, "you don't know when a woman is hitting on you?"

"I'm not in a relationship–" Davis started.

"Do you need a wingman?" Hodan interrupted. "Jamal is an excellent wingman. AJ, too."

"Aww, thanks, babe!" AJ cuddled Hodan's arm.

"He has. No. Game." Jamal enunciated in exasperation. "You can't just be good-looking."

"It doesn't hurt," Remington reasoned.

The noise and bustle of the bar did nothing to calm his rising panic. Davis was desperate to change the subject. "This isn't necessary, man. I'm good."

"We handsome men have to stick together or the system fails," Jamal promised.

"Not this again." Hodan rolled her eyes, shooing Jamal's words away. "Being hot isn't more important than being good."

Jamal pointed an affronted finger at Hodan. "That right there is why the gene pool is compromised. We, as a society, have strayed from our biological imperative to preserve the species by procreating with superior stock."

"Actually," Davis started, leaning forward in his seat, "the biological imperative is to survive. By any means necessary."

"And how are you supposed to do that with all this weak sauce? Back in the day, women had to put up with whatever they got so long as it kept them fed and sheltered. Mean, boring, drunk, lazy, trifling," he counted on his fingers, "were all things a woman endured. A happy or even content pairing was winning the freaking lottery. But if your dude was good-looking? You had a better chance at healthy kids which made it matter a little less if he was a piece of shit on the inside. Schlubby, broke fuckers can be as mean and selfish as handsome dudes can be devoted and loyal. You're talking about partnership. I'm talking about propagating the species." Jamal brought the last of his pint to his mouth.

"Fascinating. Truly amazing how you can come up with something so simultaneously feminist and misogynist. Hat tip, sir!" AJ was delighted by his nonsense.

"It's weed logic." Remington fist-bumped AJ.

Hodan waved to get AJ's attention. "Pink Sundress!" she stage whispered and they all turned to look.

"Wow!" AJ exclaimed. "She tossed the rock his way and he fumbled?"

"It wasn't so much a fumble as an expiration of the game clock," Remington clarified. "That's what set Jamal off in the first place."

"I see the problem. He clearly needs help." AJ gave Jamal an authoritative nod.

"Please stop speaking about me like I'm not here," Davis said to no one in particular. He was deeply uncomfortable with this level of scrutiny. He'd never enjoyed being the center of attention. This was agony. "I don't need help. I'm not interested in her."

"But you are interested in someone?" Hodan guessed.

Davis kept fiddling with his coaster. *Eyes down*, he scolded himself, *do not look across the bar*. This conversation was already close to unbearable. He would not be able to stand it if they pulled the truth out of him. Blessedly, the server returned with their drinks. He slumped in relief to have the focus off himself for even a moment.

"That posture doesn't lead me to believe you have any chance at bagging that hottie." AJ mused. "Why don't you show us what you're working with."

"Yeah, practice on us!" Hodan clapped giddily.

"That… isn't–can we talk about anything else, please?" Davis begged.

"Junior!" AJ waved her over, explaining to Davis, "She'll flirt with anyone."

For the love of all that was green and holy, how did this situation keep getting worse? He wasn't ready to see Junior so soon after his prodigious failure this afternoon.

A wave of overconfidence brought on by the success of working on the budget and the increased exposure they'd shared during prep for Block 7 prompted Davis to engage Junior on a subject unrelated to work. He really did want to know more about the telegraph network book. Hearing Junior say she was a fool for yearning? The irony had literally choked him. That one outburst had immediately lost him all the ground he'd gained.

"What's crackalackin', party people?" Junior and Ali arrived at the table. Davis watched Junior extinguish the flicker of curiosity at his presence as they sat. He'd put out his own at seeing Junior and Ali together.

Were the rumors about them true?

"S'up?" Ali nodded to the group at large in greeting, resting his arm on the back of Junior's chair.

"Hotspark," AJ returned his nod, "what's your stance on game vs no game when pulling tail?"

"I don't need it." He smoldered tauntingly at AJ. "I'm exotic."

Davis had always been fascinated by men like Ali, men whose appeal was powered by more than good looks. The ease with which they moved through the world was of particular interest to Davis. What would it be like to know exactly what to say to get a woman to stay and talk? To know precisely the right compliment to make her smile?

Not just any woman, he admitted, but the one studiously ignoring him right now.

"Well, Fletcher here has an appalling lack of game and isn't 'exotically Egyptian' so Junior do your flirty thing so he can practice," AJ ordered.

"And get written up for harassing the Boss' eyes and ears?" Junior asked. "Hard pass."

Davis cringed a little recalling how she'd come to that particular moniker. She wasn't wrong to be concerned. Even though Davis was an assistant, he happened to be *the* assistant and with the title of producer, no matter how frivolous Junior might find it, it made him senior to all of them.

"He's not gonna narc," Jamal assured Junior before turning to Davis, "You're not gonna narc."

"You have to tell us or its entrapment!" Hodan exclaimed.

"Oh, Cookie, a little less SVU, okay?" Junior tsked.

"Blasphemy! We need more Benson in our lives, not less," Hodan cried.

"You've been giving off a real Stabler vibe lately," AJ pointed out.

"Really?" Hodan gushed. "Thanks!"

"If you saw the smoke show he let slip, you'd feel compelled to help," AJ promised Junior.

"Maybe he's in his flop era," Junior argued. "Did you consider that?"

"Again. Right here." Davis pointed to himself, immediately regretting it.

"Yes, you are! Which is why you should go talk to her." Jamal nudged him. "Unless… you're trying to start something with your lady?"

"I don't…she's not my lady," Davis stammered.

"Okay, so let us help you," Jamal pressed.

"I thought he was game-less and therefore beyond help." Junior sipped her drink. Davis was spellbound by the path the tip of her tongue made as it caught the stray droplet of liquid on her lip.

"He might not have game but he has goals. I can work with that. Hodan's right. What you need is a wingman," Jamal decided. "Give us the rundown."

"I'd rather not." Davis tried and failed to shut down this line of questioning.

"Is she beautiful? I bet she's beautiful," Hodan asked.

"She'd have to be," AJ countered.

"Maybe. Maybe not. The attraction could be on a deeper level," Hodan argued with proverbial hearts in her eyes.

Davis was starting to feel untethered. Junior wasn't just beautiful—she was temptation and desire and he wanted his hands full of her more than was wise. Her boisterous laugh was a siren song. She had a kind word and an easy grace with almost everyone—whether guiding a lost elderly woman through basecamp or supporting a co-worker's extra-curricular projects or her easy connection with vendors, Junior had a way of making people feel welcomed. She was also a fierce opponent in possession of a razor-sharp intellect.

Was the attraction on a deeper level? He thought about how small Junior sometimes looked when she thought no one was watching, about how he wanted to hold her close and keep her monsters at bay.

Davis wasn't attracted to Junior. He was consumed by her.

"None of it matters. I don't even know if she's seeing someone." Davis tried to find a way out of this, to stop his palms from sweating.

"All you gotta do is ask. Watch." Jamal looked to the other side of the table, "Junior, you got a man?"

"I'm all the man I need." She winked back cockily.

"See?" Jamal smiled at Davis. "Easy."

"I can't do that." Davis confessed, thinking about all his failed attempts at conversation with Junior.

Besides, if she was single what was happening with Ali? There was something undeniable there. It was rare to see them together without one or the other leaning in close. Even now, Ali's thumb drew idly on Junior's shoulder. It seemed so organic; it was entirely possible neither of them even noticed it was happening.

"Because you have no game," Jamal said each word slowly like he was talking to a child.

"Speaking of all the man a body could need, guess who got traded to Memphis on a two-way contract with the G League?" AJ's eyebrows danced suggestively at Junior.

"I still can't believe you spent a year with a pro baller and my seats at the ACC didn't improve one bit." Remington shook his head, disappointed.

"I'm sorry Remy, I was preoccupied." Junior's whole body melted into Ali's side, "How do you explain a man being that fine other than proof of the gods' loving benevolence?" Her eyes fluttered as a visible shiver moved through her. "The women of Memphis are in for an awakening."

"He was doing a pap stroll with Avery Malone recently." Hodan commented while scrolling on her phone. "Think they bonded over being your exes?"

AJ snorted.

"Probably not," Junior hummed in exaggerated contemplation. "But it wouldn't be the first time. For either of them."

Ali rolled his eyes at Junior's dramatics while AJ and Hodan cackled, snapping their fingers over their heads.

Davis, however, was trying to stop the pressure building behind his eyes. She'd dated an NBA player for a *year*? And ballet's

Bad Girl–the most famously infamous dancer of her generation? Was that in addition to Ali?

There was no metric by which a professional athlete wasn't intimidating. Even a bench warmer or company dancer would be at the peak of human physicality. Add in a man like Ali, a man Davis didn't mind admitting looked like he knew exactly what his dick could do? If those were the type of people she got involved with how would Davis ever stand a chance?

"Junior, if you're still talking to him, you should mention my seats," Remington pointed out.

She waved her phone, "I'll text him right now!"

"Oh! Do you have her number? You should text her and invite her out," Hodan suggested, bringing the topic back to Davis and his lady love. "Then you could let your wingman hook you up."

"Uh..." Davis disliked where this was going.

"Jamal, tell him how helpful the right wingman can be," Hodan insisted.

"Yeah, Jamal, enlighten us," Junior snarked.

Jamal balked. "Quit being a hater, Junior. I'm acting according the rules of the system."

"Don't listen to this madman!" Junior countered. "If you like this person, just...tell them."

"It's not that simple." Davis' face scrunched in concentration. The thought of telling Junior how he felt made him queasy.

"Isn't it?" Junior raised an eyebrow.

Did he say he wanted Junior's attention? Idiot. She was waiting for his reply and Davis' tongue had tied under the weight of her expectation.

Remy laughed, "That's low-key hilarious coming from you."

Davis was missing something but the conversation moved so quickly, it kept going without him. Everything was moving too fast!

"Flirting is an art, right? It's not simply a conversation, it's also about possibility and opportunity. That's where the wingman is so clutch: they provide a low-stakes look at the possibilities. The wingman holds the door open so you shy, awkward, game-less cases can walk in and present yourselves. You have nothing to lose because the wingman does all the work." Jamal leaned back in his seat and took a big drink of his pint.

Junior whistled, "Wow, Jamal, that was actually...insightful."

"And after that System mess," AJ added.

"Don't gas him up," Remington lamented. "I have to sit through all his philosophizing. There are way more 'Systems' than there are 'Wingmans', trust."

"Fair." AJ conceded. Turning to Davis she asked, "You ready for Flirting 101 with Junior?"

"I want to talk about literally anything else." Davis' discomfort rose as he ran his hands through his hair. He already knew how flirting with Junior would end and he'd rather drink bong water than have all these witnesses.

"Eyes and Ears only wants me for my spreadsheets." Junior winked at Ali.

Ali responded with a crooked smile so devastating that for the second time in his life, Davis gave serious consideration to his sexuality.

"I think he just popped a blood vessel," AJ joked.

"Focus! I can't have my mans here pining," Jamal ordered.

"Seriously, how did we get here?" Davis said to no one in particular, placing his elbows on the table.

"You gave Pink Sundress the Heismann," AJ reminded him helpfully.

"You guys are super into football," Davis rested his forehead on his closed fists.

"Nah, it's more about the challenge of staying on theme metaphorically," Remy explained.

"A good wingman can be anyone. The point is they aren't interested in your mark, only in getting you through the door," Jamal continued, ignoring Davis, "AJ, here? She's a beast. She's got that super potent over-proof strain of Girl Next Door energy on lock. And Junior? She's the best to ever do it. She can read a situation and adapt her whole vibe to fit. Together they are unstoppable."

AJ gave a small bow while Junior waived off Jamal's hyperbole.

"Is that what this is about, you want us to get her number for you?" Junior asked him with a small furrow between her brow.

"Not even a little bit." Davis couldn't stress enough how little he wanted that.

Junior scoffed at Jamal, "Then what's happening here, exactly?"

Ali made a sound that could qualify as a chuckle, pulled a cigarette from his case and tapped the filter on the table a couple times. He lightly tugged Junior's earlobe as he stood, "I'll be outside."

"Weren't you listening?" Jamal cried

"Honestly? Not really." Junior admitted.

Sighing with great melodrama, Jamal repeated, "Davis and his lady?"

"Right. And I'm supposed to...?"

"She's not my–" Davis was completely gratuitous to their conversation.

"Give a demonstration. Hodan, what about First Date there in the corner you've been making eyes at?" Jamal offered.

"How did I get involved?" Hodan shrank into her seat.

"Because Fletcher needs to learn how to mack and we're gonna teach him," AJ answered. "You wanna meet that too-nice-ly-dressed-for-this-venue man at the bar?" Hodan gave a non-committal nod, too shy and awkward to do anything else. "Perfect. Target acquired." AJ turned to Junior. "You're up!"

"I didn't come prepared for a demonstration." Junior indicated her plain work attire as if it somehow dampened her appeal.

"Pfft. Say less." AJ maneuvered her chair so Junior could sit closer to her while she handed Junior tubes and pots and lotions from her bag. Scanning the front of the bar, AJ assessed the targets. "Oakleys, then Vans."

"What about Dockers?" Hodan asked, leaning into AJ's sightline.

AJ's lip curled in distaste. "He's strictly vanilla. Avoid that douchebag entirely. Start with Oakleys. He for sure has an Asian Thing."

Junior snuck a peek while AJ gave directions.

AJ pointed at Junior's shirt, "Off."

Davis was entirely out of his comfort zone. He looked away as Junior peeled off her t-shirt revealing the red tank top underneath. The very last thing he needed was to have a visible reaction to Junior undressing in front of him.

"Belt." AJ held out her hand.

Junior's transformation was complete. Without her belt, her pants hung lower on her hips. The light shimmer on her skin from AJ's lotion, her peach-tinted lips, and the one missed lock of hair curling at her nape make her whole look softer, breezier. Davis wanted to reach out and feel the stray curl between his fingers.

"Look at you! Camera-ready and I didn't even have to make you Say Yes." AJ cooed in Junior's face. Junior executed the complex eye roll, shrug, head tilt combo in reply.

"'Say yes'?" Davis had never felt so out of his depth. "What's that?"

"That's their thing. After reading *Year of Yes*, they use it to try to keep each other from stagnating," Hodan was happy to explain.

Then she added, "Busy just posted a throwback on Insta from when Oprah interviewed Shonda about her book."

None of that answered Davis' question, exactly, but he realized the futility of inquiring further. He nodded, accepting that those English words strung together in that order made a complete, if incomprehensible, sentence.

"Remember Oakleys, then Vans," AJ counselled.

AJ took the spot beside Davis for a better view. She and Jamal offered a running commentary as Davis watched Junior laugh and flirt with the guys at the bar. The one wearing Oakleys said something that made Junior gasp in exaggerated affront. She then turned to the one in the Vans t-shirt and lightly touched his bicep in a tacit plea for support. Davis couldn't hear what they were saying but he could plainly see how she was working them. Junior leaned over the bar to speak to the bartender, then, catching the eye of the man Jamal called First Date, hit him with the full force of her smile, tilting her head towards Vans and Oakleys in an 'I know, right?' gesture. First Date tilted his glass in salute and she looked heavenward in reply, smiling all the while. Davis felt the tingly sensation of her smile from across the bar.

"Are we sure it's a good idea for Ali and Junior to be out in gen pop together," Hodan wondered.

"Why should it matter?" Davis' attention returned to the table.

"Junior and Ali have been on and off forever." Hodan explained, "They're basically each other's gatekeepers."

"They are?" Davis asked, trying to keep his voice conversational. He'd suspected...

"They were. Past tense," AJ clarified.

"They're endgame, don't you think?" Hodan sighed. "And I never got to experience an On. Or maybe I have. I don't know, because they never tell!"

"There's nothing to know if Junior doesn't want you to know." Remington took a long swig of his beer.

"What does that mean?" Davis wondered how much he could ask about Junior before tipping his hand.

"It means there is no one better to have in your corner in a crisis," AJ elaborated.

"But?" Davis ran his hands on his thighs, waiting for the answer.

"But Junior keeps her cards close. She might spend the weekend in the hospital recovering from fighting off a roving pack of bandits and you'd never know. Don't expect her to just let you in," Jamal explained. "Not right away."

"And you're all okay with that?" Davis frowned. It was not the answer he expected.

Hodan shrugged. "We all have our things."

"She opens up when she's ready," Remington said.

"When who's ready?" Junior asked, returning to the table.

"Junior, you sit there," AJ stage-managed.

"Wait, what was the goal here?" Davis asked. "Other than embarrassing me?"

"The goal was to show you how effective we could be as wingmen," Jamal corrected.

AJ reiterated, "Junior has to successfully get First Date over there on the line. She has to open the door for Hodan." Off Davis' dubious look, AJ extended her hand. "Would you care to make a wager?"

"Don't fall for it, man," Remington warned. "She's Asian *and* Trini. That's a combination no house would bankroll. Trust me."

Davis watched as the friends descended into more jabs and mockery. The kind of hits that can only be thrown in the truest measure of friendship.

He'd always envied these displays of easy belonging. This was the closest he'd ever got to it where he was certain the ridicule would stay playful instead of the descent into brutality he normally experienced. Davis wondered, not for the first time, if he were capable of fostering that type of connection here–if he was capable of getting close to Junior.

"Excuse me." The server brought over a drink with a skewer laid across the top of the glass garnished with every piece of fruit in the bar well. "This is for the woman in the red tank top?" She indicated the bar. They all looked in time to see First Date raise his glass.

"Gimme your keys, Hodan." Junior held her hand out below the table without looking away from the bar. "Come get these when I give the signal."

Junior dropped Hodan's keys in her bag, took the skewer, and bit a piece of fruit off of it, leaving the glass untouched.

"You're not going to drink that?" Davis asked.

"Nope." She slid the glass to Davis. "You have it, Eyes and Ears. If you've paid attention, it'll be the last one you have as a single man."

Chapter 6

"HI, BUBBE!" JUNIOR SAID from the kitchen island when Ruth Rivkin came in from outside.

The bond between Junior and Roxanne's families formed after Yesenia survived the crucible of her residency under the notoriously demanding Dr. Ezra Turner.

The five Turner kids, all a perfect mix of their mother's dark hair and father's olive complexion, were always pleasant to Junior when she was at their house, but it was the youngest, Roxanne, who made her feel special. It was Roxanne she looked forward to seeing.

Junior followed Roxanne's every commandment with the slavish devotion of a star-struck fanatic. For her part, Roxanne was fiercely protective of the nerdy kid and treated Junior like the younger sibling she never got to have. She was the one bright spot in Junior's otherwise tumultuous adolescence.

Even now, decades later, when she remembered how her lonely, miserable school days stretched out endlessly before her, Junior had been able to endure it all because she had her family and she had her best friend, Rocky.

"I saw your truck out front. Why your grandfather bought you such a monstrous vehicle, I have no idea," she fretted while hanging up her coat.

Junior drove a beast of an SUV. The custom green paint job and vanity 'JUN10R' plates on her H2 made it stand out wherever she went.

"I know! It's not even remotely fuel-efficient. And with the price of gas in this economy!" Junior added to the list of her truck's crimes as Ruth neared.

"I'm sure Noah can get you a deal on a hybrid. His father-in-law owns the dealership on Davenport," Ruth repeated for the umpteenth time.

"With a Mini, some nice burly men could pick my car up and carry me to safety if I was in trouble," Junior considered, tapping her chin, accustomed as she was to Ruth's brand of brutal love. When Ruth Rivkin loved you, she was a warm wind in your sails, pushing you forward, all while reminding you not to slouch and also 'maybe try a hot oil treatment every so often, huh?' Nagging was her sincerest form of affection.

"This is all I'm saying," Ruth said, pleased by finally being understood.

Junior dutifully pressed kisses to Ruth's proffered face. "Shabbat Shalom."

"Ma, enough already!" Roxanne complained from the living room, tidying up after her daughter Ryan. Making her way to the kitchen island, she chided Junior, "Don't encourage her."

"Is your brother coming for dinner?" Ruth asked, ignoring Roxanne's words while smoothing her thick, dark hair.

"Isaac? Probably not." She endured her mother's fussing. "I thought you were having dinner with Noah."

"I was, until I thought Isaac would be here."

Junior tossed some jujubes in her mouth. "Why'd you think that?"

"She thought Isaac would be here because Ethan, mama's boy that he is, told her he would be." Roxanne leaned across the island to reach for a jujube.

"It's a crime to love your mother?" Ruth demanded, pushing the bag of candy out of Roxanne's reach.

"How did you do it, Ma? How did you get the apron strings to stretch all the way to New York?" Roxanne wondered.

Junior tossed the bag to Roxanne. "But still, why?"

"Isaac is seeing someone," Roxanne gossiped, searching for a red one. "So, *someone* is here to ask about weddings and grandchildren."

"I'm not getting any younger. I want to know my children are happy and settled." Ruth claimed with her palms up in resignation, her attempts at curbing their candy consumption thwarted. She turned to Junior. "Which reminds me, when are you going to stop all this flitting about?"

"Wha...? How did I get involved? Let's go back to talking about Isaac, please," Junior sputtered.

"I've been blessed with five healthy children and somehow only have four grandkids. I want another baby to hold while I can still stand!" Ruth complained. "Why won't your brother give me a grandchild?"

"Because he's gay and a divorce attorney?" Roxanne offered.

"What does gay have to do with me holding a baby?" Ruth asked tartly, arms crossed on her chest.

"It has nothing to do with you holding a baby, Ma. It has everything to do with him spending his days dissolving marriages in mostly contentious ways. Doesn't lead one to race down the road to family planning," she said.

"Okay, Isaac's finally admitting he's gay? *Now* can I try to introduce him to some people?" Junior had suggested this years ago but was shot down because Isaac was still semi in the closet.

"They probably all deserve better than my miserable brother," Roxanne said, then immediately turned to assuage her mother, "as perfect as Isaac is."

"Trust me—I'll choose the right person. I happen to be a superior wingman. Last Friday I got this guy at the bar and Hodan together, no sweat," she patted herself on the back. "I vow to only use my powers for good," she added with her hand on her heart.

"See? All this out at the bar and playing games. When I was your age, I had five kids." Ruth tossed her still enviable mane of hair over her shoulder.

"You were also married. To a doctor," Junior reminded her. Crossing herself, she added, "Que Dios lo tenga en su gloria."

"So? Get married!" Ruth countered.

"Pfft. I was married and it didn't do me much good," Roxanne added.

Rage still rose in Junior's throat remembering how her ex-husband beat Roxanne down with his constant criticisms and admonishments. Everything from their inability to conceive to his failed career was somehow Rocky's doing. And, as if that weren't damning enough, he'd added adultery to the pile. A life of misery and pestilence was still too good for that man. Junior wanted to look into his eyes as he suffered every wicked thing her imagination conjured.

"I have a beautiful granddaughter and, if you'd go out once in a while, maybe you could meet someone and I could have another."

It was no secret that Roxanne didn't know who Ryan's father was. They'd all taken every precaution on that long Miami weekend of debauchery to celebrate Roxanne's finalized divorce. After almost eight years of being convinced their infertility was her problem only, she never believed pregnancy was a risk. Roxanne had gathered her courage to admit what happened, bracing herself for Ruth's disapproval. Instead, Ruth kissed her daughter and pronounced the pregnancy her reward for surviving.

Because that was the other side of Ruth Rivkin's brutal love. When you crossed her there was no coming back. Once you lost her esteem, you simply ceased to exist.

"Who has time for that?" Roxanne dismissed sincerely. "Junior will make you babies to hold. Imagine how cute they'll be with big, chubby punims to squish."

Ruth looked at Junior expectantly.

"What?" Junior cried. "There are no babies with squishy punims. I'm happily single with zero obligations or expectations. It's wonderfully freeing."

Junior endured a version of this inquisition from multiple fronts. Her father came from a family of five and had twenty-two first cousins. She herself had thirteen. It was inconceivable to anyone that she'd made it to thirty-three without procreating. The only port in this storm was her mother Yessenia, who was the only daughter of an only daughter of an only daughter. It wasn't that Junior didn't want kids one day, maybe. Possibly. Conceivably. It simply wasn't a priority.

"What are you waiting for, Schatzeleh?" Ruth asked, impatient for the impending hypothetical children to arrive.

"Yeah, Junior, what are you waiting for?" Roxanne taunted, tossing the bag of candy back.

Junior considered. "I'm not sure. A feeling? When it comes, I'll know," she answered honestly. "I need to *feel* something: eyes locked across a crowded room drawn helplessly together. I need it to be...inevitable," she finished.

Ruth gave her a long, hard look. Then she turned to her daughter and asked, "Did she get this from those meshuga Duke and Duchess books she reads?"

"Probably," Roxanne allowed with a shrug. "I'm going to get Ryan from her playdate. Dinner in an hour?" She left Junior alone with Ruth.

"Jujube?" Junior offered. Ruth's face curdled in horror. She turned and wandered to the living room, leaving Junior in the kitchen with her candies.

THE NEXT MORNING, JUNIOR SUMMONED her strength to defend against her mother's attack.

"No, Mom, I know. I don't want to go." Her mother was taking another swing at her about Mass the next Sunday. It was a Saint's Day or a Feast Day or some other reason that made Yesenia believe her daughter would relent and attend. "The Lord and I are all good. Remember my birthday weekend in Montreal? Well, I met a lovely man named Jesús and we spoke to the gods all night."

Dr. Yesenia Rosales' involvement at church usually extended as far as holidays and special occasions. On a day-to-day basis, she read the blessings and affirmations as a type of meditation. This full-court press to attend a specific mass was the work of Junior's abuela. "Casual blasphemy? I should have known this is what I would get for naming you after your father," she scolded.

"Yeah? Then what does it mean that I look just like you?" Junior poked at her mother's greatest vanity. Like Junior, Yesenia turned heads when she walked into a room. So maybe in some twisted quirk of genetics, it made sense that Junior would have her mother's outside and her father's inside, which her mother was still railing about through the truck's speakers.

"Mija, what harm would it be to spend some time with your family?"

"No harm at all, Mom. Tell me where to meet you *after church* and I'll be there."

"And what will I tell your abuela?"

"Her firstborn son has corrupted her firstborn granddaughter—the bloodline is cursed, she's failed." Junior stifled a laugh at her mother's groan of pure frustration. "Estoy bromeando. Obviously. Tell her I have to work."

"Where are you now?"

"I'm dropping off some supplies at the MWC then home to relax."

"Stop on your way for some food," her mother offered.

"Aww, you do love me!" Junior needled, knowing that she'd won this particular battle in the never-ending war for her mortal soul. "It was a good joke. Admit it."

"Yes, I'm sure your father will think your jokes are hilarious while explaining them to his mother," Yesenia grumbled.

"Bye, Mom. I love you."

The call disconnected as Junior pulled into a spot in front of the Muslim Welfare Center. Still a little tired and hungover from last night's Shabbat dinner—she and Roxanne tied one on after Junior tucked Ryan in with the now infamous Queens of the North bedtime story—she couldn't wait to get home and curl up with her book about the Dominican rum heiress and the Scottish earl. Junior dug her cropped hoodie from the back seat and pulled it on before entering the Centre.

"As-salamu alaykum." Junior smiled at the woman behind the small desk in the entryway.

"Wa alaykuma assalam. How can I help you, sister?" As usual, this woman was all business.

"I have some things to drop off. I came in for the cart?"

She nodded her assent for Junior to enter the warehouse to search for the buggy. In the passageway that connected the waiting area to the warehouse, there was a long shelf on the wall where the donations were sorted and stored. Two women worked at the shelf, sorting through piles with nimble efficiency. They smiled warmly at Junior when she grabbed the cart.

Back outside, Junior lowered her tailgate and started to take off her hoodie when she heard her name. She turned into the direct gaze of Davis. She was unprepared for seeing him out of context. For seeing him at all. Still mid-sweater removal, Junior got tangled in her rush to put it back on.

"Hey," she said, a bit flustered. "What are you doing here?"

"Startling women in parking lots, apparently." He grinned.

Smiling, playful Davis was a lethal dose of handsome Junior did not have the bandwidth to process at that moment.

"Yes," she said, laughing. "And why this parking lot, specifically?"

"I think I might be lost? Jamal gave me a list of restaurants to try if I wanted 'actual, legit Caribbean food.'" Davis perfectly impersonated Jamal's cadence. "He said, 'The Real Jerk doesn't even rate'."

Junior rolled her eyes. "That is so Jamal. What does he even know about it? He's Canadian! Very, very seven generations Canadian."

"The list is annotated."

"You're definitely in the wrong place if you're looking for a Caribbean restaurant."

"The driving app was taking me through a bunch of side streets for some reason? Anyway, I noticed your truck and–"

"Here you are," she finished.

He nodded sheepishly. "Can I give you a hand?" He motioned to her trunk.

"Sure. Thanks"

They stacked the items in the cart. "Put those on the bottom and stick that by the handle," she instructed, gathering her hair in a clumsy low bun and pulling her hood up.

"What are you doing?"

"There weren't any dudes when I went in to get the cart. The woman at the desk is...intense. I would rather not raise her ire."

Davis furrowed his brow. "I've seen your hair before."

"So?"

"And you're Catholic."

"Yes. My abuela won't let me forget. Again, so?"

"So? Lots of Muslim women don't cover their hair. The rules certainly aren't stricter for non-Muslim women." He slid his hands into his pockets.

"Pfft! Tell that to the woman at the front desk. You wouldn't be so chill if she gave you the look she gave me."

"She's probably cautious with people she doesn't know," Davis reasoned.

Junior made a game show buzzer sound from the corner of her mouth. "I've been coming here every month for almost four years. Try again."

Davis assessed her. She stared right back, annoyed that he would presume to know anything about her or her relation to this place.

"You come here every month?"

"To drop stuff off, yes. Your point?" Junior was officially irritated.

"I don't have one, I guess," he conceded.

"Then I can continue? I have your approval?" Junior said, eyes wide and voice innocent as she slammed her tailgate closed.

Appropriately chastened, Davis lowered his head to take a breath. When he looked at Junior again, it was up through his lashes, causing her brain to briefly short circuit.

Davis pressed his palms together and lifted his head so that they were eye to eye. "Forgive me, Junior. That was very rude of me. I was processing you being here–worrying about observing modesty when you know you don't have to, donating to this very specific place when your efforts could be applied to any number of equally worthy causes. You don't owe me an explanation."

Junior considered letting him wallow but a genuine Dickface Apology, unprompted and in the wild, might be as rare as witnessing Halley's Comet twice in a lifetime. In the end, she shrugged off her mood.

"Get the door, will you?" She pointed with her chin to direct him.

They got the cart in and over the threshold without losing a single item. Junior parked it in the hallway, gave Davis a small wave, and turned to leave. "Thanks for your help."

"Wait, you're going?"

"Uhh, yeah? I bring the things in; I leave them there." She pointed to the hallway where she left the cart. "Then I go. Sometimes people are here. Sometimes they're in the back. That is the entirety of the transaction. No change in the system necessary."

The super-intense woman was not at her post and Junior was eager to get back to her car without enduring another of her cold stares. Davis, however, seemed to have very little concern for her distress. "I thought we..." He ran his hand through his hair. Instead, he asked, "Every month?"

"Most months. Are we doing this again? Because I'd rather not." She headed out to her car with Davis following.

"I'm curious, that's all."

Junior laughed to herself. Curious was a mild way of putting it. Lately, any solitary thing she said to him resulted in a million follow-up questions. She'd had to make a game of it or she'd lose her temper.

At work, under the glare of fluorescent lights with his buttoned-up manner and his incessant *Actuallys*, it was pretty easy for Junior to overlook Davis' handsome. She'd managed to avoid spending any real time in a room with him for so long, she could only vaguely recall his features most times. In truth, he'd been little more than a caricature of a tightly wound office drone to her. Today though, the summer sun bouncing off his dark hair, his casual clothes, and his loose-limbed posture reminded her that his brand of good-looking could be overwhelming if she wasn't careful.

"It's not that deep." She dismissed him.

"Okay, but... why here?"

"You're making it weird," she complained, but he didn't budge. Instead, he leaned on her fender and waited.

Junior let out an irked breath. "When my grandfather died, we had to empty his place to sell it. We each took what we wanted as keepsakes but I couldn't stand to toss the rest and I didn't want a company profiting financially from my family's devastation. Fuck capitalism, y'know? In the end, we each donated to a place of our choosing. Some of his clothes went to a rehab facility, his furniture went to a women's shelter. His winter coats and kitchenware came here."

Junior thought she could say it out loud, answer Davis' question without getting too close to the sore under the scab.

But how could she explain that she was heartbroken, and had no idea how to mourn? Would it make sense to say that she googled 'Syrian Refugee donations' after seeing a segment on the news and this place was the first to answer the phone? That the answer to 'why here?' was, 'because the woman on the phone was kind.' That the woman waited quietly when an unexpected sob broke out of Junior's body and chanted gentle prayers of mourning in Arabic and again in English until Junior calmed down. She tried to say it, to tell Davis with his curious eyes trained on her, but she couldn't make her throat release the words.

"Anyway," she continued, "when I finally emptied the truck, I pulled someone aside to explain what I'd brought. I asked if there was anything else they needed, knowing I had so many things I could still bring, and I was told 'diapers and formula.'"

Junior could still remember the crack she felt deep inside. She hunched her shoulders over, pressing her hands on her ribs, to protect herself from the threat of her mixed-up emotions taking over. After all this time she could not separate the sharp pain of 'diapers and formula' from the thickness of her grief and either of them could easily pull her under.

"I felt it. Inside." She fought the thickening of her throat. "After not feeling anything at all for so long, I felt that. So, I drove to the store, loaded my truck with diapers and formula, and brought it right back here. I've been doing it ever since," she finished with a shrug.

Davis' eyes flashed, fiery with emotion. "Not that deep?"

"Ask the poor bastard that had to deal with me that day. I was a snotty, tear-stained mess. It was ugly." A small shudder ran up her back.

"Please don't do that, Junior," he gripped the door frame through the open window.

"Speak the truth? My vanity can handle it," she said solemnly.

Davis would not stop looking at her.

Unable to stand the scrutiny any longer, Junior flipped her sunglasses down over her eyes and shooed Davis. "Okay, already—aren't you on a mission or something? Get off my truck."

He pushed the door closed, bringing his face to her open window. He was so close that Junior could smell the sweet, baby powder scent of him. "Based on your current location, I'm guessing Jamal is sending you to Nicey's. Turn right out of here, right at the lights, then left into the plaza with the big McDonald's at the corner."

"Do you... do you want to grab a bite?" He offered.

She appreciated the gesture. Junior could only imagine what he thought of her now that she'd almost fallen apart in a commercial parking lot, but she didn't have the energy for his endless questions and she certainly couldn't stand his pity. "My mom is expecting me. Maybe another time?"

Davis nodded his understanding. "Take care, Junior." He backed away from her truck and stood on the curb.

"Enjoy your lunch," she said lightly. "Holler if you have trouble getting back downtown." Then she put her truck in gear and drove away with Lupe Fiasco promising, rather loudly, that the sun would come up and the show would go on.

Chapter 7

"HEY JUNIOR!" HODAN WAS waiting at the freight eleva-tor with a clipboard.

"What's poppin'?"

"You know, living the dream." She pushed a stray curl behind her ear. "Didn't see your RSVP to the wrap party," she scolded. It was the last day of filming for this season and everyone was excited to have a full day off before the company-sponsored party.

Wrap parties, like chocolate, varied wildly in quality. Fortunately, Fifty-Four prided itself on its excellent treatment of the crew which meant that their wrap party was a top-notch affair. Or so she'd been told.

"I don't do wrap parties anymore, Cookie. You know this."

"You're really not going to pass through?"

"Probably not. Never say never, though. Right?"

They both turned toward the voices coming in from one of the lockups. Remy, in head carpenter mode, was finishing up with some laborers. "After break, start in suite 106. The space needs to be ready for the painters."

"Remy!" Junior called, "What's gwan'in?"

"All right, still," Remington answered, code-switching nimbly. "Hodan." He lifted his chin in greeting.

"Remy, tell Junior she has to come to the wrap party." Hodan insisted.

"Junior doesn't go to wrap parties, Hodan. She's too cool for all'at." Remington smirked.

"Now here you go!" Junior protested. "You know what we're not gonna do? Start shit with Junior."

"We starting shit with Junior?" Jamal strolled up and dapped Remington and Hodan.

"You know what your problem is?" She turned to face off with Jamal and noticed Davis standing there, looking as stern and critical as usual. It had been five days since she'd seen him in the parking lot of the Muslim Welfare Centre and Junior was glad for this return to familiarity. His budding bromance with Jamal would be a problem for her if it meant he was going to be around all the time.

"There's not enough of me to go around?" Jamal smirked, his usual cocky self.

"Not even close." She rolled her eyes. "Your problem is that you weren't raised with a healthy fear of the chancleta."

"Speak! English!" Jamal teased.

"The chancleta is universal—wielded by abuelas worldwide." Junior's voice took on a Sir Attenborough quality.

"Yo. The slipper? It's no joke. My lola is a fiend." Remington confirmed.

"I think my ayeeyo has extra pairs lying around as backup, for real." Hodan agreed.

"See? Global!" She made her eyes big and spread her arms wide.

"Is assaulting children with footwear something you all should be proud of?" Davis' face was a picture of consternation.

"If your people did it right, the threat was enough," she reasoned. "Besides, Latine problems need Latine solutions. We don't have time to negotiate with terrorists."

"You're saying toddlers are terrorists?" Davis scrunched his nose.

"Hells yes!" Hodan and Remington answered in unison.

The bell rang and the red light started flashing in the corridor, signaling for quiet on the set. They instantly dropped their voices to whispers even though they weren't close enough to the stage to be heard.

"What time are we meeting at your place?" Jamal asked Remington.

"Cocktails at six!" he said in a comically bad British accent.

"Are you gonna pre-game with us before the wrap party, Fletcher?" Hodan asked.

Davis stammered out his answer. "Oh, uh…depends on the time. I might have some stuff to do for Olivia, but maybe?"

"Aight." Jamal smiled and turned to Junior. "I suppose you're not going?"

"You suppose correctly." She made a face at Jamal. "I've seen enough of you already."

Jamal spread his arms wide and did a slow turn. "Ain't no way that's true."

"Cocky bastard." She gave him a withering look and hip-checked him. Remington and Hodan laughed at the familiar performance.

Jamal got a faraway look in his eye that meant he was listening to the chatter in his earpiece. "I have eyes on him," he said into the mic. "They're looking for you on set, Fleezy." And then returned to his mic. "He's heading in," he said as Davis nodded and hurried to the shooting floor.

"Are you guys meeting later to do each other's hair, too?" Junior watched Davis leave. "Why is Dickface everywhere all of a sudden? Did I miss a memo?"

"He's not that bad. Hangs out for Friday drinks on the camera truck after wrap and chills with everyone. I mean, yeah, he's a little goofy, but he's cool," Jamal explained.

"Someone's interviewing candidates for your spot, Rem." Junior teased from behind Jamal. "I choose you in the divorce. No cap."

"Competition is none. I remain at the top like the sun," Remy lyric'd.

Junior cooed at Jamal's sour face, "Aww. I'm sorry, 'Mal. Did I get it all wrong? My bad." She rubbed his shoulders consolingly. "Remy, will you let Jamal keep his new pet? Seems he's grown quite attached." She pressed her face against Jamal's and made puppy dog eyes at Remington over Jamal's shoulder. "Pretty please?"

"Nize it, Junior," Jamal grumped, shaking her off.

"So salty," she teased and poked him in his side until he couldn't keep his frown any longer. Remy and Hodan chuckled on the sideline. Junior looked at her buzzing phone. "I need to take this. Jamal, don't forget to send pics of your matching lewks, 'k?" She blew a big kiss to him before answering her phone.

JUNIOR WAS REALLY REGRETTING THIS Saying Yes business. She'd had no intention of going to the wrap party and was rather looking forward to a quiet night in. Her book about the Caribbean heiress faking her way into a duke's home to be her kidnapped son's nanny wasn't going to read itself. Yet, here she was in full hair and heels because she lost a bet. A bet that was very likely rigged, she considered not for the first time.

Well, if they're going to goad me into attending, the least I can do is turn up. Which is why she was wearing black cropped overalls with a lace bralette, a gold body chain, strappy heeled booties, and a bold fuchsia lip. The double-takes she got from her coworkers, the ones that even recognized her, reminded Junior that her usual uniform of straight-legged cargo pants, grey Girl Power baseball cap, and t-shirt had been doing its job.

As soon as Junior arrived at Citizen, she scanned the venue for her peeps. In the back corner, she could see that two high-top tables had been dragged behind the last booth at the edge of the dance floor. Hodan's handiwork. The positioning carved out a bit of an enclave that allowed that area to be seen and accessible while still offering privacy.

Having spotted her destination, Junior decided to do a quick lap to see what else there was to see. She heard the squeal moments before she felt arms thrown around her neck.

"You came!" Sandrine was a happy drunk. "You look amazing!"

She gave Junior another squeeze before leaning in conspiratorially. "Guess who showed up with his new young-enough-to-have-a-curfew girlfriend while his ex, here as someone's plus one, pretends she doesn't notice them? Let's get you a drink!"

She was also a bitchy drunk.

Sandrine dragged Junior to the large square bar in the middle of the room. She made eye contact with a bartender and then turned to confirm, "Vodka soda, splash of juice?"

"For color. Yes ma'am," Junior said.

"Are you just getting here? C'est un peu tard." Criticism heavy in her voice.

"Sandrine, it's barely ten o'clock! The sun set, like, a minute ago."

"Yeah, yeah." Sandrine waved her off as the gorgeous bartender came to take their order. "You're making an entrance."

"No, I couldn't get out of it. I had big plans for my couch."

"Yes, I can imagine." She handed Junior her glass, cheers-ing with big, sloppy gulps.

"Damn! This is killer."

"Matt makes an excellent drink." Sandrine eyed him lascivi-ously.

"Sandrine!" Junior gasped, turning to look at the man who looked deliciously like NHL left wing Evander Kane. "Is Matt on the roster?"

He must have felt her eyes on him because he turned into her gaze and returned her look with his bottom lip caught in his teeth.

"He'd be auditioning right here and now if I had anything to do with it. I'll settle for tonight and all day tomorrow."

"Amen. Those shoulders are...aspirational"

"Oui, c'est ça." She turned to look at Junior. "So, the rumors are true. You've been caught in a Yes."

"A) What makes you say that? and 2) Who snitched?"

"A) You're here when I know you'd rather not be and 2) It's not snitching when it's shared within The Circle."

Junior brought her drink to her temple and was about to reply but Sandrine cut her off with a hissed, "Say Yes!" before smiling over Junior's shoulder.

"Davis!" Sandrine said his name like he was the very person she was hoping to see. "Having fun?"

"I am. What a great turnout."

Junior turned to face him and his eyes bugged out. "Junior! What are you doing here?"

"What am I doing here at the wrap party or here at the bar?" She asked, confused.

"I didn't expect to see you here," Davis tried again.

Sandrine cut off their awkward interaction before it could get any worse. "What he means is that you're notoriously not a joiner and so you being here tonight is a pleasant surprise. Right, Davis?"

"Yes. It's great to see you, Junior. You look amazing," he gushed. "You both do." He hurried to include Sandrine in the compliment.

Before he could say any more, the music died and the mic gave the sharp hiss of feedback.

"Good evening, ladies and gentlemen. Thank you all for coming tonight. Is everyone having a good time?" It was Eli, the executive producer, set up on a makeshift dais beside the DJ booth. The room erupted in applause. "I want to take a minute to say how proud I am of this crew, this cast, this creative team. You're each of you, to a man, the best in the biz and I couldn't be luckier to work with you, making this show we all love!"

More hollering and cheering ensued, with complete disregard for his casual sexism. Typical. The lights went down in the already dim bar and the opening credits of the show started up on a screen set up on the opposite wall.

It was a sizzle reel of clips from the show cut in with behind-the-scenes interviews of the cast and director. There were bloopers, blown takes, and shots of the crew mugging for the camera. This got assorted jeers and laughs from the crowd. Junior looked around the room and noticed that all the execs were there. A rare accomplishment, considering.

The lights came back up and now both Olivia, the owner of the studio, and Quinn were standing with Eli.

Quinn took the mic. "There's no following that, so instead I'll say thank you a million times from the bottom of my heart. I am so lucky to love what I do and I'm so grateful to everyone for making showing up to work such a joy."

If she didn't know better, Junior could chalk Quinn's emotion up to the booze, but she appeared to be sincerely happy to celebrate four seasons of television. Quinn handed the mic to Olivia who squeezed Quinn's shoulders. "Thank you all for your hard work, peerless dedication, and commitment. None of this is possible without all of you!"

The rowdy response was deafening in the bar.

"Now let's get back to the partyyyy!" Olivia yelled into the mic. "DJ, if you please?" And with that, the lights were lowered, the music resumed its thumping, and the bartenders were back in action.

"That was lovely." Sandrine smiled affectionately at the now blank screen.

"I didn't know they were cutting footage. We agreed on the slide show," Davis frowned.

Uninterested in Davis' potential tantrum about what he did and did not know, Junior squeezed Sandrine's arm and made her escape.

"Ohh shiiit, y'all–Junior Sano is in the heezy!" Jamal shouted from the side of the bar closest to the booth they'd commandeered.

"I am, indeed, up in this bitch." Junior curtsied with a flourish of her arms. "How was the fusion spot?" she asked when she got close enough to be heard.

"So good. My drink came in a pineapple!" Hodan gushed, pulling up a picture to show Junior.

"Yummy!" Junior questioned her decision to skip pre-gaming at Patois. "I am obviously very interested in pineapple as both an ingredient and a vessel."

"Where's your drink? You didn't drive here, did you?" Hodan pouted.

Junior scoffed in response. "Did *you*?"

"God no! We're all crashing at Remy's."

"After the show is the after-party!" Remington lyric'd. His hands were up to defend himself at Junior's sharp look. "That was Hov, not Kels."

"A technicality."

"Fair." Remington admitted. "You don't come back from pedophilia."

"Serial and predatory pedophilia," Junior added.

"You shouldn't." Imani groused.

Junior offered Imani a fry from the cone she'd grabbed from a passing server which she declined.

"I'm still too full from dinner."

"We ate soo much," Hodan complained happily.

"You'll be thanking me tomorrow when this open bar fails to take you out," Remy warned, popping a fry in his mouth. "Trust me. A full belly and lots of water will make all the difference."

"Incoming!" AJ was holding a tray of precariously balanced drinks followed by Jamal, who effortlessly balanced a tray of his own.

"Shots already?" Junior eyed Jamal's tray warily. It wasn't that she didn't enjoy a night of excess. When she could be lured off her couch, she'd been known to close down an establishment a time or two. But tonight, she planned to put in enough of an appearance to satisfy the Yes she'd been roped in before employing the trusty Irish Goodbye. Shots within the first half hour were counterintuitive to her goals.

"Yup!" he handed everyone a shot.

"There seem to be far more shots than our current number suggests," Junior noted.

"Nope!" he raised his glass waiting for everyone else to follow suit. "Drink!"

"Mmm..." Hodan shimmied a little. "What was that?"

"I'll take 'things you should ask before imbibing' for 600, Alex," AJ teased.

Hodan blew a raspberry at her in response.

"I asked my boy to hook me up. This is that," Jamal explained.

"You didn't ask either?" Imani scolded him "Didn't you watch *Girls Trip*? We could all be tripping balls in an hour, trying to wrestle a tiger into a hatchback!"

"Not on that full stomach," Remington crowed. "You're welcome!"

"Also, I think that's *The Hangover*," AJ offered.

Jamal clowned, "Matty wouldn't do me like that. Come on now!"

"You know Matt the bartender?" Junior asked.

"He swam varsity. Why, you want an intro?" Jamal sounded skeptical about the possibility.

"No, sir. Besides, I think he and Sandrine have been making introductions all night." Junior pulled out her phone and texted, **'Bartender swam varsity.'** Her phone buzzed with a *Flashdance* gif of Jennifer Beals' arched body dripping wet on a chair in reply.

"Word?"

"Mmhmm," Junior confirmed.

"Nice!" Jamal approved, always happy to know that someone somewhere was getting it in. "Now if only we could get my boy hooked up," Jamal said, indicating Davis across the room. "He declined my services as wingman tonight because 'he's not built for hookups'. What kind of shit is that? It don't gotta be a hookup!"

"Since when is he your boy?" Junior asked.

"Since I took his celibate ass under my wing!" he answered.

"Why would you do that?" She could not understand voluntarily befriending the man.

"The system, Junior. The system compels me!" Jamal explained.

Imani swatted her cousin. "Leave him alone. Not everyone is out to hit it and quit it like you guys."

"I'm not a player, I just crush a lot!" AJ lyric'd to Remy's delight, bumping fists with her fellow players.

The Classic Rock contingent had thinned out and now the dancefloor belonged to the 'kids' and those drunk enough to move to anything with a beat. The transition to Top 40, Old School Hip Hop, and R&B was seamless. The party truly started when Remington and Imani burst onto the dance floor rapping along to 'Da Rockwilder' for all their worth.

Junior pressed the remnants of her drink against the side of her neck, hoping it would bring her core temperature down. Her hair had grown to its full mass and could no longer be contained. Each curl and coil reached for any molecule of moisture in the air, putting hygrometers everywhere to shame. She lifted a handful off her neck for temporary relief but the huge fans and massive A/C unit didn't make much difference this close to the action.

"Need a refill?" Davis placed a fresh drink on the hi-top between them.

"Thanks, I'm good!" She smiled politely and held up her glass.

"It's empty," he pointed out.

"Not empty." She rattled the ice cubes.

"No, I guess not," he conceded. "I like your necklace. Is that a locket?"

"It's an amulet—an Ojo de Venado." She held the one-inch gold embroidered seed. "To ward off evil energy."

"Does it work?" Davis smiled.

"Too soon to tell," she ribbed.

"I've never seen anything like it. What are those markings?"

Junior was entirely too drunk and yet not drunk enough to play Davis Asks a Million Questions. A clear head was crucial to responding appropriately. Junior leaned over the table to show him. "My initials. It's one of the markers we Panamanians use to identify each other. That, and the specific brand of crazy in the eyes." She widened hers playfully.

"I don't think you're crazy."

"That's because you don't know any better. You should be very afraid."

"I don't scare easily," Davis challenged, leaning a little closer.

She also leaned further over the table. "Loudly declaring your lack of self-preservation? Bold. Foolish."

The amulet swung between them. Davis gestured to it and Junior nodded her consent, unable to take her eyes off his mouth. Holding it in between his fingers, he answered, "My mother raised me to be brave and strong. I can handle more than you think."

With the tip of her tongue tracing her upper lip, she flirted automatically, "Your mother never met a woman like me. You should proceed with caution."

Catching herself at Davis' wide-eyed reaction, Junior gave her head a tiny shake and moved back to her side of the table. Had she... *hit on* Dickface? She'd definitely had too much to drink.

People moved in and out of their orbit making small talk. Roommates and significant others were introduced, finally putting faces with the names. Davis and Junior kept the hi-top between them but engaged with their friends and coworkers as a pair. When they were by themselves again, Junior turned her attention to the dance floor in time to recognize the song being mixed in. She instinctively found and locked eyes with AJ and Hodan, the three of them making colossal gestures of scorn, giggling to themselves from their respective corners of the party for nursing the grudge they vehemently held.

"No love for Justin?" Davis asked, taking in the spectacle.

"After what he did to Britney? To *Janet*?" Her outrage carried her words over the music. "Leaving her to shovel all that shit alone while he continued unscathed? I will *never* forget!"

"Not big on forgiveness, I see," he teased.

"Forgiveness isn't something you get because you want it. You don't deserve it, you earn it...you work for it. That squeaky bastard hasn't even apologized to her."

"You have very strong opinions about this." He seemed amused at her umbrage.

"Yep!" she said, looking directly at him. "Very strong opinions."

"About all things or just this specific thing?"

"Many things. Lots of things. Plenty of things." She gesticulated wildly.

"Switch!" Jamal called out as he traded Junior's empty glass for a full one. The glass was practically frosted, it was so cold. Junior chugged the cocktail and placed the glass on her neck.

"You really don't like me," Davis said, somewhere between a statement and a question. He seemed distressed by the realization.

Junior set her now empty glass beside the untouched drink Davis had brought and asked, "Why wouldn't I like you?"

She let her attention wander and joined the conversation beside her when he didn't answer. Smiling to herself, Junior noticed both Matt the bartender and Sandrine the man-eater were missing. A quick scan also showed that AJ wasn't around.

Like most coordinators, AJ was usually the first one at the wrap party. Unlike most coordinators, AJ delegated the responsibility of 'shuttin'r down'. AJ had always been diligent about her sleep hygiene.

"It's sparkling water," Davis said, pointing at the drink.

"Pardon?" she turned to him.

"I didn't slip anything in it if you were worried," he blurted.

"Jesus Christ!" She recoiled. Junior stared at him incredulously. Why did he always say such fucked up shit?

"Bad Bunny!" Hodan screamed and pulled Junior away from Davis before she could comment. "Come on!"

***

Davis watched as they hit the dance floor and were immediately enveloped by their group. Junior and Hodan showed Imani salsa steps just as Ali spun Junior into his arms, a move that looked so practiced–so fluid–Davis was sure they'd done it a thousand times before. A circle opened around them while they danced together during the mini-Latin set.

That could have been him, he thought. Not dancing with Junior, not holding her and moving with her like that but... closer. Closer to her orbit. He'd felt the embers of it that night at Betty's and was desperate to have it again. Instead, he was sidelined in a completely different galaxy. At this rate, he'd be lucky if Junior ever made eye contact with him again. Davis simply could not display even a fragment of chill when it came to Junior.

The DJ was having fun now, controlling the crowd, reading the floor, and layering hit after hit. Old school jams, deep cuts made popular by 90s sampling, and crowd favorites followed without a break. Junior and Imani sang along when the audio cut: "Thick legs! In shape!" and laughed when Remy and Jamal tried to teach Hodan to crip walk. Someone's drunk wife woohoo'd her way onto the dance floor, moving her body in a wide hula-hoop motion. Junior and Imani pulled her into the group and danced with her. The woman was having so much fun, it was easy to imagine she was drawn to them–to Junior. How could she not? Junior was mesmerizing.

Davis made his way to the other side of the party. While talking to Olivia, impressed that she was still at it, he noticed Junior had taken a break from dancing to get another drink. Davis started to smile as Ali made his way over to where Junior stood at the bar. The small smile died on his lips when Ali placed a hand on her hip and whispered something in her ear. Junior nodded, slammed her drink, and followed Ali to the door where Hodan and Jamal were waiting, ready for wherever the night took them.

Chapter 8

B y Monday afternoon, Junior still hadn't fully recovered from the wrap party. A bunch of people ended up at a hole in the wall and then at Remington's after that. Having chosen to drink through her hangover on Saturday and indulge in some hair of the dog on Sunday before sleeping the rest of the afternoon off, she was still rather hazy on the details. Which qualified the wrap party as a grand success.

Staring at her monitor, a little spaced and ready to clock out, small intricately hennaed hands waved frantically in front of her face.

AJ.

By the slightly panicked look in her eye and the rigid posture, Junior knew that whatever came out of her mouth next was going to be good. And probably bad. But *definitely* good. "Oh, no–what did you do, AJ?"

"Me? Nothing! The patriarchy, on the other hand, is thriving!" She was working her way up to a frothy rant. "Do you know that period poverty affects 2.3 billion people and there is no reason we can't address this issue other than 'vaginas bleed–icky!'?"

"Yes, AJ, I do know that. What I don't know is why you're here right now with that guilty look on your beautiful, unfairly glowing face."

"My skin does look great today, doesn't it? Rosehip oil. I bought some while I was at the naturopath yesterday. You should try it. A couple of drops after your toner et voila."

AJ, left unchecked, always veered towards hippy. Junior blamed her friend's inherent granola tendencies on all the time she'd spent on the West Coast. They were way too loose out there.

"That glow is youth and forbearance." Junior snapped her fingers in AJ's face. "Focus!"

"Okay, so don't freak out, but remember the wrap party? When I was in the back with Fletcher?" She winced.

Junior's hands flew to her face as she gasped. "Did you and Dickface hook up? Ohmygod–did you finally dump Kelly? Tell me everything!" Junior demanded. "Wait. My delicate constitution cannot handle knowing anything about Fletcher's o-face right now."

Junior finally understood the obsession with those pimple popping videos. She didn't want to see but could not look away. "Was he super clinical, all 'the source material suggests I insert my erect penis in your vaginal canal where I will proceed to thrust repeatedly, occasionally stimulating your clitoris until orgasm is achieved'?" Junior said in a nasal, monotone voice.

"Ew, stop!" AJ squealed. "Gross! We did not hook up."

"Okay, but...did you break up with Kelly?" Junior pressed. Then, unable to help herself: "Seriously, what do you think Fletcher would be like?" It wasn't the first time she'd caught herself wondering about an unleashed Davis.

"Junior!" AJ wailed.

"Fine! The wrap party. You were at the back with Dickface, and?"

"And he was being moderately normal. Charming, even!" AJ relayed this with a small amount of wonder in her voice. Something lurched deep in Junior's belly. A tiny wave of nausea threatened to take hold as a fragment from the wrap party came back to her.

"A whole conversation with Dickface's undivided attention? I am thrilled for you!"

"Well, not undivided. Jamal was there."

Looking at AJ, Junior realized there was more to this story and the more was probably the part that concerned her. "Out with it, AJ."

"Okay. While we were talking, he may have expressed some interest in my jewelry which prompted me to tell him about our spot which led Fletcher to ask about you, specifically. More focused curiosity, say. And *Jamal* may have suggested that we hang out together and shop for jewelry sometime soon to which *I* might have implied was a great idea." AJ's babble came tumbling out of her.

They stared at each other as the weight of those words settled around them like confetti. Or napalm.

"Nope."

"What, nope?"

"Just... nope," Junior clarified.

"You're not going to listen to the rest of it?"

"Not even a little bit." Junior started to pack up. It was close enough to quitting time and AJ wasn't going to lure her into any schemes in her current diminished capacity.

AJ rushed around to put herself between Junior and the door as though her welterweight could contain Junior's heavyweight.

"I didn't think anything would ever come of it! It was polite party talk. But then he was so sincere and he's looking for a present for his sister. So now I think I need to make good on my invitation which means I need you to hang, just once, on purpose, with Fletcher."

"I'm going home now. I'm going home before your crazy seeps in and infects me, too," she said over her shoulder, side-stepping around AJ and out into the hallway.

AJs voice followed Junior down the stairwell. "Good talk! Let's revisit tomorrow!"

JUNIOR WAITED IN FRONT OF Balzac's Coffee Roasters for Davis to arrive, lamenting how few of AJ's Yeses ever broadened her horizons. The specter of this outing to the Distillery District had loomed over her all week. AJ's apologetic text explaining that she'd be late, but would join them later turned Junior's scone to paste in her mouth. If she wasn't a thousand percent sure that AJ would rather crawl over hot coals and broken glass than subject herself to one of Junior's moods, she would have accused AJ of doing this on purpose.

As it was, she was only here because AJ's mouth wrote a cheque Junior somehow became responsible for cashing. The payback Junior planned to extract would be epic.

"Hey, Junior. Is Adrienne inside?" Davis greeted her.

"Hi." Junior appreciated that Davis didn't feel entitled to the familiarity of the name AJ. "She's trapped in Chinatown or something? It wasn't clear. She'll meet us later."

"Oh. Okay." He looked around nervously.

"If you want to reschedule, I get it. It's up to you," Junior affected nonchalance, willing him to, in fact, choose to do this another time.

"No, it's all right. I mean, it would be great if you're still willing? I'm looking for a gift for my sister. I thought I'd try that jewelry store she mentioned." A spark of hope flashed across his face.

"Birthday?" Junior guessed.

"A belated birthday/graduation combo gift," Davis clarified.

"You missed your sister's birthday *and* graduation?"

"I know," he rubbed his neck, "but I plan to have something when she comes to visit next week."

"Why am I not surprised?" Junior stared at him for a moment, somewhere between laughing and scoffing.

"Easy, Judge-y. I sent flowers and called her. We don't live in the same city and, if you recall, I was a little busy at the beginning of the month," he defended himself. "Besides, she starts her graduate program almost immediately. Nothing changed after she shifted the tassel on her cap."

"That's almost twenty years between you and your sister. Is it only you two?"

"Ouch!" he clutched his chest. "I just turned thirty-four, thank you."

Junior was surprised to learn he was only a year older than her. *Being profoundly annoying must really age a person.* "Come on. Let's solve your problem."

She led him to Transformed, a small, found-object jewelry store beside the fancy kitchen place. "I love it here," she told him, pushing through the stained-glass door. "Even when I place an embargo on myself, it's still fun to look at all the pretty, shiny things."

"Magpie! How are you, darlin'?" Max's throaty welcome never failed to make Junior smile. "I see you brought a friend!"

"Not a friend." Junior gave the word the same emphasis, correcting her quickly. "A someone from work who needs the perfect gift for his sister." The last thing she needed was Max getting any ideas and gossiping to their mutuals.

Junior watched Davis take in all of Max's glory. At sixty, she had come out later in life with zero concession to gender conformity. She was wearing a denim jumpsuit unbuttoned to her navel with a statement necklace, zebra print loafers, cocktail rings on seven of her ten fingers, and her signature square-framed reading glasses perched atop her bald head.

Junior chastised herself for not warning Davis. She forgot that the fluidity Max chose rankled the kind of people who could only live in a binary. As Junior was herself a multitude of things simultaneously, she never understood trapping yourself in a small, limiting box. But then Junior remembered exactly how Davis reacted to her when they first met and she braced for impact.

If he hurt Max's feelings, Junior wouldn't be held responsible for her actions.

Davis flashed a genuine smile. "There are so many great things in here that I don't know where to begin!"

"Aren't you a treat?" Max enthused. "It's for your sister? Why don't you tell me a bit about her?" She came around from the worktable to lead Davis to some options.

Junior left Davis in Max's capable hands. If there was anything the shop owner loved more than placing the perfect piece with the exact right owner, Max hadn't found it yet.

Junior's phone buzzed in her pocket, signaling that her abuela had sent another Bible passage on a floral background. She replied with a perfunctory **'gracias a Dios'** and vowed to never forgive her cousin Claudia for teaching their grandmother how to use WhatsApp.

Junior kept scanning the display cases knowing that if she let herself, she could buy six different pieces and not have a single regret. She was close to trying on a pearl ring when Davis was suddenly beside her with his gift chosen, wrapped, and paid for.

"Ready?" He smiled.

The store's phone rang. Junior made eye contact with Max as she answered the phone and, with a wink, she waved goodbye to Junior and Davis.

"Wow! I never thought I'd meet a drag queen." Davis shook his head in wonder as they stepped outside.

Junior looked at him sharply. "And you still haven't," she bit out.

"No, I guess it's not the same when they're not all done up. My sister loves *Drag Race*. She'll flip!"

Of fucking course.

"Hey!" She snapped her fingers in his face. "She is not a drag queen." Junior immediately regretted many of today's choices. But mostly she regretted agreeing to AJ's reckless need to be helpful, if not for which, Junior wouldn't be standing here right now. She looked Davis in the eyes and said slowly, "Max is a trans woman, not a drag queen."

"Oh," he said and gazed out over Junior's head.

He must be updating his CPU, she thought to herself.

Then he had the nerve to say, "Actually, I believe the term is 'woman of trans experience'," without a trace of self-awareness or irony.

Junior scoffed in disbelief. "You really can't help yourself, can you?"

Davis smiled at her, abashed.

With a small shake of her head, Junior checked for an update from AJ and decided to get a killing time snack.

***

Davis followed Junior to a bakery where, upon entering she announced, "Snack Time!" She immediately zeroed in on the cinnamon roll. "Bingo," she said to herself. Turning to Davis she offered, "Want anything? It's not as good as Leigh's but still. My treat."

"Oh, uh…Thanks. I shouldn't." He looked around awkwardly, trying to figure out how to not crowd her in the tiny space. He felt as though the baked goods were plotting against him.

"Suit yourself." She shrugged and took a big, enthusiastic bite when it was handed to her. Junior moaned her satisfaction. "You are missing out," she said to him around a mouthful of the gooey confection, licking icing off her lips.

"I don't think I am," he valiantly maintained eye contact. The sound she made—for a pastry!—was so decadent, so indulgent, he might never again know peace. God help him, his eyes dropped to her sticky, icing-glazed mouth. Joined with her moaned satisfaction, now on loop in his brain, Davis was uncomfortably aware of her proximity to his tightening pants.

Junior gave an unbothered tilt of her head. "Let's go," she said, pulling more manageable pieces off to pop in her mouth.

They wandered through the different shops and boutiques, stopping for Junior to buy stationery, a linen-scented candle, and some witch hazel. He was fascinated by the eye-watering way she spent money. In each store, Junior held up things for Davis to see or smell or sample and he gamely did as he was told.

They continued to wander through the alleys and stalls. Seeing some kids clamber onto a peace sign sculpture, Junior asked, "Your sister is, what, twenty-five? It's still a nine-year difference," Junior pointed out. "That seems like a lot."

Davis laughed. "Have you been thinking about that this whole time?"

Junior gave an unashamed shrug.

"I don't know. My parents just sort of…are. There was no plan, apparently, with either of us. They got pregnant when they got pregnant. My mom and dad met in middle school, started dating, and have been together ever since. They like to remind us that they've only ever kissed each other. It often comes after one of us goes through a break-up. Teddy's usually," he smirked. "My mom likes to say 'Your heart knows when it's found the last kiss you'll ever want'."

Junior melted at his mom's sappiness. "You haven't left a trail of broken hearts all over the country?"

"Hardly," he admitted. "I'm usually the heart that's broken."

"Seriously?" Junior's eyes widened.

"Why is that surprising?" Davis chuckled self-consciously.

"Well, because you're so–" Junior caught herself before finishing her sentence.

"Oh, this is going to hurt, isn't it? Go on, rip the bandage off." He took comically loud, deep breaths.

"You're so, you know, how you are...Mr. Corporate Ladder, has to have the last word, always correcting people and stuff?" She winced a little. Davis couldn't tell if she took any joy at having to be the bearer of that particular bit of news. "I guess I figured you'd be super critical in a relationship."

"Really?" Davis' scalp prickled with his discomfort.

"I mean, kinda? Like you'd be all–" she cleared her throat and said in a stern, low-pitched voice he supposed was him, "'I'm sorry, you poured the brandy in a sherry glass. This isn't going to work out,' or 'your reliance on the nonstandard synonym irregardless has made me question our future together', or 'ATM Machine and PIN number are redundant acronyms and I can no longer abide your use of such', or—"

"God, stop! Please. I get it." Davis cringed, appalled that she thought that about him.

Of course she thinks that, a voice scolded him. *What else do you expect when you can't keep your foot out of your mouth whenever she's around*, the voice added grimly.

"Oh! I thought of another really good one! 'Actually–'"

"Okay, that's enough!" He talked over her and covered his ears, pulling the plug on her performance.

They made their way to a bench and took a seat, setting their purchases between them. Junior pulled out her phone and tapped out a message. "AJ's close," she said and then returned her full attention to him. "I take it I was way off base?"

"Yes. And no."

"How's that?" Junior asked.

"I..." he started and then reconsidered, unsure of how to make her understand. He didn't want to ruin this time they'd spent together, especially since he'd so rarely managed a conversation without stepping in it and completely alienating her. They were having a good time. The truth about his life and where he came from would put a damper on what was an otherwise pleasant morning.

"What?"

"I was a late bloomer. In everything. It took me longer than the other kids to learn to read and then when I did, it took me even longer to grasp the bigger picture of the words," Davis said, deciding to tell his story. It couldn't be worse than her believing he was an overbearing blowhard.

"You mean reading comprehension?"

"Yeah, exactly that." He smiled sadly. "The teachers all strongly suggested my mom look into remedial training for me, but Mom wouldn't have it. She fought that school every step of the way. It was a struggle to learn how to learn, but we found the key to unlocking my brain. I read out loud all the time and I used lots of repetition. I don't have to tell you how popular it made me."

"I bet those kids were spectacular assholes." Junior empathized, a knowing look in her eye.

"They really were!" Davis agreed. "It wasn't enough that we were poor and lived off the grid. I had to be dumb, too." He laughed mirthlessly. "When Teddy came along, my sister Danielle, my mom was ready to fight the fight again. Except Teddy could read at three and wrote words in neat block letters at four. She got to school and was smarter than kids grades ahead of her. Which didn't change much for my mom because she still had to march in that school and demand they take care of her kid."

"Were they assholes to your sister, too?"

"Things were just different enough by then that she had an easier time of it than I did." Davis looked down at his hands.

"A small mercy?" Junior offered.

"It was," he allowed. "I, on the other hand, never really had an opportunity to socialize when I was a kid because I needed every waking moment for my schoolwork. Playing a sport or joining a club was an hour each night away from my lessons that I honestly couldn't afford. Then, when I was older and it became clear that my learning disability had no bearing on my intelligence, I was obsessed with proving to those teachers who said I'd never amount to anything that I was as smart as any other kid. Smarter, even! I threw myself into my studies at the expense of almost everything else." He shook his head in disdain.

"When I finally started to meet people in university, started to date, I was terribly awkward. My helpful observation that, for example, 'PIN number' is a redundant acronym was met with derision. My need to really, truly study was seen as an unwillingness to have fun. And my limited resources prevented me from participating in anything that required any type of cash outlay."

"That sucks," Junior lamented.

"It did. Then it didn't... it is what it is, I suppose." Davis shrugged, meeting her eyes for the first time since he started his story. Their gazes remained locked until they heard AJ's flustered voice.

"Sorry I'm late. I totally forgot that I promised my mom I'd pick up the wonton wrappers she likes from one very specific place down there, and I planned to go before acupuncture, but they weren't open so I had to go back, and of course, by then Chinatown was chaos," AJ said in one gust of breath. "Have you guys had lunch already? Please say no, I'm starving!" she whined.

"We haven't. Any cravings?" Junior asked Davis.

"Um, I think I'll pass. You two go on."

"Oh, Fletcher." AJ was crestfallen. "Don't go."

"Honestly, I've got a bunch of stuff to do still. It's fine!" The gods know he hadn't planned to tell Junior all of that but she was such a good listener and he was desperate for her to understand. He silently pleaded with her to let it go, hoping his discomfort wasn't all over his face.

"… If you're sure." Junior sounded unconvinced.

Davis waved the bag from Transformed. "I am. Thanks for your help, Junior. I know she'll love it."

"Hey." She smiled at him. It wasn't her dazzling smile or even the tight smile he normally received. This smile was filled with commiseration and sympathy, the type to soothe a toddler with a skinned knee—one that shared a postal code with pity. "See you around."

"Enjoy your lunch, ladies." He waved at them before turning to leave.

Of all the things he'd said and done to damage his chances of getting close to Junior, it would of course be the truth about his childhood that delivered the death blow. For as long as he lived, he'd never be able to explain his unforced error.

***

Sandrine let out a cloud from her vape. Junior sniffed the air. "Cotton candy?"

"Candy apple," Sandrine corrected.

"Does it taste like a candy apple?"

Sandrine shrugged and pulled on her vape again. They'd decided to eat their lunch outside at the picnic tables and lingered, taking advantage of the perfect late June weather–bright sun, low humidity–and the rare quiet in the office. The workdays were shorter and the lunches were longer now that they were solidly in wrap mode.

"Will you have any time off?"

"I've booked a month in Vieques," Sandrine answered.

"Good for you!"

"At least there are three months between seasons this time." Sandrine turned at the sound of an approaching car. "The Twins," she noted.

Imani and Jamal made their way to the picnic table.

"Anything good at the sale?" Junior asked.

"Nah." Jamal lowered himself on the bench beside Junior.

"We went over to the *Odyssey Street* set sale," Imani filled in for the visibly lost Sandrine.

"But it was too space-y so we didn't get anything," Jamal added before shouting, "Fleezy!" as Davis exited the building.

Junior had seen him briefly in the hall and wondered if he regretted telling her about his life. Learning they'd both had lonely childhoods toppled the final brick in her wall of scorn toward Davis, giving way to a protectiveness she couldn't fully explain.

Junior was both impressed and appalled by the way his easy smile suggested the confession was a distant memory. Either he was an exceptionally good actor or he'd truly moved on. She simply couldn't relate—the good Lord knew she didn't let herself be vulnerable that way. Not anymore. Not for a long time.

"Quitting time already?" Sandrine teased as Davis approached the group.

"I wish. I'm headed to Fifty-Four."

"Ah. Enjoy," she said, emitting another candy-scented cloud.

"How's it going with your lady?" Imani asked boldly. "Any progress?"

"Imani!" Junior chided.

"What?"

"Davis has a lady?" Sandrine was intrigued.

Jamal clarified, "We're trying to get him his lady."

"More accurate to say Jamal is overly invested in an unhealthy and unprofessional way," Junior scolded the twins.

"But..." Sandrine's curiosity overruled her sense of propriety. "It's not working?"

Junior rolled her eyes and leaned back against the table, annoyed with her friend's prying. His love life was certainly none of her concern.

Davis cleared his throat. "I um... I think I have to throw in the towel."

"Why?" Imani cried.

Well, okay, maybe Junior did want to know more. Davis was so tight-lipped about this person, she half wondered if he'd made them up to get Jamal off his case.

"What happened?" Jamal demanded, pulling out his phone.

"I've just accepted that it's time to let it go. She'll never see me that way."

"Let me guess. Your game-less ass tried to talk to her and messed it up," Jamal accused.

"Game-less? What is that?" Sandrine's face scrunched in confusion. Her constant struggle with English slang was the price of the effortless chic of being half French and half French-Canadian.

"There was a crazy hot woman at a bar and Davis wouldn't take her number," Imani filled in.

"That's not at all what happened," Davis complained.

"Cole's Notes." Imani waved off the rebuke.

Junior threw her head back and laughed. "You weren't even there!"

"The gist is that Davis is turning down women left and right because he has his heart set on one specific woman," Imani summarized. "But he's not making progress there, either."

"Ah, okay. Game is confidence with women. Like swagger?"

"Correct," Jamal said, checking his phone.

"D'accord." Sandrine nodded before turning her sympathetic gaze on Davis. "And you don't have this, Davis?"

"I do! But I need to move on. It's time. I need to be done," he explained, flustered.

Junior noticed Hodan walking toward them. With all the censure she could muster, Junior asked Jamal, "You called in reinforcements?"

"I texted AJ," he answered.

"AJ is in an assets meeting. She sent me to take notes and represent her interests," Hodan explained.

"This is insane," Davis grumbled to himself.

"I don't want to say this is your fault because... how could you have known?" Junior consoled Davis. "But you should never have let him in." She jerked her thumb at Jamal. "Now? It's Vampire Rules: you either put up with him or you have to kill him."

Jamal gave Junior the hand as Imani and Sandrine chuckled. "What we need is to get her on your turf, surrounded by your people."

"Yes. A kickback at his place," Imani agreed, twin braining with her cousin.

"Then we could all be your wingman!" Hodan clapped.

Sandrine pulled on her vape again. "Parfait. We can help to show you in the best light."

"You got a yard, right?" Jamal confirmed. "It works best when it's outside."

"Is it private? With grass and trees and stuff?" Hodan asked, texting with the speed of one who communicated exclusively by thumb.

"Just private will do," Imani countered.

"I'll roll through to scope it out–see what we're working with," Jamal finished.

Davis tried to regain control of this runaway train. "Whoa, wait! Hold up a sec."

Junior took the straw from her drink, mimed stabbing Jamal in the heart, and mouthed *your choice* to Davis. She knew all too well how the best intentions could get washed away in the tide of enthusiasm.

"Calendars up, people," Imani ordered.

"I do not want to have a party at my house," Davis said to completely unconcerned ears.

"It's not a party. It's a kickback," Imani corrected him. "In, say, two weeks? After Canada Day long weekend."

"Works for us!" Hodan confirmed, consulting her phone.

"Bien." Sandrine smiled.

"Let your people know, Bossman," Jamal slapped Davis' shoulder. "You're having a soirée!"

"Good luck, Eyes & Ears. Sounds like you're going to need it," Junior said to a shell-shocked Davis as she gathered her things.

Chapter 9

"Junior!" Davis was surprised to find her on his porch in the setting sun. "What are you doing here?" She was wearing a yellow shirt dress with leather loafers and there was a lollipop protruding from her cheek. Her hair, in two low pigtails, blew slightly in the breeze.

"Jamal had to do some stuff with Remy, so you're stuck with me," she said as though it explained her presence at his home in any way.

"Stuck with you? For what?"

"Scoping your place for the kickback? Remember last week? Jamal didn't forget."

"I sort of hoped he had," Davis admitted.

"Then you shouldn't have given him your address."

"I thought we'd have a beer or something and I could talk him out of it." Davis had been looking forward to having Jamal over. He enjoyed Jamal's antics and hoped they were becoming friends outside of work.

"No such luck. Is now a good time? I'm not disturbing you or keeping you from your side piece, am I?" Off his look, she amended, "I won't take long. Five minutes tops."

"I don't have much of a choice, do I?" he asked, sullen.

"You do, you just choose not to exercise it," Junior reminded him.

"My choice is murder or letting you in to help plan a party I don't want?"

She smiled brightly at him, waving her purple lollipop. "See? Always a choice."

"Let's get this over with," Davis sighed, put upon. He was sure he could manage five minutes without saying anything too ridiculous. He'd done it before–three times, now!–he could do it again. He would invite her in, she'd look around, and she'd leave before he put his foot in his mouth. Then he could get back to his evening of... well, trying to get over her.

"So, this is where the magic happens?" Junior said when he opened the door wider.

"Magic?" he moved to let her through.

"I'm guessing you didn't watch a lot of Cribs back in the day," she joked as she stepped out of her shoes.

"Not really, no."

"It was a show on MTV where you'd get to see inside famous people's homes. It became a thing for the celebrities to say when the camera team went into their bedrooms."

"You're in the foyer."

"Eyes and Ears, observant as ever!" Junior replied. He watched as she looked around, taking in how the white walls and warm wood flooring created an inviting space, the large windows that let in a lot of daylight, and his sturdy couch and matching armchair faced off over a dark wood trunk that served as his coffee table.

There were some accent pieces that, with the rug and throws, created an overall look one might describe as 'southwestern'.

"Would you like something to drink? Water? Tea?" he offered politely, leading her further into the house. Five minutes, he reminded himself. Don't make a fool of yourself for five minutes.

"This is not what I expected from the outside," she mused, accepting the offer of water.

"What did you expect?"

"I... I don't know," she answered honestly. "I didn't give it that much thought."

"The Great Junior Sano, stumped," he teased. "I don't know what you're looking for but you're welcome to search until you find it. Let me go get you that water."

"Do you live here alone?" she asked.

"Mostly. My sister crashes when she's in town. It's technically her house too, but she's more of a silent partner."

He had a small workspace under the window in the corner of the living room, facing the neat, compact yard out back. Dropping her bag on the chair, she peered out the window. "Is there another way back here? Or do you have to go through the house to get to your yard?"

"There's a gate at the side down the driveway," he watched her from the kitchen.

Turning, she saw that his laptop—so different from the sleek tablet he carried all the time—was running a slideshow of pictures from the sets, the crew, and some schematics from the art department. "Were these for the wrap party?" she called.

"Kind of? There were a couple of ideas on the table," he said, coming toward her.

Junior smiled at a picture of herself filling the screen. She was at her truck in the production office parking lot with her hair down, lit perfectly by the setting sun. "When did you take this, Sneaky?" Brazenly, she pressed the spacebar to pause the image.

"Junior, wait!" Davis cried, too late. It wasn't a slideshow but a screensaver. The lock screen opened up to the picture of her–hands in her hair and her face tilted to the sky, oblivious that she was being photographed.

"What the hell?" Junior asked, alarmed.

Davis put the glass down and showed his palms. "I can explain."

"Can you? Because I'm trying very hard not to freak out."

"I know this looks bad," he tried.

"You think?" She was tense. Wary.

"I took it on the day we met. I was surprised that you were Jaime Sano and I... I got overwhelmed. I over-corrected and made it worse. I spent the rest of the day kicking myself. That night, I saw you in the parking lot running your fingers through your hair. You looked so blissed out. There was no one around and I... I acted impulsively," he admitted.

Sometimes, when he was lying in bed or sitting at his desk or even vaguely still in any way, the mortification of that day heated his skin like a fever. Determined to make a good impression, he had learned little tidbits about as many key crew members as possible so he could sprinkle the factoids in during an introduction.

Jaime Sano, Jr. wasn't supposed to be a woman. She wasn't supposed to have a smile that disrupted his equilibrium. She wasn't supposed to derail his thought process to the extent that he could only dwell on the surprise of her gender instead of her stellar reputation, the impressive handling of her workload, or literally any of the dozens of things he could have said at that moment.

When he spotted her in the parking lot, he had intended to speak to her, to try to apologize and salvage their terrible interaction. Then she leaned on her truck and loosened her severe topknot. He'd heard her contented sigh and his knees almost buckled. The moment seemed private and he was embarrassed to witness it even though he didn't dare look away. No matter how he berated himself, Davis couldn't delete the photo.

"That's disturbing."

"I know!"

"Seriously, it's really creepy." She stared at the picture more intently.

"I promise I don't skulk around taking pictures of you—of anyone!—I behaved rashly."

"That takes some of the creep factor out, I guess." She sounded like she was trying to convince herself. "It still doesn't explain why you kept it, why this is your wallpaper…" she trailed off.

"Can you really not guess?" His voice was low. Davis was standing on a ledge waiting to be pushed. "I like someone."

Junior looked at the image again as the realization hit. "She is beautiful. A little fragile. When she smiles, you feel it all over. You can't get close to her. You always say the wrong thing. You aren't built for casual hookups." Junior looked at Davis now, all their interactions laid bare between them. "You're going to give up on her because she'll never see you that way."

Davis stepped closer to her. Everything was out in the open. She could laugh in his face. She could run screaming. The truth was out and, no matter what happened next, there was an odd relief in it.

"Junior," he said softly. His hands twitched at his sides to reach for her, but he pulled them back at the last moment. He was standing in a minefield. The wrong move—the wrong shift of his weight—and this could detonate.

Junior was transfixed by the photo.

"Do you understand now?"

She nodded.

"Do you want to talk about it?" he asked hopefully.

She shook her head.

"Are you still freaking out?"

"A little," she whispered.

Davis moved even closer. "Junior, please don't worry. This doesn't have to mean anything. We'll go back to how it was. We can pretend this never happened." She hadn't looked up from the screen.

"What if... what if I don't want that?" She looked at him then.

His breath caught in his throat. Of all the outcomes, her showing the slightest interest never even entered the realm of possibility. "If you don't want to pretend it never happened?" he asked, unwilling to leave such a crucial detail to interpretation.

She nodded again.

"We can do that, too," he rushed to reassure her. "We can do whatever you want."

Her attention had returned to the photo. Davis wondered if Junior could see what he did. The woman in that image was ethereal. She was beautiful. She was also a little vulnerable.

"Do you want to leave?" He moved to the other side of the window so her path to the exit was unobstructed.

She shook her head.

It was solidly night outside now. The faint outlines of his lawn that had drawn Junior to the window in the first place had vanished and all they could see was their reflection in the glass.

Davis turned to her, slowly, afraid of spooking her. "Do you want to stay?"

She nodded to his profile in the window.

"We don't..." He shook his head to start again. "I don't expect anything from you. I know this is... a lot. We can just... sit for a minute."

She faced him, still confused. "It was me?"

"Yes," he answered softly.

"You never said anything."

"I might have if I thought there was any point," he said somberly. "I didn't think you could stand me."

"I couldn't. You're an insufferable pedant," she said as though in a trance.

"You couldn't." Davis chose to focus on her verb tense instead of her description. "But now?"

Junior looked away, shy. "Now? I find myself gamely tolerating your pedantry."

Davis let out a relieved breath. Maybe, he hoped, this ordeal could end in something other than ruin. Allowing some of the tension to leave his body, he unclenched his jaw and stretched his neck. Moving to put the kettle on, he said, "I'm going to make some tea. Do you want some?"

Junior shook her head.

"Okay. I'll be back in a minute." Absently, he rubbed her shoulder. The tiny squeeze meant to convey comfort sent a shiver through her, causing Junior to flinch. Their eyes locked and Davis pulled his hand away.

"I'm sorry! I didn't... I wasn't..." He tripped over his words, putting the offending limb behind him.

"You can touch me," she said, stepping closer to him.

He shook his head and kept his hands to himself even as she stood beside him. "I meant what I said. You don't owe me any-thing."

"I know."

"And how I feel about you doesn't have anything to do with your feelings for me." He closed his eyes against the proximity of her.

"Agreed." She waited for him to open his eyes. "Still, it's okay if you touch me. If you want to."

"If I want?" He choked. "You have no idea what I want," he muttered to himself.

"What do you want?" Junior moved even closer to him.

Davis opened his eyes to her expectant gaze. Did she think he could answer when she was so close? He could smell the sweet smoky scent of her and he doubted she understood the weight of the invitation she offered. He couldn't touch her, he knew that, but God how he wanted to.

"Will you tell me?" Junior quietly asked again, when he didn't answer.

Everything else was on the table. He was already certain that facing her again would be impossible, no matter his promise that nothing would change. Why not this? Why not tell her?

"You, Junior. I want you," he admitted.

She stared at him blankly.

Perhaps that was too obvious. He tried to elaborate, "What I want, Junior, is to know everything about you. I want to know about every single song and book and show you love—even the ridiculous ones. Especially the ridiculous ones. I want to roam through market stalls with you. I want to make you laugh. I want to feel the weight of you in my arms. I want to fall asleep beside you, wake up beside you. I want to feed you breakfast in bed. I want you to beg me to stop. I want you to beg me to never stop. I want you sweaty and sticky and breathless beneath me. I want all of you, Junior, in all the ways I can have you."

He'd let himself get carried away—said too much, too soon—but the words were out and could not be put back. Davis forged ahead. He held her shoulders and brought them eye to eye. "But more than all of that, I want to kiss you. That's what I want."

Her breathing was shallow and her eyes were unfocused, but she managed to nod.

Holy mother, did that mean she understood his ramblings? Was it acceptance of this bizarro world they'd fallen into? Did she want him to kiss her? Davis' brain almost short-circuited. He'd spent an embarrassing amount of time thinking up scenarios that ended with her kiss. He'd imagined her mouth would fit against his perfectly. Fuck, he wanted to kiss her.

"Say it, Junior." Davis was barely hanging on to his composure. He wanted her explicit consent. "Say yes."

"Yes," she breathed.

Davis brought her to his mouth in a gentle brushing of lips, a punctuation, before pulling away to assure himself this was happening.

"Again," she said on a sigh.

He kissed her, this time tasting the lollipop as he explored her mouth. She surrendered to his kiss, her body melting into his, her tongue following where his led. This was all he'd wanted–Junior in his arms while he feasted on her soft, sweet lips–and he would stay here, as long as she let him, enjoying the best thing he'd ever done.

"More," she whispered when he pulled away to catch his breath.

Seeing the desire in her eyes was all the encouragement he needed. Davis cradled her head and took full possession of her mouth, kissing her hungrily. Junior arched her body to get closer to him. Davis wrapped an arm around her to lock her body against his. His other hand tilted her head further back for better access to her kiss. Her hands were on his neck, on his shoulders, across his back, pulling him closer. She whimpered when Davis broke their contact to run his tongue down her neck. Feeling a shiver roll up her body when he nibbled at the base of her shoulder put a wicked glint in his eyes.

Now that he had permission to touch her, Davis' hands moved all over her body. He'd been called up to the majors and was ready to make good on the opportunity: his hands on her breasts while he nibbled her ear; a fist full of her hair pulled aside to gain access to her throat, planting wet open-mouthed kisses there; her nipple between his fingers as he caught her bottom lip in his teeth; his thigh pressed against her crotch as she wriggled and squirmed against him. He used every part of his body to overload her senses.

"More," she insisted.

He ran his hand up the back of her thighs, slipping under the hem of her dress, plying her with deep, searching kisses. He slid his thumb into her underwear and groaned when he found her wet and ready. Junior writhed and moved her hips to chase the perfect pressure of his thumb. She struggled with the zipper of his jeans, moving his hand from her body so she could finally free his erection from his clothes. Davis sucked in a breath at Junior's touch and she gave him a sloppy, teeth-clashing kiss as she took him in her hand, stroking firmly.

"I need…" she tried, again. Davis pressed her back to the window, undoing the top three buttons of her dress, his mouth never leaving her body. He completely blanketed her as his one hand held her throat so he could trail kisses down her neck while his other hand returned to make delicious mischief against her clit.

He logged every moan and sigh coaxed from Junior's body. Every place he touched, every sound she made, was a vital detail. The way she exhaled when his teeth grazed her collarbone. The hiccup that escaped when she guided his two fingers inside her. The low rumble in her throat when their tongues collided. And now he would add the soft hum she made when he closed his mouth around her nipple.

"Tell me," he groaned into her skin, running his lip along the swell of her breast, slipping his tongue into her bra to tease her.

Davis would do anything, give anything, she asked of him. With erratic breaths, Davis pleaded, "Tell me what you need, Junior. Let me give it to you."

"I need..."

She wriggled free and leaned over to clumsily root through her bag while Davis pressed kisses on the back of her shoulder, keeping a tight hold on her hip for balance. Straightening, Junior pulled his face to hers and kissed him hungrily. She tore open the foil packet and, catching his lip in her teeth, rolled the condom on the full, hard length of him.

"Fuck. Junior," he hissed.

"Correct. Fuck Junior," she challenged.

He did not flinch from her stare. Instead, Davis returned his hand to the waist of her underwear and gave the flimsy material a forceful tug. Junior moaned into his chest as he hoisted her on the sill, hooked his elbow behind her knee and entered her in one smooth push. Their pleasure echoed in the dark room–hers rolling her eyes; his rumbling through him and weakening his knees. He rested his forehead against hers struggling to regain his focus. The feel of her, God, he was un-prepared–lacked the imagination–for the bliss of being allowed this access.

Junior spurred him to action when she wrapped her other leg around his hip and grabbed his arm for balance. Taking the hint, Davis set a punishing pace into her eager, waiting body, his thumb never wavering from its task. She closed her eyes and tipped her head back against the window.

Davis took the invitation to kiss her shoulders, bite behind her ear, and run his mouth along her jaw. The pressure that had been building finally bubbled over and Junior clutched at him wildly. Davis put his mouth to hers and greedily swallowed every moan and cry and whimper as she came undone. He stilled inside her letting the last waves of her climax crash, both of them laboring to get their breathing under control.

He kissed her softly on the lips. "Was that what you needed?" he asked, caressing her face.

Junior's eyes fluttered open, unseeing. When they regained their focus, she smiled at him and nodded.

He put more gentle kisses on her eyes, her temple, and her forehead. "Good." He placed another soft kiss on her lips. Davis lifted Junior off him and the window sill, discarded the condom, straightened his clothes somewhat and reached a hand towards her. "Come on, let's go upstairs."

Junior stepped unsteadily toward him with a look of confusion.

"What?" he asked.

"Go upstairs?"

"Do you want to stop?" Davis' expression moved from anticipation to concern. He didn't want anything less than her enthusiastic participation.

"Uhhh..." Junior pointed at the outline of her body left in the steamed window. It gave him a small thrill to see that proof even as it already started to fade away. "You're still... I mean... you threw the condom out," she stammered.

"Junior," he said, infinitely patient, "do you want to finish what we started?"

"We may have different definitions of the word 'finish'."

"I don't think we do," he reasoned.

"Then that was...?" she motioned again to the window sill he'd very recently had her pressed against.

"A release?" He shrugged. "It seemed like you needed to take the edge off." Seeing her dangling at the mercy of the pleasure he'd given her was both humbling and supremely gratifying.

"But you didn't?"

"Junior," he held her face gently and brushed his thumbs along her cheekbones, "if you think my first time with you was going to be a quickie against a window, you haven't been paying attention. I want you naked. I want you sweaty and sticky and breathless," Davis repeated since it appeared she had forgot. He gestured between them. "We still have all of our clothes on."

She searched his face. Satisfied with whatever she was looking for, she said teasingly, "When you put it like that, I guess I'd better go upstairs."

"And get naked," he added, relieved.

She wriggled, letting the tattered ruins of her underwear hit the ground. "And get naked," she confirmed cheekily as she headed up the stairs.

Davis looked around in disbelief at the direction his day had taken. Hearing Junior's exaggerated, "Oh, so *this* is where the magic happens!" He decided that whatever transpired to put her in his arms mattered less than him doing everything possible to keep her there for as long as possible.

But how was he to do that when his hands shook with nerves? The expression 'butterflies in my stomach' was insufficient. The feeling was closer to a school of fish swimming madly around in his guts. Trying for calm, Davis took a deep breath. He'd kissed Junior! He'd held her, and kissed her, and felt her come apart in his arms and now she was heading upstairs. To his room. To his bed.

Releasing his breath, he desperately tried to slow the pounding of his blood.

Davis made his way quickly up the stairs, forcing himself to tread lightly down the hall. Everything about this evening was so far beyond his wildest imaginings. And even though he knew she'd be there, finding Junior on his bed still stole his breath and sent shockwaves through his frazzled system.

"You're still dressed. We agreed to naked." Davis didn't recognize the low-pitched commanding voice that came out of his mouth, but Junior seemed very pleased by it.

"You're still dressed."

"I just got here."

Junior raised herself onto her elbows. With a smile that skirted the boundaries of depravity she gave a casual lift of her shoulder. "I thought you'd want to do the honors."

He did want that. There were few things in the world he wanted more.

"Come here." Davis gestured to the side of the bed closest to where he stood.

She pulled a coil from her pigtail straight and let it bounce back into shape. "Why don't *you* come *here*?'

He took the two steps to bring his thighs to the edge of his mattress and waited for her to come closer. Instead of moving, Junior gave him a silent 'Can I help you?' with her perfectly threaded brows.

With one knee on the bed, Davis reached for Junior's ankle and tugged. The giggle she let out when she fell back on his duvet was a playful tinkle of laughter that Davis immediately logged in the Sounds Junior Makes file he'd been compiling for the better part of a year.

"Well, Eyes and Ears, what are you waiting for?" She wriggled in impatient invitation.

His body, still amped from the sex intermission and tired of waiting for his brain to catch up, asked the same thing. He took a minute. One minute to memorize the sight of Junior splayed on his bed in the moonlight. One minute to appreciate the momentous occasion.

"I'm waiting for you to stop squirming and put your hands above your head."

"Oh, really?"

Davis leaned over her and gave her a deep, greedy kiss. "Yes, really. Arms up, Junior."

"Yes, sir." She made a show of crossing her wrists as she lifted her hands above her head.

He separated her hands and with a quick nip of her jaw, scolded, "Behave."

"Make me."

The need in her voice made him impossibly, painfully, harder. He didn't think he was capable of making Junior Sano behave, but he knew he could make her come. So that's what he set about doing.

He removed her dress, leaving her in nothing but her bra, and proceeded to follow every curve and dip of her body with his hands and then again with his mouth. He kissed and nibbled and stroked while she begged him for more. He licked and sucked her nipples through her bra, removed it, then licked and sucked her bare skin.

Finally, he relented and gave her exactly what she cried for.

More. Harder. Again. Faster.

Slower.

They came together in a tangle of tongues and teeth and limbs again and again until Davis didn't know anything but the feel of her skin against his.

Junior, in the throes of climax, was like tapping into pure, unfettered pleasure. He'd had to remind her to breathe, as though her body was so committed to receiving its pleasure even basic functions were discarded. It was so intoxicating, he was mesmerized as he brought her to orgasm with his hands, twice with his mouth, and this last time with his dick.

When his body could hold off no longer, Davis tipped over the edge. His own orgasm hit him like the surf along the shore, pounding and relentless, taking no notice of anything in its path.

He shook with the force of it while Junior did her own share of licking and kissing as she purred her encouragement, telling him how good he felt steadily throbbing inside her, pleading with him to keep coming, keep filling the condom, as she brought herself to orgasm with her fingers. And also his dick, he thought dazedly, for a third time.

Junior rolled onto her stomach and lay her head on her folded arms while Davis hurried to the washroom. Returning to his bed, he pressing his entire body along her right side. They lay together in the silence, enjoying the delicious uselessness of their muscles, and waited for their frontal cortexes to come back online.

He was lit up like a Roman candle. His entire body thrummed, as if taunting his brain with a smug 'See? Get on board, Over Thinker!'. His brain, also a bit fuzzy, reluctantly ceded the point. Sex with Junior had been phenomenal. He'd never been so turned on, never felt so connected–never climaxed so hard!–in his life. And still, this right now–a sleepy Junior tangled in his sheets and smiling at him–was the most transcendent experience.

"I can't believe you're here." His voice was soft as his hands roamed aimlessly on her skin. "How are you here?"

"It's definitely not how I saw this errand playing out."

"Errand?"

"I was supposed to be doing kickback recon. Not doing... you."

Davis had forgot all about that. Was that earlier today? He didn't want to acknowledge the passing of time. The world around him could wait. All he wanted was to stay in bed with Junior.

"I can't complain too much."

"You have complaints?"

"Definitely not about this." He pressed his mouth to hers for a kiss. Her hair was soft against his palm, her curls barely contained by her hair tie. He wanted to turn on all the lights and look at her, take her all in, but that would require him to get out of bed. Discarding the condom was enough of a chore. Davis refused to leave the bed while Junior was still in it. Not again.

"You really didn't want to have that party, huh?"

He walked his fingers up and down her spine in a meandering path.

Davis did not like the implication and quickly corrected her. "Sex with you wasn't my solution to getting out of it."

Junior raised her head enough to kiss his forearm in acknowledgment. "Still, calling it off will be even easier now that you've had your lady."

"Had the lady?" He stopped his wandering hand. At her furrowed brow he matched her posture, laying on his belly with his head on his folded his arms facing her, "Or, do I have the lady?"

"Fletcher..."

Davis barreled forward before she could finish her sentence. "I don't... I'm not good at being casual. I really like you and want to get to know you better." They both let out a little chuckle at their current level of familiarity. She reached over and gave his bicep a small encouraging squeeze. "I don't know what happens next."

"I don't know either. I didn't expect any of this."

She didn't expect any of this? Davis hadn't been on solid ground since he'd opened the door to find her on his front porch. If you'd given him a million dollars and infinite guesses, he still wouldn't have accurately predicted this ending to his day. Junior naked and whispering in his bed was a dream he'd only recently given up on for its sheer futility.

"I know I'm alone in my feelings and sex doesn't change anything—"

"Not... alone. Maybe just... not as advanced?" Her interruption came in low and halting, as though she'd stumbled to the truth while speaking.

He chose his words carefully. "Does that mean you want to see where this goes?"

"It means I need to figure it out."

That was encouraging, wasn't it? He knew he wasn't going to get relationship status after tonight, but his stubborn brain wanted her to spell it out. He wanted the chasm between hating his guts and potentially being his girlfriend to start closing with this first step.

He stole another soft kiss. "Can we figure it out together?"

"We do work well together," she smiled against his lips.

"We do, don't we?" Davis pulled her close, settling her into his side, and held her until she fell asleep.

***

Junior's head was spinning as she blinked into the darkness. Davis' steady, slumbering breath tickled her neck. As she squirmed, he pulled her closer to his side, removing the precious distance she'd managed since waking in his arms.

How did she get here, lying in a disheveled mess in Davis Fletcher's bed, tucked up against him, while her torn underwear lay abandoned on his living room floor? The whole thing was too absurd to contemplate. He'd confessed his feelings and offered her a cup of tea like they were going to sit on the couch to discuss their favorite colors.

Davis Fletcher had been into her for who knows how long. He'd been interested and then convinced himself that he had to move on without once making a move or indicating even a platonic interest. All this time he'd harbored these feelings. All this time he'd watched her from afar without ever hinting at anything more than a polite acquaintanceship. She'd only intended to stay long enough to make sense of it all.

But he was so adorable as he stammered his apology for touching her without consent, assuring Junior that his feelings had no bearing on hers. Then he was incredibly sexy with all his sweaty begging talk. And the kiss... Davis was a good kisser, damn him!

Her need had always been a greedy, impetuous thing—and Davis fed and nurtured it until it took on a weight and shape of its own. The more she needed, the more he gave her and, like a wildfire, Junior's need consumed everything in its path.

It didn't matter that the small part of her still capable of clear-headed reason had screamed for her to stop or, at the very least, slow down and remember that Davis wanted something she could not give. This was not a simple case of two bodies giving and taking pleasure. This was a man who wanted commitment and he wanted to try having it with her. And even knowing she could not adhere to something so lofty, her need still demanded that she take everything he was willing to give. Junior had no excuses or explanations—she'd chased her pleasure into a ludicrous situation. Again.

She couldn't take all the blame for what happened, though, could she? Yes, Davis was smart and affable. But his kind, consideration only highlighted the fact he'd fucked her like a deviant god of sinful carnality. Junior couldn't remember the last time she'd been so well-used. Her body was so wonderfully loose and achy, she seriously contemplated waking him up with her mouth so they could do it again.

No.

She knew better. Davis only thought he wanted her. The reality of her never matched people's expectations and while Junior didn't have a problem with Davis knowing what she looked like without any clothes, she couldn't allow him to see her naked.

Nothing about this situation could be categorized as reasonable and Junior cringed thinking about the scope of this fuck up. Luckily, she knew exactly what to do when visiting Bad Decisionville: give the slip in the middle of the night and hope like hell the three months between seasons would be enough time to recover from this phenomenal lapse in judgment.

Slowly, with practiced skill, Junior escaped the warmth of his embrace. The cooler air already worked at clearing her head. She took one last look at his sleeping face—he really was an uncommonly handsome man—and searched for her dress in the dark. Blessedly, her bra had landed in the same vicinity. With her clothes clutched to her chest, she slipped out of his room, and made her way stealthily down the stairs. Grabbing her underwear off the floor en route to where she left her purse at his desk, Junior quietly buttoned her dress while stuffing her feet in her shoes.

Satisfied she'd recovered all her belongings, Junior let out a long, silent breath before leaving his house.

It had been fun but it absolutely could not happen again.

***

Davis turned, searching for the already familiar weight of Junior's body pressed to his. She was gone. He didn't need to open his eyes to know. The sound of her truck's ignition rumbling to life beneath his open window answered for him.

It was disorienting. Her scent lingered on the sheets that were still warm to the touch, so how could those be her headlights flooding his dark, quiet street when she didn't even say good-bye?

Davis was wrong. This was the most surreal thing that'd happened since he'd found her on his doorstep.

He could admit his thoughts of bringing her coffee in the morning may have been fanciful. He was prone to getting carried away where she was concerned. But she'd said they'd figure it out together, hadn't she?

Davis finally let his eyes open to face the truth he already knew.

That's not what she'd said at all.

And what was he supposed to do now? Text her and ask why she left? Demand that she come back? Would he have bothered with sleep had he known this one fever dream of a night was all he'd have with her? He debated with himself, the chance to kiss and caress her versus the perfection of feeling her snuggled next to him, instead of admitting how bitterly disappointed he was.

His brain gave his body a haughty sniff as it chided him for naive hopes. Not that his body noticed. It was too busy fighting the bitter churn of acid in his stomach. Or was it bile from his liver? Either way, it was a hot misery he felt in the back of his throat.

He'd watched her for months. Davis knew she offered the illusion of intimacy but didn't really allow people to get close to her. Her easy smiles and playful touches were smoke and mirrors. It was his number one obstacle to getting to know her. Well, number two. Junior believing him an insufferable pedant was definitely the larger obstacle.

He knew all of that and still fell victim to it anyway.

Because he'd believed her when she'd said he wasn't alone in his feelings.

But she hadn't even said good-bye.

Chapter 10

LITTLE AGGRAVATIONS PREOCCUPIED MOST of Davis' day. Quinn had presented an excellent six-episode outline and Fifty-Four was totally on board with her vision until Eli complained that it was too 'Feminist Manifesto'. Added to that was his frustration with his dealings—could he even call it a relationship? – with Junior.

He'd asked her, that first night, what happened next. He'd done a fairly good job, he thought, of reiterating that he wasn't interested in a fling. He'd tried casual relationships before and he invariably tangled sex with emotion to his own detriment. She said she needed to figure some stuff out and that this, them, in the understatement of the year, was unexpected. She said she would figure it out and then left while he slept, disappearing for five days.

They'd been together a handful of times since then. Always after dark. Always at her whim. Always she slipped away before sunrise. And always he was disappointed that she hadn't stayed.

He told himself that it was the talking late into the night that confused the issue and that if she'd got up and got dressed afterward instead of the murmured exchanges they shared, naked and tangled in each other, it wouldn't sting as much come morning. But the truth was that she was still circling cautiously, afraid to land, and it chafed.

He looked at the window, remembering, as he often did when he thought about her. A hand moved languidly in his periphery and caught his attention. Someone was in his yard. "What the?" he muttered, sticking his head out the back door. "Junior?"

She was sunbathing topless on one of his lounge chairs.

"Oh, hey!" she looked up at the sound of his voice. "I hope you don't mind that I waited for you?"

"Waited?" Davis was caught off guard and very, very distracted.

"I know we didn't have plans or anything," she continued. Plans. He almost laughed. "What are you doing back here?"

"I had a bit of stuff to do at the office. It was a ghost town, by the way. Pete mentioned that you'd just left, so I thought I'd swing by." She stood and stretched, her dark nipples beckoning, before continuing, "But, of course, you weren't here." She picked up her purse and cell phone in one hand and her discarded dress turned beach towel in the other.

"I had to return my production vehicle," he said dumbly. He couldn't gather his thoughts fast enough to even remember if he saw AJ's assistant while he was at the office. Obviously, he had if the man was updating Junior on his whereabouts.

"I was going to wait on the porch, but some old vidajena was giving me greasy eyeballs and I didn't want to have to slap one of your neighbors, so I came back here." Stepping through the doorway, Junior reached on her tiptoes to kiss Davis hello. "That chair was so comfy and the sun felt so good. I couldn't resist."

"What if someone saw you? What if I wasn't alone?"

"Someone like who, your side piece?" she teased, plopping her pile of belongings on the couch.

"Literally anyone, Junior." Davis stepped onto his deck to quickly scan for neighbors who may have got an eyeful.

Davis returned inside to find her standing in the middle of the room, half naked, looking pensive. He watched as Junior took in her surroundings, having never seen his place in daylight, the accent pieces seemed to be catching her eye. Beautiful woven throws hung over both the couch and chair. A large, beaded mat was on the coffee table under four clay pots of assorted size and wholeness. The painting of what looked like swaths of color but was, in fact, an abstract rendering of a teepee housing a fire on the plains.

"He calls you Chief," she murmured to herself, still scrutinizing his living room.

"For the love of God, Junior, put some clothes on! I can't concentrate."

"This is literally nothing you haven't seen before."

"I definitely haven't seen you naked in my living room."

"Not naked. Topless." She tsked, pulling her dress from the pile on the couch. She continued to take in the space as a whole. "Which has been perfectly legal since the 90s."

Davis made his way to stand behind her.

"Eli calls you Chief," she said again.

"Let's talk about what these underpants are doing for me." He groaned into her hair, removing the dress from her grasp and dropping it on the floor. He'd never get tired of feeling the softness of her tightly coiled curls. It was, after all, part of his ongoing investigation into the source of her sweet smoky scent.

She leaned into his embrace, exposing her neck. "I didn't figure you for the white cotton briefs type."

"Seeing you in them, I am easily swayed to a pro-cotton brief position." He grazed the column of skin while he looked out at the room over her shoulder.

"Why does Eli call you Chief?" she asked directly.

"Eli thinks it's funny because my mother is Cree."

"You're Indigenous?"

"Non-Status, yes." He turned her and kissed a trail along her neck.

"And you're okay with Eli's casual bigotry?"

"Junior, I have a handful of your ass and a hard-on that can only be described as biblical. I do not want to talk about Eli right now."

That got her attention. "Biblical, eh?" She reached in to judge for herself. Davis quirked his brow, awaiting her verdict. She wrapped her hand around the base of his erection, leaned up to his mouth, and asked, "Then what do you want to talk about?"

Davis ran his hands down her sides, delighting in the feel of her. "Did you know," she said cheerfully, "that the sash the Bonhomme Carnaval wears is a nod to the Métis ceinture fléchée? I learned that in Grade 6 Social Studies."

"I don't want to talk about that either." He kissed her hungrily. What he wanted was to feast on her body while the sun shone through his blinds, lighting his way.

"Rude. I worked very hard on that project!" She pouted when they parted.

"I don't want to talk about twelve-year-old you, either."

"Ten," she corrected, reminding him of her skipped grades. "You should probably take these off." Junior tugged at his shorts. "I know how you feel about having sex with your clothes on."

"You do, do you?" he said as he brought her mouth to his.

Junior broke from his kiss to pull his shirt over his head before undoing his shorts. "Yeah," she breathed, "I do."

He pulled her to him, eager to feel her sun-warmed skin against his. Davis' forearm was a brace on her spine, keeping her flush against him. There was no space between them but still he pressed her closer to his body, kissing the side of her face.

"Do you want to talk about how I know that?" she teased, looking at the corner where they shared their first touch.

"Nope," he said and, without warning, hauled her up and over his shoulder.

"Put me down!" Junior shrieked, trying in vain to wriggle free. "You'll throw your back out!"

Junior wasn't a small woman. She could generously be described as pear-shaped. It was this bottom-heavy silhouette—her height coupled with the way her hips flared out from the noticeable dip at her waist—that played into the illusion of slimness. Still, Davis slung her over his shoulders with seeming little effort.

"Nope," he said again, biting her on the ass cheek closest to him, before taking her upstairs to show her exactly what he did want to talk about.

"Go on, ask." Davis pressed a kiss on top of Junior's head.

"Ask what?" she craned her neck to look at him.

Holding her in his arms this way, with the afternoon sun spilling into his bedroom, created a new intimacy between them. In the daylight, he could see that her lips were a little swollen from his kisses and that there was a dazed, satisfied, sex-drunk look in her eyes. When he ran his hands along her body, he could see—not just feel—where her skin pebbled in goosebumps. He liked being able to look at her this way, fully and completely.

He smirked at her. "I don't know what it says about me that after that"—he tugged the sheet Junior was tangled in—"you're still thinking about Eli. I can feel the questions radiating off you."

"What can I say? I'm a complex creature capable of holding multiple thoughts simultaneously. I can experience a headboard rattling orgasm *and* wonder why you allow his racism to go unchecked."

"Yes, and I was hoping the headboard rattling orgasm would put all other thoughts out of your head. There are many things I'd rather discuss with a woman post-coital in my bed."

"Yuck. Don't ever say that to me again."

"What should I say?" He kissed her.

Junior would not be deterred or distracted. "Why do you pretend to be white when you're not?"

"I don't pretend. I don't bother correcting people." His hands drew indecipherable shapes on her skin. Confessions uttered in the many lush spaces of her body had quickly become his new religion.

"Semantics," she accused.

"Not really. I have never and would never deny my heritage. I'm proud of who I am. I don't need to announce it all the time," he explained.

"Weird," Junior answered.

"Why is that weird? You don't run around saying you're Black all the time."

"That's not even remotely the same. There's absolutely no way to identify me as anything other than a Black woman."

"Right. I look like what I am, too."

"Are you being willfully ignorant? Because I cannot overlook that, even in the face of all the orgasms."

"Obviously it's not the same. I know that. What I'm trying to say is that I do look like what I am but people choose not to see it because my skin isn't brown."

Junior looked at him and, taking in his wide, sharp cheekbones, his full lips, his deep-set eyes, and strong brow, conceded his point. He absolutely read as Indigenous.

Funny how a little distance, a simple lack of reference, robbed him of his entire identity. Back home, where Indigenous people are more densely populated, it was never a question. There were too many people who looked like him living their everyday lives for Davis to be thought of as Other.

"I guess if you're going to have a misapplied identity, it's hard to beat 'straight white guy'."

"The only real benefit is not having to answer stupid questions or being held to a standard based on some superficial benchmarks."

"Newsflash, Sapó: that's literally the privilege of whiteness. You get to be an individual instead of a representative of your entire race."

"Fair point."

"Still doesn't explain why you let Eli say that shit to you," Junior pressed.

"Fuck that guy. He is on his way out. He knows it, too. That's why he uses petty manipulations to make himself feel less obsolete. Everyone knows his time has passed. It's only Olivia's loyalty that keeps him in his position."

"And your silence," she accused.

"My silence buys his silence. I won't have to pretend I'm not insulted when people ask if I 'got in' through some rehab outreach program or when they gush at how jealous they are that I don't pay taxes and got to go to university for free. Which I didn't. Most of us don't, by the way." He didn't want the bile of repeated generational injustice spilling onto this moment. He also couldn't pretend it didn't exist.

"Why did you say you were non-status? You're Cree," Junior wondered.

"My mom was enfranchised when she married my dad."

"That's so fucked up," Junior acknowledged. "She can appeal that now, can't she?"

Davis shrugged. "She says the government can't take something that wasn't theirs to give and she's no less Cree because of who she married."

They lay quietly for a moment before she spoke again. "I'm not trying to engage in a contest of Who Has It Worse, okay? All I'll say is: you are uniquely positioned to do something about the Elis of the world. Your white presenting privilege will make sure the words are heard in a way they are not when coming from marginalized voices."

"That's just it, Junior. He already knows I'm a marginalized voice so my words will not be heard in any other way. He'll make sure of it. Trust me, he'll get what he deserves."

"That is historically inaccurate."

"Maybe. But I will deal with Eli my way."

***

"Morning!" Junior called out from the side entrance of her friend Leigh Bridger's shop. "I've come for books and baked goods!"

"I was gonna call you later. Are you still good to cover for me next week? Wednesday afternoon and Friday evening?" Leigh wiped down another table in the café section of her bookstore.

Leigh was notoriously reluctant to ask for help. She'd carry insurmountable loads in silence to avoid being perceived as an inconvenience yet somehow didn't see shouldering all of her family's dramas as anything other than her responsibility. Knowing continued attempts to get Leigh to see the flaw in her logic would fall on deaf ears, Junior chose helping in any way she could—whether Leigh asked for it or not.

"Absolutely," Junior confirmed, heading straight to the counter to pilfer a square of fudge from the display case.

"Thanks, you're a lifesaver."

"Are you kidding? It's not every day your baby wins an award!"

"My baby's daddy is getting an award for athletic achievement," Leigh corrected, "But yes, we're excited."

"Meh." Junior deadpanned, "I was invested when I thought it was Langston."

"Langston? I can count on one hand the number of times that boy displayed any form of athleticism in his twenty-six years of life."

"Your son has always been wise beyond his years," Junior reasoned. "He should write a book–Winning at Life Without Breaking a Sweat: The Langston Coffield Story!"

Leigh let out a gleeful chuckle. "Speaking of soon to be published books, there are galleys for you to pick through." Leigh motioned to the new shipment visible on her desk, as she continued her opening rituals. Junior wandered over to paw through the stack. "I thought you were stopping by yesterday?"

"I got distracted and lost track of time." Junior's voice was muffled from behind the walls of Leigh's office.

"Mmhmm." Leigh finished with the last of the tables and made her way to her office.

"You don't know–I could have been doing any number of things!" Junior protested too much. "I could have been with AJ saying Yes!"

Already knowing the answer, Leigh asked, "Were you?"

"No."

Junior had no idea what had possessed her to show up at Davis' yesterday. She'd stripped the phrase 'one-night stand' of all meaning and now she'd brought it into the light of day? The plan was to peel out of Bad Decisionville like a thief in the night, not stroll down Main Street perusing real estate! She hadn't even set up any ground rules because there wasn't supposed to be a second time. Or a third. Or yesterday's sixth.

Davis didn't ask any questions whenever she appeared on his doorstep. He only held her close, kissed her breathless, and made her cry out her release. And after, when she was flushed and limp and sated? Davis whispered his idle musings into her skin. Things like *you were in the stairwell the first time I saw you and I thought* please *don't work on Elysian, I won't survive it* as he trailed kisses up her spine. And *you hold your breath when you come like you're bracing for impact* into the crook of her neck. Or *I can't quantify the ways I want you but you could figure it out, couldn't you—that magnificent brain of yours could calculate the ways* with his face on her stomach. Unable to resist, she'd address his random thoughts and before she knew it, they were talking and sharing and giggling in the cocoon of his bed. It was devilry!

Leigh chuckled while she got herself organized. "Does this distraction have a name or did you bother?"

Rolling her eyes in protest, Junior huffed. "Knowing a name and forgetting it in the interim is not the same as never knowing it."

"Isn't it?" the ever-responsible Leigh challenged.

Junior sighed and leaned on the filing cabinet. She always loved the beginning of new relationships when everything was exciting. The tremor of anticipation rushed through her like a drug.

New conversation, new routines, new touches and kisses, all kept her attention for a time. Unfortunately, that feeling always wore off and she was left feeling nothing at all. The nothing usually started small. Maybe she wouldn't get excited when their name flashed across her screen. Or a kiss didn't elicit the same thrill as it used to. Sometimes she would balk if they tried making plans too far in the future. Other times it was a caress that didn't cause butterflies. Eventually, the nothing grew and grew until she couldn't even muster up enough interest for sex.

No matter how long they lasted or how they ended, Junior always remembered each beginning fondly. You didn't need a name for that.

"No, Leigh, it's not," Junior insisted.

"Mmhmm."

"Whatever." Junior pulled some books from the pile of galleys. Leigh laughed, placing the newest release in the series about the Victorian-era girl gang that moved seamlessly between Mayfair ballrooms and Covent Garden bars on top of Junior's growing pile. Junior gasped in delight. "Gracias, mijita!"

"You're welcome, you chaos demon," Leigh replied affectionately. "I don't care about the random sex–you know that, right? You're a consenting adult." Junior looked up at the familiar face and waited for her to finish. "It's how arbitrary it all seems that worries me. Life doesn't have to just happen to you."

Junior nodded.

Leigh was right. This thing she'd started with Davis would be no different than the others. The novelty of it all–the sheer peculiarity of getting involved with Dickface–would wane, like it always did and she would look back and remember that moment in his living room with a smile. Junior did not doubt that this entire situation was fleeting. And since it was going to end anyway, why couldn't she stick around and enjoy the ride? So long as she was careful, there was no reason this couldn't be a satisfying summertime interlude.

Standing at the fork in the road, Junior chose to have a couple more dances with the devil before leaving Bad Decisionville for good.

"Leigh, is there quiche? I'm going to sit at my tree." Junior smiled, packing her books in a tote. "It's the perfect day for a picnic!"

Chapter 11

"**S**HOULD I BE CONCERNED," Junior murmured, her breathing still labored, "about you perpetuating the stereotype of Indigenous people's wanton desires?"

"I believe that bit of fiction is only reserved for our women." Lying behind her limp body, slowly softening inside her, Davis bit gently behind her ear.

"Stop biting me," she whined.

Davis froze. "Did I hurt you?" He was always so careful with her.

"No, I'm okay," she reassured him.

"You don't like it?" he asked, angling himself to see her face. When she didn't answer, he smiled wickedly. "You don't like that you like it?" He ran his hands up her sides, kissing the column of her neck and gently bit her jaw. She clenched around him and moaned softly. "What a shame to have to give up such a delicious reaction," he murmured, "but I'll stop biting if you want me to." He caught her earlobe with his teeth and she shivered. She buried her face in the mattress and shook her head, aroused and embarrassed.

"Hallelujah!" Davis reached an arm beneath her body, bringing them both to a seated position, her back against his chest, settling her between his legs.

"I've been fed a pack of lies. You claimed to be a starry-eyed romantic, unlucky in love. And now that I'm helplessly in your thrall, you've revealed yourself a practiced Lothario!"

Davis chuckled against the back of her neck. "What can I say? You inspire a certain...enthusiasm in me."

"Your enthusiasm is well received." She ran her hand along his thigh. "I'm curious about your mastery in the face of your previously claimed status as an outcast."

"It's true, I struggled in the beginning to find my place. I didn't fit in—for so many reasons. Then I met Suneetha when I was still an undergrad and she was in second-year med school."

"Gag," Junior mocked.

"You have a problem with the name Suneetha?"

"I think it's a beautiful name. I was pre-emptively barfing for the 'went through the Kama Sutra with my Indian girlfriend' part of the story," Junior said derisively.

"Wrong cliché, Smarty-pants. Why reach for an ancient Sanskrit text when the play on Indian and Indian is such low-hanging fruit?" he kissed her temple.

"Ew, seriously?"

"Oh, yeah. It was actually kind of impressive, looking back on it," Davis mused.

"So, you and the good doctor..." Junior nudged, not needing any more detail on the ways people could be cruel to each other.

"Being with Suneetha, highly focused and ambitious, was like finding the key to unlocking campus life. She never complained about how much time I spent studying or working and I never felt pressured to take her out. We went for cheap beer and shitty pizza or a low-budget dinner party with her friends sometimes. But otherwise, we stayed in, doing homework and having sex. It was great."

"I bet," Junior teased. "Playing doctor with a doctor? Can't beat that!"

"I spent a lot of time learning about the human body's many erogenous zones," Davis whispered, pressing the ridge of Junior's ear between his thumb and forefinger.

"Where is she now?" Junior's breath hitched in her throat. "I'd love to send her a fruit basket or something." If she was the one that taught Davis how to do the thing with his tongue and pinky finger, Junior would happily lavish the woman with gifts and cash prizes.

"I wish I knew," Davis admitted.

"What do you mean?"

"Growing up the way I did makes something like university feel inconceivable. Everything was bigger and louder and more crowded than I'd ever experienced. Suddenly, I'm responsible for all this money and there are temptations everywhere. I could have easily fallen victim to any number of things in my eagerness to fit in. She was a lifeboat. I owe her so much and she has no idea." He ran his mouth along Junior's neck. It'd been weeks and his touch still ignited that inexplicable thrum to her skin.

"Then what happened?" she asked, her breathing shaky.

"Nothing happened. I guess... I didn't believe her when she told me that our arrangement was temporary. After almost three years together, I thought... She always said we had an expiry date." Junior felt him shrug. "I was naïve enough to think that something about me would change her mind."

"I guess that's the downside to being with a focused, ambitious woman." Recognizing it would be bad form to bring it up right then, Junior made a mental note to make sure they were on the same page about the parameters of this fling.

"Yeah. The worst part was realizing I didn't have a single friend of my own. I mean, yes, I knew people and could kill an afternoon in the commons and there were coworkers I could crack jokes with, but my actual friends were all Suneetha's and when we split, even though it was amicable, I didn't know how to bridge that gap."

"But you have friends now, right?" Junior asked.

"Yeah, I guess," he reluctantly allowed. "It's hard for me to connect with people. I'm still not great with navigating that stuff. It's uncomfortable when I get it wrong so I generally keep to myself."

"What about Remy and Jamal?" she reminded him.

"They're your friends," he deflected.

Junior knew what that confusing loneliness felt like. She wouldn't let Davis suffer it unnecessarily. "You hanging out with them has nothing to do with me. You're an insufferable pedant–I certainly wanted nothing to do with you!"

"Is that right?" Davis grinned at the familiar rebuke, clamping his arms around her torso.

"God, yes!" she continued teasing. "I did my level best to avoid you at all costs!"

At that, he flipped her on her back and pinned her in place. "I'd noticed." He leaned in and kissed her, tugging the sheet off.

"It didn't stop you in any way, though, did it?"

"Can't say that it did," he admitted against her mouth.

"And now I've rewarded your bad behavior with my attention and naked overtures," she struggled against her rising arousal as he kissed a path down her body. Being on the receiving end of Davis' determined focus was an onslaught to her senses.

"I do feel very rewarded." He flicked his tongue in her belly button, letting out a little hum of enjoyment at the sound of her hissed pleasure.

"I suppose I only have myself to blame for your continued effrontery."

"I suppose so." Davis grinned, then lowered his mouth and gave her clit the full scope of his insolence.

JUNIOR WOKE UP DISORIENTED. Aside from the few hours in the morning when they'd had a picnic at the Rosetta McClain Garden, a favorite of Junior's for its mix of city and nature, and two breaks for food and facilities, they'd spent the entire day in this bed. His head was on her stomach, his left arm along her side, his right arm under her shoulder as though he had started the climb up her body when the strings were cut and he lay where he fell. She ran her fingers gently through his hair, unable to move any other part of her body without disturbing him.

He stirred. "Hi."

"Hi." She smiled at him, still running her fingers through his hair. "Did you have a good sleep?"

"What time is it?" His voice was scratchy from his nap.

"I have no idea. I can't reach my phone," she said softly.

"Shit. Sorry. Did I crush you? Why didn't you wake me?" He immediately lifted himself off her.

"I'm fine. What about you? That can't have been comfortable." Junior was certain there was a crick in his neck and a numb right hand he wasn't mentioning. Davis prioritized Junior with a single-mindedness that bordered on pathological.

"Literally falling asleep between your legs? It doesn't get any better." He raised her leg and kissed above her ankle.

Davis adjusted himself on the bed, pulling Junior to his side covering them. "My seventeen-year-old self would have borne his virginity with much more fortitude if he knew he'd one day wake up naked with the prettiest, most popular girl in school."

Junior snorted her laughter. "I was not the prettiest or even remotely popular in school."

"You don't expect me to believe that," Davis said, tracing abstract patterns on her back.

She shrugged. "Believe what you want. I'm saying that seventeen-year-old you should get it over with: take that nice girl to prom, book a hotel room and cover it in rose petals for the big deflowering, because seventeen years later he is in bed with a fraud."

"First of all, it is very sweet that you think I could have afforded a hotel room or enough flowers to spread any petals anywhere, even if there was a girl who was willing to go to prom with me."

"If we're pretending you would have been happy to wait seventeen years for me, let's also pretend that you rented a limo and went to prom."

"A limo, too?" he laughed. "Is that how you showed up to prom?"

"I didn't go to prom."

"Really? You didn't?"

"Uh-uh." She shook her head. "I could have, by then. I probably should have," she said more to herself.

"Why didn't you?" He continued drawing lazily on her skin.

Junior thought back to her time in school. It was all so fraught with her unfulfilled dreams and wasted efforts.

"I didn't want to risk being disappointed," her answer was equal parts honest and cryptic. She tried again to explain. "School wasn't fun for me when I was younger."

"I can't imagine." He kissed her shoulder and said softly, "Trying to get through the day with a horde of pubescent boys throwing themselves at your feet."

Junior knew that he was goofing around, that he had no idea what her childhood and early teens were like, but she was trying to tell him something and he wasn't listening.

"Were you always handsome?" She challenged, willing him to understand.

"You mean did I always look like this? Yeah, kinda," Davis said easily. "I was scrawnier, certainly, but yes, I always looked like me. Why, do you find it hard being so beautiful?" Junior felt an edge to his teasing now.

Enough! She shook herself free of his embrace, sitting upright, arms clasped around her knees. "No, actually, it's really fucking easy being beautiful, if you want to know the truth. I highly recommend it!" She didn't bother hiding the venom in her voice.

She shifted herself to the edge of the bed, away from the feel of his skin. How was he not understanding her? Wasn't this loneliness something they had in common? After all his talk about seeing her, about wanting to have her wholly and completely, he was like everyone else–blinded by the package with no interest in the contents.

This whole thing was a colossal mistake–she should have pulled the ripcord that first night like she'd planned. "Where are my clothes?" she muttered to herself, remembering that their clothing had started to come off on the stairs. She sprang to her feet. Her voice was barely above a whisper when she headed for the door. "I need to go."

***

"Junior!" Davis called after her but she didn't stop.

She must have heard the commotion of him trying to pull on some shorts and barrel down the stairs because she was looking up at him when he appeared on the landing. "Junior, what just happened?"

He watched her, her top and skirt back on but her bra and underwear in her hand and wanted nothing more than to return to bed where they had playfully enjoyed each other all day.

Getting her text that morning instructing him to meet her out front in ten minutes was already such a deviation from their established nocturnal routine that he hadn't stopped to ask any other questions before hopping in her truck. He was satisfied simply to be wherever she was.

They'd walked hand-in-hand through the garden and then ate together under a large tree. Junior had confided it was her favorite place in the whole city. She and her grandfather used to sit under the same tree and talk about every and anything at all.

When they'd returned from her thoughtfully planned picnic at the park, she leaned over the console of her truck to kiss him. Sure that she meant it as goodbye, he'd impulsively suggested she come inside. Her laugh bubbled from deep in her throat as she said, "It's either that or I come right here," and deepened their kiss.

Now she was searching the darkening room for her things so she could leave him.

"Junior, please. Stop." He made his way to her as she stuffed her delicates in her bag and hung it on her shoulder.

"I had fun today," she said without meeting his eyes. "I'll see you around, okay?"

"What does that mean?" His volume hid his rising panic.

She continued looking through him.

"Please. Please, just tell me why you're mad. I was joking before. You have to know that." He reached out and gently held her wrist.

"I do know that. I do." One side of her mouth lifted in a shadow of a smile. Pulling out of his grasp, she hunched her shoulders over and pressed her hands on her ribs, the way she did in the parking lot the day she told him about her grief.

"But I did something wrong?" It was more of a statement. An acceptance of the inevitable.

He watched Junior pull herself together. "I was trying to tell you something."

"Okay, so tell me." He tugged on her arm.

"You kept joking about how beautiful and popular I must have been, but I wasn't. Not even close. I was a shy, awkward, rule-following bookworm who dreaded going to school because I had no friends. A chubby little girl who was picked on for eating weird food and talking funny, whose parents didn't allow simple character-building activities like sleepovers or summer camp, but spoke openly about sex work and structural inequality," she said, chin raised in defiance. "I was so lonely. I was paralyzed by the fear of never figuring out why the kids at school hated me. Then one day, puberty hit and I was hot. Nothing else about me changed. I still ate weird food, still read ahead on the assignments, and still talked funny. Somehow none of it mattered anymore."

Her voice was harsh and far away as though she were lost in the memory of their arbitrary, unfair response to her overnight transformation. "Somehow it was 'totes adorbs' how nerdy I was. For long, painful years I wondered when it would all get taken away. When would they realize that they let the wrong girl in and banish me back to my place, lurking in the shadows?" She looked at him now, desperate.

He tried to convey his understanding with his eyes.

"Now, I know it's all a fucking game. A game I am very good at playing." She laughed ruefully. "But I owe it to the twelve-year-old who begged her parents for a 'normal' birthday party. The girl who waited at a kitchen table crammed with chips and chocolates and pop to win over her classmates that didn't show? I owe it to her to keep playing."

"It might have been who you were but it's not who you are now," he tried to inject a level of surety in this voice that belied the fact that he didn't quite understand.

"Isn't it?"

"It doesn't have to be."

"Why? Aren't you still the dirt-poor half breed with a learning disability and something to prove?" The viciousness of her words was softened only by the hollowness of her delivery.

Davis turned away from her, but he wasn't fast enough to stop the words from landing in his chest and seeping out like a slow-burning poison in his veins.

He was still the dirt-poor kid who didn't fit in properly and the life he built for himself in this city that had chewed up and spat out so many small-town dreamers before him was a testament to his drive and ambition.

Oh, he understood *exactly* what she'd been trying to say.

When Davis looked at Junior again, she was ready for confrontation. He placed his hands on her neck, kissed her chastely, and said, "Yes. I am."

Davis wrapped his arms around her and held her close while she let the fight drain out of her. He held her quietly, rubbing his hand up and down her spine until the sky went from navy to black, the tiny bulb on the range hood the only light to see by. Davis ran his finger between the strap of her bag and her shoulder. "Can we get rid of this now?" he asked, his voice low and hopeful.

"No."

"No?" He was disappointed of course, but he knew such an uncharacteristic display of vulnerability would trigger her flight instincts.

"Can we get something to eat?" Junior mumbled into his chest.

Relief flooded his system. She was going to stay. She'd opened up to him, fought to make herself understood, and was choosing to stay.

Davis placed a tender kiss on her temple. "Yeah, okay. Lemme get dressed."

She picked up this morning's discarded shirt and tossed it at him. "There. You're ready."

"We're naked under our clothes."

"Everybody is naked under their clothes," she shot back.

"You know what I mean. Your underpants are in your bag."

"What, are you going to hand out flyers announcing it? Come on, I'm starving!" she cried.

Davis relented and followed her out the door in search of something to eat. The truth was, he'd follow her anywhere–undergarments be damned.

***

Later that night, she told him the story of her failed birthday party. She told him about how she begged her parents to break tradition and, though her abuela protested, her grandfather swayed her parents to her cause. She'd given an invitation to everyone in her grade, but no one showed. Her shame was magnified when her mother announced that she would, indeed, have to go to school on Monday. Junior was convinced the bullying would be unbearable but it was worse than she imagined: they'd been completely indifferent to her missed party. Had they teased and taunted her, she'd have known they hadn't shown on purpose. The all-encompassing apathy hurt way more.

That's when Junior started to intently and keenly watch people. She figured that there was something obvious that she was missing and if she paid enough attention, she could reason it out and make things better. Like any other equation, she needed to solve for X.

She watched what they ate, how they gestured, and when they laughed. She watched who sat where. She watched how they spoke and how they danced. Junior watched and watched until she was so good at noticing things, she started to anticipate their reactions.

Like that, her attempts at quelling the bottomless emptiness of her school day turned into a fun game of strategy. The schoolyard was a chessboard and she was one of those savants who could see five or six moves ahead, predicting with uncanny accuracy when an Emma would fall out with a Sarah or when a Jack would provoke a Thomas.

"You're a puppet master!" Davis hovered between impressed and horrified.

"It's more like the end of the Matrix where all the information is there all the time? I have to focus on something to see it clearly," she clarified.

"Making your superhero origin story your disastrous twelfth birthday party," he continued as though she hadn't spoken, enjoying the drama he was spinning too much. "You'd be called something cryptic like The Seer or The Watcher. And your arch-nemesis would be... hmm." He paused, contemplating.

"Grocery store sheet cake?" she offered.

"What? You don't like sheet cake?" he gasped, truly horrified by this admission. "That's the real tragedy of this story!"

"I insisted on having the biggest one my father could find. I pitched the whole thing in the trash that night and it mocked me every time I went to throw something out."

"Those were a cornerstone of my youth. All special occasions were celebrated with a small, circle grocery store cake. My mom had to drive almost an hour to the one place that carried them, which is what made them a treat."

"That's lovely." She kissed his chin.

"So... you never had another birthday party?"

"Oh, I had all kinds of parties. I just stopped inviting unworthy people to them."

It was also when Junior began to turn resolutely inward. She figured that she would never be disappointed if she never had expectations. No one could let her down if she didn't ask anything of them. She learned to stop voicing any desire for anything, convinced that it would prevent her from ever experiencing that scalding humiliation again.

"I had a full-scale gala for my Quinceañera. My nineteenth and twenty-first birthdays were also bangers. My 30th birthday involved liability waivers and NDAs," she added mysteriously.

"I'd pay good money to hear about that party," Davis said low in her ear.

"Ironclad NDAs," she repeated, squirming from the heat of his breath on her skin.

"Then I guess I'll have to wait until I'm worthy enough for an invitation."

"I've been known to throw a party at a moment's notice under the very flimsiest of pretenses: balloons, confetti, streamers—the whole nine yards," she teased, running her hand across his chest.

"I promise that I will show up to any party you invite me to."

"Goldfish wedding, hamster graduation, stuffed animal dance recital...?" she continued, dragging her nails toward his increasingly apparent erection.

"Any party at all," Davis vowed, his voice thick. "You invite me, I'll be there."

"Even the party in my pants?" she asked suggestively.

"Especially the party in your pants."

"I hear everyone's coming," she finished the puerile joke with her hand wrapped firmly around him.

"They aren't yet." Davis hoisted her on his lap and brought her mouth to his. "But give them some time and they will be."

Chapter 12

"A RE YOU GOING TO go to Marta's wedding?" Claudia asked.

Their cousin Martina, the youngest of their tío Enrique's kids, was engaged to some hotshot investment banker that she met at a charity event in Miami. "I don't think we have a choice," Junior smirked, taking a sip of her drink. They were having lunch on a patio close to Claudia's office in Toronto's bustling financial district.

"No, you're right, we don't. My mom was talking to her mom and it sounds like she's trying to keep it classy, which means small wedding party!" Claudia pumped her fist in triumph.

Having a large family meant there were constant events. Until Junior's youngest cousin Silvana was born, Regina Sano had thirteen grandchildren, which was a curse twice over. A curse because thirteen was an unlucky number, the weight of Judas' betrayal still heavy after all these years, and a curse because though she didn't have the least number of children among her siblings, Regina had the fewest grand- and great-grandchildren. Now, with fourteen grandchildren, her abuela worried slightly less about the various omens of impending doom. What Junior always itched to point out, but knew better than to try, was now each of Regina's fourteen grandchildren had thirteen first cousins.

"Are you sure? Tía Concha is an unreliable source. So is your mother." Junior didn't dare get her hopes up. "Have you spoken to Martina directly?"

Claudia jammed the last mouthful of salad into her face and shook her head.

"Hmmm… I will remain cautiously optimistic."

Junior smiled as Claudia finished her lunch. Between Claudia's general disinterest in humanity and her anxiety-fueled bouts of depression, she was totally oblivious to the attention she attracted. They looked almost nothing alike: Claudia was short and busty whereas Junior was tall and modestly endowed; Claudia's hair fell in big loose waves that lacked the commitment to fully curl whereas Junior's hair wrapped around in gravity-defying coils. They had similar complexions but the only thing they had in common was their eyes if anyone bothered to notice. It was second nature to add 'our dads are brothers but we look like our mothers' immediately after stating that they were cousins.

"Have you seen Lalo's baptism pictures? He is so delicious!" Junior squealed. "I went over there on the weekend to warn Alma–"

"El ojo?" Claudia finished.

"Abuela is spun out that Eddie's family put 'blue strings' on the baby for protection. Or something? I don't know. I can't hear about it anymore."

"Alma said the huayruro seeds serve the same purpose. Abuela's just annoyed that it's the Peruvian evil eye and not a Panamanian one."

"Por favor!"

"Never mind all that. Tell me all about whatever it is you've got going on! And make it quick, I have to be back at work in twelve minutes." Claudia smiled at the waiter removing their dishes.

"What I have going on? I'm going camping, as you know. Thanks for getting these from your brother, by the way." Junior laughed, waving the security fob and padlock key to Fernanda's storage locker. "I might not understand your sister's choice to spend all her time counting frogs in the rainforest, but at least now Diego won't be the only one getting use out of her stuff."

Her cousin had joined a conservation excursion in Costa Rica after university, married the founder, pushed out four kids, and never looked back.

"You've been to Nanda's. She's not exactly fending for herself against the elements," Claudia said, reminding Junior of their visits to her sister's sprawling, sustainable farmhouse.

"No, certainly her house is gorgeous, but she actively chooses to sleep outside. On the ground!" Junior's lament made her cousin snort.

"True. That is a choice," Claudia agreed. "What about the other thing?"

"Other thing? I have nothing going on. I'm off until I go back to work at the end of September. You know that already." Junior answered, confused.

"I'm more interested in this freshly laid vibe you've got going on." Claudia sipped her ice water. "The chisme, Hammer. Spill."

Damnit. Claudia could smell gossip like a truffle pig. "There's nothing to tell. I'm seeing someone. It's good. He's different. A bit annoying, but good." Affection warmed her cheeks, unbidden.

"Will you bring him to dinner on Sunday?"

"Fat chance, Claudia." Junior shook her head. "That's not what this is."

"Then at least tell me his name."

"No." Junior scoffed. "If I wanted everyone to know about him, I would have told them myself."

"Harsh," Claudia's pout turned to a mischievous smile, "but fair."

"Shall we pay? You have three more minutes."

"And you're headed back to Mystery Man?" she taunted.

"As a matter of fact, yes. The lay is not as fresh as it could be." Junior winked as she gestured for the bill.

After lunch with Claudia, Junior went to Fernanda's storage locker to pick through her old camping gear, squeezed in a mani/pedi, and stopped to pick up a falafel plate from Davis' favorite spot.

He'd been working hard on the show and even went so far as to borrow oral histories of popular television series from the library for any hidden insights they might reveal. When she got to his place, Davis had his phone on speaker while Eli gave him notes. Eli was in fine form today, power-tripping for all he was worth, dropping no less than four ignorant things in the last half hour alone. Junior, sure, each time that Davis would say something, was disappointed each time he did not.

The call finally ending, Eli said to Davis, "You won't be the low man on the totem pole anymore, Chief. Take my advice and watch yourself out there. You can't even talk to a woman these days without it turning into a hashtag me too witch hunt!"

There was a bit more back and forth before Eli said, "Let's circle back next week to see how this goes, okay?" and disconnected the call.

"Seriously?" Junior seethed.

Davis, distracted with his work, misread Junior's reaction and huffed. "You should hear some of the garbage that comes out of his mouth. It's unreal."

"I did. It was impressive how you stood up to him when he made some of his more outrageous comments. The one about diversity hires was a real showstopper!" Eli's belittling of Davis' suggestion to post the entry-level positions at the Native Canadian Centre of Toronto was particularly vicious.

"Junior, please." Davis immediately went on damage control. "I told you, he's a relic on his way out."

"Doesn't sound like he's on his way out. Sounds to me like he's fundamentally involved in the development of your show. This is your big plan to weed him out? Co-sign his bullshit until he dies or someone finally brains him with the coffee maker?"

"I don't co-sign his filth!"

"You don't stop it. By not challenging it in any way, you're making a choice!" She could not believe the kind of shit Eli felt comfortable saying. That Davis, of all people, gave him the space to say it. All of the shitty things he'd endured, all the stories he'd shared with her, and he was willing to simply kowtow to this madman?

"Don't start, all right? I'm not going to engage him in a debate, Junior. I'm not going to validate his garbage by giving him a chance to air his 'side'. You know as well as I do, arguing only legitimizes that asshole." Davis sneered.

"I don't need you to debate him. I need you to shut that shit down instead of all that nothing you're currently doing!"

"I'm not doing nothing!"

"What are you doing? Because it wouldn't cost you anything to correct him."

"I promise you that being forgotten about–being completely erased from his seat of control–will hurt him more," Davis insisted. "In the meantime, my work will speak for itself."

"Or, just a suggestion, demand accountability for the harm caused!" Junior's voice rose with her frustration. She was angry and confused and she didn't know what to do with the outrage pooling in her system. She didn't know how to defend someone who eagerly accepted their torment.

"Storming the castle might work for you but it's not my style. I refuse to give Eli any of my energy," he countered. "Don't worry, next time I'll grab my headphones and spare you the pain of listening to him." Davis tried to lighten the mood but it did not land as intended.

"You think that's the problem–that I heard it and not that he said it?"

"Eli says stupid shit all day long."

Junior's eyes were murderous. "That is the wrong fucking answer, *Bossman*."

"I have to work with Eli until we get the green light and are out of development. I have to work with him."

"And then what? You say to Olivia, 'Oh, no, I don't require Eli's input on this project any longer as I, an untested rookie, can handle it all on my own because I've been reading books on the subject!' That how you see it shaking out?"

"Don't be mean," he warned.

"Oh, so you can speak out when you don't like something someone says," she snarked. "Good to know!"

"What makes you think only your way is the right way? I am telling you that I've got this."

"You're not insulted? It doesn't bother you at all?" Junior tried a different approach. She was desperate to get through to him. She couldn't see a way this fling worked if Davis' response to injustice was wholesale complacency.

"How can you ask me that? I've been eating his shit for years. But I have to be smart about this, I can't go off whenever I want to, consequences be damned."

"You are Olivia's most trusted assistant. She is giving you the chance to lead an entire property. If you're saying she doesn't know, which is problematic on its own, by the by, then you tell her! She can do something."

"And what if she doesn't? Or worse, she backs Eli? What do I do then?"

"You think she'd do that?" The possibility Olivia could mentor Davis so personally yet still abide this cruelty he suffered appalled her. "Then she's made her choice. At least you'd know where you stand."

"Right. And then?"

"Then you leave and work somewhere else!"

"Where?" he challenged.

"I don't know!"

"Your big solution is I burn all my bridges on the way out the door to... elsewhere? Is that it?" he reproached her.

Junior sighed. She had to find a way to show Davis that he deserved more than this. That he could demand better than this. "You're smart and well-liked and good at your job. You can go somewhere else if you had to. You've had a taste of production now—be a production manager or a line producer."

"I want to create a show from the ground up. I want to find stories and develop them and create entire worlds for people to escape to. I don't want to figure out whether the grips get a pre-call or what to do if an actor misses their flight because they're wasted in Cabo. If I leave before I get this chance, then I leave as Olivia's Assistant, not as a Creator and Executive Producer. If I leave before I make this next step, Eli wins. He wins and I'll have thrown everything away for nothing. That cannot happen. Do you understand me? It can't."

"But—" she started.

"No. No more, Junior. Promise me you'll let this go." He pulled her onto his lap so they were eye-to-eye.

"If you–"

"Promise me," he insisted.

"I promise."

"What do you promise?" he arched his brow.

"I promise to let you deal with this your way because you have a plan that is not my plan," she droned.

"Junior," he pleaded.

Though Junior hadn't followed the path her parents set for her, she knew politics were more than fifty percent of the job in corporate life and still knew all the rules of the game. If she were being truly honest, she relied on those skills almost daily even though the general vibe of a production office wasn't as brittle. She could admit she understood his point without agreeing with it.

Meeting him square in the eyes, Junior offered, "I promise, Sapó, to stay out of it."

"Thank you." He kissed her face. "Okay, go seethe over there. I have to finish this." He kissed her again before nudging her away from the table.

Junior made a big show of flopping onto the couch. When she saw Davis looking at her, she gave an exaggerated scowl.

"Twenty minutes. Thirty tops," Davis said, smiling at his desk. "Then you can give me the cold shoulder up close."

"Hmph!" she replied, settling in to wait for him with her book about the tinned goods heiress who married an impoverished earl.

Chapter 13

Things between Davis and Junior finally started to settle into a familiar routine. They both continued to live their lives—she off for the summer, he working on development for the new series—and spent time together without much discussion or fanfare. They managed to quietly fit each other into the open spaces of their lives. Sometimes she was available for dinner, other times she had plans. Sometimes he invited her for lunch, other times he had to work.

From the outside, there was no indication that their lives even crossed paths. Junior packed up every trace of herself each time she returned home, never leaving so much as a hair tie behind. No matter how much Davis grumbled that his house wasn't a hotel, she kept showing up with her stylish duffel bag in tow. It was better, she insisted, because this way she wouldn't accidentally forget something she'd need when she was at home. Davis countered that she could simply have two of a thing, that he'd buy whatever she needed—an offer Davis knew she recognized for being as grand as it was sincere since he did not, as a rule, spend frivolously. Yet still she demurred.

The night before she was to go camping in Algonquin Park without indoor plumbing or fixed shelter, an exercise in mindfulness and meditation about which AJ's Reiki practitioner was evangelical, Davis checked her supplies. Correctly surmising that Junior had never 'roughed it' a day in her life, Davis was concerned that she wouldn't be adequately prepared. Worse, he worried that Junior would have walked into a sporting goods store and been sold a bunch of useless, poser crap. He should have known better—she'd done her research and bought exactly what she needed from the very top of the line.

Junior had purchased a lightweight all-season tent and footprint, a Therm-a-rest sleeping pad, a silk sleeping bag liner, a lantern, a folding table and chair, and two different headlamps. All told, Davis figured she'd spent close to four grand on gear, clothes, and equipment for what amounted to a long weekend's worth of activity she'd likely not partake in again. "Let me see you put the tent together."

"Again?" she cried.

"Please, Junior, humor me." They'd pushed her furniture out of the way so he could see the fully pitched tent.

"Maybe I should just take the hammock," she grumbled. "Historically, my people are hammock users."

Davis smirked at this announcement. Junior's use of *my people* could mean anything from Panamanians specifically to Latin Americans generally to people from the Caribbean to Black people of the greater diaspora. Sometimes it covered multiple groups at once. One time it meant first gen Canadians with ESL parents. Even with context, there was no sure-fire way to discern her meaning and he'd learned it was pointless to try. She refused to be pigeon-holed by anyone.

"You also bought a hammock?" Davis was stunned by the cavalier expenditure.

"Kyle said the tent might be easier but the hammock would be more comfortable. He didn't mention that you would be here harassing me to put the thing together over and over again or I might not have bothered," she pouted.

"Who's Kyle?"

"The guy at Sail? He said that I could bring any of it back so long as I didn't use it outside. Maybe I'll do that instead. It's less stuff to pack," Junior reasoned, cementing her decision.

Davis pinched the bridge of his nose and sighed. "Junior, you choosing your fancy new insulated camping hammock doesn't mean I won't want to see you use it. I want to make sure you'll be safe."

"Aww, are you worried about me?" she cooed.

"Very!" He opened her first aid kit to double-check its contents. "I didn't realize your saying 'Yes' to 'fun, broadening of horizons' included this level of extremes."

"I've been to Algonquin before, you know."

Davis stared at her, skepticism all over his face. "It's not at all the same thing; you were working on location, Junior—all your meals were catered!" A laugh sputtered out of him, landing somewhere between disbelief and exasperation.

"And we also rented a place once—" the words didn't get all the way out before she conceded his point. "Okay fine, I guess," she muttered under her breath.

"Come on, Bear Grylls. Let's find somewhere to hang your hammock," he said, kissing her temple.

After they'd tested both her ability to set up and break down the tent, as well as tie, hang, and lie in the hammock, Davis moved on to her safety kit. She had an impressive collection of things already. Her cousin Fernanda's old cast-off backpack, solar-powered battery charger, UV water purifier, and crank light were still in excellent condition. He checked the sharpness of her knife and proffered a multi-tool, insisting it was worth carrying around and not needing it rather than the alternative. He also insisted that she carry a length of duct tape wrapped around a pencil, a transistor radio, and, hilariously, a deck of playing cards. Once Davis was satisfied that Junior could use, pack, and haul all of her things, they were ready to call it a night.

"I always forget that you're a Wilderness Guy under all of that buttoned-up Office Guy." Junior laid out brand new travel-sized toiletries and toothbrush for him to use.

"Ah, yes–centuries of knowledge and carefully preserved traditions held sacred by our elders and lovingly passed down through generations boiled down to...Wilderness Guy," he teased.

"You know what I mean!" She hip-checked him and he tugged on her bun in acknowledgement.

Watching as she began her nighttime routine, it struck Davis how natural being with her was for him. He enjoyed hearing about her day and the way she honed in on little things about his. He wondered if she held back out of habit or if she had a genuine aversion to joining their lives. Was there something Junior was waiting for? Was there something he could do to give it to her? He was willing to push at that bruise one more time.

"You know... my skills as a so-called Wilderness Guy keep me more sharp and adaptable than Office Guy." He leaned on the wall behind her.

"Is that so?" she smiled at him in the mirror.

"It is. It's important to be able to change course, adjust your route, when the original path is obstructed."

"Mmm."

"Out of curiosity, what are you going to do with all that after?" he asked casually.

"After what?" she said to her reflection, swiping a cotton ball soaked in witch hazel across her face.

"After I leave."

"I don't know, throw it out?" she shrugged.

"I won't have finished any of it."

"So?" her brow creased.

"So? Wouldn't it make sense to leave a small stash of things here for me to use whenever I stay over?"

"Hijo de puta!" She muttered, cursing herself for falling into his trap. "I cannot believe you're starting this again. First of all, you staying here tonight wasn't planned and if you felt strongly enough about it, you could call a car to take you home and save these precious toiletries," she pointed out. "Secondly, because you, like many North American men, have bought into the myth of gendered clothing, you don't have a bag or purse or satchel to hold an emergency kit of supplies. Your loss. Lay it directly at the feet of the patriarchy, by the way." She stepped on the pedal of her garbage can and dropped the cotton ball in it. "Third, if it means that much to you to keep this random generic sampling of things, be my guest." She faced him with her arms crossed over her chest.

This righteous vexation–her eyes full of challenge, her posture defiant–always heated his blood. He should probably scratch beneath that surface.

"Maybe an evening packing your gear helped me realize how very passionate I am about travel-sized toothpaste," he cracked.

"Is that what this is all about?"

He brought his shoulders to his ears, "Maybe?"

"Far be it from me to stand in the way of your passions." Junior leaned over and pulled out a mesh basket from under the sink. "We have one for whitening, one for total oral health...this one's for sensitive teeth." She pawed through the samples from the dentist, holding them up to his inspection.

"How about I use yours?"

"My what?" Her eyes widened in alarm.

Davis stood in front of her, their toes touching, and said, "Your toothbrush. We can share."

"That's disgusting." She shuddered, dropping the toothpastes back into the basket.

"I thought about it and I'm beginning to see your point. I'm willing to pivot. Why have two of all our things? You should use my toothbrush when you're at my place and I'll use yours when I'm here."

"Stop it. That's not funny, all right? I put that in my mouth!"

"You put other things of mine in your mouth." He tapped his chin thoughtfully. "It makes a certain kind of sense, don't you think?"

"I'm going to barf if you don't knock it off." She heaved a little in earnest.

"Let's start now." He reached for her toothbrush.

"Absolutely not!" Junior clutched it to her body and fled. His hysterical laughter followed her down the hall. He knew he'd pay for that bit of torment; Junior would make sure of it. But as he wiped the tears of laughter from his cheeks, he had no regrets.

Chapter 14

COMING DOWN THE STAIRS as AJ and Quinn were catching Roxanne up on some gossip, Junior announced, "I think Leigh is here."

They were gathered at Roxanne's for the season finale of the delightfully trashy Turkish soap they watched as a group.

After her thirtieth birthday weekend, the bond was cemented between Junior's disparate group of friends and these binge-watch evenings, better than any book club, became cornerstones of Junior's calendar. They'd tried watching it on the phone, and even once via video chat, but it wasn't the same. In the end, they agreed that they would wait until they could all gather together to watch the shows.

They'd got stuck in a British TV loop with the series about the five teens who were given powers after being struck by lightning during community service directly after the one about the young writer who doesn't quite remember what happened to her after night of hard partying in London. Leigh eventually broke them free with the series about a teen South African swimming star who may have been abducted at birth.

"And Claire, too!" Claire said from the doorway, entering the house right behind Leigh. "Parking was a bitch. Why do you pay so much to live here if you can't put your goddamned car anywhere?" Claire demanded in her signature profanity-laden style. The petite hospital facilities administrator hated the term biracial, explaining instead that she was a Black woman with a white mom, had a love of salty treats, salty language, and maintaining her rigorous fitness regimen equally.

"Why did you drive? Parking in The Beach always sucks." Leigh pulled a cloth out of her case to clean her glasses. "And now you can't have a drink."

"I'm not drinking tonight," Claire made her way into the den to announce, "because I'm fucking pregnant!"

"For real?" AJ gasped.

"For real!" Claire admitted as the smile broke across her face while her friends squealed and cheered and wrapped her in a big, messy hug. "We went to our first prenatal appointment yesterday. Fourteen weeks!"

"Thelonious!" Junior hollered, clapping her hands. The friendship that started out of convenience, them being the girlfriends of double-dating best friends, took root and grew a foundation of its own. Now, neither woman spoke to either man yet were fiercely loyal to each other. Junior was thrilled for Claire, even if she did worry that the baby would be born in a cross-fit gym.

"What are you saying?" Quinn asked.

"She should name the baby Thelonious–boy or girl!" Junior insisted. "They could be Theo for short!"

"I will do no such thing," Claire said adamantly, flopping her body on the couch. "No matter how iconic Sir Monk was."

"Booo," Junior grumbled.

"I haven't even wrapped my head around it yet. I'm still in a bit of shock. Holy balls, I'm going to be a mom! I need you to talk about something else for a minute," Claire begged.

"It's a sign. Why, this very afternoon Junior and AJ were room monitors at Ryan's art class. By the time your baby arrives in the world, AJ'll be a pro toddler wrangler, primed and ready!" Roxanne teased.

"They were so cute, you guys!" Junior could hardly contain herself. "They made little paper fans with popsicle stick handles. There was paint and glitter glue and stickers and teeny feathers everywhere!"

"I can still feel their slimy little hands on my skin." AJ shuddered.

Junior and AJ were having dim sum when Ryan called to ask her aunt to come to her art class. Never missing the opportunity to indulge The Kid, she readily agreed. She Yes'd AJ into service but, after the class, added the promise of foot massages in recompense.

"Adversity builds character. Shake it off, soldier," Leigh ordered. Having completed her time in the trenches, Leigh also wanted nothing to do with small children if she could at all avoid it.

Claire laughed. "So, no babysitting from you two betches. Got it."

"We need a change of topic," AJ ordered.

"Drinks?" Roxanne asked the room. "I've got a Sauv Blanc and a Malbec on the go."

"Lemme help!" Quinn popped up. "Your pours are too big!"

"Don't listen to her, Rocky. I like your pours," Leigh countered.

"Agreed!" Junior called after them.

"You're supposed to get five glasses out of a bottle," Quinn reminded them.

"Pfft!" AJ laughed. "Not where I'm from."

"Me either!" Leigh chimed in.

When you factored in the breaks needed for AJ and Quinn to dish about people they'd worked with or rumors they'd heard, for Roxanne and Claire to rewind and ogle any sexy bits, and time for visiting, 'come over and watch some TV' was roughly a four-hour commitment. They were now rounding the corner on hour six. Claire's baby news, the cottage getaway Roxanne was embarking on in a couple days, and AJ's new flame with Girl Kelly (plus Junior's obligatory bashing of kicked to the curb Boy Kelly) was keeping the party alive.

"Okay, Angels. I must bid you goodnight. My evening takes me elsewhere." Junior stood from her place on the couch and stretched.

Leigh squinted at her. "Where are you going?"

"Chasing dick, where else?" Claire laughed.

"You take that back! I do not chase dick. Rather, dick makes itself available to me," Junior said with a flourish.

"It's been so long, I wouldn't even know what to do with one if it was laid out on a platter," Roxanne sighed.

"What happened to Tow Guy?" Junior asked, alarmed that she missed something happening with Roxanne.

"You were dating a toe guy?" Leigh made a face. "A podiatrist or a fetishist?"

"No, I was banging a tow truck driver."

Leigh nodded. "Yep—that makes more sense."

"But now it's over?" Quinn asked.

"Never mind that, I want to hear about your thing," Roxanne said to Junior.

"It's not A Thing, it's just...a thing," she answered, not wanting to get into any more detail about whatever it was that was happening with Davis.

"Should we get the stamp?" AJ shimmied.

Roxanne and AJ liked to joke that the brave souls who entered Junior's bed should be stamped with a best before date so that they wouldn't be surprised when her interest waned and they parted ways. Often it was a clean break since Junior never declared intentions towards church bells and a distant future. But sometimes the poor darlings were so blindsided by her seeming sudden change of heart that it got unpleasant.

Junior considered it. She wasn't ready to talk about Davis. She worried that if she looked too closely at it, the spell would be broken. Too much focus on the way Davis erroneously believed always having her favorite fruit on hand would curb her candy intake or the weekend getaways she planned to nearby destinations because Davis enjoyed exploring local oddities might upset the balance. Junior shrugged and said, "It's not necessary."

For now, she would return to the happy bliss bubble he'd created for her and leave the outside behind.

Chapter 15

Davis looked over as Junior giggled.

"Would you rather fight one horse-sized duck or 100 duck-sized horses?"

Davis considered the options. "Easy—a horse-sized duck."

"Agreed." She was scrolling through her socials, stopping now and then to show him a funny video or meme. Often, she simply chuckled or made a scoffing noise to herself and kept scrolling. A moment later she asked, "Do you think a hotdog is a sandwich? There's heated discourse on the matter."

Davis loved debating obscure, ultimately meaningless topics with her. They could argue for hours about whether Kermit and Piggy's progeny would be hatched or birthed, or if 'salad' inherently implied fresh produce. Her phone made a now-familiar chime.

"Rocky says hi," Junior smirked at her phone.

"Rocky says hi...to me?" he asked, surprised.

"Uh-huh."

"Your best friend Roxanne told you to say hi to Davis?" he clarified.

"Essentially."

"The way Sapó *essentially* means 'Eyes and Ears,' but literally means snitch?"

"Technically 'Eyes and Ears' also means snitch, so...," Junior was unapologetic.

"She doesn't know about me." Davis was a little disappointed. He hadn't thought Junior was singing in the streets like some animated fairy princess but part of him hoped that she'd confided in *someone* about them.

"Rocky knows that I am not alone and that I am not alone at not my house and that I've been not alone at not my house for some days now and she said to say hi."

Davis accepted this as the gesture it was. She had told Roxanne, however obliquely. "Tell her I say hi back."

She typed his reply and nodded to herself before returning to her book about the amateur astronomer who gets hired as a governess to two precocious orphans.

Davis pulled her feet in his lap and absently rubbed them while he worked. Junior was one of the smartest, savviest people he knew and she'd never once conflated his slow reading with his level of intelligence. Which was probably why he didn't feel the sting of embarrassment he normally felt when having to read with an audience.

There were always emails and story notes and logistics to get through. It was a lot, but Davis had never felt surer about the shape his life was taking. Junior smiled up at him, wriggling her toes against his stomach and at that moment, he knew this was everything he wanted.

"What?" she nudged him with her foot.

He let his head fall back on the couch and closed his eyes.

"What?" she asked again, more insistent when he'd taken too long to answer. He felt the weight of her scrutiny. Before he could address it, she straightened on the couch. "I'm gonna go," she said, pulling her feet from his lap.

"What? Why?" Davis held her ankle in a vise-like grip, his eyes clear and focused on hers.

"You seem busy."

"Junior," he chided, turning his head back to the ceiling. She hadn't even tried to be convincing.

"I mean, you have a lot going on. I don't want to get in the way." This, at least, sounded believable.

"C'mere." He tugged on her ankle until she was in his lap. Davis rested a hand on her hip and squeezed gently. "What's going on?"

"Nothing!" She squirmed under his gaze. "I just think I should go," she said, looking past him.

"Look at me." She huffed her annoyance and rolled her eyes a little before settling into the eye contact. "Do you have somewhere to be?"

She shook her head.

"Do you want to leave?"

She shook her head again. "No."

"Good. I don't want you to leave either." He squeezed lightly. "So... what's going on?" His voice was gentle and steady but he remained focused.

Davis waited quietly for her to gather her thoughts. Junior's skittishness was as familiar to him as the sound of his own voice. He had no idea what had spooked her, but if he let her run now, he'd lose the hard-fought ground he'd gained. It was the same when he wanted Junior to have keys to his place as was the weeks-long battle of wills to get her to leave things there when she spent the night. Looking at her now, her hair piled on top of her head in what she called a pineapple, wrapped in a silk scarf, wearing a ratty tank top and pajama shorts she pulled from a drawer in his room, he was certain this too would be worth it once they got to the other side.

"You looked drained. I thought it would be easier for you if I left. So, you didn't have to ask me to," she finally admitted.

Davis ran his hands up her sides until he was holding her shoulders. "How very considerate of you." He pulled her in for a kiss. "I honestly can't think of anything I want less," he said against her lips before kissing her again.

"I'm sure there's something." She pouted at his playful mocking.

Davis caught her lip in his teeth. "Uh-uh."

"Gallstones?"

"Do I want gallstones less than I want you to leave?" The laughter in his voice egged her on.

"World War?" she offered.

"I don't think you're doing this right." He took her mouth again.

"You want war?" she challenged.

"Aren't you always saying we can never achieve global harmony under capitalism? We might as well wait out the carnage here." He kissed a path down her neck.

"A system that prioritizes the wealth of a few over the basic needs of the many by monetizing the planet's finite resources is unsustainable," Junior managed through increasingly ragged breaths.

"Noted." He held her lusty stare. "Stay."

"Like a labradoodle?"

Davis smirked with one side of his mouth, relieved. A snarky Junior meant the panic had subsided enough to make way for her trademark mulishness. "No," he bit behind her ear. "Like a woman who likes spending time here, with me."

"Tell me what made you so upset."

"I'm not upset. I'm on my way to being very, very happy." He pulled the neckline of her shirt down and flicked his tongue on her chest.

"Before," she insisted, moving a little out of his reach. "You were fine, then you were deflated. What was that?"

"I wasn't deflated. I was contemplating."

Junior shifted off his lap and tucked herself along his side. Wrapping his arm around her, she settled her head on his chest and left her legs across his lap. When she stilled, he continued softly in her ear. "I was thinking about you. About how right it feels having you here. About how happy I am with you."

"What's to contemplate?"

Feeling her stiffen, he kissed the side of her head. "The fact that I knew I couldn't tell you that without sending you running for higher ground." Junior opened her mouth to protest, but the words died in her throat. "What makes you run?" There was no criticism in his voice, only genuine curiosity, a desire to understand her.

"I'm not running away, necessarily. Sometimes my feelings are too big to feel all at once. I need time to figure it out," she admitted self-consciously.

He nudged her encouragingly. "What were you feeling?"

"I... I don't know—I was enjoying being here like this. Then you got that look on your face and I thought... I thought you wanted me to leave or something."

Davis kept running his hands on her back. "And that made you want to run?"

"No! It made me mad! I was angry and I wanted to leave before you could kick me out!"

"You were mad at me for what you thought I was going to do and leaving...?"

"Was going to let me be hurt in private!"

Davis was almost there. "Why didn't you ask me before jumping to wrong conclusions?"

"I did–twice! You flopped your head back on the couch!"

"And it didn't occur to you that I might need to think about something first?"

"Then you should have said that," she sulked.

Davis raised his brow at her obvious double standard.

"What?" she cried. "You're the one constantly throwing your feelings around like glitter at the peelers! How am I supposed to know when you need time to work something out?"

"I didn't need time to work my feelings out, I needed time to figure out what to do about yours."

"I don't know what to tell you, Sapó," she said quietly. "My feelings are a mystery to me, too."

He brought her head to his chest and resumed running his hand down her back. "Let's make a deal." He kissed the top of her head. "Instead of leaving whenever you're having a Big Feeling, maybe you can try to tell me about it. I want to be able to talk about this stuff with you, Junior."

"I don't know if I can do that," she admitted to his shoulder.

His chest tightened. "You don't think you can talk to me about your feelings?"

"I don't think I can process mine and metabolize yours at the same time. You *want* so much all the time. It's overwhelming," she answered eventually.

Davis took a deep breath and considered her words. He did want so much all the time. It was easy to forget that, comparatively, this was all new to her. The disparity plagued him–he didn't know what to do, too impatient to close that distance.

"Okay. I can try to keep my Big Feelings to myself a bit more." He offered the only feasible middle ground he could think of.

"Until we get better at sorting through your Big Feelings, I'll keep mine to myself."

"That's not right either. I don't need you to stop expressing your feelings. I need you to keep your feelings separate from mine. We won't always feel the same thing at the same time and that has to be okay."

She was right, he admitted. The reason he was put out was because he worried she would not react the way he wanted. "That is a surprisingly mature read on the situation from someone who claims to not have a grasp on her feelings," he teased.

"Complex, remember?" She tapped her temple. "It may also surprise you to know I have been described as temperamental."

"I think there's a pool in the office on who draws first blood: you or Walter," Davis said with unreserved glee.

"Stop saying that! It's not that bad!" Junior hid her face in his chest.

"At one point in Block 3, I was sure we'd have to file an actual worker's comp claim." He was barely holding back his laughter.

"The man is impossible!" she complained righteously. "Colors from a designer chip book for a dark, medieval tunnel? Ridiculous!"

Davis grabbed her face and kissed her with all the joy he felt for her, this complicated, messy, stubborn, brilliant, silly, beautiful woman. "Junior, are you happy?"

"Yes, of course."

"Are you happy with me? With us?" he clarified, having fallen victim too many times to Junior's proficiency with semantics.

"I am," she smiled at his specificity.

"Then let's be serious about this."

"You want me to wear your pin? Do you have a letterman jacket? We can't go steady until you proffer either or, preferably, both," she gushed, teasing him.

It wasn't how he'd planned to broach this, but they were here now. Might as well power through. "I want us to be together. For real. No hiding, no games."

"We are together," she pointed out.

"No one knows you're here, Junior."

"Everyone knows I'm here. I told you, Rocky said hi. Maybe not this specific address, but they know. Trust me, we should keep it that way for as long as we can."

"I don't want to be a secret," Davis countered. He wanted nothing more than to be able to hold her, press his lips against hers, whenever the mood struck him.

"I'm not asking you to."

"Junior." His voice was reproachful. "We'll be back at work on season five soon. You're starting next week!"

"Yeah, so?"

"So? I should lie to everyone all the time?" he asked, irritated. He wanted to be able to answer 'how was your summer' with something along the lines of 'perfect! I spent it all with Junior'.

"Think of all the lies you told your side piece as practice for this moment," she teased.

Davis untangled himself and set her on the other side of the couch. "How many times do I have to tell you to stop joking about me having someone on the side? You are it for me. There is no one else," Davis said through gritted teeth. He knew she was deflecting but he was not in the mood for irreverence. He was tired of this compartmentalizing she insisted on. He couldn't find the humor in Junior's refusal to take the next step. Not now.

***

She'd pushed him too far.

Junior had tried to not let her suspicious nature get the better of her. She'd tried to shake it off when she'd felt the shift in his mood. After all, her lips were still swollen from his bruising kisses. But the man who'd very recently had his head between her thighs had been replaced by one who seemed weary. Resigned.

She'd thought it was work. Davis was under a lot of pressure so Junior did her best to keep the separation between Church, her loyalty to Quinn, and State, this... involvement with Davis clear. She knew Quinn and Davis had their own relationship and she didn't want to color it. It was partly why Junior had convinced herself keeping their relationship private made sense.

Whatever it was, it had been her cue to leave.

At least, she'd tried to leave. But she'd never been able to resist sexy Determined Davis. Had it been dorky Rules & Regulations Davis, she could've dismissed him with an eye roll. Or goofy Silly Davis who was easily distracted from his purpose. She could even ignore thoughtful Caring Davis if she didn't look too closely at why she did.

No, instead it was sexy Determined Davis–the Davis who demanded she look at him when he entered her in one thrust. The Davis who held her down in this very spot an hour ago until she shook from the pleasure. The Davis who talked her through her climax, promising all the ways he planned to have her yet. It was that Davis who'd pulled her to him–never taking his eyes from hers, patiently waiting until she admitted, reluctantly, one very true thing: her feelings often came to her in a torrent and she latched on to the first one she could identify, regardless of whether it was the most relevant or most true–who was harder to ignore.

Another very true thing? She would have been in her car on her way home by now if he hadn't held her, soothed her, with his calm and his kisses. It had unnerved her and she'd felt the walls closing in. She'd needed a bit of space, a little levity, to distance herself from the enormity of it all.

But she'd pushed him too far so now it was her turn to do the calming and soothing. "Who's asking about your personal life, Sapó?" She straddled his lap.

"You know what I mean, Junior." He closed his eyes against the pressure of her body on his.

"Claro." She kissed him behind his ear and murmured, "But it's not an issue as you've just admitted no one is asking."

"They will ask. You know they will," he insisted.

"Who, Jamal and those guys?"

Davis nodded.

"You can tell them you got the girl! She came for your earnest good looks but she stayed for the way you slang." Junior rocked her hips playfully against his for emphasis.

"I'm not saying that."

She kissed the corner of his mouth. "Tell them the truth: it's still new and you're taking it slow."

"And when they ask about her?" He pressed.

"They haven't asked her name yet, have they? They're unlikely to start now."

"I can say anything I want so long as I don't say it's you?"

"Don't be churlish. I'm asking you to keep our private life separate from our work life until we're ready to let those outside influences in."

"I am ready!" he exclaimed. "That's what I'm telling you. I am ready to take this all the way. I have nothing to hide."

"I've been there before, Sapó. Dating someone at work? I've been there before. It's a lot of pressure. Not to mention the power imbalance of our jobs. There's a level of scrutiny that I'm simply not ready to expose us to. Not yet. I want to protect what we have for as long as I can." Junior ran her palms against his chest and pressed a firm kiss on his lips. "Okay?" she asked.

Davis looked into her pleading eyes. Wasn't this what he wanted? Didn't he just ask her to trust him with her feelings?

Did she need to go into detail about what happens when you run into a colleague you haven't seen in a while and they ask about the person you're no longer dating? Or how unpleasant it was when people, in an attempt to show their support, report back every detail of that person's actions? She could tell him that sometimes people took a twisted satisfaction in a break-up, scavenging for any sign of distress to feed the machine and how she hated knowing people speculated about those details behind her back. She would, of course, though she hoped this was enough.

"I'm going to tell my sister."

"Sure, of course," she agreed.

"And we're only keeping it quiet at work? Only for now?"

"Yes."

"Okay," he nodded.

"Okay?"

"Okay," he confirmed.

Junior kissed him before teasing, "One day, when you admit I was right about this, I won't even say 'I told you so'!"

JUNIOR SAT ON A BENCH on Queen Street, enjoying the late summer sun while her niece wrestled with the vagaries of choice.

"Maybe if we sit upside down, the decision will come to our brains faster. Should we try it?" Junior suggested to Ryan.

"Okay!" the child beamed.

Junior twisted herself on the park bench so her legs dangled over the top and her head hung off the seat at an angle that would certainly cause her grief later.

"Like this?" Ryan copied her aunt's posture.

"Excellent!" Junior adjusted her so there was less risk of sliding off the seat and cracking her skull wide open. "So now we need to think our thoughts all over again and see what happens."

They were at Jimmie Simpson Park. It'd been an hour since Ryan's swimming lessons ended and they were still debating whether to have soft serve with all the bells and whistles or regular ice cream with fancy flavors. Ryan couldn't decide and now the french fries that were supposed to help them choose were finished. "So, which do you think you'd like more?"

"Do both places have sprinkles?"

"I don't remember if Ed's has sprinkles," Junior answered honestly.

"Can I have two flavors?"

"You can," Junior confirmed.

"Okay," Ryan folded her hands serenely on her stomach.

Junior nodded solemnly and watched as Ryan's face scrunched in concentration and laughed to herself. There were worse things than spending an afternoon at the park while her favorite little person decided which kind of ice cream to indulge in.

As they hung from the park bench, the clouds rolling lazily by, Junior's mind wandered. She needed a haircut. Or maybe some highlights. She contemplated taking Ryan to get their nails done later, once the great ice-cream determination was settled. Though at this rate, that might have to be postponed to another outing.

Junior brought one leg off the back of the bench to scratch behind her calf and felt the telltale stubble there, and added 'leg wax' to her list of things to schedule.

Did Davis not feel that? Did he feel it and not comment? Did he feel it and not care? It would be so typical of him to decide that her stubbly legs were the sexiest thing that ever happened to him. She wondered what he'd think if she got a Brazilian.

Ugh! She gave her head a shake, chastising herself. This was neither the time nor place to be entertaining such thoughts.

"Junior?" Davis was suddenly standing over her.

"Hey!" Had she conjured him with the power of her mind? It seemed as plausible an explanation as any for why he was suddenly there, colliding her worlds. She struggled to right herself, woozy from all the blood rushing from her head. "What are you doing here?"

"I could ask you the same thing." With laughter twinkling in his eyes, he indicated the park bench she'd dangled from.

Trying to get her bearings, Junior gave her head a small shake. Davis loved the falafel plate from Tabule and was probably grabbing something from the nearby restaurant. If not for this delay in ice-cream procurement, their paths wouldn't have crossed.

"We're trying to get the decision to our brains faster by being upside down," Ryan explained. An 'obviously' was strongly implied.

Junior, remembering herself, scooped her niece up off the bench and into her lap.

"I see," Davis answered. "What kind of decision?"

Ryan eyed him warily. It was one thing to speak when an entire Auntie Junie separated them. Now, without that buffer, where he could reach out and touch her, Ryan was deeply uninterested in further conversation with this interloper.

"It's okay, my love, he works at my work." Junior smoothed Ryan's curls behind her ears.

"With Remy?"

"Yes, with Remy," she confirmed.

Davis extended his hand, attempting to reach her on common ground. "Hello, my name is Davis. You know Remington?"

Ryan looked at his outstretched hand. Her furrowed brow seemed to say 'get a load of this clown' even as her mouth replied, "Remy is mishpocha."

"Family," Junior explained to Davis' confusion. "And you might as well put that away. She's clearly not going to shake your hand."

"That's not very nice." Davis attempted to guilt Ryan into action.

"Luckily for us, the goal isn't nice. It's autonomy," Junior said, pride giving an edge to her voice. She placed a small supportive kiss on the child's temple. "And Ryan has *chosen* not to shake your hand."

Junior was openly critical of niceness. She'd told him multiple times that it was a moral failing—a disingenuous quality weaponized against women—prioritized over good or kind which were better, more valuable, traits. He knew she found people who trafficked in nice untrustworthy. They made her uncomfortable. Why Davis would be surprised she steered her niece away from adopting the insurmountable character flaw was beyond her.

He nodded his understanding. "May I sit?" He'd asked Junior but was looking at Ryan, who'd been blatantly staring at him. Finally, she shifted to the other side of Junior in acquiescence.

"So, Remington is family," Davis repeated.

Ryan took in his casual posture on the bench and said, "Yes," before adding, "I got him his house."

"You did?" Davis asked, skeptical.

Ryan nodded proudly. "I stayed very still and didn't make a sound and Auntie Junie said I was his success key."

"The Key to His Success, Muppet," Junior corrected with a chuckle.

"There's more to that story," Davis mused.

"Short version?" Junior offered. When Davis nodded, she continued. "When Remy was ready to put an offer in on his house, his realtor said the sellers wanted the house to go to a family, so we went with him to the second viewing."

"You pretended to be his family?" There was clear criticism in his voice.

"We are his family," Junior corrected. She remembered their meeting so clearly. She was sure that if she closed her eyes, she'd open them to find herself inside that awful bar where Roxanne had taken her. "I told you how we met? How we became friends?"

"At a retirement party for a costume designer. Jamal and Remington saved you from unwanted advances," Davis answered.

Roxanne dreamed of becoming a costume designer and she'd worked her way onto an in-demand team, giving her lots of opportunities to learn and grow. Newly graduated Junior, earning a small salary running her grandmother's estate, had yet to decide on a career path and the pressure to join her father's firm was unbearable. Spending a rare night out with Roxanne was the perfect distraction.

At the bar, Junior had found herself on the receiving end of a drunken leer. Unsure who was a co-worker and unaware the 'corporate culture' she understood did not apply, Junior hesitated over making a scene among Roxanne's peers. Unfortunately, the snaggle-toothed man with the receding hairline took her continued proximity as an invitation to start a dialogue.

It was Jamal, sitting a few stools away with Remington, who stepped in with something smartassed about life giving you signs if you were sharp enough to read them. Snaggletooth stood up, appreciating neither the implication nor the interference, in a peacocking display of machismo. Jamal stood up, then Remington stood up. Snaggletooth, realizing he'd overplayed his hand, quickly sat down again. Jamal also sat down but Remington stayed standing, staring, until Snaggletooth skulked away.

Junior thanked them for their help but they amicably waved off her gratitude. Jamal explained they were happy for any excuse to tell off most of the people there. If Roxanne thought it odd when Junior returned to the table with them in tow–Jamal she knew, Remington she didn't–she didn't say. Instead, the four of them laughed and talked and drank and unknowingly planted the first seeds in Junior's mind: *maybe this is where I'll fit.*

"We stand up for each other. It's what we do."

"You were his wife and kid?" Davis amended.

Junior looked down into Ryan's bottle-green eyes and shrugged. "Remy carried her throughout the visit while she slept. Dark, curly hair and genuine doting can disguise multitudes."

A curious expression Junior couldn't decipher crossed Davis' face before he leaned over to smile at Ryan. "You must have done a really good job!"

"I did!" she beamed.

"Yes, you did," Junior repeated, squeezing Ryan affectionately.

They sat together on the bench, taking in the activity around them. In the distance, the sounds of the ice cream truck floated on the breeze. "Auntie Junie, I still can't know!" Ryan blurted with the deep and powerful exasperation wielded by five-year-olds.

"It's your choice. If you don't want to, 'no' is also an option." Junior reminded her.

"Pick?" Davis asked. "Not lunch, right?" he asked, indicating the empty fry box.

"That was our deciding snack," Ryan explained. Again, the 'obviously' was strongly implied. In Ryan's short five years of life, she'd already taken Junior's penchant for having a snack for every occasion as gospel–walking snacks, thinking snacks, car snacks, waiting in line snacks–there was simply no task that could not be improved by a snack.

"We're deciding between hard ice-cream at Ed's Real Scoop and soft-serve at Sweet Jesus," Junior clarified, pointing in the directions of the treats. "It's Ryan's choice. It's probably the last weekend the pickup window at Las Carnitas will be open, what with it being after Labor Day and all."

"I see," Davis' brow furrowed in contemplation. "When I have a hard time with a decision, I like to make a list. Have you tried that?"

"Yes!" Ryan wailed, giving the word two extra syllables.

"What's on your list?" he asked with genuine interest in the five-year-old's dilemma. Junior settled in a for another round of Davis Asks a Million Questions. She'd come to accept that it wasn't a practice reserved solely for her–he simply enjoyed a good old-fashioned chinwag.

"Sprinkles," she counted on her fingers, "flavors, and pointy or flat cones."

"Hmmm..." Davis considered. "Those are all things you like about ice cream. What you need is a list to help you figure out which one is better."

"That's obvious: soft-serve," Junior answered with a decisive nod. "It's easy and fun."

"So is scooped ice cream," Davis countered.

"Too much effort," Junior dismissed. She gathered their mess and handed it to Ryan. "Ponerlo en la basura."

As Ryan skipped over to the trash can, Junior brushed off the salt and fry shrapnel in her lap before noticing the set of Davis' jaw. "What?"

"He works at my work?" he said with a shake of his head.

"Seriously?" Junior asked in a huff. "You're mad about that? What, did you want me to say 'It's okay, my love, I had his privacy in my mouth this morning'?" she hissed sarcastically, using Ryan's word for genitals.

"Or," he scowled, "'this is my friend, Davis' could have also worked, as an alternative."

"I was caught off guard, okay?"

"You were caught off guard from having to introduce me to someone in your life? I thought we were doing this, Junior. We agreed we would tell people."

"Yesterday! We agreed to it *yesterday*." Junior could not believe he was getting bent out of shape about this. Did he expect her to start announcing it to people, willy nilly? Obviously, she needed to ease into it. Her family and friends were a cat's cradle liable to tangle at the slightest provocation. Did he really think she'd start with her niece of all people? "She's five years old, Sapó, it's not an issue, all right?"

"She's not old enough to understand that I might mean something to you? Does her mother know? Really know?" he pressed.

"Does Mommy know what?" Junior swallowed her sharp retort as Ryan climbed back on the bench, putting herself between Junior and Davis. The action was not lost on either of them.

He schooled his features before answering, "About your ice cream decision."

"That's against the rules," she said. "When I'm with Auntie Junie, we do what we do and we eat what we eat and Mommy can't ask or get mad as long as I'm in one piece."

"And no hospitals are involved," Junior added, wrapping her arms around her niece.

"Living entirely without accountability at every turn. Great," he sniped under his breath.

Junior cut her eyes at him. If he thought she wouldn't throw down in front of this child, he'd better think again. "Have you made your decision?"

"Yes." Her face screwed up in concentration. "I think so."

Davis gave Junior a hard look and then turned to Ryan. "You should know that soft serve may be fun and easy but there's no substance to it. It is made of artificial ingredients. Scooped ice cream may be harder to eat but it's satisfying. It is made with real ingredients. Sometimes you have to put in a bit of effort if you want something real." He glanced pointedly at Junior and said, "You should try it."

Junior rose and swung Ryan onto her hip. "Say goodbye, Muppet," she urged, a note of peevishness in her voice.

"Goodbye, Mr. Davis," Ryan said, holding her fist out to him.

Davis tapped hers dutifully.

"No!" she shook her head "You have to make it explode!"

"Jamal?" he asked Junior.

"Ali," she corrected, too annoyed to quite meet his eye.

Davis bumped his fist against hers and then spread his fingers wide, making loud, comical explosion noises to Ryan's giggling delight. "Bye. Enjoy your ice cream," he turned and walked away, leaving Junior to deal with the implications of his admonishment.

SHE'D BEEN PREPARED FOR passive-aggressive barbs the next time she saw him but instead, he'd spun her into his arms and danced her around his living room. Junior was so prepared for a cold war; it took her days to accept their spat really was squashed before she finally let it go. Which was probably why she felt so blindsided now.

It was the Friday before Junior officially started on season five. She liked having the extra day to get everything set up and fully operational. Since Art and Construction started before everyone else, this small amount of prep allowed her to hit the ground running. If she didn't load in on her own time, she'd lose an entire day to the process instead of a couple hours and she hated feeling unsettled. Sandrine always scolded her for working for free but Junior argued making her life easier was worth it.

In his capacity as associate producer, Davis wouldn't start for another couple of weeks. In his capacity as Olivia's assistant, however, he was in and out all the time–as evidenced by the wide smile plastered on his face as he ambled over to where she stood with AJ.

"Hey, Junior." Davis said with more volume than she felt necessary. Dios, had he leaned toward her? Junior's posture stiffened. Her face showed her abject horror at his attempt to embrace her in the middle of the production office.

"Fletcher." Junior said coolly, hoping it would encourage him to dial it down.

He recovered well enough with a bright, "Hi, Adrienne."

"What up, Bossman?" AJ had no problem matching his boundless energy. "Need me to unlock your office?"

He ran his fingers through his hair and gave her a lopsided grin, "No, I'm passing through on Fifty-Four business. Thanks, though."

"How was your hiatus? Did you work the whole time?" AJ's friendliness was her worst quality. Junior maintained her cheerful indifference.

"It was good. We," Davis seemed to catch himself before finishing with "Olivia had a lot going."

"Is that why you didn't have the kickback? You were too busy?"

If Junior thought his almost hug was a lot, the glance he shot her was intolerable. She arched her brow, awaiting his response.

"I was never having the kickback. That was Jamal being...Jamal."

Junior turned to face AJ. "Did you hear that? It is possible to say no to Jamal. People do it all the time."

"But saying yes is so much more fun!" AJ shimmied her delight.

"Speaking of Yes, are you all ready for tomorrow's ride?" Davis asked with a toothy smile on his face.

Junior stared at him. Had he lost his mind? How did he plan to explain having that information? Was this the other shoe dropping? Him forcing her hand at work, making it so that people had no choice but to notice something between them and start asking questions? If he wanted this game of chicken, she'd make like Peter the Apostle and deny, deny, deny.

Pretending she wasn't affected, Junior tsked to AJ, "You need to stay off social media."

"We're supposed to be fundraising, Junior."

"Actually, it's on the production calendar." Davis supplied helpfully.

Junior's incredulous gaze washed right over them both.

The office phone rang and AJ hustled to the closest desk to answer it.

Junior scolded Davis under her breath, "What do you think you're doing?"

"Catching up with friends at work?"

"Don't play coy with me! We weren't friends before, why would we suddenly be friends now?"

Davis absorbed the blow with visible effort. That might have been harsh, but she was feeling rattled. If Davis couldn't keep it together now, what would happen when everyone was milling around?

Junior swung her bag on her shoulder, checked her phone and announced to no one in particular, "I gotta go."

AJ made her way back over to them and hugged Junior's side. "Are we still on for a movie later?"

"Yep."

"I'll text you when I'm done the walk through with building management." Straightening, AJ waved at Davis and went back to her office.

Junior made her way down the stairs knowing Davis followed. When they got to the double doors, she looked around to be sure they were alone and pulled him to the corner. It was only the illusion of privacy. They couldn't be seen from the hallway but they were in full view of anyone coming through the doors or standing in the lobby. "Get it together, man. You almost gave the game away."

"I'm not supposed to speak to you at work? That's ridiculous!"

"You can speak to me all you like. You're not supposed to know things about me."

"Junior–"

"Our work lives are separate from our private lives. That's what we said, remember?" He'd had a lot of heat for her when she hadn't applied the rules to his satisfaction. It'd be wild for him to complain now the shoe was on the other foot.

"I'm not going back to you scurrying away whenever I approach." The words came out of his clenched jaw. "I won't be ignored by my girlfriend."

"I'm your girlfriend?" Junior gave a sultry batting of her lashes. At his flinty stare she dropped the act. "I'm not going to scurry off, Fletcher. I need you to remember there are certain things you theoretically shouldn't know and to act accordingly."

He was quiet for a moment as he faced her in the protection of the building's vestibule. On an exhale he admitted, "I didn't think it would be so hard to see you and not touch you."

This man.

Junior softened. She cupped his cheek in her palm and he closed his hand around her wrist, leaning into her touch. She was so used to hiding behind her carefree flirty image, to keeping almost everything about herself locked away from the general public, it didn't occur to her the kind of compartmentalizing she practiced would be difficult for him. And if he'd found her alone, could she honestly say her reaction wouldn't have been different? "I'm sorry, Sapó. I know I'm asking a lot of you."

"Maybe," he brought their hands down and clasped them, "But I get it."

"It won't always be so difficult. Sometimes entire days went by where we didn't see each other, remember?" She gave his hand a squeeze and teased with a wry grin, "Those were my favorite."

Davis stepped closer and insisted, "Not a day went by where I didn't see you, Junior."

She was lost in the intensity of his stare. It landed on her skin like a cool mist.

"Oh." The word was barely sound.

One of the heavy doors crashing open reverberated down the empty hallway. She jumped, pulling their hands apart, putting a more respectable distance between them. With a quick, frantic glance around Junior let out a long, slow breath when she saw they were still alone. One hand clutched her chest in effort to slow her racing heart while the other pressed her forehead.

Davis reached for her hand again, rubbing his thumb soothingly along her knuckles. They stood together, the hum of the fluorescent lights drowning out the other sounds around them, until she felt settled.

"It'll be okay, Junior. I'll get my head around it and it'll be okay." He gave her hand a final squeeze and, with a determination she'd come to recognize, walked out into the warm September sun.

He'd figure it out.

He'd manage. For her.

A tiny alarm started in the back of her mind warning her she might be in over her head.

Chapter 16

Davis wondered how Junior fared with her ride. She, Hodan and AJ had signed up for a challenging, yet achievable fifty-kilometer charity bike ride along the Gardiner highway and up the Don Valley Parkway ages ago. For some reason, the race lining up with the autumnal equinox was a huge factor in AJ's decision-making. He'd thought to send a quick text but at the last minute, called instead.

"Jaime Sano," she answered.

"Hi, it's me," Davis said, "Why'd you answer like that?"

"I'm on my bike and couldn't see who was calling."

"Sorry!" he stammered. "I was calling to see how it went. I didn't think you'd still be riding."

"No, we're finished. I'm headed home now." She sighed, obviously content with her morning. "It's gorgeous out."

The plan had been for Remington and Jamal to load Junior, Hodan, AJ, and their bikes into his pickup after the race and drive the cyclists home. "What happened? Why didn't you call me?" Davis stopped himself from asking more questions. He knew exactly why she hadn't called. Though her friendship with AJ, Hodan, Remington and Jamal (who generally came as a package deal) existed outside the walls of their office, they were being slotted in firmly in the At Work category of people knowing about their relationship.

"Nothing happened. Remy and Jamal were there as planned, the handsomest pit crew around! We all went for breakfast and I decided to ride home after, that's all," she explained. "The bike path along Lakeshore is practically a straight line to my place."

"Why don't you come over? It's much closer."

"How about a little later? I'm in serious need of a shower."

"You know, I happen to have the components required for bathing right here. The hot water, soap, lotion, and towels are even housed together in a separate room for comfort and convenience."

"How practical!" Junior gushed. "Maybe I will stop by. If only to see this feat of modernity firsthand."

"Prepare to be amazed!"

Eleven minutes later, Junior dropped her bike in Davis' backyard and stepped inside. His back was to her as he put dishes in the cupboard.

"You stretched, right? It's really important–" Davis lost his train of thought as he watched Junior toe off her shoes and toss her gloves and helmet on the table by the back door. She was sweaty, her hair matted, her face flushed from exertion, and still, she was so beautiful. "That's what you wore?"

Junior looked down at her white zippered cycling jersey with colorful squares along the left side and black spandex shorts. "I know," she conceded. "We probably should have worn the event jersey but Hodan wanted us to match," she explained as she walked to the sink to wash her hands.

"What do I have to do to get you to wear this exclusively in this house?" he said from behind her, running his hands over the slinky fabric. She turned to see the appraising look on his face. He brought the zipper down and kissed the notch at the bottom of her neck. "I also like this zipper. More of your clothes should have zippers."

"Don't." Junior pulled away. "I stink!"

Davis pulled in a deep breath. "I like the way you stink."

"I need to shower," she reminded him.

"Yes, I'm trying to help."

Junior looked down at her unzipped top and back up at Davis, brows raised.

"I'm trying to make the effort of a shower worth your while… finish getting you dirty first, you know?"

He kissed her, his tongue greedily searching for hers. She braced her hands on the sink behind her for leverage as she angled toward him. Davis tasted the salt on her skin, licking as he went down the column of her throat. She arched further when she felt the warmth of Davis' mouth through her bra.

He kissed her again, managing to find some restraint when he pulled her lip into his mouth. "Is my Rouleur feeling a little tender?" he ran his hand along her seat, pressing their bodies closer together.

"Yes," she gasped. Whether she was answering his question or responding to the sensation of his hand on her ass was debatable. Junior put her arms around his neck and pulled him closer, chasing the friction through the thin fabric separating them.

"That won't do." Davis reached down, gripped the back of Junior's knees, and dragged her up the length of him enjoying the shiver of pleasure as she moved over his erection. Locking her legs on his waist, Davis kept one hand underneath her and the other hand on the back of her head. "We should take this party upstairs immediately," he said, bringing her mouth to his.

He slowly walked them up the stairs. And though he couldn't completely see where he was going with Junior's mouth on his, he was taking enormous pleasure in the way each movement bumped his body against hers, causing her to moan and whimper in his mouth.

Davis kissed her up the stairs, down the hall, and to his room. He kissed her while he lowered himself to the bed and carefully settled her on his lap. He kissed her, his hand never once leaving the back of her head, as she writhed and rubbed against him. He didn't stop kissing her until he heard her tiny sob. "One... Two... Three..." He counted quietly to himself, his lips moving on her throat, waiting for the gentle tremor to shake her body. "Mmm," he hummed to her collarbone. "That is an excellent start."

"I was promised a shower," Junior reiterated as Davis proceeded to undress her, pulling the zipper down and sliding the jersey off her shoulders.

"If I recall, I simply stated that components required to bathe were here. I did not promise access." He nipped her shoulder. "Besides, we're not finished getting dirty."

Davis laid her on the bed and continued undressing her. Pulling her socks off, he nibbled her ankle then trailed kisses to the back of her knee. He reached for her bike shorts and slowly peeled them off. "I mean it, Junior—I don't think I can handle knowing you're wearing these in public."

"The Lord will not suffer you to be tempted above that you are able," Junior teased, tugging at his shorts.

He hovered over her for a moment, holding her gaze. He adored this woman. The way he wanted her should have been worrying. It didn't seem reasonable to be this affected, yet he honestly didn't want to do a thing about it. He pushed himself slowly into Junior's exquisite body and, not for the first time, wondered what he would be willing to give up if it meant keeping her in his life. "We are about to find out," Davis whispered into her skin.

THAT NIGHT, DAVIS WOKE UP disoriented and frantic after someone punched him in the jaw. The sound of Junior crying out in pain sent his heart pounding.

"Junior! What's wrong?" He gripped her shoulders, fully alert. "What happened?"

"It hurts!" she cried, pawing at her legs. "It hurts so much." Another spasm of pain must have gripped her because she caught his temple when her head snapped back.

At least he'd found the assailant.

"Junior. Junior! Look at me." He held her head. "Your muscles have seized. We have to massage them." He pressed his thumb into the rock-hard mass of her leg and she shrieked. "I'm sorry, I'm sorry, I know it hurts but you have to try. Can you try?" He kissed the top of her head.

Junior made a feeble attempt at working through the knotted muscle. "Good. That's good," Davis encouraged. "We need to soak your legs to loosen the muscles. I'll be right back, okay?"

As she nodded her understanding, he placed a quick, firm kiss on her lips before forcing himself to move. On his way to the kitchen, he detoured into the bathroom to start filling the tub, adding a hefty pour of lavender Epsom salt. Davis sped down the stairs, grabbed a green juice from the fridge and the bottle of painkillers and raced back to his room. The sight of Junior curled up in a ball, mewling in pain, nearly undid him.

Placing the juice and the small bottle of pills on the night table, he scooped her into his lap uncurling her legs. "I'm here, shhh, I'm back." He wiped the tears from her face. "Can you take this?" He offered her an ibuprofen that she washed down with the pressed juice. He ran his hands soothingly on her back.

His heart finally slowed enough for him to piece things together. After Junior had had her shower, loudly refusing his offer of help, she'd settled herself on the couch to tell Davis about the charity bike ride. He hadn't noticed at the time, but Junior spent the entire afternoon and evening watching TV, eating dinner, and chatting, curled in a ball. Now he chided himself for missing the obvious.

"Let's go," he murmured, lifting Junior as he stood.

"I can walk, it... you don't have to carry me."

"I don't mind," he answered with his lips on her face. It wasn't a kiss, necessarily, but Junior leaned into it.

With Junior balanced on one leg, Davis sat on the edge of the tub and swished his hand through the water. "Okay, it's ready." He turned the tap off, lowered Junior's pajama-clad body into the tub and pulled her legs straight when instinct brought her knees to her chest. The residual panic still tightened his voice. "Keep your legs in the water."

Junior nodded and leaned back on the tile. They sat in silence—Junior with her eyes closed and waiting for the drugs to work, Davis facing her on the floor mirroring her positioning.

"I think I elbowed you in the face." Junior cringed.

"And also head-butted me." Davis exaggerated rubbing his temple, laying it on thick.

"Ugh. Sorry."

They continued in a peaceful silence until the tinny chirping of Davis' watch went off. He tested the muscles on her thigh and was pleased to find them pliant. "How are you feeling?"

"Better. Thank you." She still looked wan.

"Let's get you out of there." Davis pulled the stopper and grabbed a towel. Helping her up, Davis leaned forward so Junior could use his body for balance. He tapped her left leg, indicating that she should raise it into his waiting hands. He ran the towel up and down, taking the opportunity to move her leg back and forth, bending and twisting and kneading the muscles from her quad to her calf as he dried her skin, before lowering her foot to the floor. He repeated his ministrations on her right leg then wrapped the towel around her waist when he was finished.

"Is this knowledge Gym Guy or Wilderness Guy?" Junior asked, pulling her pajama shorts off to drip dry in the shower.

"Both?" he offered. "Probably more Wilderness Guy."

"Don't think I didn't notice that in my moment of weakness you chose to feed me vegetables." She levelled judgement at him.

"You noticed that, huh?" He grinned.

"Honestly, I was sure you were going to force some type of vile tincture down my throat, so I guess I got off easy."

"If I thought you'd drink it, I'd make you a raspberry leaf and chamomile tea right now."

"No need. Look." She marched aggressively on the spot. "The magic of modern medicine!"

"Get dressed, Big Pharma. You're going to sit with a heating pad for a bit."

***

Junior changed into a light pink terry romper, settled cross-legged onto the bed, and smiled at him. "My abuela would be impressed. She's a big fan of dirt teas."

"Yeah?" he pulled her legs straight and laid two towels on her lap, ignoring her indignant huff.

"Why does that surprise you? Lots of cultures embrace the roots and bark method of healing. Besides, her grandmother was from Guna Yala so she holds it a bit closer."

"Guna Yala?" Davis laid the heating pad on Junior's outstretched legs.

"The Indigenous province of the Gunas in Panamá. My abuela's Abuela was Guna. When you trade recipes, make sure she knows your knowledge comes from your Cree side. Regina Sano will not take a white dude explaining shit to her lightly."

"I guess it didn't occur to me that you would have such 'roots and bark' origins."

"I don't. My father is a mathematician and my mother is a surgeon. All linear facts all the time."

"Okay, so your mother added a little science to her roots and bark, as you call it. Still a healing bent."

"My abuela is my father's mother. My Grandma, my mother's mother, was not inclined towards healing or nurturing of any sort." Junior said with a hint of laughter.

"Why do you call your mother's parents Grandma and Grandpa? I mean, why do you say it in English? Weren't they Panamanian too?"

"They were. I don't know why." Junior shrugged. "Maybe because my mom was born and raised here? It's hard to explain." Junior searched for the words. "My grandmother cared a lot about appearances and prided herself on her ability to speak fluent, almost accent-less English. By the time I came around, I think my mom chose English for her because that's what she'd have wanted, you know?"

"You don't even speak accent-less English," Davis teased, sitting on the edge of the bed beside her.

"Funny, right?" Junior chuckled. "While my mom was a resident under Roxanne's dad, Dr. Turner, I spent my formative learning-to-speak years with a couple of old folks who grudgingly spoke English, so," Junior thickened her accent, "I have a very good excuse."

"If your mom was raised here and your dad in Panamá, when did they meet?" Davis asked, picking at the narrative hole Junior forgot to plug.

Junior looked contemplative. "Get my phone."

It wasn't a huge secret–it wasn't a secret at all, really. Junior wasn't embarrassed, she was merely private. And people were weird about money. And she hadn't mentally prepared herself to let Davis in on this particular detail. And it didn't change anything about who she was, only how people reacted to her. She didn't have time to keep coming up with more reasons because Davis handed Junior her phone. She gestured for him to sit beside her, and queued up a video. "Mr. Fletcher, meet my grandmother, Paolina Garza."

She turned the screen to him, knowing the name wouldn't mean anything to Davis but that he would absolutely recognize the hysteria of a red carpet.

"Holy shit." Davis appeared transfixed by Junior's grandmother as the camera followed every move. Even with hundreds of bulbs flashing, Paolina practically floated across the red carpet exuding elegant refinement. "That's your grandmother?"

Junior nodded. "The story is long and complicated but the answer to your original question is my grandmother returned to Panamá when she was cast in *Corazón de Vidrio*, 'Heart of Glass'. It was supposed to be a guest spot but the fans loved her, the cameras loved her, and the producers were smart enough to build a storyline for her. When it became clear she was going to be there for a while, my mom and grandfather joined her there after my mom finished high school. She went to university in Panama City."

On the screen, Paolina signed autographs for screaming fans, blessing each one with her undivided attention for the time it took to scribble her name on a poster.

"At some point, my mom and her friends went to Santa Catalina for Semana Santa. A group of locals tried to hustle them, thinking they were tourists."

"Why would they think that?" Davis asked.

"Santa Catalina is a very beautiful but very remote coastal town. At the time, it wasn't a place outsiders would spend Semana Santa. Add in their English speaking and it screamed tourist."

"And what is Semana Santa?"

"Holy Week. The week leading up to Easter. Big holiday in Catholic countries. Huge. Think Spring Break with religious processions. Anyway, one of the boys from the area convinced his friends to stay with him during the holiday. He was happy to find some gullible tourists to dupe for their entertainment. They tried it with my mom and her friends. Not only did she lay into them in Spanish, but she did it in their dialect. My dad was among the hustlers and fell hopelessly, instantly in love. Or so he claims. My mom says she didn't remember him being there that day." Junior shrugged.

Davis kissed the side of her face, "Falling for a Rosales woman that doesn't know you exist? I can relate."

She leaned into his caress.

"And that was it? Happily, ever after?"

"Yes. And no." Junior smiled coyly. "They tell different versions of the story but the common thread is the two groups merged and spent the entire holiday together, and my parents were a couple. They separated at the end of the break either so they could figure out how to overcome the obstacle of living on different coasts, or because it was over and pointless to pursue anything while living on different coasts. Some months later my dad made his move, but my mom was dating someone else."

"Ouch!" Davis empathized.

The video ended frozen on Paolina. If Davis was searching for Junior in her grandmother's face, he wouldn't find her there. "He obviously didn't give up since you're here, plotting revenge against me for the high crime of putting vegetables in your bloodstream." Davis kissed her scowling face.

"Treasonous!" She glowered, hamming it up for her audience of one.

"Your mother is a doctor! How did you get away with this high fructose diet?" He laughed.

"This woman," Junior tilted her phone to indicate her grandmother, "was super strict with that woman. A lot of focus on what my mom ate and how she looked and what she wore resulted in a delightful loosening of the reins when she became a mother herself. Plus, my aforementioned exposure to the old people who maintained the old ways meant that the yucky leafy vegetables were easily cast aside for the yummy starchy ones. And now that I'm a grown-up, I can eat whatever I like!"

Davis pulled the heating pad off her legs, laughing at her grand declaration. "Okay, Grownup Adult Lady. You're free."

"Finally!" Junior cracked and immediately brought her knees to her chest, leaning into his side.

Davis held her close and kissed her temple. "Thank you for introducing me to your grandmother."

Junior looked up at him and smiled. "You know, usually when people find out, they have very different questions." She knew Davis would ask her a hundred questions–Junior was so used to fielding his endless barrage no matter how inconsequential her words–but she was surprised at their direction. Then again, it always amazed her to notice the things Davis noticed.

"Yeah? Like what?"

"Like what kind of famous she was and what that means for me in the present day." Junior shrugged.

"Aside from the near-militant hold you keep on your privacy," he teased, "it doesn't seem to mean anything for you in the present day."

He always paid such close attention, didn't he? Junior spent so much time making it clear that while she may have had a famous to-a-highly-specific-demographic grandmother, her parents were as plain and boring and regular as they came. Which meant she was as plain and boring and regular as they came too.

Junior understood the freedom having money provided. She didn't have to work to live a life of comfort many people struggled to achieve, which was partly why she did work and why she vocally advocated for the more vulnerable around her. There was almost zero risk to Junior to speak out, so she did—loudly and often. She may have been born into the body of a queer Black woman of Latin American descent—a veritable straight flush of underserved identities—but she used the privilege of wealth, the only ace she held, to its fullest extent.

"Very keenly deduced, sir. We have more than some, not as much as others."

"And all because your grandmother was beautiful and talented," he finished.

It would be easy to think that. Most people did. The truth of the matter was Paolina Garza might have been the fame, but her grandfather, Javier Rosales, was the fortune. Their family's security came from trade and shipping. Any vestigial notoriety was pure nostalgia and it had absolutely nothing to do with Junior. Hell, she'd never even met Paolina Garza!

"And don't forget ruthless. Beautiful and talented and ruthless." Junior decided against correcting him. He knew enough and the rest of it changed nothing. "Tell me, Fletcher are you going to continue this dereliction of duty while you gawk at celebrities or will you get off your ass and feed me?"

Chapter 17

"**S**HOOT." JUNIOR UNTANGLED HERSELF from Davis' embrace on the couch. She'd bought a sushi-making kit and spent the night foisting her creations on an enthusiastic Davis. Recovering from their shameless gluttony, she'd lost track of time. "I have to go."

"Why, what's wrong?"

"I promised AJ I'd dress up and my costume is at home. She's very committed to Halloween this year–there's a contest for best Individual *and* Group Costume."

"You dress up for Halloween?" Davis was delighted by the prospect.

"Don't get any ideas. It's the same every year: The Devil in Disguise based on the song by the usurper Elvis Presley."

"The usurper?" he scoffed. "Really?"

"The *King* of Rock?" she scoffed right back in his face, brow arched. "Really?"

Davis shook his head and chuckled at her uncompromising stance on issues of cultural currency and appropriation. "What does that look like?"

"I wear all white like an angel to 'disguise' my devil horns."

"You can't leave early in the morning?"

"I'm sorry, Sapó." She kissed him. "I'll make it worth your while, I promise."

"That's more like it. Let's get rid of these pants." He leaned her back on the couch.

"Tomorrow. I will make it worth your while when you see my costume tomorrow." She laughed sympathetically at his pouting face.

"Okay. Tomorrow," he said as she gathered her things and slipped out the door.

She hadn't lied when she described her costume to Davis. What she didn't clarify was that her outfit was usually a white scoop neck t-shirt and stylish white track pants. Today, though, she put a bit more effort into bumping up her angelic look. The possibility of seeing Davis school his reaction, of provoking him when he could do nothing about it, inspired Junior to pull out all the stops.

Junior got what she wanted when he turned the corner into the production office. She'd worn a white bikini top under a white tailored shirt with the top three buttons undone to reveal multiple gold chains. The shirt was tucked into skin-tight white jeans. With half her hair up in two buns behind red glitter devil horns, matching red glittery lipstick and custom fronts completed the look.

The slight stutter in Davis' step and pained expression was more than worth forgoing anything solid for lunch lest her pants split from the pressure. Junior purposefully leaned over Hodan's desk to maximize his view and his torment.

He nodded a general greeting as he passed her in the main production office on his way to the boardroom. Her phone buzzed in her pocket. **'What's in your mouth?'**

Junior smiled and made sure he could see her take the selfie, her open mouth the only part of her face in the frame, revealing the gold caps and three small diamonds across the top of her front teeth.

'Worth your while?' she texted with the attached picture.

'I wouldn't call anything about that angelic'

'Imagining how they feel?'

'Behave'

"Liam!" Junior put her phone away and clapped excitedly, intercepting him en route to the stairwell. "I heard you were trying to find the perfect nude lip for your J Lo?" His roller derby team was called Livin' La Vida Lopez.

"Hey, Junior." Liam, the camera loader, smiled, looking snazzy in his black suit and skinny tie. "Can't have too many pale gloss options."

Most departments had made an effort to coordinate their outfits: the camera department were the Reservoir Dogs; AJ's production office were The Flintstones; the Grips dressed as the Scooby Gang; Sound were Ghostbusters; the ADs turned up as the Belcher family from Bob's Burgers; the Costume Department showed up as Pink Ladies from Grease 2; and Hair and Makeup were Kiss, which seemed like home-court advantage.

The Twins showed up as the super-cousins Kal-El and Kara Zor-El which meant they were giddily pulling their shirts open at the chest all day. She thought the Electric department was Fight Club based on Ali's Tyler Durden look, but when she saw the gaffer in a yellow Hawaiian shirt and the genny op in a hospital gown under a brown velour sweater, she realized they were various Brad Pitts.

The winners of the group costume would be chosen by secret ballot and announced at the end of the day.

"Match the color to your nipples and it will be your perfect nude. A beauty blogger I follow swears by it! Trust me."

"Really?" Liam seemed equal parts skeptical and intrigued as he continued toward the stairs. "This could be a game-changer."

"We can't let the Bronx Bomber go out there looking anything but flawless. It's what Jennifer deserves." Junior smiled.

Ali had joined Junior in the common area of the production office to loiter a bit during the downtime of crew lunch.

"You can figure that out at the makeup counter?" Ali frowned considering the logistics.

"Oh, yeah—we just whip them out at Sephora." Hodan rolled her eyes.

Junior nodded and winced.

"How long have you been wearing that grill?" Ali shook his head at her like she was a wayward toddler. She made a huffy show of defiance which earned her a stern, "Yalla."

"I'm fine!" she complained, clearly not fine. "Déjame!"

"Yalla." Ali pointed to the arm of the chair in front of the large window. Their bilingual bickering was proof of how far gone she was.

***

Davis was leaving the boardroom when he heard a sound he recognized coming from Junior, in a very specific context. He turned the corner to find Ali standing between Junior's legs. One of his hands tilted her head back while the other searched her mouth with some funny-looking pliers as she held onto his belt loop.

"Isn't it supposed to just snap off?" AJ asked, supervising the ordeal.

"It is, but her stubborn ass doesn't listen ever and now it's stuck," Ali grumbled. With the pliers in her mouth, Junior made an indecipherable retort conveying her dissatisfaction. "There."

Junior groaned when he removed the jewelry, running her tongue over her teeth with relief. "Thanks, Hotspark!"

Ali wiped under her lip to fix her smudged lipstick, wrapped the freed grill in the stained tissue and put it in his shirt pocket before settling on the chair.

With no small amount of anxiety, Davis noted the ease and familiarity shared between Junior and Ali. The realization that it didn't register to either of them, Ali's hands on Junior in such a casual display of intimacy, Junior's lack of physical boundary–even now, she sat between his legs, leaning against him, laughing and joking with everyone completely unaware–didn't make it easier to witness.

The very worst part was wondering whether she'd put a stop to it if Davis asked her to. If he pointed it out, confessed how it made him feel, would Junior fix it? He thought she would. Hoped she would. To find out, though, he'd have to say it out loud. He'd have to admit it to her and risk her refusal, and he could not bring himself to do that.

"Okay, but that's why vampires are the worst...they've been alive for centuries and they're trolling high school hallways? Why would anyone ever go back? High school suuucked! Besides, what's Bethany gonna talk to an immortal being about, AP Physics? Those dummies thought the earth was flat!" Junior complained as Davis tuned into the conversation.

"True love compels them, Junior!" Clarke, the new office PA, insisted.

"Don't bother, Clarke. She does not believe in vampires as a concept. You're screaming at the ocean," Hodan advised.

"I want to know what Count Suck Your Blood was doing during slavery. The holocaust? Internment? Vampires aren't tormented enough if you ask me." Junior sniffed.

"Then what's your monster of choice?" Pete, AJ's assistant, asked her.

"Probably ghosts. Unsettled souls," Junior answered and reflexively kissed a black stone on one of her necklaces.

"I thought you weren't religious." Pete pointed to her obvious reliance on the talisman.

"She's not. She's superstitious," AJ clarified.

"What's the difference?" Clarke asked.

"One doesn't restrict my present-day freedoms for the vague and uncertain promise of future reward."

Davis could not imagine a more perfect encapsulation of Junior Sano. "You don't want to wait and see?" he asked, unable to resist joining the conversation.

"No." Her mouth twisted with impropriety. "I'm not great with delayed gratification." She held his gaze and everyone else in the room disappeared from his awareness. He immediately compiled ways to put that to the test. Junior always relinquished control of her body in pursuit of her pleasure. Davis was certain he could experiment for hours.

"What the...?" Hodan's voice behind him broke the spell. He turned, at the same time as everyone else, to see Noella, the annoying location manager, get off the elevator in a garish polyester jumpsuit and walk towards the kitchen.

"Noella, what are you wearing?" AJ asked, instantly reacting to the giant plastic afro that accessorized the outfit. "We specifically made it clear that people's culture and identities are not acceptable costumes. Please take that wig off."

"Uh, I'm a disco diva? It's not a cultural identity," she said smugly.

"The afro needs to come off, Noella." AJ's tone lacked all patience. "Some people might find it offensive."

"Are you serious? It's offensive to have afros?"

"It's offensive for *you* to have it, Noella. You need to take the wig off," AJ said slowly and clearly.

"People are not costumes," Clarke clarified from her desk. "It's not that difficult."

"I don't even understand. Suddenly there are so many rules about what you can be for Halloween." Noella protested.

"Your costume shouldn't appropriate or fetishize any individual or group of people, Noella," Clarke explained. "You shouldn't need to change your hair texture or skin color to achieve the look."

"Sucks for you then, doesn't it, Junior? Your costume choices are limited to welfare queen, stripper, druggie, or gang banger," Noella giggled as though it were a joke they were both in on.

"What?" Junior shook her head in disbelief. Why Noella chose to focus her buffoonery on Junior, who hadn't said a word since Noella walked through the office, was almost more shocking than her disgusting stereotypes.

Ali kissed his teeth and waved Noella away with a, "Nah."

"Oh, don't be so sensitive. I was joking, gawd!" Noella huffed.

The temperature in the room dipped precipitously as Junior's eyes narrowed into cold dark pools. Ali didn't move, other than to place his hand on the small of Junior's back as she stood, but Davis was suddenly very aware of his every exhalation.

"What is your problem?" Junior demanded.

"I don't have a problem. I'm just saying it's ridiculous. The whole point of Halloween is to be something you're not for a day. If these are the new rules then you'll only be allowed to dress like whatever Scarborough housing project you're from. Where's the fun in that?"

There were gasps around the room. "You're out of line, Noella!" AJ scolded.

"That was your one," Junior said, her voice calm.

"That was my one what?" Noella asked, planting a hand on her hip.

"Junior, can I speak to you, please?" Davis called from across the office. Things were spiraling wildly out of control and he needed to do something before it exploded.

"That was the one time you get to say racist shit to me without getting slapped." Junior ignored Davis and remained focused on her attacker.

"Of course! That's all you people do is throw accusations of racism around for every little thing. I'm not racist. I'm telling it like it is."

"I really hope you enjoyed your little scene, Noella, because while there's a zero-tolerance for violence policy in the office, out in the wild? I will dog walk you across the parking lot the next time that trash comes out of your face. Bet."

"Junior?" Davis tried again.

Noella stood her ground, leaning into Junior, arms folded across her chest. "Is that supposed to be some kind of threat?"

Junior put herself directly in front of the location manager. They stared at each other while everyone stared at them.

"It's not my Blackness you should be afraid of, pendeja," Junior sneered in Noella's face. "Ask about me."

Davis' heartbeat pounded in his ears. Junior stayed squared off against Noella, daring her to respond. Davis couldn't tell if Ali's hand at her back was his way of encouraging her or calming her.

"Junior!" Davis called sharply, desperate to put a stop to all of it. Noella jumped at the sound of his voice, breaking the standoff.

He turned and headed to his office once Junior moved to follow him. He stood in the doorway to usher her in, then closed the door behind them.

"Don't you ever do that to me again," she hissed, outraged.

"I wanted to make sure you were all right."

"She's the one you should be worried about." Junior glowered.

"I don't care about her!"

"You don't care about me, either." Junior's eyes flashed dangerously.

Davis' head jerked back. "How can you say that? You're my girlfriend, of course I care about you!"

"You watched that woman say that foul shit to your girlfriend and did nothing? Said nothing? I'm not your girlfriend." Her lip curled in disgust.

"I cannot yell at her for being shitty to my girlfriend," he sighed heavily.

"I just told you—I'm not your girlfriend," she said coldly. "I'm also, evidently, not an equally valued member of your crew who *deserves*, by the way, to be protected against such abuse in their workplace!"

"Junior—" he tried, but she kept going.

"You're supposed to call that shit out when you see it because it's the right thing to do whether or not you're fucking the victim! This is exactly why I didn't want to tell people about us. If you cannot even treat me like a person when no one knows we're together—if you cannot even establish a baseline of moral character—what do you think happens once we're in the open? I'll tell you! It will look like you were punishing her because we're sleeping together and not because she's an asshole who shoulda got her shit rocked!" Junior whisper yelled. "All you had to do was acknowledge that she was wrong and you didn't!"

"Obviously Noella was out of line, but maybe—"

"Fletcher, if you finish that sentence I will push you, this desk, and that chair right through the god damned window, I swear to fucking Christ." She closed her eyes and held her head.

Davis thought he'd seen Junior angry before. He'd seen her rail at the news and rant into her cell phone in three different languages. He'd learned to steel his body's lusty reaction to her fiery tirades as she stomped through his home or slammed doors in her condo. Even her arguments with Walter that echoed through the office were insubstantial bluster now that he was witnessing true fury pouring off her.

"Junior," he started but didn't know what to say.

"I told you already that I will not overlook your willful ignorance. This," she pointed between them, "does not override that."

"You're going to walk away because I wanted to stop you from doing something you'd regret? Something you couldn't take back?"

"I will never regret telling a bigot to get fucked. Never!" Junior got in his face. "I will walk away from this, from you, to stand up for myself every time! You don't get to have me while simultaneously dick-riding for the people who would hurt me. That is not how this works. And if you don't understand that by now, if you don't know that fundamental truth about me, then you're the one about to do something you can't take back."

"I'm not saying you shouldn't stand up for yourself but we are at work, Junior. You can't run around assaulting people in the office! There are ways to go about this."

"If racists got slapped more often, they'd think twice about spewing their garbage. Not that it matters now. You've signaled to her and everyone in that room that her behavior will suffer no consequences."

"I did not!"

"No? How do you think it looks that one of the producers barked at me to come into his office after witnessing that altercation, hmm? No reprimand for her, just me being dragged back here behind closed doors. Who do you think that action assigns value to without the context of our sex life? What about the six people who witnessed the authoritative way you handled that, huh?" She watched him expectantly as she counted out the marginalized identities of the group in question. "Two Black, one Asian, three Muslim, two queer, and three women. You think they feel like you give a shit about any issues of discrimination or ill-treatment they might face?"

Bull's-eye.

Davis slumped in his chair with his head in his hands.

"Excellent work, Fletcher. I feel very cared for. Enjoy caping for the status quo," she spat, leaving him there without another word.

Many truths came crashing down on Davis in the wake of Junior's furious departure. It stung that, in the moment, Junior looked for her boss and not her boyfriend to come to her aid. What hurt more was that she was right.

When Olivia gave him the title last season, he assumed it was to distinguish him from a 'coffee and dry cleaning' assistant. Sure, he had more responsibility and his opinions carried some weight but, in his mind, he was still 'just' Olivia's assistant.

This horrible experience drove home that his role as producer, hopefully soon executive producer, meant his preference for keeping his head down and quietly doing his work in the face of any and all ugliness was no longer an option.

***

Junior returned to her office and rolled her shoulders a couple of times while taking deep, cleansing breaths to let as much of the irritation out as she could. Stuffing a blow pop in her mouth, she focused on the piles in her inbox. Prioritizing the various forms and envelopes on her desk was exactly the mindless task she needed to help her calm down. Some of the heat of her irritation went away but the sting of it remained.

She wished she could give a damn about Noella, but Junior simply couldn't. Exchanges like that were so common-place—from the affable assertions that she 'must miss the warmth of back home' during the winter to 'you're Latina? But...you're Black' to the more blatant 'no, but where are you *from*?' Junior had always been subjected to these insidious reminders of her place.

They were too common, too nonsensical, to warrant any more than an eye roll and a possible snide remark in response. But today was something else. It was one thing when she thought Davis did not stand up to Eli, specifically. No matter how it rankled she understood that his job security factored into how he chose to deal with those problems. But this? Where Davis' role as producer gave him the authority and the autonomy to act but still he didn't? This was a problem she could not get around.

"Are you okay?"

"Yeah." Junior smiled wryly at AJ. "I never could stand her."

"I don't think you'd even made it down the hall before Clarke was in Marin's office to report Noella's behavior." AJ perched on the edge of Junior's desk.

"Clarke did?" Junior shook her head unsurprised. At twenty-four, a new addition to the office this season, Clarke was exactly the type of person who understood her privilege, how it could be wielded in service of others, and the structural barriers in place that actively prevented true intersectionality.

"Yup. Then we had to explain dog-walking to Pete. That was a good rabbit hole to send him down," AJ laughed.

"Has Marin said anything?" Junior worried that this narrative would be turned against her and mentally prepared herself for everyone's eagerness to see Noella's aggression as a simple misunderstanding–or worse, an overreaction on Junior's part.

"She asked us what we saw and made some calls. Why, did Fletcher give you shit?"

"No. He said he was trying to prevent further escalation." Junior rolled her eyes.

"I bet he has no idea he saved a life. Or, I guess, until you talk Hotspark down, her life is still at risk," AJ teased her about Ali's protectiveness before leaning over for a hug. "You're good?"

"I'm good," Junior confirmed.

"Incoming," AJ whispered, rising. "Later," she said on her way out as Marin and Davis walked into Junior's office.

"Junior." Marin used her concerned voice. "I heard what happened and wanted to make sure you're okay."

"I am, thanks."

"I want you to know that I've had a brief chat with some of the people who witnessed your...disagreement–"

"Noella hurled racist insults at Junior. It wasn't a disagreement," Davis corrected.

Marin stiffened slightly, corrected her wording and continued. "With some people who witnessed the verbal assault. By all accounts, Noella was the aggressor. I also understand that you, *in defending yourself*, promised physical retribution. Neither act is acceptable under our Zero Tolerance policy. If you agree, Noella will be required to issue you an apology which will put an end to further action for either of you."

Junior understood that Marin wanted to find a fair and equitable solution so she could put it away as quickly and quietly as possible. She also understood that Noella was getting off easy. "I agree."

"The apology should be in public," Davis interjected.

Marin's questioning glance mirrored her own.

"She made her vile remarks out loud and in front of everyone. She was wrong in public–she should apologize that way, too."

Marin considered his words and decided. "That seems reasonable. Junior?"

Junior was speechless and could only nod her assent. She had not thought him capable of that level of nuance and awareness. It was a pleasant surprise.

"On behalf of the production, I apologize that you were subjected to that behavior. Noella will be spoken to."

Another nod.

"Thank you, Junior," Marin said and left her office.

Davis tipped his head and followed Marin down the hall.

Junior's phone buzzed in her pocket. **'I was worried. I panicked and I handled it wrong. That doesn't mean I don't care about you. We're on the same side.'**

'Are you doing your Other Ways now?' she wrote back.

'As a matter of fact, yes.'

'What does that look like?'

'Making sure it is clear that you were the victim of racist violence and not just on the losing end of an argument, for starters.'

'Impressive.'

'And keeping Eli in the dark so it will be handled with care and consideration.'

'Smart.'

'Also currently advocating for a mandatory sensitivity seminar to be added to her apology.'

'Diabolical.'

'Come over tonight so we can talk properly'

'Can't. Busy.'

'Busy plans or busy mad at me?'

Junior smiled to herself. He knew her so well. **'Both'**

'Will I see you this weekend?'

'As soon as I'm done being mad at you'

'And there's nothing I can do to speed up the process?'

'First week in November is big for my people. Can't be rushed.' She typed with a wry grin.

'Is there room for me to join you in these Independence Day celebrations?'

'Not currently but I will keep you posted.'

"Who are you smiling at?" Clarke asked, arms full of green script pages.

Junior put her phone back in her pocket. "I heard that you went toe-to-toe with the establishment. Pretty hard-core, using that Speak to Your Manager energy against Noella."

"It's my birthright. Noella deserved to be on the receiving end." Clarke shuddered. "That was intense. You were so cool, though. I would have had a full-on panic attack."

"As if! *You're* so cool. If only you chose better celebrity crushes," Junior teased.

Clarke stuck her fingers in her ears and laughed. "I don't know what to tell you. I can't explain it–it just is!"

Junior's phone buzzed again. **'I remain at your disposal'**

Reading the text, she shook her head and said, "Tell me about it."

Chapter 18

JUNIOR HAD BEEN CRAVING ceviche. It was probably her body's way of regulating her sugar intake in some twisted version of obtaining balance. She had consumed a worrying amount of Halloween candy in the last couple of weeks even by her own standards. She'd stopped by the market and got everything she needed, not trusting Davis' pantry staples to provide in her time of need. They'd ordered in a lot lately and the few times they did cook, it was something quick and simple.

And, if she was being honest with herself, she wanted to do something nice for Davis who had been trying so hard. Junior knew she was holding herself at a distance and she knew he felt it. Davis had got too close and the depth of the hurt and disappointment he'd caused had taken her by surprise. Flings shouldn't hurt. She needed to recalibrate the parameters of this situation so she could continue to enjoy this thing they were doing, risk-free.

She unloaded the bags from her trunk and, walking to the house, tried to remember how much of the Milagro was left. Junior was pretty sure she hadn't finished it. She hoped she hadn't. When Junior put the key in the door, it swung open. She looked around before stepping cautiously inside. "Hello? Sapó, your door is open!" she called from the foyer.

"Hello?" a woman's voice answered.

Curious suspicion replaced Junior's caution. She headed into the house. "Hello?"

"Hi!" A young woman with long dark hair and a golden complexion over a familiar face smiled at her from the kitchen. "You must be Junior. I'm Danielle."

Junior could see the resemblance between Davis and his sister. Her brows were meticulously shaped and not as heavy as her brother's, but there was no denying they were family. It occurred to Junior that Danielle must be the connecting piece in the line that joined the two worlds. There'd be no denying Davis his heritage with his sister around.

"Yes, sorry, of course! He always calls you Teddy. It's nice to meet you. I hope I'm not intruding. I can go if you guys have plans," Junior offered.

"No, please. I'm the one that's intruding. I needed to get away for a minute and it's easier to come here than to go home." She gave a piteous smile. Davis had said that his sister suffered broken hearts often and Junior guessed this was a case of that.

Junior remembered being in that type of all-encompassing love. She was twenty-one and completely infatuated with the gorgeous guy who'd relentlessly pursued her. Ali Mansour was smart and sexy and a little bit dangerous—so unlike anyone she'd ever known—and he wanted her. He wanted her and he'd let the world know. She gave herself to him so completely that when they broke up after two years, she was physically sick for a week.

Within a month, he came crawling back and publicly prostrated himself for her forgiveness. The thought that he could have caused one tear to fall... she should only cry happy tears, he'd lamented. He couldn't look at himself in the mirror knowing that he'd brought her even a moment of pain. She was the only one for him, he'd said, and he was wrong to ever question that.

Junior was powerless against that display of atonement. All of that passion and fire must mean something, proved something, about the strength and purity of their love. Junior spent the next five years chasing that rush through higher highs and lower lows. Finally, she admitted to herself that something was missing, would probably always be missing, and tearfully begged him to let her go.

Junior put the bags on the counter and started to unpack. "I was going to make dinner. If you don't mind a little chaos, I'm happy to have the company." If there was one thing Junior was good at, it was giving sound relationship advice that she herself did not follow. She would pay as much or as little attention as this broken-hearted co-ed desired.

But first: tequila.

***

Davis walked in an hour later to delicious aromas from the kitchen and salsa music blaring from the speakers. He inhaled deeply and smiled to himself. Junior.

It had been fraught between them since his mishandling of things at Halloween. She no longer trusted him, if she ever did, to move their relationship to the next level. Yes, they'd talked and he'd apologized, but Junior had pulled away from him. Despite her physical presence or claims she'd made to the contrary, she'd emotionally shut him out all the same.

Coming home to find her cooking in his space like she belonged in it was encouraging. Proof that a thaw had started to melt the frost that had settled between them. "You still haven't taught me how to–"

Stepping into the kitchen, Davis came to an abrupt halt, observing the scene without comprehension.

Junior was adding something to a pot while Teddy sampled from the cutting board, the two giggling like old friends.

"Doodle!" his sister cried when she noticed him. Danielle stumbled over and threw her arms around him. "Junior is sooo pretty! You didn't tell me she was so pretty! She's making ceviche and arroz con pollo and she told me dicks are everywhere and not to be sad because I'm a bad bitch and I can get another one whenever I want. And I can, you know? Because I am a baaad bitch!" she nodded to underscore this tipsy proclamation.

"Hey, Teddy." Davis looked at Junior who had pulled her lips into her mouth to keep from laughing. "You got my sister drunk and told her dicks are everywhere?" He pointed the remote at the speaker to lower the volume.

"I did no such thing. The tequila got her drunk. You Fletchers need to work on your tolerance." She took a sip of her drink.

"And the dicks?" He stifled his laughter.

"Dick is a low value commodity. That's just math."

Danielle tugged on her brother's arm. "Doodle, smell me! Junior said I would feel better after I took a bath and I used her stuff and I smell so good and my hair is so soft! Touch it! Soft, right?"

Her eyes were glassy and she slurred a little, but mostly Davis could tell that she was happy to no longer be carrying her burden alone.

"Oh! I wanna show you something. Wait here!" Danielle tripped up the stairs and hollered, "I'm okay!" before they heard her stumble down the hall.

Junior tried to hide her giggling behind her glass. Davis leaned in and tasted the alcohol on her lips. "You gave her straight tequila?" he laughed.

"She's a grad student. I thought she'd be better at it. Lesson learned." Junior took another sip and set her glass down.

"Are you going to fill me in?" He kissed her again, holding her against his body, hips aligning with hers.

"She was here when I arrived and visibly upset. Mike, or Mick? Mark? Some jackass with an M name told her they were just having fun but he didn't see a future for them," Junior sneered, "So I did the only logical thing when a member of the sisterhood is in crisis: blind, unwavering support."

"Thank you," Davis put a kiss on the side of her head as she leaned against him.

"Anytime, Doodle!" she let out a boisterous laugh when he groaned. "Don't worry, Sapó, I know that Doodle Bug and Teddy Bear are family names. You don't have to worry about me using them." She pat his face affectionately and turned to check on the pot.

Davis schooled his features from the blow Junior unwittingly dealt. He knew she meant that she wouldn't betray the confidence of it.

Still, it hurt. After all this time, he'd hoped that she would start speaking about the future when she referred to them. Instead, it was one more example of the mess he'd made, the impediment to their progress, by disappointing her.

"Here you go!" Danielle started from the top of the stairs. She was giddy with anticipation. "Open it!"

"Teddy, it's amazing. You made this?"

She beamed at her brother. Danielle had been learning to read the Cree language. Their mother taught them what she knew by speaking it at home but they didn't read or write the language. Danielle had made a panel with the first word they'd both learned to read.

Junior looked at the beaded fabric Davis held up with the artfully designed symbols. "Is that Cree?" she asked tentatively.

Danielle nodded.

"It means Family." Davis smiled at his sister.

"You like it?" Danielle asked, taking it from his hands.

"I do. Thank you."

"Thank you? For what?" She frowned at him.

"For making that for me." He reached for the panel that she twisted out of his reach.

"I didn't make it for you."

"Then why did you give it to me?"

"I didn't. I said I had something to show you. How does that mean you get to keep it? I'm not even finished yet!"

Just like that, they devolved into a heated round of bickering.

"Okay, Fletchers, let's eat!" Junior called, halting their quarrel with the promise of food.

JUNIOR WAS IN THE BATHROOM getting ready for bed with Danielle sitting cross-legged on the counter on one side, sniffing and inspecting the tubes and pots and vials Junior laid out, and Davis leaning on the wall on the other. They'd made it through dinner with lots of laughter and anecdotes, but then at the sink when they were washing and drying the dishes, another spat broke out and Junior left them to it, choosing to watch TV upstairs.

"These are both toners?" Danielle asked, holding up two bottles.

"I bought that one first but didn't like the feeling on my skin after. Try it. If you like it, you can have it. I've been meaning to throw it out," Junior admitted.

"And this?" Danielle held up a spray bottle.

"A stupidly expensive moisturizing spray that I'm not sure works."

Danielle hopped off the counter and rummaged through her toiletry bag. She laid out her few items and started her evening routine in the mirror beside Junior.

"You Fletchers sure like hanging around together in the bathroom. Is there something I should know?" Junior chuckled.

Danielle shrugged while pinning her hair back "There's only one bathroom in our tiny house. You get used to having people in your space all the time."

"What's your house like? Your brother doesn't ever talk about where you guys are from. Only that it's up north and remote."

Davis laughed at Junior's blatant attempt at wheedling information on their childhood from his sister.

"I mean, that's all there is to say. Our dad built the house before either of us was born and didn't factor teenagers into the floor plan. Our parents' room is in the front of the house, our rooms are in the back, and you don't have to get out of bed to have a conversation with anyone." She laughed.

"She's exaggerating." Davis rolled his eyes for Junior's amusement. Because he didn't do it enough for it to be an effective indicator of his derision, it looked more like an aggressive batting of lashes.

"Not really," Danielle insisted. "Okay, we weren't all living in one big bed and eating cabbage water like *Charlie and the Chocolate Factory*, but we live on one level off the grid. My parents still don't have Wi-Fi. Can you imagine?"

"I didn't have an upstairs or downstairs at my house either." Junior smiled. "Or, well, I guess there's sort of a downstairs. More halfway down and to the left," she considered. "Technically, I still don't have one."

Davis laughed. Junior's apartment probably had the same square footage as his house. "Your condo doesn't count."

Junior gasped at the bottle of translucent purple liquid Danielle doused her cotton pad with. "Gross–that is basically dyed rubbing alcohol! Where'd you get it, the dollar store?" Junior took the cotton swab and the open bottle and pitched them in the trash. "Here. Use this instead."

Danielle's eyes flew to Davis' in uncertainty. Davis gave her a small, reassuring nod.

People always claimed they understood what he meant when he explained that he grew up impoverished and then proceeded to say the most callous things about the places and services he relied on to survive. They didn't understand how living in scarcity wore you down in every possible way.

To this day, Davis felt a small pang of anxiety whenever he splurged on a 'non-essential' item. He still went over his bank transactions, monitoring his balance with every purchase made. He still worried that one unexpected bill would send him back to the bottom of the pit he struggled so hard to climb out of.

Watching someone cavalierly throw away an almost full bottle of anything was outside the scope of comprehension for the siblings who used every single thing to the very last drop.

"What?" Junior asked, picking up on their tension.

Davis stood behind her and rubbed her shoulders. "Junior," he reprimanded softly to her reflection. He watched her as the admonishment made its way across her face like liquid on litmus paper.

When the penny dropped, she turned to him, stricken. "I'm sorry," she whispered.

He dropped a quick, light kiss on her lips. "I know."

"Danielle, I am so sorry. I didn't mean to… it doesn't matter what I meant. I'm sorry." Junior took one of Danielle's hands in hers. "Seriously. I don't think before I speak sometimes."

"Most of the time," Davis butted in, which earned him an elbow to his gut.

"No, it's all right. I know you didn't mean it like that," Danielle said weakly to the mirror.

"It's not. I said a shitty thing," Junior insisted.

"I'm not mad, honest. I… sometimes I'm able to forget, y'know? Just for a little while." She gave Junior a watery smile. "It always sucks when I remember."

The adrenaline of packing up and going to her brother's unannounced had dimmed, the fancy bath products had faded, the tequila had worn off, and Junior had thoughtlessly made Danielle feel less than, probably not unlike that jerk, Mitch. Junior hugged her tight and looked at Davis over her shoulder. "You know what? I think we need a slumber party."

"Huh?" The Fletchers asked in unison.

"A slumber party! We can stay up all night and talk shit about exes and have snacks and watch movies. What do you say?" she asked Danielle.

"I guess?"

"Let me check with Claudia and Silvana," Junior said, thinking out loud.

"Wait, you're going to invite your cousins here?" Davis was dumbstruck. Of all the ways he thought he'd meet members of her family, 'slumber party for his broken-hearted sister' wasn't even on the first six pages.

"Don't be ridiculous. We're going to go there. Or my place. Probably their place." Junior pulled up her phone, but before she could dial, Davis put a hand on hers.

"Slow down a minute. You're leaving and taking my sister with you?"

"We're going to have a slumber party. We can't speak freely with you there, Sapó." She gave his cheek the 'silly boy' pat. "Don't worry, I won't tell your sister anything about you that she doesn't already know." Junior tapped the screen and hollered, "Wapin'?" Junior moved her face from the speaker and said to a bemused Danielle, "Go pack your stuff, we'll leave in twenty," before going to Davis' room to pack her bag.

Once the plans were in place, Junior hung up the phone and faced a dour Davis. "Don't make that face at me, okay? Please. She was feeling better and I wrecked it. I need to make it right."

"By taking her to your cousin who hates strangers and is a stranger to her—as are you, not for nothing—for a slumber party?" he asked, voice full of sulky reproach. He wrapped his arms loosely around her waist and tried a different tack. "I have a better idea. You just finished reading about the half-Indian tailor and his bluestocking horse lady. I bet one of your dazzling book recaps will make her feel better."

"Claudia dislikes groups of strangers. One *guest* won't be a problem, trust me."

He was sorry that his sister was hurting. It didn't mean he was willing to sacrifice a night with Junior for a heartbreak that wasn't going to crack the top ten in her lifetime. He opened his mouth to argue but Junior cut him off.

"Listen. If she had anyone she could trust at her stupid school, that's where she'd be right now. You wouldn't have known anything about Mick or Mark or whatever his name is until she was seeing someone new. She sat on a bus"–Junior shuddered a little–"for six hours so she could get away. Are you still listening?" She stared at him expectantly.

Junior had repeatedly told him about her worry for women who didn't have the support of other women. A woman without female friendships was vulnerable, she'd said, lacked the strengths and insights sisterhood provided. Though her adolescence was tough, she'd always had Roxanne and her cousins, and had met Leigh when she was in university. Knowing you were loved and trusted enough to be told the truth unconditionally was a power Junior believed every woman should have. She was now apparently trying to give it to his sister.

When he nodded, she continued, "What she needs is the drunken camaraderie found in the women's bathroom of every club and bar in this city. In the absence of that, we're having a slumber party. She needs to complain about what a piece of shit he was. She needs to talk about the time he refused to kiss her after she swallowed his seed or anytime he chased his pleasure and left her behind or whatever other limp-dicked bullshit he unquestionably did. She needs to miss him and hate him and plot vengeful things against him in a way that can only truly be done with other people who know the misery of dating cis men."

"Can you not? I don't want to think about Teddy having sex with anyone."

"Exactly," Junior tilted her head, considering. "And maybe you're right and she's never had a dick in her mouth, but I wouldn't take those odds."

Davis's entire posture clenched trying to fight off the visual.

"When will you be back?"

"Lunchtime? We can take Danielle to Dynasty for dim sum before I head home."

"You're not going to stay?"

"Sure, why not? There'll be no action here, no action there—what's the difference, right?"

"Wait, what?" he stammered. This surplus of baby sister creating a deficit of naked Junior was not how he saw his weekend playing out.

"Let me get this straight, you don't want to acknowledge that your sister has been knocked into the drywall with her panties around her ankles, but she should have to hear all of your noises?"

"I can be quiet," Davis said and kissed her deeply. He moaned a little when she swirled her tongue against his. Junior ran her hand up his thigh and cupped him firmly. He growled, pushing her against the doorframe.

"Quiet, huh?" she said, smirking and ducked from his grasp into the hallway.

"We'll see you tomorrow, Doodle!" Teddy called from downstairs.

"Goodnight, Sapó!" Junior added and led Danielle out to the waiting car.

Chapter 19

THE WEEK AFTER JUNIOR'S annual holiday brunch was a blur of work, shopping, family, and Davis.

What started as a simple potluck gathering of friends and family had evolved into a feast of sweet and savory dishes, fresh fruit, cakes, and cookies. This year the table had been packed with lumpia, pancit, fried shark, foole, tamales, maraq digaag, latkes, tourtière, two kinds of ham, four kinds of rice, quiche, and brisket—all washed down with alcohol enhanced everything: Baileys in coffees, vodka in juices, bourbon in teas, and rummy eggnog for the purists. She'd hosted a riotous seventeen people around her dining room table.

Davis had been annoyed and disappointed when she explained that there'd be too many streams converging between friends and family for him to attend. How would she even explain it? His presence would raise too many questions. The last thing she needed was for Claudia to make some reference to Danielle or for Claire to invite him to another spin class. Even the ever-practical Leigh would've counselled that discretion was the better part of valor. It wasn't the right time, she'd insisted, they needed to get through the chaos of the holidays before going public at work, and he'd relented.

An insidious voice had needled her all day. As it got louder, it sounded uncomfortably like guilt.

Junior balked.

She wasn't ashamed to be with Davis! What was one afternoon, a handful of hours, really, in the balance? Certainly not enough to be an indictment of her and their... affair. This was just separate from that, she told herself and shook off her uneasiness.

That night she'd admitted to him how much she'd missed him all day and he'd shown more grace and tact than she would have had the situations been reversed.

They'd spent every night since at Junior's because she'd had so much to do. Among many other things, she'd discovered Davis was an ace gift wrapper. What he lacked in speed, he made up for in sharp, clean corners and perfectly aligned patterns at the seams. Junior found it admirable, especially because she operated on a 'get it done and cover any sins in ribbons and bows' method. Now, finally on top of her Holiday To-Do List, they'd spent a productive night at his place packing his suitcase.

"Are you ready for Monday? You have everything you need?" Junior asked through a yawn, as she settled into bed.

"Yeah, I think so."

"And you promise to explain to your family why I didn't wrap their presents?" she asked, not for the first time. She'd twisted herself in knots worrying about how gifts to his parents would be received. They didn't know her, maybe didn't even know about her, but it seemed more awkward to send something to Danielle without including them. Besides, it was the season of giving and who didn't like getting gifts?

"They aren't even expecting anything from you. They aren't going to be mad that you didn't wrap it in frills and bows."

"Sometimes they get weird at security and start flagging shit for nonsense reasons."

"I'll wrap them before I hand them over. Don't worry." He put a quelling kiss on her forehead.

"You're back on the thirtieth?" she settled into his embrace.

"The morning of the thirty-first. If you don't already have plans, I'd love to do something together."

"I'm not a big fancy New Year's person, Sapó. I'm more of a 'Chinese food in my pajamas binge-watching a show until the ball drops' kinda girl."

"Sounds perfect," he said on a contented sigh.

"Then you, sir, have yourself a date." She yawned again, closing her eyes.

"I could not be happier." Junior could hear the smile in his voice. "When do you want to open gifts?"

"You got me a present?" She feigned surprise. "Why, Mr. Fletcher, I don't know what to say!"

"Before or after I go home, Meryl?" He shook her playfully.

"Let's do it now!" All her sleepiness was pushed aside at the mention of gifts. She was equal parts nervous and excited for Davis to open his.

He laughed in disbelief. "You want to open presents now? I practically had to carry you up the stairs."

"Just say you're not ready and stop making excuses," she challenged, getting out of bed

"Hmph. You're on." Davis went to the chest of drawers and pulled out a small flat box the size of a picture frame. "Well?"

Junior scurried out of the room and returned with an unwrapped box. "You first!" she bounced on the bed. "If you don't like it, you can exchange it—no worries at all." She was already bracing herself for rejection.

"I'm sure it's perfect." He kissed her cheek. He carefully opened the box. Under a comical amount of tissue paper, he pulled out a grey cashmere scarf. "Junior, it's—" His stunned expression was reward enough. "I've never owned anything this nice before."

"I figure since you refuse to zip up your damn jacket, you need a proper scarf to keep you warm." He pulled the scarf out of the box and smoothed his hand over the soft, thick, luxurious material. "That color will go with your normal coat or your Canadian Dinner Jacket, which I cannot believe you seriously wear in public and like I said, you can change it if you want a different color or want something else entirely."

"No, I want this one." He pressed a firm kiss against her lips. "Thank you. It is beautiful."

"Yeah?" She smiled shyly. Her money wasn't a factor between them—it never came up because they had no financial entanglements. Dinners out, weekends away, the odd thoughtful 'thinking of you' purchase were all within a scope that kept them on equal footing. This, though, was shining a klieg light on the disparity. She wanted to spoil him with the material things he continued to deny himself and hoped it wouldn't ruin the ease they'd enjoyed.

"Yeah." He kissed her again. "One day I'll bring you up to Red Lake so you can experience actual cold."

"No thanks. This cold is cold enough! Red Lake can be a summertime visit," she said, rubbing her hands with anticipation. "My turn!" She snatched the package from his extended hand with devilish glee. She made a big show of examining the box to discern its contents. She shook it and held it up to her ear and even smelled it before tearing through the paper. "Hmm."

Inside was a disc of wood, roughly two centimeters thick and as big as her hand, cut on the diagonal. A simple but realistic rendering of her tree was carved into the wood. The leafy branches curved up and out to the edges of the disc while the trunk grew out of a stylized root system. As she turned the disc over to see the other side, something in the roots glinted in the lamplight. She looked again and noticed that a shallow groove was etched into certain lines in the roots. Pressed into the grooves was a gold chain creating the lower-case letters j r. Junior. But also: Javier Rosales.

"You made this? Is this...?" She was overwhelmed by the gesture.

"I was going to make you a picture of your tree, but when I went there to sketch it, some branches were down and I thought..." One side of his mouth twitched in uncertainty. "Do you like it?"

Junior could only nod as tears spilled down her face.

He explained, "Max helped me with the inlay. She said the necklace can be removed without any damage."

The necklace, a gift from her grandfather for her Quinceañera, had snagged on her coat and broke on the day he died. Junior had took as an omen and refused to have the chain put back together.

A hiccup-y sob escaped. He pulled her close while she cried and clutched the wooden keepsake he'd made to her chest.

Junior thought of all the little pieces of her he would have to have gleaned and stored away to create this. All the little facts that would have been cobbled together, some from long before they were a They, over many conversations and thrown away utterances. Davis quietly and diligently collected all these things and turned them into a beautiful token.

"Thank you," she said through her tears. "This means... thank you."

"I was so worried you'd notice that a piece of your necklace was missing before I had a chance to give this to you." He kissed her temple, rubbing circles on her back.

"How did you do this? *When* did you do this?" she asked, wiping her face.

"Growing up the way I did gave me the time to master the art of woodworking, though it has been a while since I've done anything like this," he admitted. "And you don't spend nearly as much time here as I'd like." He smiled with his lips pressed against her temple.

"I can't believe you had time for this."

But she could.

He'd spent hours and hours sketching and planning and carving, all while thinking about her and how he hoped she would receive it. Hours and hours concentrating and focusing on getting it exactly right. Hours and hours pouring himself into this gift for her. Because even though she didn't know what to do about it, she knew what it meant.

Davis loved her and he'd carved his love into a hunk of her favorite tree to give to her.

She leaned the disc on the night table on her side of the bed before moving the boxes aside to turn on Davis' lamp.

"What are you doing?" he squinted at the sudden light.

"I want to see you," she answered and settled herself on his lap to kiss him. She kissed him for all the things she could not say, for all the feelings she could not yet express. Then, as she felt the first stirrings of his desire, she kissed him to encourage his wanting and the need to satisfy her own.

Davis shifted beneath her, moving the blanket from between them and placed her more securely on his lap.

His hands moved over her as he kissed her, his tongue searching and claiming hers. Davis raised her off his lap to rid himself of his pajamas and, with her now on her knees in front of him, caught her breast in his mouth through her nightgown. Junior let herself get carried away by his masterful command of her body, by the way he always committed himself to her satisfaction.

"No, like this," Junior corrected when he tried to shift her onto her stomach. Davis repositioned himself against the headboard while Junior pulled her nightgown over her head and tossed it blindly across the room.

"Come here." He caught his lip in his teeth as Junior straddled him. He captured her mouth and kissed her deeply as she lowered herself onto him. Davis' moan came from deep in his throat.

Junior set a slow and steady pace, aware of his every pulse and throb. She put her arms around his shoulders, keeping their bodies close so that her breasts rubbed against his chest as they moved. She hissed when Davis put his hand between her shoulder blades and pressed them even closer together. "Yes."

Davis' other hand caressed her thigh, up to her hip, across her back, and squeezed her ass. She moaned so he did it again, squeezing and pulling gently during her downward motion. Neither Junior nor Davis shied away from the sustained eye contact as they held onto each other, looking away only when their eyes rolled in pleasure or when they shared a scorching kiss that sent shivers down their spine.

Junior wanted to stay here, like this, where she could understand and decipher these feelings–his hands on her body, her mouth on his, their tongues intertwined, their ragged breaths–this desire.

Both of his arms pulled her toward him creating delicious friction.

"Junior, I'm going to... I'm–I can't..." His eyes were nearly black with his arousal. His muscles were taut from the tension of holding himself back.

"I–I need..."

"What do you need?" he breathed into her skin. "Tell me what you need."

She needed him to understand that he couldn't say it to her—that if he wanted to hear her say it back, he could not say those words to her. She needed him to accept that this, right now, was her way of acknowledging his feelings. She needed him to realize how much he meant to her even if she wasn't where he wanted her to be. But she couldn't say any of that. She didn't know how. So, she moved with him, feeling his lips on hers, keeping their eyes locked, bodies pressed together, and whispered, "Take me with you," as she kissed him desperately.

He leaned forward slightly changing the angle of his hips to allow himself a long, slow thrust, grinding against her where their bodies connected. On the third pass, she broke. Junior threw her head and breathed through the first wave of her climax.

"Those are my noises, Junior," Davis growled.

He ran his mouth along her neck to where it met her shoulder and bit down as another wave of her climax hit. Junior let out a sound of such primal pleasure that Davis followed her over the edge, shouting out as his own orgasm twisted and contorted his body.

When he'd caught his breath, he held her face and kissed her. "I can't believe I have to leave you tomorrow."

"You don't have to leave me right now," she said, looking into his eyes.

"No, I'm not going anywhere right now." Davis nestled her to him, pulling the covers awkwardly over them, and they lay that way—connected and connected—until they fell asleep.

***

For the first time in many years, the ungodly departure time from Winnipeg—always the cheapest during the holidays—was something Davis was grateful for. He'd have the morning to recover from his travels and still spend the day with Junior. Having spent his entire visit trying to imagine her in Red Lake, he was eager to see her again.

When he got home, he found Junior curled up asleep in his bed. He watched her sleep for a moment, thrilled that she'd spent the night there without him, before taking a quick shower and joining her.

"You're home," she smiled sleepily.

"Shhh… it's still early." The thrill ballooned in his chest. He was home and so was she.

"I'm awake now." She yawned and snuggled closer to him, fast asleep.

They spent the next four days together, inside and partially clothed. Playing house with Junior was a dream he didn't want to end. Sadly, Monday arrived entirely too soon and they had to part.

"Will you come back tonight?" He kissed her slowly against the front door.

"I have to go home, Sapó. I need clothes and stuff." She moaned into his shoulder. "And now I need to leave for work. You do, too! Stop this." She kissed him back, her tongue greedily searching for his as she arched closer to him.

"I'm stopping. Are you?" Davis' voice came out in a low rumble from his chest. He put his hand under her sweater and raised the cup of her bra and kissed her while running his finger along her covered breast. Junior arched into his touch. Her skin was always so soft, he never tired of the feel of her. "Because it doesn't feel like you're stopping."

"You are making a mess," she breathed, writhing against him.

"Show me," he whispered in her ear. Junior guided his hand passed the waistband of her pants and down between her legs where he explored her wet warmth. "Jesus!" he slammed his fist on the door above her head. He was plagued by indecision–fall to his knees and drink his fill or pin her to wall and sink in to the hilt.

"See what you've done?"

Davis covered her mouth with his. Junior, apparently in no way conflicted about what he should do, slowly slid his fingers inside her while the heel of his palm rubbed delicious friction right where she needed it. He kissed her feverishly as she rode his hand. "You feel so good," he groaned.

Her head fell back when the lightning struck her spine.

Groaning as she clenched his fingers, Davis pressed feather-light kisses on her face and said, "Watching you let go like that is…" He kissed her lips softly. "I will never get enough of it."

She smiled around the kiss. "Lots of honeyed words from the man who intends to send me out the door a squishy mess."

"That's a small price to pay."

"Says you," Junior sniffed. She kicked off her boots and pulled her pants down.

"What's happening?" Davis hadn't taken a sick day in four years. Junior disrobing in the foyer could break his streak. He'd already started composing his out of office message. Olivia was a huge believer in staying home when you felt ill, she'd have no follow up questions.

"I can't go to work like this, Sapó! I have to change." Junior hustled up the stairs and quickly washed off. She returned to Davis and her discarded pants and proceeded to get re-dressed.

"That's not going to get you out of this house any faster," Davis lustily reached for her.

She laughed, dodging his grasp. "Do not touch me, Sapó. I have to go!"

"Junior, you're wearing my boxers. You can't just do that and not expect me to react!" If anyone had ever asked him about whether he thought Junior could fit into his underwear, he would've laughed at the sheer insanity of the question. In what world would such a thing occur? But here she was with the material drawn high on her legs, stretched to its capacity, as it struggled to contain the bounty of her ass.

"Then you should have let me leave in my own clean, dry underpants. I can't do nothing for you, man." She gave an impish shrug. "I'll call you later." She reached up and placed a quick kiss on his lips that he deepened. She pushed him away. "Nope. Down!"

"Okay, okay. I have to go... deal with this." He indicated his state of arousal. "Kiss me."

Junior eyed him warily.

"No more playing. I swear."

She kissed him goodbye and he watched her pull on her boots and coat and rush to the office.

As her truck backed out of the driveway, Davis thought he might need to call in sick anyway.

***

"Did you see the Variety roundtables? What did you think?" Pete asked the room at large. AJ's first assistant included Junior in the conversation since she was taking a break from the piles of invoices mutating on her desk by having a visit in the production office.

"I didn't watch any, but I caught the highlights," she answered with a bit of distaste.

"You didn't like it? I thought it was a good mix of women on the TV panel. Finally, a bit of representation!" Clarke added. AJ and Junior scoffed at each other and then turned to Clarke to explain.

"The thing about representation," AJ started gently, "is that it can still be pretty exclusive when you're looking to check boxes instead of having an organic grouping of people."

"Yeah," Junior continued. "Like, all that talk about more Latine representation is good and necessary. The problem is that they never mean–just off the top of my head–Alycia Pascual-Peña, Y'lan Noel, Gina Torres, Jharrel Jerome, Michaela Jae Rodriguez, or Sarunas Jackson. They mean Eva Longoria and Pedro Pascal or Sofia Vergara and Oscar Isaac. It's always Ana de Armas and never Ariana DeBose. Which is fine but then don't pretend that you mean Latine when your definition is so narrow, you know?"

"It's even worse for Asians. There's this myth that Asian men aren't hot, which is a fucking joke. And then to add to the insult they never mean Riz Ahmed, Dev Patel, Hasan Minhaj, or Rahul Koli but then have the nerve to suggest that the kind of Asian they do mean–Manny Jacinto, Alexander Hodge, Pierre Png–aren't the sexiest things on legs!" AJ threw her hands up. "There are so many hot Asian men outside of the narrow, fragile Hollywood definition."

Clarke nodded her understanding. "I would walk away from this desk, no questions asked, for Hyun Bin."

"Oooh, who's that?" Hodan asked, typing quickly. "Yes. That is the correct answer!" she said when his image loaded on her screen.

Junior pulled him up on her phone and showed AJ.

"I think I would fire you if you didn't," AJ approved.

"Then I'm forced to ask: do you not know that Chris Pang exists? It's an easy replacement–you wouldn't even have to change the initials you carved into the desk," Junior harangued Clarke.

"The Charlie's Angels guy? I will also walk away from my desk for Chris Pang," Clarke admitted. "Satisfied?"

"Hardly. But the things I would let Smaran Sahu do to me, illegal in thirty-seven countries, would go a long way." Junior sighed.

"How did you guys get here from 'TV Actress Roundtable'?" Pete, the only male on AJ's team, was long used to this type of hyperbolic debauchery.

"Oh, Pete—do you want to talk about hot chicks? We can do that too. I would wholeheartedly let Megan Thee Stallion tie me to your desk and spank me!" AJ teased him.

"Obviously," Clarke agreed.

"Ooh, did you see the Yumi Nu cover?" Hodan offered.

"How can all of that luscious be stored in one woman?" AJ wailed.

"See, Pete? Equal opportunity thirsting!" Junior pointed to the side of the office currently breaking three of the seven sexual harassment policies.

He shook his head, laughing.

"What's equal opportunity thirsting?" Davis said as he and Quinn were passing from the writer's rooms to the executive suites.

"You know, lusty gawking?" Quinn said to him. Junior contained her smile. Of course, Davis would be the one person under the age of sixty that didn't know what thirsting was.

"And you're all...thirsting?"

"Not all of us," Pete said chipperly. "But Junior is willing to break international law for someone named Smaran Sahu and Clarke will quit her job for a Hyun Bin."

"Don't forget Megan," Hodan said.

"Of course. They are all willing to be tied up by Megan Thee Stallion," Pete reported.

"Obviously," Quinn agreed.

"Also, Junior was choosing violence, as usual, by harassing my team about their thirst choices." AJ leaned on Junior's shoulder.

"If you're talking about me trying to save Clarke from herself, then yes. What would you have me do?" She kissed the top of AJ's head. "I just want better for you and your Yes Button, Cookie." Junior gave her thumb a small lick and winked at Clarke who shook her head in disbelief as a furious blush spread to her hairline. "And on that note," she bowed to the delighted giggles of AJ, Quinn, and Hodan, "I will return to my invoices."

Hours later, Junior was working away, head down, deep in concentration and gnawing on the end of her scarf. There was always something hanging out of her mouth–a lollipop or popsicle stick, licorice, a pen, the string of her hoody. Davis had teased her about how appalled he was to find her disgusting habit adorable.

"Will I see you tonight?" he said from her door while tapping away on his tablet.

She looked up at the sound of his voice, surprised. "Yes."

"Good. Because I have plans for that scarf," he said provocatively and walked away without once looking at her.

Junior flushed. She thought she'd closed the case on the subject of 'tonight' but even before hearing Davis' steamy counteroffer, she'd changed her tune–willingly forgoing reason and responsibility for one more kiss, for one more touch. For more him.

She shook it off and made a note to remind him that those types of thoughts intruding during her workday were problematic. Dangerous, even. Yes, she would reinforce their boundaries. As soon as they were done with the scarf.

Chapter 20

"YOU GUYS, I THINK he might have developed some game after all," AJ commented while watching Davis with a pretty blonde in the corner.

They were at Betty's to make Ali pay up on a lost bet, something about the Halftime Show, and Junior was feeling out of sorts. This was the first time they'd both been out with the group since she and Davis started their thing and she hadn't expected to feel so... exposed.

AJ and Imani were making observations about Davis' easy posture, charming smile, and the woman eating out of his hands. The blonde moved to show him something on her phone and he leaned over to see the screen.

Davis was curious by nature. They'd spent hours shooting the breeze with perfect strangers because he was endlessly fascinated by life. Junior was sure he had no idea how that type of focused attention could be a balm to many people. She couldn't begin to guess what he was talking to that woman about–her labradoodle? The flooring she was sourcing for her new kitchen? A sunburn that looked eerily like a club sandwich?–because his level of interest would be the same.

It wasn't something people would know about Davis, but she did. Because she knew him.

Because he was hers.

"You can tell a lot about a guy by the way he leans," Imani announced.

"You cannot," Junior grumbled.

"You can!" she insisted. "Look at the line his body is making. It's solid but loose. There's an ease to the way he moves." Davis was wearing a navy crew neck sweater with a pair of well-worn jeans that hung perfectly off his hips.

Hips that drove her to both the edge of the mattress and her sanity mere hours ago.

"And his hand on that bottle," AJ added. "It's a nice, firm grip with his fingers spaced comfortably apart. He's not choking it but there's no chance it falls out of his hands either."

Imani agreed. "Now you're talking. Those hands around your neck, with a little bit of pressure as he folds you like a sheet? Yes, please!"

"You're married!" Junior scolded.

"Since when are you such a prude?" Imani laughed. "For the sake of this exercise, we are in a world where Davis might know exactly how to put it down. And in this world, where I would be willing to risk my reputation and my career to sleep with a producer, I am not married with kids. Better?"

"Did you see the way he put the bottle to his lips? You think he gives good head?" AJ asked before Junior could answer Imani. Then she added, "If it's a made-up world, why does he still have to be the producer? Can't he be just a guy in a bar?"

"I suppose," Imani conceded. "But maybe him being the boss is part of the draw here? I can't tell. I'm too thrown."

"Thrown by what? What are we looking at?" Hodan joined the table.

AJ gestured. "Fletcher and that blonde."

They looked over at the same time Davis tossed his head back and laughed at something the flirty blonde had said.

"You think he hooked up with his lady?" AJ asked without taking her eyes off him.

"No. Remember, he said he had to move on," Hodan reminded her. "And we didn't have the kickback. Besides, he wouldn't be with Blondie if he got his lady."

"True," AJ agreed. "Imani might be right, Junior. He might know what he's doing."

"This is so offside." Junior knew she shouldn't be annoyed. It wasn't anything they hadn't said before. Junior had said way worse—about Davis himself!—and knew it was all harmless conjecture. She could tell them he does, in fact, know what he's doing, has a god-tier vertical game, doesn't sacrifice quality for quantity, and likes to maintain control at all times. But she didn't. She wasn't ready to give up this thing she'd found, that she'd got to have all to herself. "What, do we all have a thing for Fletcher now?"

"Not at all," AJ admitted. "It's a simple recontextualization. We're acknowledging that he might be the type to wrap Blondie's ponytail around his fist while he blows her back out. No different than when Nick Jonas went away all purity rings and came back cut with serious 'I fucks' energy."

"Right?" Hodan agreed. "'Chains' is a vibe."

"Where is Remy? I need a sane person," Junior muttered.

"He went to help Ali carry the next round," Imani answered.

***

When Davis joined the others, they were in a heated discussion about the Oxford comma—the lyrics to a song were the linchpin to the argument.

"There are seven factors!" AJ slammed her fist into her palm. "The kid not being his and everyone knowing are two separate factors."

"That's the same factor," Jamal insisted.

"An Oxford comma makes them separate!" she exclaimed.

"No one has ever given this so much thought," Junior said, dismissing them both. She was on edge. If the others noticed, they didn't mention it. Davis tried to catch her eye but she refused to look at him.

"He specifically asks the listener to 'add up all the factors'", Remington countered.

"Okay, count 'em up," AJ said.

Hodan and Jamal put their hands up as Remy repeated the lyrics, not for the first time, Davis guessed, while they tallied with their fingers.

"Five," Hodan said at the same time Jamal said, "Six!"

"Wait," Hodan checked. "Is his dad a factor?"

"Yes," everyone seemed to agree on that much, Davis noticed.

"Then six," Hodan amended.

"Seven," AJ enunciated.

Jamal turned to Davis, "Weigh in, Bossman. Is everyone knowing your kid ain't yours one insult or two?"

"Uh... Do I know the kid isn't mine?" Davis tried. "If I didn't already know, I'd take it as two insults."

"Oooh—good point," Remington allowed.

"It doesn't matter what he thinks," Junior practically sneered.

"No, it doesn't. Because the answer is *seven*," AJ exclaimed, stepping nimbly around Junior's hostility. Davis tried once again to check in with her but she, again, refused to make eye contact.

He'd promised to 'not be weird' tonight and even went so far as to arrive separately. He hadn't tried to touch her or talk to her outside of general group interactions, despite the way her outfit taunted him, yet something was clearly wrong.

"Hi, Davis?" He looked up into the face of the blonde he was speaking with earlier. "We're headed out, but here's my card if you want to talk about it some more."

"Thanks, Emily." He slid the card into his wallet. "I'll be in touch."

She smiled at him, giving the table a nod of acknowledgment before turning to join her friends at the door.

"It's really over? You gave up on your lady?" Hodan was crushed.

"What?"

"You and *Emily*"—AJ gave the name more emphasis than necessary—"looked pretty cozy."

Was Junior mad about that? "She's a kinesiologist. I thought she could help on the show."

"Real smooth. 'I'm a TV producer and would love to talk more about an opportunity'" Imani teased.

"Here we go." Davis shook his head good-naturedly. "She's married with kids."

"Maybe she lives in a world where that doesn't matter," Junior spat.

"Why you gotta play with my heart rate? You're out here homewrecking?" Jamal cried.

"I'm not homewrecking." Davis took a swig of his beer.

"Then you're still pining?" Hodan asked, somewhere between hopeful and skeptical.

"I'm not pining," he answered before realizing his mistake. "I'm not talking about this."

"I guess congratulations are in order," Junior said with forced cheer. "To your hookup!"

"We didn't hook up," Davis said to the side of Junior's face. What the hell was her problem? Why was she pretending they weren't talking about her.

"I'm so confused. Did he get his lady or not?" AJ asked Remington.

"Yeah, Bossman." Junior's snarky tone made Davis cringe. "Don't keep everyone in suspense. Did you smash, or...?"

Junior looked right at him then, eyes filled with confrontation. He had no idea what game she was playing, but it needed to stop. He held her gaze a moment before repeating, "I am not talking about this with you. Any of you."

He tried to tell how the response landed but Junior shrugged and turned away from him, closing the door on any further attempts at contact.

Imani tipped her glass to Davis. "Chivalry isn't dead!"

He returned the salute and took another sip of his beer. AJ, Hodan, and Remington had somehow returned to whether there were six or seven factors, Jamal and Imani were discussing something about their mothers, and Davis was trying to control the urge to drag Junior out back and keep her there until she snapped out of it or they both suffered frostbite.

Ali made a clicking sound in the back of his throat that caught and held Junior's gaze. Judging by the way her eyes narrowed at him across the table, he was successful at communicating *some*thing. At this point, Davis didn't care who was able to get through to her so long as she came back to her senses.

They stayed like that, her back stiffened by defiance, him slouching, but full of warning until, finally, the impasse was broken. Ali said something that sounded like, "Bi sharafak," which she ignored. He said, "Khallas," and she responded with a stubborn tilt of her chin. Ali lifted his brow slightly in challenge.

Junior rolled her eyes and got up in a huff. "I'm going to the bar. We're still on Ali's dime, remember?"

"Yes, I certainly do!" AJ crowed. As Junior passed AJ, Davis noticed the little squeeze of reassurance AJ gave Junior. It was impressive watching Junior's hackles visibly smooth and her entire posture change. He wasn't sure if he should feel vindicated—clearly wasn't imagining her mood—or annoyed she'd so spectacularly shut him out.

"Be right back." Ali left in the opposite direction.

Coming here tonight was a mistake. He decided he'd finish his beer and leave. He could not touch or speak to Junior at home without having to watch her do shots at the bar with an adoring group of strangers.

"Any word on the pickup?" Imani asked.

"Not yet. We hope to hear soon—once the episode has been delivered."

"You don't have to wait until it airs?"

"Not this time. It has always been pitched with a mid-season air date so if it looks good, if it seems like it has legs, we'll get the go-ahead," Davis explained.

"And if it doesn't?" Remington asked.

"If what doesn't?"

"If they don't go forward with the spinoff," Remington clarified. "Do you go back to Fifty-Four?"

"Word," Jamal piped up, "they cast you out of the tower to mingle with us rabble. Will they let you back in?"

"Um...I didn't lose my job at Fifty-Four. Technically, I added *Elysian* to my existing job." Olivia was effusive in her praise at his success on season four. When Davis broached returning to *Elysian* for season five, he'd felt her pride like a warm summer rain soaking him to his skin.

"Boo! Stay in production with us, where the fun is," AJ insisted. "Can you imagine working corporate in-house? I'd rather drink bleach!"

"It's not as bad as all that." Davis chuckled, her hyperbole reminding him of Junior. When he scanned the bar to find her, she was holding court, gesturing wildly.

"Admit it. We're more fun!" Hodan needled.

"That you are," Davis agreed.

Junior's laughter made its way over the din of the bar. It was too loud, too shrill, and it rang false to his ear. She had a small crowd eating out of her hand as she relayed some anecdote. Davis couldn't stand how over-saturated she seemed. Her natural dazzle, the thing that made her so captivating, had been turned up too bright, too loud, that reeked of an effort that both annoyed and disappointed him.

"I'm gonna head out," Davis announced to the group.

"Already? Hotspark's still on the hook for another round," AJ said.

"I'm good. Imani'll drink mine for me."

"As a favor to you," she said solemnly with her hand on her heart before dissolving into tipsy giggles.

Remy bumped his forearm against Davis'. "All right man, later."

"Be easy," Jamal did the same.

"Say goodbye to Ali for me, wherever he is." Davis looked around.

Hodan pointed. "On the patio. Smoking and seducing, per uzh."

"Ah. Well, anyway." Davis got up and headed to the bar. He made eye contact with the bartender, placed his order, and waited.

"I was going to bring the drinks over, Impatient!" Junior flirted at Davis.

"Quit it, Junior," he said without looking at her. "You've made your point."

"What, you're mad?" she pouted, still flirting.

"Enough!" Davis was out of patience. "Let's go."

"Go? Go where?"

He looked at her then. "Home."

"I can't leave yet!"

"Yeah? You're having a blast here playing this ridiculous game, are you?" She wouldn't meet his gaze. Davis had nothing else to say to her. "Goodnight, Junior."

He was a caged beast pacing the sidewalk while he waited for his car. He fumed the whole ride home. The driver took one look at him and did not say a word, the entire transaction taking place in tense silence prompting Davis to leave a generous tip and five-star rating for the driver's trouble.

His mood hadn't improved after his shower, so he filled the kettle for tea. It wouldn't clear his mind but the motions—measuring out the leaves, waiting for the water to boil, steeping the liquid—gave him something to do with his restless energy. Just holding the warm mug and breathing in the fragrant steam provided a small measure of comfort. He stood there in his dark kitchen leaning against the sink until his tea was stone cold.

Davis had rinsed his mug and set it on the rack when he heard the key in the door. He watched as Junior slipped off her heeled boots, hung her purse, coat, and scarf on the hook, and quietly made her way through the house.

"It's late, Junior, and I'm tired."

"Dios! You scared me," she whispered, clutching her chest. "Why are you standing in the dark?"

He didn't answer her, so she made her way to where he stood in the kitchen. "You forgot your water," she said, placing the bottle on the counter.

"You came here to bring me a bottle of water?" Davis wasn't in the mood. He'd rather she go home if she was going to play games.

"No, I brought the water because you left without it. I'm here because…" She searched for what to say.

"I didn't even want to go tonight," he reminded her.

"I know."

"I was happy to stay home. You could have gone without me."

"I know, okay? I know! I thought I was ready–that it would be like it is at work, but then I saw you with that woman–"

His lip curled in disbelief. "You turned into a snarling beast because I spoke to a woman?"

"No, not–"

"I watch people literally trip over themselves to get to you and I say nothing, do nothing, as they flirt and buy you drinks and generally fawn all over you. I make banal chit-chat with a woman one time and you're blinded by jealousy?" There was no way Junior thought he was interested in anyone but her. The idea of it was too ridiculous to contemplate. "Seriously?"

"I wasn't jealous of her!" Junior made a small flouncy motion with her hip. "She was cute or whatever, but that flaca wasn't your type."

Davis could not believe that she had the temerity to be indignant. If he wasn't so annoyed, her audacity might have charmed him. "Then what the fuck happened tonight?"

"I don't know!" she yelled. "It was the whole thing! It was seeing you, in the wild, with everyone else seeing you, too. You were giving off big King Orgasm energy–"

"I don't even know what that means," his interruption did not affect her nonsensical babbling.

"–and I was annoyed that people could see it, that they could see what was supposed to be my thing only. And then those guys were talking about your hands and how you lean and your stroke and I was–"

"You were jealous?" he asked, piecing it together.

She took a deep breath to compose herself. She looked him in the eye and admitted, "I was jealous." Then she added quickly, righteously, "But not of that flaca!"

For all the incomprehensible strings of words that poured out of her mouth, none of them was an apology. "You flew into a jealous rage," Davis advanced on her.

"Had an outsized reaction," she corrected, backing away from him.

"Flew into a jealous rage," he repeated, "because your friends were objectifying me?" He backed her against the counter, his hands resting on either side, caging her in. He watched her struggle to form a counter-argument. "Which wouldn't have happened if they knew about us?"

"I defended your honor," she said primly.

"You defended my honor by treating me like shit?" He leaned down and bit her shoulder a little harder than playful. Junior's breath hitched in her throat and her body arched to his. "If that's you defending me, I'd rather you not bother," he said into the curve of her neck.

"I almost said something tonight," Her body trembled with anticipation. She wrapped his fingers around her throat, holding his gaze. "When it was posited that your hands here would be arousing based on the way you held your beer."

"What stopped you?"

"It's none of their business."

"Junior." Davis stilled. One way or the other, this was the last time they were having this conversation. She might bristle at the ultimatum but Davis was tired of pretending he wasn't top-to-bottom in love with her and was fed up with the cloak and dagger routine. Moving his hand from her neck, he said, "You have to tell me, right now, are you in or not?"

Junior wrapped her hands around his waist and hid her face in his chest for a long moment. Davis waited patiently for her to speak while trying to calm his racing heart. "This is good, what we have, right? I mean... I..." She took a deep breath and started again. "I like that I can close the door and leave everyone and everything outside. What if letting everyone in ruins our perfect, special thing? I'm not hiding you, Sapó, I swear." She looked up at him, her big, coffee brown eyes moist and pleading. "I'm hoarding you."

This woman was going to destroy him. Davis kissed the top of her head and whispered, "Something's gotta give, Junior. Please."

He didn't know what else to do but beg her.

"I know." She nodded. With a tremulous voice, she asked, "Just... I... can we talk about what it will look like, going forward, telling people?"

Of course, his analytical flight risk needed a plan. She needed to think through all the angles, anticipate any major obstacles, before she could wrap her mind around it. It might take a conversation or two, but it was a yes. A way forward. A victory.

He lifted her onto the counter, stepped between her legs, and smiled. "We can do that."

Junior took a fortifying breath before bringing her lips to his for a kiss that quickly lost its tenderness. She wrapped her legs around his hips, trapping him. Davis responded by grabbing her hips and pulling her close enough to feel his phone buzz in his pocket. "You should turn to the side a little to let your phone do some of this work," she said into his ear, her recent moment of vulnerability forgotten.

"When I have you here ready to apologize?" Davis smiled devilishly. "Let it go to voicemail."

"Was I apologizing?"

"Definitely. Apology first, then an evaluation of my stroke. For the record, of course." He grazed his teeth along her jaw.

She wiggled against him, "Let's have that stroke eval right now."

"First things first."

"Are you withholding sex for an apology? That's beneath you." She ran her fingers through his hair. "Which is unfortunate, because I'm trying to be beneath you."

He knew she was trying to distract him from her bad behavior, and that she was, in her intractable way, apologizing. "Are you using sex instead of apologizing?"

"I thought the apology was implied and the sex was the acceptance of such."

He trailed kisses along her throat. "Unfortunately, unlike you, I am a simple creature capable of holding only one thought in my head at a time. Without your explicit apology, my performance might suffer and adversely affect my evaluation."

"Ha!" Junior barked. "Well played, Sapó."

"I speak only the truth."

"I am very, deeply, sincerely," she paused when his phone buzzed again, "going to replace Leroy with your phone."

"Leroy?" The corner of his mouth dipped in a frown. She held his gaze until he connected the dots. "You named your vibrator Leroy?"

"Of course. Leroy is a king!"

"I thought I was the king of your orgasms," his mischievous mouth still trailed kisses along her body.

"Threatened?"

"Encouraged," he said, taking her mouth fully.

When his phone blew up again, Junior broke away to reach in his pocket. "Sapó," she said softly. "It's late. Answer it."

Davis looked at the screen and went on immediate alert. "Teddy? What is it?"

Something was very wrong–he was sure Junior could hear his sister's panicked voice through his phone. She tried to slip away to give him privacy, but he pressed his hand on her stomach to keep her close. While he tried to both reassure and question Danielle, he let the feel of Junior's hand up and down his arm anchor him.

"Shit!" Davis exhaled, tossing his phone on the counter.

"Hey! Be careful–Leroy doesn't like to be mishandled," she scolded him. Bless her, she was trying to keep his mood from tipping completely over.

"Now my phone is Leroy?"

"All vibrators are Leroy." She nodded, still running her hand up his arm. "What happened?" She rested his head against her body, her head on top of his. "Tell me."

Davis inhaled deeply before filling her in. His dad was found lost and disoriented by some campers almost twenty kilometers away from home. Somehow, his dad had managed to recall his name and his daughter's number, but not where he lived or his wife's name.

"I was home at Christmas! How did I miss it? How could my mother keep this from us?"

"It doesn't happen all at once, Sapó. He might have been totally fine then," she said, consoling him.

"He was diagnosed two years ago!" he snapped. "My Mom was forced to come clean when Teddy confronted her. He was missing all day!"

Junior overlooked the fear and the worry behind his sharp tone and held him closer. "Where is he now?"

"The campers got him to a ranger station. That's who called Teddy."

"And your mom?"

"I don't know."

"Does he need to go to a hospital?"

"I don't know."

"What are you going to do?"

"I don't know!" he exploded, moving away from her embrace, resting his head on the cupboard door. "Fuck, Junior, I don't know!"

Chaotic thoughts raced through his head and he couldn't hold one long enough to process the information. His father's life had been at risk because his mind was slowly deteriorating. His mother had been lying about it all for years. And now his father was in a hospital with who knew what type of injuries.

It was too big to contemplate. Everything hurt.

After a moment, Junior slid off the counter, made her way to the small desk by the back window and grabbed his agenda, his tablet, a pen, and a pad of paper.

A new panic rose. "Where... I'm–what are you doing?"

"You said you don't know. So, let's figure it out. Come. Sit." She settled herself on the couch.

"I shouldn't have snapped at you. I'm sorry, okay? But, I don't–"

"Siéntate." She thumped the cushion beside her. "I'm not good at feelings. I'm not good at having them or talking about them. Hell, I'm not even good at feeling them. I was awful tonight and you didn't deserve it. But this?" She indicated the mini work-space she'd set up. "I'm very good at this. So, let me help. Please?"

The unfathomable news about his father had blindsided Davis. He was furious with his mother, worried about his sister, and so, so tired. Yet despite that, maybe because of it, he went to sit beside a clear-eyed and focused Junior, drawn to her regardless of his inner turmoil.

"Go through this," she handed him his planner, "and see what's on deck for the next three or four weeks. Most of it can probably be done remotely, so only note anything major."

"Three weeks?" he said, a little dazed.

"You don't know what you're walking into."

Davis nodded and got to work. Junior kept a steady stream of questions to focus him—closest airport, did he need accommodations, was there a vehicle or did he need to rent one, were there neighbors or extended family to inform—and two hours, a couple of exchanges with Teddy, some drafted emails, and a momentary break in his composure later, they'd nailed down a plan.

"Should we hire a car to get your sister to the airport?" She yawned, losing her fight against sleep.

The 'we' sent a small thrill through his system despite the chaos. The unexpected bond between Junior and Danielle had shocked and pleased him. "Maybe? Who knows how reliable the dirtbag she's currently entertaining will be," he said, yawning in reply.

"And what about the dirtbag you're entertaining?" her voice was thick with exhaustion. "Or would you prefer to have a car arranged, too?"

Davis leaned over and placed a small kiss on her temple. She burrowed further into the couch, already asleep. He watched her for a moment, tempted to close his eyes and settle in beside her, but the sky was the pink of dawn. Soon the entire room would be flooded with light and, more than anything, he needed to sleep.

He carefully removed her earrings and bracelets before lifting her and carrying her upstairs. Junior would be mad about sleeping without fixing her hair or removing her makeup, he thought as he undressed her, but then decided that she'd be more miserable if he woke her now than if he waited until the morning. Davis climbed into bed beside her and pulled the duvet over her shoulders, before succumbing to sleep himself.

Chapter 21

T HE RIDE TO THE airport was slow and uneventful as they
crawled along the highway.

"Can I ask you a personal question?" she asked out of
nowhere.

"Uh oh." Davis laughed.

"People get very weird about money and I don't want to upset
you."

"Now I'm super looking forward to the question," he deadpanned.

"Your dad only uses cash, right? He doesn't have a bank account or anything? So how did he buy the land your house is on?
How did you and Danielle make it to university? How did you buy
your house?"

"That's more than one question," he teased.

"Not really. It's all variations on the same question," Junior
asserted.

"I guess that's true. Um... the land I believe had been in my
grandmother's family for generations. My mom inherited it and
my parents built on it. They worked for jobs that paid cash, as

you said, and paid some bills and kept basic food in the house. We grew what we could and hunted and fished and chopped trees for heat and stuff to supplement that. I got a job and opened a bank account when I was sixteen. At seventeen, when it was clear that I could make it to university, but was too poor for student loans, I applied for every single grant I qualified for at the insistence of the local librarian."

"The library? What were you doing at the library?"

"That was my job. And my only source of internet. I spent all my time there either working or studying and researching," he explained. "The grants got me in the door and I worked two jobs to stay afloat." He didn't often talk about all the things he managed to achieve despite his huge disadvantages, all of the information that he gleaned from talking to people who were willing to take a chance on him.

"And my house was another bit of luck and timing. I knew a woman who volunteered at the NCCT, Tara, who worked at the Royal Bank in the loan office. She told me about Power of Sales, where banks sell foreclosed houses? She was making conversation, not thinking I would have the kind of money needed to even try. But I did. Sort of. Teddy and I came into a small inheritance from my grandfather's sister and I convinced her to let me invest her money. Then I asked Tara for the list and to help me figure out how to get a mortgage. I put an offer in on the ones I could afford and that's how I got my house."

"How did you even know you could do that?"

"That's just it, I didn't know. Tara was talking about all the ways lower-income people are excluded from these types of opportunities. If she didn't take me under her wing, I would probably still be living in my basement apartment."

"Wait. You took whichever house they let you buy?"

"Yeah." He laughed. "There were a ton of steps and a lot of trial and error but that's the gist of it."

"Wow!" Junior shook her head in amazement. "You went through all that because your dad is a survivalist?"

"No. You can't understand," he said, protective of his father and his childhood. "My Dad comes from generations of poverty. Growing up, he saw how banks messed his folks up with fees and charges and loans they could never repay. He felt the pinch of choosing food over heat or shelter over electricity. He watched my grandparents work until they were so tired, they couldn't stand and still not have enough to make ends meet."

It wasn't lost on Davis that the poverty people love to ascribe to Indigenous folks came from his white father. "It is unimaginably hard to pull yourself up the socioeconomic ladder–the entire deck is stacked against you. When my mom inherited those four acres, he truly believed he'd found a way to break the cycle and beat the system."

"Kinda like 'I do not want what I do not have'?" Junior offered, trying to understand.

He took her hand and squeezed it.

"Yes, exactly. I'm the first person in my dad's family that has ever gone to university. I'm the first to have a job that pays enough to cover my cost of living while still having a little left at the end of each month. I can go to the grocery store and pick anything I want off of any shelf, which is a giddy feeling compared to what I had as a kid. But any time I buy something that could be deemed even moderately extravagant, stomach-churning anxiety tells me I'll regret having spent that money when all this gets taken away. It's irrational, I know, but the fear of failing–of losing Teddy's future on a gamble–keeps me from loosening the reins."

They drove in silence, holding hands the rest of the way. When she pulled into the airport parking, he felt her hand tighten in his.

She parked her truck and walked with him to the gate, while the tension increased in his body.

"Hey." Junior tugged his arm at the bag check. "Look at me." Junior smiled her brightest smile. He usually felt the tingle of it all over his skin. Now it was a faint glimmer in the gloom of his mind. "You made your way from the outskirts of your tiny town to the biggest city in the country. There are high schools here with more people than the population of your hometown, do you understand that?" She took his other hand in hers. "You have accomplished so much, against all odds, by the sheer force of your will. You are going to get through this, too, okay? You will figure it out." She kissed him once. Then again. "Call me when you land in Winnipeg."

"I will." He crushed her to him desperately, then turned and walked through security without looking back.

As promised, Davis kept in touch at every step of his trip home. When they checked in at the hotel, he chided her for the liveried driver and hotel upgrade to which she staunchly said, "You already have a layover. Why would you add to your misery by staying at a Comfort Suites?"

"Those are excellent value for your money. Plus: waffle station," he retorted.

"Pfft."

"And the limo? With the dude holding Teddy's name on a sign?"

"1) How else would you know your accommodations had changed? and B) I figured she'd enjoy it."

"You didn't have to do that. I can email you the money." In Davis' experience, the wealthiest people happened to also be the stingiest.

"Don't be an asshole, Fletcher. It's a gift. An act of kindness. You know what those are, right?" At his petulant huff, she continued, "So, enjoy a good night's sleep on a superior bed in your upgraded suite with pre-arranged room service before your transfer to the airport tomorrow, and leave it at that."

"I'm so freaked out, Junior–I don't... I just..." He admitted.

"Shhh..." she soothed. "You have to get there first. Worry about that. You can pick a new thing to worry about once you're there. We'll make a list so you can spread your worry out equally," she teased.

"Thank you," he was plagued by the unknown. "This is all so difficult. I don't know what I would have done without you."

"You should eat something. Maybe go for a steam in the sauna, it will help you sleep." She deflected his praise. "Call me later."

"Junior? I–"

"Call me later," she said again, cutting him off.

"Okay." He exhaled. "I will."

And so it went. They texted all through the day and spoke every night. Davis and Danielle knew immediately that they would stay at home while they figured things out. They'd had some heated conversations with their mother who still refused to accept the severity of what happened, acknowledging only that it could have been worse and how she would adjust accordingly by maybe getting some new locks on the doors. When her children pointed out the dangers of that option, she shrugged and said simply that they would figure it out. Davis couldn't tell if she was ignoring reality or if she was downplaying it for their benefit. Either way, getting his mother to even consider looking at care homes was a non-starter.

Three days after his incident, the day after his children returned home, Charles Fletcher was released from the hospital, a little pale but in otherwise excellent spirits. He was lucid and clear-eyed, which only reaffirmed Deidre Fletcher's convictions. She doted on her husband and together they insisted that the children were overreacting. Charles joked that he would have 'turned left at Albuquerque' sooner if that's all it took to get his heartbeats home. Davis was annoyed and frustrated that neither of them seemed to be taking this seriously.

One short week later, Davis and Danielle got a glimpse of their mother's life. Charles was storming through the kitchen yelling, "Tell me where you put it! I know I left right here, Linda. It didn't grow legs and walk away so just give it back!" as he slammed cabinet doors and tore through drawers. "How many times do I have to tell you to stop touching my things?" he raged.

"Charles," his mother tried for calm authority, "I am Deidre–Didi–not Linda. You haven't had that switchblade in over forty years."

"Who the hell is Linda?" Danielle whispered to Davis.

"Dad's sister, Aunt Lou?"

"Aunt Lou's name was Linda?"

"Not sure. He called her Lindy-Lou, I think? She died right after I was born," he answered tersely. He was paralyzed by the scene in front of him.

"You're lying!" he yelled in Deidre's face and continued tearing through drawers until he pulled one right off its track. It fell to the floor in an unholy clatter of cutlery.

"Dad!" Danielle shouted and put herself in between her parents. "Dad! Stop it!"

The noise startled Davis into action. "Teddy, get Mom out of here!" He pointed to the dining room. He got in his father's face. "Outside, now!" Davis had no idea what he was going to do outside except possibly freeze to death, but he needed to snap his dad back to reality somehow.

Davis threw a coat at his dad and watched him pace furiously. "It's so typical of Lou to do something like this, you know? I promised Didi that I'd show her my switchblade. I can't show up tomorrow without it. I won't!" Charles kept on this way, spewing muttered abuses against his sister until, suddenly, it turned into fond reminiscing. "Your aunt was always doing stuff like that. She worked my nerves!" He laughed. "I found it hidden in her boot, of all places. Can you believe that?" He shook his head. "Anyway, I took it to school and your mother was very impressed, just like I knew she would be. I got my first kiss that afternoon. On the cheek, of course, but it was plenty." His smile was so wistful, so full of love for the woman he'd been menacing moments ago.

"What happened to the knife, Dad?" Davis asked, his throat thick with unshed tears.

"Lost it along with some other mementos when my pack got stolen in Churchill." He shrugged, then looked at his son as if seeing him for the first time. "Why are you outside, Doodle Bug?"

A cold emptiness wrapped around Davis' chest making it hard to breathe. He managed a small smile. "I had to get some fresh air, clear my head a bit."

"Girl trouble? Your sister mentioned you've been seeing someone. A real stunner, I hear."

"She is," he allowed, as the despair threatened to choke him.

Davis talked about Junior all the time and even introduced them by video during the holidays, so his parents could thank her for her thoughtfulness. She and his father bonded over her understanding of the trap of capitalism and the ineffectiveness of a centrist government for the worker class.

"Well don't stay out here too long. I'm going to check on your mother. She's been so worried ever since I was admitted to the hospital." He clapped a hand on his son's shoulder and headed inside, leaving Davis alone to reckon with his future.

That night, unable to do more than plead for a distraction, he listened to Junior's reassuring stream of babble. She filled the silence describing the photographer she'd booked for Quinn's upcoming birthday dinner; how intolerable she found the erasure of Panamá in the discussion of Reggaeton since it was the literal birthplace of the genre; how outrageous it was to learn that she befriended people who not only liked, but willingly chose, watermelon Jolly Ranchers when watermelon was objectively the worst flavor of all Jolly Ranchers; how she was still thinking of maybe getting highlights or, instead of that, shaving her head bald; and how she planned to re-watch the entire How To Train Your Dragon series of films, as it was one of the few theatrical trilogies that improved with each entry.

Junior chatted away, structuring her conversation so that Davis never had to do more than grunt to participate, while silent tears spilled down his face.

"It's bad, Junior. It's so bad and it's only going to get worse," he managed when he could finally speak.

"I'm sorry, Sapó. I'm so sorry." She tried to console him. "Is your mom ready to talk about options?"

"Probably not. I don't even know what the options would be for them. It's not like they have savings or retirement plans of any kind and my mother refuses to be separated from my dad. She won't leave him." He was despondent. "I... I don't know what we do now."

***

Danielle came up with an answer of sorts a couple of nights later when she announced at dinner that she'd bail on grad school to stay home and take care of their parents. What started as a bit of incredulity on his part had devolved into a full-scale brawl between the siblings with their parents trying, and failing, to mitigate the damage.

He was in such a state that night that Junior could hardly follow along as he raged. She would never have known always-in-control Davis was capable of this type of wild diatribe. Hearing him fracture this way startled her. She didn't dare interject or offer any alternative to his reasoning. She simply listened, endured, and tried to think of the right words to say.

Davis always knew what she needed, always said the perfect thing when she was feeling unhinged. She wanted to do that for him now. When he finally paused for breath, she told him the one thing she really needed him to hear right then. "I miss you so much, Sapó."

Junior heard the small hiss he made as some of the fight seeped out of him. "Why would you say that to me?" he asked her, dazed and voice cracking. "When I'm half-crazed from missing you?"

"It's a big feeling I'm having. You told me to tell you whenever I was feeling them," Junior said, grateful that her plan had worked.

"And now is the time you choose to do as I ask?" he teased, a small amount of levity finally returning to his voice.

"What can I say? It takes me a couple of tries to get the hang of new things."

"It does not."

"It takes me a couple of tries to get the hang of new things I do not want to do. Better?" she amended to his amusement.

Davis took a sobering breath. "God, Junior—you were right. I had no idea what I was walking into here. And between this and trying to keep on top of things at work, I'm so stressed out."

"Don't overthink it, Sapó. You're there to help, not take over. It sucks and it's frustrating, but if your parents don't want to listen to you, there's not much you can do." Junior worried the mounting pressure would be too much for him.

"I know you're right, I do, but I can't let it go. I'm really worried about my mom being alone with my dad when he loses it for real."

"You'll get through this. We'll figure it out. Try to get some sleep. This will be more tolerable after you have a proper night's rest." She didn't know what else to say and didn't enjoy feeling so helpless.

***

The next couple of nights were less fraught. It seemed that everyone in the Fletcher household had tacitly agreed to a truce and navigated around potential landmines as best they could. When Davis got the news that the network wanted to go ahead with thirteen episodes of *The Mothers*, he sent Junior a green traffic light emoji. She responded with a gif of a party blower unfurling. His family was happy about his success and, even though they didn't fully understand what it meant, they celebrated at dinner with cake and ice cream, the Special Occasion marker of his youth. Davis knew exactly what this 'promotion', as his mother had called it, meant. He was going to get, among other things, a new contract as an executive producer.

Junior sent him another text later that evening that read, 'I've got something for you,' with multiple files attached. His parents didn't have Wi-Fi so Davis relied on his data. Being so far from town and its surprisingly updated cell towers meant sometimes attachments took forever to load. It was a pain for work. And now, when he was on the edge of his seat with anticipation, it was torture.

After helping clean up from dinner, Davis retired to his room and tried to load the attachments again. Junior had sent him application forms: grants and financial assistance packages for poverty level patients and medical requirement info for a home in the Kenora area. Davis had looked into subsidy programs to the local care facilities, but his parents were too poor to qualify for those. The ones they did qualify for were either too institutional to ever consider or had years-long waiting lists. He'd had no idea other options were available to them.

"How did you manage all of this?" he started as soon as she answered the phone. "This is amazing!"

"I'm uniquely motivated to work towards your return to the city," she teased. "Have you started on the applications yet? There's a deadline."

"No, I just opened them now. I'm gonna be honest, I thought the attachments would be something else..."

"Like what?"

"Like...you suggested a celebration when I told you about the pickup? Maybe I thought it was a picture of you or something."

"You thought I would send dirty pictures to your parents' house?" she asked, scandalized.

"Not dirty pictures to my parents, Junior. Sexy pictures. To me."

"Why would I do that?"

"I honestly did not expect this reaction, especially considering that thing you did with the ice and the mouthwash that time," he goaded her. These little glimpses of Junior's polished upbringing amused him. All of her private schools, fancy events, and proper etiquette meant she sniffed judgmentally at breaches in societal standards like dress code. The contradiction was impressive.

"That was in my own space that I pay for where I can do whatever I like. Not your childhood home where your entire family can hear each other breathe through the walls!"

"Uh, I'm pretty sure your neighbors heard something through the walls that night," he bragged.

"Weren't we talking about filling out applications to care homes?" she wondered aloud, pointedly. "They are time-sensitive which means they require immediate attention."

"I've chosen another topic."

"If you want to discuss that topic further, you'll have to come here to do it."

"Oh, I'll come there all right. Trust me, Junior, I will not be talking when I get close enough to put my hands on you. This septic tank is thirty percent my DNA."

"You're talking real reckless, sir. You have a lot of paperwork to plow through. I suggest you pump your brakes before things get heated."

"Too late. Things got heated when I thought you sent me nudes and now it's all I can think about."

"You just admitted that you didn't need the pictures to gum up your mother's pipes," she countered.

"I certainly did not *need* them. I know what you're doing."

"Trying to cool your ardor?"

"Stoking it. Plough. Pump. Pipe."

Her giggle sounded muffled. Davis switched the call to video and was rewarded for his hunch. Junior smirked mischievously at him from her bed, propped up by the sea pillows she slept with. Her phone was clipped to the reading arm attached to her headboard and she had one earbud in. "Okay, guilty," she admitted with her bottom lip caught between her teeth. "But you do need to stop now."

"What is it you're always saying to me, 'Don't start none, won't be none'? You started some."

"You're the one who started that nudes talk. All I did was send you some bureaucracy to handle."

"What can I say, I find paperwork sexy." He flashed her a dangerous grin.

"Quit it, Fletcher!" she scolded.

"Go get it, Junior."

"Go get what?"

"Leroy. Go get Leroy." Davis' voice was hoarse. This impulsiveness was something only Junior brought out in him. He'd spent his entire adult life trying to maintain the levelheadedness he'd become known for, yet this woman constantly had him blurting out whatever thought crossed his mind.

"Absolutely not."

"If that's what you want. I'm sure we can manage without it, but things will be better with an extra point of contact."

"We are not managing anything right now, Sapó. You're going to hang up your phone and take a cold, restorative shower and go to sleep."

"I definitely will do that. Immediately after, I will do that."

"How would that possibly be enjoyable for you? Or, are you also going to–" She arched her brow.

"Junior, right now, if a stiff breeze passes over my crotch I'm liable to shoot a hole through the window. Get Leroy."

Davis watched as she considered protesting again. Seeing him this way, a little demanding and a little desperate must have swayed her. He missed the feel of her and spent more nights than he cared to admit pretending she was wrapped in his arms. There was no way she didn't know that.

Junior fumbled around her nightstand. "Here you go!" She presented it for Davis' approval.

"It's black," he stated the obvious.

"Observant as ever, eh Sapó?" Junior teased. "This one is whisper quiet and has many speed settings."

"We're only going to need the one. Turn it on low. Good. Take off your clothes, lie back, and close your eyes."

Junior proceeded to follow Davis' instructions.

"Lay it against your neck, then slowly run it down and along your collarbone." The silicone was a bit resistant at first, catching against her skin at times until she got the hang of the speed and pressure that worked. Davis had her repeat this on each side multiple times until he instructed, "Now run it gently up and down your chest, just the tip, between your breasts." Again, it took a moment for her to figure out the pressure she needed to apply. "Angle it a little, yes like that, and run it under and around both breasts in figure eight." This one didn't take any fiddling to get right. She was immediately stimulated by this action.

"I love that your breasts fit perfectly in my hand. Exactly right," he breathed in her ear. "I like feeling your nipples harden in my palm."

A soft moan escaped her lips.

"Roll the length of the vibrator along your nipples, Junior."

She pressed her thighs together.

"Stop that," he scolded. "Leave them open."

Junior let out a frustrated whimper, but she left her legs apart as she continued to taunt her nipples. The stiff, hardened points looked indignant at being roused without his mouth there to attend them.

"I know what you need, Junior. I promise, I will give you what you need," he vowed to her, his voice thick with lust.

With her eyes still closed, she nodded her acceptance.

"Bring that down your side to your hips, then cross your body at your bikini line, then up your other side. That's right, nice and slow." Davis could no longer ignore the wet he felt through his track pants. He grabbed the head of his erection and held it firmly. The groan that escaped could not have been suppressed even if he had the capacity for such a feat. Junior's eyes opened as she paused with Leroy between her breasts.

"I thought you weren't going to do that," she teased.

"I wasn't," Davis admitted. "You're just so fucking sexy."

"Let me see," she demanded huskily.

Davis moved his phone so she could see his fist tightly holding the very top of an angry erection.

"You should probably take your pants off, or at least free that beast from its confinement, and enjoy this properly," she advised.

Then, in an act that had to be in blatant violation of all Geneva conventions, Junior waited until Davis was looking at her to dart her tongue out to rest on the tip of her vibrator. He tried to squeeze his eyes shut before the image was scorched in his mind's eye but it was too late.

"Now," she continued innocently, "where were we?" She adjusted her phone angle before settling back in bed.

"Close your eyes," Davis started again.

"But I want to see," she argued.

"I'll let you know when there's something to see. Close your eyes."

"Okay," she murmured. "What do you want me to do?"

"Lay it against your stomach, pointing downward from your belly button. A little lower."

She let out a small hum of pleasure.

"Yes, right there," he encouraged her. "Now run your fingertips along your thigh, up the back and down the sides"

Junior raised her knees so she could reach easier.

Davis warned her with a gruff 'Don't' or a stern 'Behave' whenever her hands got too close to relieving the pressure building inside her.

Another whimper escaped her lips as she pulled her hands up her sides and back down her thighs. "Please," she begged.

"Look at me," he said low in her ear. "I want you to slide Leroy, slowly, once, all the way in."

Her hips moved off the bed to accommodate the action. With the head of the vibrator pressed at her opening, her whole body shuddered at the sensation.

"That's my favorite part," Davis said, holding her gaze. "That first thrust is always so hot. Slowly, Junior. Slowly."

She moaned long and low, deep in her throat, sending a hot spasm through Davis' body as she slid the vibrator deeper.

"Don't let it slip out," he said through clamped teeth.

He could tell by the way she'd thrown her head back that she'd done exactly as he'd asked.

"That feels so good, doesn't it?" he asked.

"Yes," she sighed.

"Christ, you've made a liar out of me, Junior because I am so very jealous of your vibrator," Davis groaned and started to jerk himself off in earnest. "I want to be the one inside you. With my tongue. With my hands. With my dick."

It wasn't enough to hear her ragged breaths or to see how she caught her bottom lip in her teeth, he wanted to feel the shuddering tremors roll over her. He wanted to taste the salt on her skin and smell her desire clouding the room. He missed her so much. This wasn't nearly enough.

Her hands were everywhere as her body writhed and she rode her vibrator. "Please," she begged, "please."

Her back arched off the bed and her breathing was labored. Watching her reach for her pleasure, begging him for it, was delicious torture. If he could hold a complete thought, if he were capable of analyzing the situation, he might acknowledge this was a torment for her too. As it was, he was aware of only two things: how hungry for him Junior looked as she watched him pump himself into his hand, and how very turned on he was by the sight.

"Now, Junior." He choked on the words. "Now."

She did not need further explanation. Junior slid the length of her finger along her clit, bringing the tip to exactly where she needed it most. A sob escaped when the force of her climax hit and contorted her body.

"Yes... just like that...good. Breathe, Junior, slowly. Shh... Didn't I tell you I'd give you what you need? God, you're so beautiful, you have no idea. Breathe, Junior." Davis kept up a stream of tender declarations as she recovered from her orgasm.

He watched her struggle to control her limbs enough to switch off her vibrator and pull the covers over her damp skin.

"Wow!" she said, still catching her breath.

Davis chuckled. "I cannot believe we wasted all these nights not having sex."

"I thought this was specifically a celebration," she teased.

"Say the word, Junior, and I will find something to celebrate every single night."

Her smile was tender. "What I need is for you to get your family sorted and come home."

Home.

Until Junior, the word always meant the big sky of Red Lake. Now? It meant wherever she was.

"I'm working on it," he said, sobering.

"You'd better go put those clothes in the washer before you're forced to have an awkward encounter with your mom."

"I don't know... I was such a late bloomer she didn't have to deal with that when I was a teenager. Maybe now is the time for that milestone."

"Okay! You suggesting that you and your mom bond over your cum stained clothes is exactly where I leave you, Sapó. Good night."

"Good night, Junior. I–" he caught the words before they slipped out.

"You... what?" she asked, tiptoeing around the declaration he'd left hanging out there.

"Nothing. Have fun at Quinn's party tomorrow," he finished. "Sweet dreams, Junior."

Chapter 22

JUNIOR HAD TOYED WITH asking Davis what his boss wanted with her, but since he didn't mention it, she didn't either. The date and time of the appointment with Olivia Young had shifted constantly, Junior almost convinced herself she'd escaped the ominous meeting.

The request was obviously in response to something that had happened at Quinn's party last weekend, but Junior couldn't figure out what. She'd never shared more than an acknowledging smile the rare times they passed each other in the halls. Junior wasn't even sure that Olivia knew who she was or what she did until their conversation at Quinn's party.

"Jaime, thank you for coming—am I saying that right? Jaime?"

"Yes. You can call me Junior, though. Everyone does." Junior appreciated that Olivia wanted to make the effort but placing too much emphasis on the pronunciation was almost as bad as saying it incorrectly.

"Well, Junior, thank you for coming. I know that we've been a bit hard to nail down so I appreciate your patience."

It amused Junior to imagine replying to one of the many schedule changes that took this meeting from its original Monday afternoon to its current Friday morning with 'Piss or get off the pot, lady' as if she had any choice but to make herself available to the studio head. "Not a problem at all. I'll take any excuse to get out of the office," she said amiably.

"Please, have a seat." Olivia gestured to the stylish leather armchairs in front of her glass-topped desk. Her office was airy with large windows overlooking the bustle of downtown Toronto. Junior was surprised by Olivia's decor. She'd expected heavy, dark wood furniture with jewel tone upholstery. Instead, it was filled with modern glass and chrome accents, and colorful abstract paintings on the walls.

The built-in bookcase was a tasteful clutter of framed photos of Olivia with family and with notable persons; various awards including five Gemini, two Genie, a Peabody and several others Junior didn't recognize; copies of her books and some gorgeous special printings of famous tomes; two autographed Blue Jays baseballs, presumably from the '92 and '93 World Series; and, randomly, a lava lamp.

Her space was a Rorschach test that would either intimidate or inspire. If Junior squinted–made a few small changes in furniture and content–Olivia's office was not especially different from Yesenia's.

"I really enjoyed our conversation the other night. I was impressed with your perspective. You brought up many valid and vital points."

Junior tilted her head in acknowledgment, unwilling to speak until she knew what Olivia wanted.

"It was a lovely evening all around. All that love in the air," Olivia continued dreamily.

"Quinn and Sebastian are very good together," Junior agreed.

"And you and your young man." Olivia leaned in, as though gossiping with a girlfriend. "Ali is quite handsome. You two make a rather fetching pair."

Jesús Christo ayúdame, Junior thought to herself. "Ali and I are friends. We aren't a couple."

"Oh? I thought... You two seemed... Well, anyway." She gave Junior an appraising look before moving on. "You know, when I started Fifty-Four Media the world was very different. I had achieved so much and yet had to smile politely as I watched men less qualified, less capable by almost every metric, get promoted ahead of me again and again."

Things weren't so different now, Junior wanted to point out but held her tongue.

"I look at your generation and I'm amazed to see young women chase their ambitions unfettered."

"Many of us have women like you to thank for that," Junior answered diplomatically, still unsure why she was there.

Olivia waved the sentiment away. "I'm satisfied to know that I was brave enough to walk through the doors that were held open for me and secure enough to not shut those same doors behind me. I bring it up only to illustrate how the landscape has grown and shifted since then. Take your place with us on *Elysian*."

Junior's heart rate spiked a little.

"Your contributions haven't gone unnoticed. Because of you, because of the job you created with your singular talent, all our stylized series going forward will adopt the design tracker position. And I know other shows are looking at implementing the position, too. You've made an indelible mark, Junior."

"And...you're asking me to teach other people my singular talent?"

"Touché." Olivia smiled. "I'm asking you to speak about your experiences."

"My… experiences?" Junior hedged.

"Yes! Your experiences as a woman who carved out a space for herself, identifying a need and rising to the challenge of filling it despite the obstacles. We are participating in the summit to address diversity and inclusion in film and television. I think you'd make an excellent speaker on the subject, given what you've achieved on *Elysian*. I'm sure other women would find it as inspiring as I do. What do you think?"

All that she'd achieved…as a twofer, Junior thought bitterly, realizing Olivia was referencing her race and her culture.

Junior was all too familiar with this brand of feminism. The kind touted by a specific type of woman, in service to a specific type of woman, at the exclusion of the breadth and scope of all other womanhood. The needs of 'other' women–Black, brown, Indigenous, queer, poor, trans, informally educated–were used as props and never centered in the greater conversation. The 'other' women were welcome to the Cause so long as they got in line and didn't make too much noise, so long as they remembered to be grateful they were even allowed in the room to witness the conversation. Those were the 'feminists' who wrapped themselves up in respectability, wielding the charge of sexism like a shield against legitimate criticism and who halted the movement as soon as their specific needs were met.

And the part that stung was that Junior knew–she *knew*–Olivia rolled her sleeves up and got down in the trenches. Her reputation and her community engagement spoke for themselves. The city was filled with people who had a story about the myth and legend of Olivia Young. Anything ranging from how she gave them their first break, to the time she spoke at their school, to a workshop she funded that changed their life, to a panel they saw that she was a speaker on, to the sheer reverence for the numerous awards and accolades she had accumulated in her decades-long career. Olivia Young was an institution all on her own.

Which is why this? This implication that Junior's job, the niche she carved for herself using her singular talents, had anything to do with her race or her culture, as though Olivia could take any credit for it at all, was a slap in the face.

The mere fact that Olivia had thought it laudable to hold Junior up as a brave example of perseverance to an isolated act of racism instead of acknowledging the myriad ways Junior and marginalized people like her navigated structural and institutional biases daily pissed her off. To frame the conversation they'd had about the way micro-aggressions were, by design, supposed to be big enough to hurt the target but small enough to conceal the shooter as vital and valid, only to then suggest being Black and/or Latina was an obstacle in the environment she was going to be praised for creating? It was a tone-deafness Junior could not excuse.

Junior had tried the genteel approach. She'd tried casting oblique aspersions and they didn't land. All her veiled civility earned her was the offer to do more work publicly propping up the rotten system! Olivia wanted to hear about Junior's experiences? She wanted Junior to speak truth to power so other women could be inspired? Fine. Junior would give Olivia exactly that, with plain language and all the fire in her belly, starting right this minute. "What I think, Olivia, is this whole thing reeks of performative self-congratulation."

Olivia blanched. "Would you care to elaborate?"

"Yes, I think I would. Thank you," Junior said before pulling the pin and lobbing the grenade.

HOURS LATER, IN HER OFFICE, a little cross-eyed from reading reports, Junior fished her phone out of her pocket and smiled. "Hey, you–how's it going?"

"Where are you?" Davis asked her.

"At work. Where are you?"

"Pleased to find my house spotlessly clean. Disappointed that all traces of you have been scrubbed away."

"I took all my stuff out for the cleaners this morning. You weren't supposed to arrive until Sunday!" She was suffused with joy–Davis was back!

"I came in early so we could spend the weekend together."

"Really? For future reference, I prefer my surprises a bit more telegraphed."

He laughed at her umbrage "When can I see you?"

She almost blurted, Now! "I have to finish one thing then I'll be right over. An hour–two, max."

"Okay, see you soon. And Junior? I hope you're not wearing anything you're overly fond of."

A small shiver stole up her back. "I'll start undressing in the car," she pledged, and got back to work, determined to complete the pile in record time.

En route to his place, Junior considered going home to change into something more tempting. On the rare times Davis lost control, driving heedlessly into her body–moving as though possessed, pressing her, frenzied, against any surface that would hold them–he'd still avoided damage to her clothing. After that first night, he hadn't acted with such... recklessness. Maybe the right outfit could inspire some. But the thought of delaying their reunion for another hour was out of the question. Junior couldn't wait to feel his arms wrap around her, shutting everything else out.

That's all she needed–a few hours alone with Davis, just the two of them–to settle the stress and worry she'd carried since his phone rang all those nights ago. After that, they could open the doors and let the world in. She'd tell him about Olivia's bullshit offer and maybe extract some type of sexy penance if it turned out he knew and hadn't warned her. They could attempt a 'soft opening' on Sunday if he was feeling up to it... brunch, maybe?

She pulled into his driveway. *Whatever. We have all night to figure it out.*

"Lucy, I'm hooome!" She called out to the quiet house. Junior walked in to find Davis folded in the armchair holding his head. She could feel the anger radiating off his entire body.

"Is it true?" He asked, voice tight, not looking at her, "Did you do it?"

"Do what?"

"I called Olivia to say I'd be in the office on Monday unless she needed anything. She had an awful lot to say about you and your big moment."

"I..." Junior started. *Fuck.*

"Tell me you were drunk. Tell me you didn't blow up my life for sport. Give me anything, Junior. I'll believe you." He pleaded miserably. "Just tell me you didn't do it."

"I was going to talk to you about it, face-to-face."

Goddamnit, Olivia! Why would you broach something this sensitive on the phone?

Fuck, fuck, fuck!

Chapter 23

SHE'D BOUNCED INTO HIS house like she hadn't a care in the world and found him in the same position he'd been in since he got off the phone with Olivia, what, an hour ago now? Two?

Davis didn't bother with any pleasantries. He summoned all his will to get the words out before looking at her. He was desperate for Junior to come up with an acceptable reason, any plausible excuse, so he could lift his head and look at her with something other than sick disbelief. Instead, she was stammering her words.

"It wasn't a conversation to have over the phone."

He spread his arms wide and leaned back in the armchair. The desire to fall at her feet and bury himself in the feel of her clashed violently with the part of him that couldn't bear the sight of her. "Let's have it, then. I'm all ears!"

He watched with dread as emotions cycled across Junior's face. She took a moment to settle herself on the couch, then started. "Olivia approached me at Quinn's party to talk about what happened with Noella last year. I didn't think it left the production office, so I was surprised that Olivia brought it up."

Davis gave her an incredulous look. Junior was too smart to play dumb.

"I didn't know. Marin said it was over so it was over," she said in answer to his unspoken criticism. "I explained to Olivia that those types of insidious attacks are entirely too common and that more than anything, I was worried about being painted as the aggressor instead of the victim." Junior swallowed.

He already knew all of this. He tapped his fingers, waiting for her to tell him why.

"I explained that I wasn't even worried about losing my job–it was a consequence I was willing to face–as long as the truth was heard and handled fairly. She asked questions, I asked questions. It was good. Then we took our seats for dinner and I thought that was that. My one and only conversation with Olivia Young."

"So, you didn't bring Ali as your date?" Davis sneered.

"No! I mean, yes, but–"

"You didn't spend the whole night flirting with him? Putting on a show of affection in front of my boss and our colleagues?"

"It wasn't like that! You know it's not like that!" she insisted.

"You didn't disappear with him because you were, and I quote, 'so enchanted with each other'?"

"That was about something else." Junior rushed the words out but she wasn't saying anything Davis wanted to hear.

"Something else like what?"

Junior's mouth opened and closed again.

"Why would Olivia think you two are together? Why would she suggest you're in a secret relationship you don't want made public?"

"What?"

"Wait, let me guess–you're trying to protect what you have? Worried about the power imbalance of your job?"

"How dare you?" she hissed, standing over him.

He rose to meet her with a mirthless laugh. "How dare I what, wonder how much longer you plan to string me along?" He kept going as Junior opened her mouth to respond. "The crazy thing is, I don't even care! I don't!" His arms flew out from his sides. "I don't care that you walk all over me or that you've fought this relationship every step of the way. I wait for you to decide when I can be taken out of the box and I let you! I let you make me a liar and, God help me Junior, I don't care! I put up with all of it because I convinced myself some of you was better than nothing, that it was worth it in the end, because I still remember the ache of wanting you without any hope of ever having you."

"What are you talking about? You have me." Junior argued.

"I want all of you, Junior."

"You have all of me!"

"No, Junior, I don't. Because if I did, you wouldn't exist so completely independent of me and our relationship that an evening with Olivia, my boss and mentor, ends with her thinking you're dating someone else! Do you have any idea how fucked up that is? Can you imagine how that makes me feel?"

"But I'm here! I'm yours!" Junior took a step toward him but he backed away.

"Then I want more. I want more than this." He gestured between them.

"You want and you want and you want. You're going to suffocate me with your want! There is no more, Fletcher. This is it!" Junior dragged her hands down the sides of her face.

He closed his eyes as the truth dawned on him. She didn't think there was anything else to give because she didn't think anything was missing. If he never pushed it further, she would happily stay with him, in a dark, cordoned-off section of her life and, to his shame, he would let her.

"I love you!" He pressed his fists against his stomach when she didn't answer. Fuck! This wasn't supposed to be the way he told her. "I am so in love with you Junior, I can't see around it!"

She lowered her head.

"You have nothing to say?" He was an exposed nerve, pacing blindly in the small living room. Junior loved him, he knew it–he *felt* it while they were apart–and he'd raced home to her to claim it... only to face this betrayal? "How could you do this to me?"

"I didn't do anything to you. That's what I'm trying to tell you. I didn't–"

"You didn't use me for your case against Eli? After I told you to leave it alone? After I begged you to drop it? After you *promised me* you would?" His voice kept rising, out of his control.

"*She* called *me* to her office. *She* asked *me* what I thought," she yelled.

"Yeah? Olivia asked you what you thought of Eli specifically, did she?"

"I was calling out bigotry in the workplace. I was trying to show the implicit bias that needs to be addressed if Fifty-Four is truly going to evolve the way Olivia wants." Junior pleaded for his understanding. "After what happened at Halloween, I thought you would understand!"

"After what happened at Halloween, I thought you would understand that there are other ways to handle these things, Junior!"

"I did it your way. I talked to Olivia!" Junior said with a small amount of ridicule in her voice.

She could play all the word games she wanted; he was not going to fall for it. "Ever the crusader," Davis mocked. "Righting the wrongs of the hopeless and downtrodden."

She closed her eyes and took a deep breath before trying again. "Just... please, just listen."

"Listen to what? To you explain how jeopardizing my job and everything I've worked for is worth it if you get to have another Hero Feather in your cap? Can you explain how letting me handle it, how keeping your promise, was entirely beyond your ability?" This wasn't happening. Davis felt unmoored.

"Olivia is being awarded for being a trailblazer. She asked me to speak about 'my experiences' on a diversity panel. I told her I couldn't participate and that a performative display of inclusion was no solution if her entire foundation was corrupted."

"Still waiting for what that has to do with me," he muttered, his voice hard.

"It has everything to do with you! How can she be championed for bold, innovative hiring practices when the very environment she created is run by toxic patriarchy?"

"I have asked you repeatedly to leave me out of this. Can you honestly not see that this is a no-win for me? You've forced me to either fight the gatekeepers or absolve them when I want to do neither."

"You should want to fight!" she challenged.

"I fight. I fight my way."

"You fight?" she scoffed. "You clear your throat and wring your hands and have lots of concern. You don't fight."

"Junior, not every altercation requires a battering ram, okay? This is not some in-house airing of grievances. Olivia takes this shit seriously. There's going to be an inquiry. Legal will be involved. The staff of Fifty-Four and all Fifty-Four's productions will be interviewed thanks to your big moment."

"Good! He deserves to face some fucking consequences."

"Are you listening to me?" Davis demanded. "I could lose my job. I don't have a pile of family money to land in—I could lose everything!" He could not believe they were having this conversation. Junior was smart and compassionate and knew all about his complicated relationship with money. What would possess her to drag him into this?

"Of course, I'm listening to you! I'm telling you that you're freaking out about nothing. This isn't the end of the world, it's the beginning."

She might as well have offered him the chance to be castrated on national television, for all the sense she was making.

"Why are you mad, huh? Seriously. Why?" With her upper body tilted towards him, she was righteous indignation personified. "Because now Olivia knows Eli is a piece of shit and has actively been a piece of shit to you? You just said there's going to be an inquiry. Are you suggesting you won't be forthright when asked about his behavior? That you'd cover for Eli?"

In frustration, he clutched his head in his hands. "No, I'm not saying that–"

"Then you're worried about nothing! This won't come back on you. I promise."

"You. Don't. Know. That." He looked at her with disdain. "Your promises might not be worth a damn, Junior, but my reputation is! This could blowback on me as a whistleblower, which is the quickest way to get fucking blacklisted! I can't afford a scandal!"

His whole life he'd learned to keep his head down and avoid notice. Whether it was the kids at school who mercilessly teased him, his teachers who looked for any excuse to hold him back a year, or the local authorities who never seemed sure how much his white Dad neutralized the 'stain' of his Indigenous heritage–Davis did not court attention. Nothing good ever came from being in the spotlight. Not then, and certainly not now.

"You're the victim, Fletcher! What scandal?"

"Any scandal!" Yelling at her wasn't making a difference, yet the words flew out of his body with a force he couldn't stop.

"Look, I get that you're upset. You prefer to hide behind your passing privilege–"

"Hide!" he spat. "I'm not hiding. I'm trying to survive! I'm trying to create something! I want a meaningful seat at the table so I can change things from the inside."

"That doesn't work–it takes too long. This is happening *now*! Marginalized people shouldn't have to wait and suffer in silence, too afraid to speak up because they have too much to lose!"

"What about what I have to lose?" he roared in her face. "I'm sorry that my life's ambitions are moving too slow for you!" Who was this woman? Did she spare him even a moment's thought before wreaking this havoc?

"This isn't about you!" Junior yelled back, unrepentant.

Davis recoiled as if she'd slapped him. "I guess that's the problem. None of this is about me for you." This realization brought new devastation. When would he accept the cold, hard facts and stop projecting? Junior didn't love him. She couldn't possibly care about him and still be capable of this. "You leave destruction in your wake and never once look back to see who's cleaning it up."

"If it needs to be torn down so it can be built up properly then that's what has to happen."

"Is this a game to you? After everything I told you, everything I've been through–is this all a big joke?" The pressure building behind his eyes was clouding his vision.

"No, it's not a game. I am trying to help! Don't you see? If the abuser is welcome, then the victim is not. The Elis of the world have their poison baked in. It colors everything! You and Quinn were creating something from scratch and he changed the very tone of your show when he called the outline a 'feminist manifesto'! You think you can get rid of him quietly with your scalpel but the damage is deeper than that. It all has to be rebuilt. It needs a sledgehammer!"

"And whatever happens to me in the process–to Teddy–is collateral damage? You talk your big anti-establishment talk but you're nothing but a dilettante slumming for kicks. A bored little rich girl meddling in people's lives for entertainment." He didn't bother to control the sneer that accompanied his words.

"Fuck you!" Junior hissed at the low blow.

"Yeah, fuck me!" He shot right back. "How pathetic do I have to be to love you when you don't give a shit about me?"

"You don't seem to mind being pathetic when it's in pursuit of your relentless ladder climbing. Maybe if you loved me like one of Eli's boots you keep licking it wouldn't be such a struggle!"

He stared at her, not knowing what to do with the ruin crashing down around him.

Davis couldn't hold on to the fracturing pieces of his stability while this callous creature wore the face of the woman he loved. "You should leave," he seethed, holding her gaze. "Right now."

It was only after the door slammed shut behind her that Davis crumpled on the couch, all the fight gone, and reality truly set in. He'd told her he loved her and kicked her out of his house in the same conversation. As much as it hurt–he felt like he'd been run through with a length of rebar–he wouldn't take either thing back.

Chapter 24

"**C**HICAS!"

"Sí, Abuela?" the cousins called from the couch. They waited for the instruction they knew would not come as their grandmother busied herself with the house full of family. Alma's son Eduardo kicked his legs in amusement as Junior tickled his round belly.

"Hi, Lalo! Hi!" she cooed.

"Just make one of your own, already." Claudia rolled her eyes.

"When Alma has made me this one to play with?"

"Wait until Eddie hears that we did all this for you." Alma's sarcasm was noted and ignored.

"Ay, Alma–look at how cute he is. You make good babies, prima. Maybe don't go back to your computer nerds and make some more of these instead!" Junior gushed to the baby.

"The computer nerds need me. Who else will translate what your father and his actuaries are crying about if I'm not there?"

"Lalo, don't you want some company?" Junior said as baby Eduardo grabbed a fistful of her hair.

"Maybe if you showed your Davis this side you would be with him instead of harassing me," Alma sassed.

"Claudia!" Junior scolded. "En serio?"

"What? Silvana was texting with Dani and I noticed something about a fight."

Junior rolled her eyes and exhaled noisily. She was happy that Danielle and Silvana were friends. They were closer in age and seemed to hit it off at the impromptu sleepover. What Junior could do without was the notoriously gossipy Claudia, who would end up with a bullet in her head if the alternative was keeping a secret for more than twenty-four hours, having access to any insider information.

"It's true? You and your secret boyfriend broke up? You can't always be sure with this one." Alma tipped her head in Claudia's direction. "But since you're here after church…"

"I come to lunch all the time!" Junior scowled at Alma. "And I don't know what we are. We got into a fight last week. Things were said and I haven't spoken to him since."

"What happened? Silvana won't ask and I can't always figure out what they're talking about," Claudia asked shamelessly.

"Chicas?" came the call from the kitchen again.

"Sí, Abuela?" they answered.

"Ven aquí."

Junior hauled Lalo on her hip and followed her cousins to the kitchen. The dishes and platters piled high with rice, stewed chicken, dumplings, patacones, fish, black beans, and pink potato salad were ready for the table.

"I'll go tell them we're ready," Claudia said.

Junior handed the baby to her grandmother's waiting arms and set the table with Alma.

"Tell me what happened, dale, before La Chismosa comes back," Alma whispered across the table.

"Nothing. I answered a question his boss asked me and mentioned him when he asked me not to and he's mad about it." Even her own comically incomplete explanation implicated her.

"Did he get in trouble?"

"No! Which I pointed out, by the way. He kept saying how bad it could be instead of focusing on the good that will come out of it."

"Pero, like... *did* good come of it?" Alma pressed.

Junior stopped short. She hoped good would come of it. She believed good would come of it. But she didn't really know if it would.

Alma gave her a charged look. "Did you do the Hammer thing where you bang and stomp and crush instead of listening?"

"I am not a hammer, Alma," she retorted.

"Jaime the Hammer," Alma sing-songed the childhood taunt. "And let me guess, you didn't apologize because you're right and he's wrong?"

Going solely on behavior, there was no way to tell that Alma was four years younger than Junior. She was always more mature, more steadfast, even as a girl. It was especially annoying, now that Alma was a mother, to put up with her reason and practicality.

When Junior didn't answer she pressed, "You didn't, did you?"

"But I *didn't* do anything wrong. He should apologize to me!" Junior insisted obstinately. She'd zealously held on to her anger so she wouldn't be forced to acknowledge any of the other feelings clamoring for her attention.

"You said he asked you not to say something, but you said it anyway. At the very least you should apologize for that, no?"

And there it was. The truth in its simplest form: Junior promised him. She had given Davis her word and hadn't kept it. If Junior admitted Alma was right about that, what else would she have to admit? She nodded her head in acknowledgement.

"Now the question is, do you say sorry and go back to missing lunch because you're 'working' every weekend," Alma made the finger quotes around the word, "or will your schedule suddenly open up because you're a stubborn Hammer?"

Junior rolled her eyes and threw a napkin ring at her cousin instead of examining her situation. She would feel her other feelings at a later, more convenient time.

***

Davis was tired. Hopefully tired enough to go right to sleep. He'd been pushing himself to the point of near physical exhaustion to keep from focusing on the shambles of his personal life. He ran more laps, swam more lengths, and lifted heavier weights to fill his time and clear his mind. The inquiry at Fifty-Four had started in earnest and Eli was on a paid suspension while the lawyers and external investigators did their work. As far as he could tell, no one had linked him directly with Eli's ousting and all he could do was hope that remained the case.

Davis had no love for the man, no desire for this to end with anything other than his complete and total annihilation. No matter how unlikely that outcome was, it was no less than Eli deserved. But that was the problem with toxic people–if they couldn't control you, they tried to control how people saw you. Davis didn't want Eli to have any ammunition to either worm his way out of this scrutiny or drag Davis down with him.

He'd almost made it to the top step before he noticed her.

"Hi," she offered tentatively.

"Hi," he said, somewhere between surprised and annoyed. It had been close to two weeks since their fight, since he'd last seen Junior.

"How are you doing?" she tried.

"Fine."

"I heard that the inquest has started. Are you okay?"

"What do you want, Junior?"

"Can we talk?" she asked softly. "Or, I guess... can I talk?" Her hoarse voice was an indication of her exhaustion.

Davis took a deep breath but she started in before he could reply. "I said some things I should never have said." She stepped closer to him. "I wish I could take all of it back."

"All of it?" Davis challenged.

She sighed. "All of our fight. All of the hurtful things that I said."

"But you don't want to take back what you did—the literal cause of our fight."

"I did the right thing the wrong way. Doesn't that count at all?" she pleaded.

"Selling me out was the right thing?"

"Defending you. Standing up to a bully! I never meant to hurt you," she insisted. "Never," she added fiercely.

Davis killed the smile before it had a chance to fully form. The sound of Junior's accent, her dropped *h* and rolled *r*, was only ever noticeable when she was too distracted to suppress it. He'd found it so cute, hearing it for the first time, when she was soft and sleepy beside him. He'd convinced himself that hearing her accent was proof that she was letting her guard down, that there was something substantial between them. Another in a long list of ways he'd lied to himself.

"What do you want me to say, Junior? All is forgiven, let's chalk it up to bygones?"

"I want you to say that you know I wasn't sleeping around."

He looked away from her, holding himself as rigidly as he could, and nodded.

"I want you to say you didn't mean what you said about not mattering to me." Junior put her fingers on his jaw and forced him to face her. "I want you to say that we can work this out." She raised herself on her toes to keep their gazes locked. "I want you to say that we can try."

"Junior, I–" Davis' throat worked as he tried to find the words to scold her for this breach of his body boundary. He wanted to assert the emotional distance between them now that she'd collapsed their physical distance.

"I want you to tell me how to make this right–that you'll let me make this right," she said, her mouth hovering in front of his, a dare and an invitation.

The feel of her breath against his lips was too much. His resolve, an untested theoretical exercise, crumbled in the reality of her presence. Davis closed the distance, his lips on hers in a bruising kiss, pushing her back on her heels. Junior sighed her relief into his mouth and melted against him.

Her display of need and vulnerability was an accelerant. Davis' kiss went from one of hopeless resignation to wholesale abandon. He kissed her forcefully, demanding full access to her mouth. His tongue searched hers, bold and unfamiliar.

Junior's kisses were always sugar-sweet. She was never more than an hour removed from having eaten some kind of candy. Tonight, she tasted cool and minty, the newness of which only added to his urgency. He angled her head so he could better take possession of her, so he could fill all the spaces created by their separation.

Davis pressed her against the siding, wedging her between his house and his body so her feet barely touched the ground. His kiss was less punishing but no less consuming. He placed his hands on her hips before sliding them up her sides, under her coat, desperate to touch her. It had been ten days since he'd seen her, three weeks since he'd brought her to a shuddering climax on the phone, and six weeks since he'd last held her.

"If you keep that up," she groaned with her lip caught in his teeth, "things are going to get awkward for you and your neighbors."

Had he been so foolish to think her absence was something he could get used to? To hear her voice heavy with need almost undid him. His breath made little clouds in the cool night air as he panted. God, he'd missed her.

"God, I've missed you." He said, resting his head on hers.

"I'm sorry, Sapó." She raised her face and inhaled the familiar baby powder scent of him. "I should have never spoken to Olivia," she said, punctuating her words with soft kisses along his neck. "I'm sorry."

"You're sorry for speaking to Olivia?"

"And the awful things I said. I'm sorry I let it get so heated."

Davis stiffened. He wanted her to apologize but this wasn't it. Apologizing for speaking to Olivia was as meaningful as a thief's apology for breaking the window when they burgled your house.

Davis' heart cracked all over again.

After everything he'd said to her, didn't she understand what she'd done wrong? He'd confided in her all his fears and anxieties. They'd spoken about the way he grew up and all the barriers he overcame to be here. He'd told her, in no uncertain terms, what was at stake for him. And she put all of that at risk because she didn't want to give a speech.

If she didn't understand that, what else didn't she understand? If she didn't see how she'd jeopardized him, what else would she take for granted? What other ways would she blithely compromise him?

"You still don't get it." He stepped away from her in a daze.

"I don't get what?"

"You don't even think you were wrong, do you?" he accused her.

"I do! I broke my promise and talked about Eli when you asked me not to. I know it was wrong. I'm apologizing for that," she said, losing her grip on the conversation.

"You really don't understand why I'm upset." If it weren't happening to him, he might have found the disconnect fascinating.

"Then tell me! Let's go inside and talk about it, okay? We can just talk," she pleaded, reaching for him and clasping his waist. When he didn't answer, she tried again. "Please, Davis. Say yes."

It figured, he thought miserably, that this would be the first time he heard her say his name. The sound of it on her lips, in her real voice, with her accent lengthening the *i* just enough to make it sound new and unfamiliar, was a pleasure he hadn't even known he'd gone without. That small, unexpected thrill burned through the last of his defences, and he knew.

He knew that if they went inside, the threat of sinking into her warm, delicious body dangling like a sword over his head, he'd never have the strength to resist her. He would be drunk and heady from their reunion after six long weeks apart. The excitement would sustain him, would cloud his mind until, eventually, they ended up right here again, with her not having any motivation to change and him too weak to force her. He would forgive her, and keep forgiving her until there was nothing left of him.

Davis had to end this now while he still had the self-respect to manage it.

"Damnit, Junior," he grumbled and kissed her again. A slow, sensual kiss that had an air of finality. He leaned his forehead against hers as he controlled his breathing.

"Wait, please. Talk to me. Why won't you talk to me?" Her eyes, glassy from unshed tears, searched his for an explanation.

His hands itched to pull her to him, but the sting of his realization kept him from giving in. "I'm sorry, Junior. I can't." His face crumpled. "You should go."

Junior's eyes were wild with confusion and he ached to soothe her. The impulse grew as he watched her pull herself together—her shoulders back and spine straightened. With one last look over his shoulder to the door that had never before been closed to her, Junior turned and walked away.

Chapter 25

"AUNTIE JUNIE?" RYAN SAID, poking Junior in the side.

"Yes, my love?" Junior answered without taking her eyes off her phone.

"Should we have a snack?"

"It's almost time for dinner, Muppet," Junior gave a distracted reply.

"Okay!" Roxanne cut in. "Ryan, go tell Bubbe dinner will be ready in twenty minutes. Go, now, please!" She said to stave off any whinging. Turning to her friend, she said sharply, "Out with it!"

Junior put down her phone and looked up. "Out with what?"

"You're ignoring The Kid? Don't get me wrong, it's about time. I told you always giving her your undivided attention was a mistake. They need a certain amount of neglect."

"I wasn't ignoring her."

"She asked you for a snack. She's never had to ask you before."

"I'm a little distracted, I guess," Junior admitted. Even though she'd shown up tonight seeking Roxanne's counsel, things were worse than even she realized if a five-year-old could tell she was off her game.

"Yeah, no shit. I want to know why. I'm guessing it has something to do with Sergeant Deep Dick?"

Roxanne sometimes gave Junior's partners nicknames–Hang Time, Crusher, Percival–and this counted as one of the more ridiculous ones.

Junior rolled her eyes.

"What, he should be Colonel Deep Dick when he hasn't even earned the privilege of me learning his name? I think not."

"My issue isn't with the rank you assigned, Rocky."

"What, then? What's your issue?"

"I think... I think I messed up, Rox," Junior said, almost to herself.

Roxanne sat beside Junior on the couch. "Whatever it is, it can't be that bad."

Junior tried to compose herself. This part was always the hardest. As had been proven time and again, saying it out loud made it real. And if this was real, the way she missed him, Junior wasn't sure how she'd recover. "So, you know how Eli Gorman is a bigot and a misogynist?"

"You mean the schmuck who speaks to my cleavage any time I have the honor of his company? Yeah, I know," Roxanne confirmed. "I think everyone except Olivia knows."

"Um... Olivia might know now. I may have told her. I definitely did tell her after Quinn's birthday-turned-show-pickup celebration," Junior rambled before composing herself. "Olivia called me to her office to ask me if I'd speak at a panel on Diversity and Inclusion as part of a greater celebration of Fifty-Four's strides in that arena."

"Yuck."

"I know. Five seasons I've worked on the show and she couldn't pick me out of a lineup and then one conversation at a dinner party and she's asking me to speak publicly?"

"I don't know about that. Olivia may be in the dark about what a dumpster fire Eli is, but she would have already scoped you out if she decided to approach you about the speech," Roxanne countered. "Quinn makes it sound like Olivia is always on the lookout for people to mentor."

"Too late now, because I told her that the awards and accolades were essentially meaningless since she turned a blind eye to the rot at the core of her business. I told her that her loyalty was exactly what gave Eli the cover to behave so boorishly. I had examples and footnotes and citations at the ready. And then, because I smelled the blood in the water, I added all the racist things he constantly says to Fletcher."

"Racist things to Fletcher?"

"Yeah. He's Cree and Eli's always at him with 'Chief' this and 'time for a powwow' that and 'earn your place on the totem pole' the other."

"What a waste of a human." Roxanne shook her head. "Good for you for speaking up!"

"Except, apparently, Olivia is a real one and wasted no time calling an inquest of my allegations. She told Fletcher what I said, demanding to know if it was true and why he didn't trust her enough to go to her with it."

"Damn. Respect." Roxanne nodded her approval. "That's how it should be!"

"No, you don't understand." Junior shook her head. She fought against her cowardly throat and willed the words out. "I promised, Rocky. I promised him I would leave it alone and because I just fucking had to twist the knife... He's so mad at me. I mean really, really mad. We yelled and screamed—it was awful. In the moment, I was in Mach, y'know? I was too busy being righteous to feel the break happen. And then even after that, I was too outraged to pay attention. It wasn't until later when I—"

"Wait. Wait, wait, wait. Are you… were you sleeping with Davis Fletcher?" Roxanne asked, wide-eyed. Junior nodded, her whole body numb. "Sergeant Deep Dick is Dickface? Is that what you're telling me?"

"Yes," Junior said on an exhale.

"How do you say 'bury the lede' in Spanish?"

"Shut up!"

"I will not!" Roxanne whisper-yelled. "I thought it was a nameless hookup when this whole time it was Dickface?"

Junior buried her face in Roxanne's lap. "He wouldn't take my calls and my texts went unread, so I went there," she admitted from the darkness of her cocoon. "The way he looked at me when he told me to leave? I see it all the time, Rocky." She whispered, "What am I going to do?"

"Junior." Roxanne pulled her up and held Junior's head so they faced each other. "Did you catch feelings for a Booty Call?"

Junior freed herself from Roxanne's grasp, indignant. "He wasn't a Booty Call. It was… we were… in a relationship." Junior felt the weight of the word, the implication of it, in her mouth and found it unwieldy.

"You were in a relationship. With Davis." Roxanne repeated.

Junior gave a half-hearted shrug. She couldn't properly qualify what they shared. Everything about him was so unexpected, so completely out of left field, that even now when it was seemingly over, Junior had no idea the scope and breadth of the thing they created. She only knew that she was still quite protective of it in a way she was unable to reconcile.

"So, he was your boyfriend?" Roxanne tried to absorb the information.

"Uh… sort of?" Junior hedged.

"I need you to explain to me what's happening in that twisty brain of yours."

"Nothing is going on. We never labelled it, that's all," Junior defended herself.

"You were 'in a relationship' for three months and it never came up whether you were exclusive or what was happening between you?" Roxanne almost shouted.

"Six," Junior corrected under her breath.

"I'm sorry," Roxanne blinked rapidly. Her unnaturally pleasant voice was a warning to proceed with extreme caution. "Six what, Junior?"

"Months. Over the six-ish months, we did discuss our exclusive, monogamous status, went to the clinic for an STD screen so we could eighty-six the condoms, and talked about taking things to the next level. I wasn't ready to go public when he asked me in September and we got into that whole thing at Halloween and so we... kept on doing what we were doing. Then we agreed to go public but he had to go home to deal with some family stuff before we could, we had it out when he came back, I tried to apologize, things went kaput, and voila, here we are." Junior's hands flopped in her lap.

"You are un-fucking-believable." Roxanne snorted.

"Rocky, please, okay? I know I messed up–just tell me what to do." Junior had followed Roxanne's every directive, without question, for twenty-nine years. Now more than ever, Junior needed her guidance.

"What to do? Junior, after six months you can't even call him your boyfriend. You need to figure that out, babes."

"Why does everyone want to talk about their feelings all the time?" Junior whined. "I don't know what you want me to say!"

"Did he love you?"

Junior nodded, as tears sprang to her eyes and closed her throat. Roxanne hugged Junior to her shoulder.

"Did you love him?" Roxanne asked softly, stroking Junior's hair.

Junior felt a sharp stab in her ribs as she tried to inhale. Did she love him? She willed her tears not to fall. "I can't... I don't... I don't have the bandwidth for that right now, Rocky. I can't."

She was standing too close to the truth. She couldn't bring herself to talk about loving him now that she'd lost him. Roxanne held her in the quiet until the pain in her ribs subsided.

"Is Auntie Junie sad because of Mr. Davis?"

Unwilling to remain excluded from the action any longer, Ryan tiptoed closer to the couch from her eavesdropping perch on the stairs.

Roxanne arched a brow and smirked. "They've met?"

"Nope. Don't even." Junior straightened. "He, by chance, happened upon us after swimming lessons," Junior explained, shutting down the implication.

"We were having a deciding snack," Ryan added. "Mr. Davis said soft ice cream isn't real and that Auntie Junie should try something real even if it's hard."

"Is that right?" Roxanne gave Junior a knowing look.

"Yes, but I still like soft ice cream best," Ryan announced, loyal to her aunt no matter what.

Junior pulled Ryan in between their bodies. "Me too, Muppet. Both are good, though."

"Yeah. They both are." Ryan considered. "Then why are you sad, Auntie?"

"How can I be sad when you're here?" Junior gave her niece big, sloppy kisses all over her face.

Over her daughter's squeals of laughter, Roxanne warned, "None of this goes away just because you don't want to deal with it."

"Ugh, you're no fun!" Junior groused.

"Mooooom," Ryan complained.

"Don't Mom me. Your aunt is avoiding her responsibilities."

Squinting, Ryan looked between her mom and her aunt, trying to figure it out.

"Ryan Aviva, go get my purse please." Junior looked at Roxanne as Ryan scrambled off the couch. "We need a thinking about our feelings snack!"

"OKAY. I THOUGHT ABOUT IT and I'm clear on my feelings," Junior announced as she strode into Roxanne's house the next afternoon, kicking off her boots and shrugging out of her coat at the door.

"Hi and welcome! How are you doing on this fine day? Can I offer you a refreshment?" Roxanne bowed solicitously.

"I'm angry. Really, very angry."

"Oh, good. The second stage is always the funnest," Roxanne muttered.

"Anger is Sad's bodyguard," Ryan recited from the couch.

Junior looked at Roxanne, who shrugged in response. "Daycare."

"Oh, Muppet, my Angry is here all by itself." Junior gave her niece a bright reassuring smile.

The night before, three generations of Rivkin women had surrounded Junior while she tried to sort through her feelings, desperate to find an emotion other than despair to cling to. They held her and comforted her and fed her while she did her best not to fall apart. Junior could have stayed the night at Casa Rivkin. They offered and strongly suggested, repeatedly, that she do so, but Junior wanted to be alone, in the safety of her own house, when the tears finally fell. As she'd always done, Junior called to let Ruth know she made it home safely. Ruth ended the brief call with a soothing, "Things will work out the way they're meant to, Schatzeleh. It's B'shert."

Today, Ruth's Little Treasure didn't feel so warmly inclined toward destiny.

She'd gone through the motions of her nighttime routine while working out her feelings. She missed him, she knew that. She regretted that she'd hurt him and hadn't been able to make it right, she knew that too. As she climbed into bed, she heard his voice complaining about her many pillows, arguing that it was as clear a capitulation to capitalism if ever he saw one, and it made her smile. It was this bittersweet nostalgia, this mawkish 'live, laugh, love' brand of craft store sentiment that carried her to sleep.

Her nostalgia, however, had warped in the night and when she awoke all Junior felt was anger. Her fury was so clean and pure she vibrated with it. Junior's rage was molten and it burned her tears into a billowing steam signaling to all and sundry that Mount Sano was about to blow, causing destruction the likes of which were unseen since Pompeii. It was this rage that carried her back to Casa Rivkin.

Roxanne smirked. "So now you're angry."

"Yeah. I'm incandescent! Wouldn't you be? He tells me to lay off. He makes me promise, right? And I don't so he's pissed. Fine. But I apologized. I go to him and I say I'm sorry for what I did and it's no good? I literally said, 'I am sorry for speaking to Olivia,' and he says I don't get it? I made a promise, I broke it, which was wrong of me, and I apologized. What's to get?" Junior threw her arms in the air. "Fuck that guy!"

"Swear jar!" Ryan crowed.

"Here." Junior fished a twenty out of her wallet and gave it to her niece with a kiss on the top of her head. "For all the bad words I haven't said yet."

Ryan's eyes widened in amazement. Even with her elementary grasp of math and currency, she understood that there were a lot of quarters in a twenty-dollar bill.

"Go put that in your piggy bank. The swear jar is closed right now," Roxanne said.

As soon as Junior thought Ryan was out of earshot she started in again, "Can you fucking believe that asshole? The absolute gall! Like, are you shitting me? All his bullshit about talking through my feelings! I asked him–begged him–to talk about it, to tell me what to do and he just fucking doesn't? That cock sucking dick-face!"

Roxanne whistled, impressed. "How long were you holding that in?"

"This is freeform, baby–like jazz. We're going where the words take us."

"Oh, boy," Ruth said, having heard Junior's tirade as she came up from the basement. "I said to your mother, I said 'how lucky you are that your daughter is so quiet and sweet, not like my vilde chaya.' Maybe I spoke too soon, huh?"

"Yeah, maybe!" Junior agreed, nodding and pacing maniacally.

"I need to call in some reinforcements. This is bigger than me," Roxanne said, reaching for her phone. Junior kissed Ruth, then stomped past Roxanne to the treat shelf in the kitchen. "You're wasting the call, Rox. I'm fine. But if you insist on an intervention, tell them I need chocolate. Lots and lots of chocolate."

"Ryan! Get dressed, Zeeskeit. We're going to your Uncle Noah's," Ruth said and kissed Roxanne on the cheek. "Let me know if we need to stay the night." She ran her thumb across the spot she kissed and asked, "Are you using the moisturizer I got you? You can't afford to be careless."

Moments after Roxanne hit send on her message to The Alibis group chat, Junior's phone rang. Ali.

"I'm fine. Honest," she assured him before he could start. "I messed up and it caused a bit of grief but I'm okay," she tried for calm, knowing that she had to convince him to stand down. "I mean, if I can handle Olivia thinking we were a couple at Quinn's party then I can handle anything, right?" she joked, hoping to distract him with something light and inconsequential, but she wasn't as successful as she'd hoped.

At least he was no longer worried and said he would stop by later.

By the time she got off the short call with Ali, the messages in The Alibis group chat were piled up like poker chips at the high roller table. Leigh couldn't make it because she had an order to prep. Claire, already a week overdue, was willing to risk the visit if they guaranteed that her baby wouldn't be born on Roxanne's floor. Quinn and Remington suggested vastly different interpretations of 'bring chocolate.'

In the intervening hours, Junior sat on the couch, quietly and methodically demolishing bag after bag of candy as an eerie calm settled over her. She told herself she wasn't angry. Sure, it didn't end the way she thought it would, but when does it ever? These were her consequences and she would face them then move on.

Junior couldn't unring the bell now that Roxanne had put the word out, but she could explain what happened and begin the process of putting this whole thing behind her. So, she waited. She waited for everyone to arrive so her Over Him could begin.

Chapter 26

"ARE WE REALLY NEVER going to talk about her? We're going to pretend this is totally normal and everything is A-Okay?" Danielle asked for what felt like the thousandth time since Davis told her about Junior. They were walking back from lunch and she gestured to encompass his entire being. "We'll just ignore the general state of you?"

"There is nothing to talk about, Teddy. I'm fine." Why should he be the only one he lied to about his feelings?

"Have you told Mom?"

Davis' face shuttered. "I'm going home because I want to see what's going on with my own eyes and I'm taking advantage of Dad's consult with Dr. Redwood to force Mom to keep the appointments I set up to tour care homes."

Dr. Redwood had bought a hundred acres of land from the Crown and then, through grants and funding, built two dozen buildings, a common area, and a medical facility. The idea was that senior citizens with full mobility would have a better quality of life if they were able to maintain some independence. Once their mobility suffered, they would be moved out of the cabins and into a more traditional care home setting of the medical building.

"I'm not going home for a chat about my social life."

"Doodle," Danielle admonished as they turned onto his street. "Are you telling me Mom has no idea? She didn't say the thing about 'the last kiss you'll ever want'?"

Davis gave a deep, weary sigh. "Remind me again why you're here?"

She opened her mouth but didn't speak. Following his sister's distracted gaze to the figure lounging on his front steps, Davis muttered, "What now?"

"You know him?" Danielle asked with more interest than Davis found necessary.

"Unfortunately," he confessed.

"It must be like an oasis back here in the summer. All tree-lined and sun-dappled and shit," Ali said with his face to the sky. It was one of the mild and sunny false starts to Spring that happened every March. Winter hadn't fully relinquished its hold yet Toronto fell for the ruse every time.

"What are you doing here?" Davis cut him off.

"Rude. Aren't you going to introduce me?" Ali made eyes at Danielle.

"Hi," she beamed and held out her hand, "Danielle."

"Ali. The pleasure is definitely mine," he smoldered.

"Teddy, wait inside. This won't take long."

She shot her brother an annoyed look but did as he asked. "See you later, Ali," she said over her shoulder, heading into the house.

"Inshallah." Ali's body twisted to keep his eyes locked on hers.

"That's my kid sister, dude."

"Sorry to break it to you, my man, but there is no kid there."

"Gross. What do you want?" Davis demanded.

"Peace in the Middle East, for real. I got people all over the region and shit's stressful."

"What?"

"You asked what I want." Ali shrugged and turned to look Davis in the eye. "What I want is the wrong question."

"Yeah? What's the right question?"

"How do I know where you live?" Ali fished his smokes out of his pocket.

"Trust me, that was next."

"I wasn't sure I could find it again, to be honest. It was dark last time and I wasn't paying attention on the way here. We were at Betty's shooting the shit as we do. I got the signal from this dime in St James Town. We'd been texting for a while, but she works nights at the hospital so our schedules didn't sync, y'know? Still, I had a good feeling. Junior asked me for a ride."

Davis had never heard Ali speak so many words consecutively. "This cannot be why you're here."

Ali offered the pack to Davis, who declined, before he put one to his lip. "Junior lives in the other direction but she's steady making moves on the low, so I didn't think nothing of it."

"Anything," Davis corrected absently.

Ali let out a tiny huff of a laugh. "It's a good thing you're so pretty."

Davis gestured for him to continue, accepting the reprimand.

"Junior didn't tell me who lived here and I didn't ask. But it was late and I wasn't driving off until I was sure she was safe. When the door finally opened, she fully jumped into someone's arms. It was dark in the house and I couldn't tell who it was. As I started to drive away, all the lights turned on." Ali flicked his lighter a couple of times before it caught. He pulled deeply on his cigarette and finished, "That's how I know this is your house."

Davis remembered the night vividly. He and Junior had notched another round in their cold war over her having the keys to his place and he was ready to take his frustration out on whoever was ringing the cursed bell. When he stumbled to the door, he was surprised to see Junior on his porch. He'd barely got the door open when she launched herself at him. Before he knew what was happening, she was in his arms, kissing him. Davis tried to clear the threshold to close the door by leaning Junior against the wall and had accidentally pressed her on the panel of light switches.

Ali watched Davis, making sure his meaning landed.

"What, you're here to gloat?" Davis asked hotly, shaking off the memory of that night burning him all over.

Ali squinted as the smoke rose from his cigarette and shifted to make room for Davis to sit. "Nah, it ain't even like that with me and her. Not anymore. Not for a long time."

"And I should believe you?"

"You should, Bossman. I wouldn't do you like that. And more importantly, neither would Junior," Ali insisted.

"I don't know what Junior would or wouldn't do," Davis didn't bother masking the petulance. He'd planned a future with a woman who didn't exist. The reality of it still stung.

Ali raised his face to the warm spring sun once more, blowing out a long stream of smoke. "Did she ever tell you about us? About how it went down?" Off Davis' look, he said, "No, of course she didn't. She's a G."

"Listen, man, I appreciate you coming down here to defend your friend or whatever but–"

"She did you dirty, I get it. I'm not making excuses for her."

"Junior told you what happened?" Davis was skeptical. He couldn't imagine Junior confiding their relationship to Ali before Roxanne. Then again, he hadn't expected her to send their lives up in flames, so what did he know?

Ali laughed to himself. "Nah, I just... she was your lady, right? Your beautiful mystery? And after all that you got with her? She would have had to play you foul for you to walk away. She needs to answer for that on her own."

Davis was embarrassed at how keenly Ali had deduced what happened between them, which made him even angrier. "How do you know I walked away?"

"I don't. But I'm guessing since Olivia thought me and Junior were together, you did too. I can't have that on my conscience."

"Okay, great, message received. I'll see you around, I guess?"

"I didn't know how to be with a woman like that." Ali took a drag, ignoring Davis' attempts to dismiss him. "We were mad young. It feels like yesterday sometimes. Twenty-one isn't old enough to know all the ways a relationship could be. I didn't know what any of it meant. She would walk into a room and have three, four guys sweatin' her. I got off on having a beautiful girl dudes wanted and then blamed her for being a beautiful girl dudes wanted. We'd throw down and break up then get back together–real telenovela shit. It was like that for years, me pretending I was worthy of her and her pretending I didn't constantly disappoint her. The bitch of it is that when it was us, chillin' at home or doing the family thing–keeping it low-key? It was the realest. No one could touch us."

"And you thought you'd try again, see if it sticks this time?" Davis didn't want to have this conversation. He didn't want to think about Ali and Junior together and he didn't want Ali's sympathy. What he wanted was to be left alone to wallow in his misery.

"You are not hearing me, my guy!" Ali pointed his cigarette at Davis, punctuating his words. "There is no us. I love her. Real talk, I will always love her and I am telling you it is not like that. We exist because Junior decided to salvage something out of the wreckage."

"I see. Perfect Junior can do no wrong and I'm the bad guy for standing up to her?"

"Junior? Perfect?" Ali let out an ugly laugh. "Far from it. Shit–she's stubborn, judgmental, can hold a grudge like you wouldn't believe, she eats like a child, she gets cruel when she fights dirty, and she lets dogs lick all on her face and mouth." Ali cringed at that last point of contention.

"Those are kisses." Davis wanted to refute Ali's assessment of Junior's character, to defend her against the harsh critique. Davis thought about the fun he'd had letting some trivial, low-stakes disagreement–spurred by her judgmental outrage or childish eating habits–turn into a high-octane expedition through the city for things like 'the best beef patty'. Nothing Ali said was untrue, necessarily, it just wasn't the whole picture.

"I don't fuck with dogs. That shit is haram." Ali shuddered. Davis thought it best he not point out all the other acts expressly forbidden in the Koran that Ali routinely participated in. "I'm not saying she's perfect. I'm saying, for the right person, the person who can see through to the real Junior inside, she's worth it."

"But you're not him?"

"Not the way she needs. Maybe the biggest regret of my life. Time will tell." Ali shrugged, standing. Davis rose to face him and he continued, "We're older and wiser now, yet the maturity gap didn't close–she still wants to keep it low key and I still want to be where the action is. Our paths are parallel which is its own blessing. Mashallah."

The door opened and they both turned to see Danielle.

"Ew!" She sniffed the air. "Were you smoking?"

"I know, filthy habit." Ali bowed his head in mock chagrin.

"It is," she agreed. "You should quit."

"I should. I haven't found the right motivator. Maybe you could help me?"

"Okay, that's enough. Thanks for stopping by. See you around." Davis shooed Ali down the steps, putting his body between his sister and his friend. He didn't know which was more surprising—that he'd used the word friend or the realization that it was true.

"It was nice to meet you," Danielle said from around her brother.

"A true delight," Ali responded, turning to head down the street.

"Hey, man," Davis called out. "Why did you really come here?"

Ali smiled proudly. "Good question!"

"And?"

"Rocky rang the alarm—she rallied Junior's people. She's probably gonna blow up your spot. I thought you should know."

"She's going to blow up my house?" Davis asked in disbelief.

"Nah." He chuckled. "Your secret life with Junior might not be a secret for much longer. Though with Roxanne it could be the other thing, too," he acknowledged as he turned to amble toward his car, whistling a soft melody as he went.

"Was that Junior's ex?" Danielle asked curiously when Ali's car pulled away from the curb.

"She told you about him?"

"Not specifically. At the slumber party, she mentioned that she was with a guy back and forth for a long time and that no matter who broke it off or how long they were apart—a week, a month, a year—he always found her and she could never say no when he asked for her back. It seemed... intense. Silvana told me there were two separate times they seemed headed down the aisle."

Davis considered this. Though he didn't have a clear timeline of her relationship with Ali, he understood that they shared an intimidating bond born from their immense history. It didn't make it easier to watch them together, Davis just knew there wasn't anything he could do about it.

Danielle gave her brother a pitying shake of her head. "If that's him, if that's the guy she was talking about, then you're even more delusional than I thought."

"What's that supposed to mean?" He was struggling against thoughts of Junior intruding when he wasn't prepared for them.

"You said she came to you to apologize, to try again after you tossed her out–"

"I didn't toss her out." He rubbed his temples against his sister's grand proclamations.

"But she came here to try to fix things?" she repeated.

"Your point, Teddy?"

"Are you joking? Did you see that guy?! I would follow him off a cliff if he asked me," she said dreamily. "Seriously, I would let him stub his cigarettes out on my naked body. He could literally chain me to his bed and–"

"Teddy! The point?" Davis was not interested in his sister's fantasizing.

"The *point* is that Junior never went to him. She cried and drank and screamed and moped, but she never went to him." Danielle stared him down, waiting for Davis to get it. When he didn't ', she rolled her eyes aand said, "She went to you."

***

Slowly, everyone trickled into Roxanne's, mingling around the kitchen island and nibbling on the Food Network caliber charcuterie board Roxanne threw together and the yummy bits and pieces of baked goods AJ picked up from Leigh. Junior was ready to put this whole episode behind her and enjoy an evening with her friends.

"So, spill! What happened?" Remington asked when they were all assembled and settled.

"Nothing *happened*, per se. My blood sugar was low and I might have overreacted a bit," Junior started. She figured keeping it light and easy would make it easier for them to absorb the truth about her and Davis.

"You? Overreact? I won't believe it!" Claire clutched her imaginary pearls.

"Picture an unhinged superhero tearing through my house with lightning bolts flying out of their eyes," Roxanne added.

"Part of that was because our boss, the big boss, Olivia pulled me aside to ask–"

"Errr–my bad. That was me." Quinn cringed. "She asked me about you and Ali and I drunkenly said, 'They'll always have Paris.' It seems I didn't do a good job of relaying humor." Quinn hid her face behind her hands. "Sorry!"

"Huh?" Junior hadn't intended to bring that up at all. It had nothing to do with anything.

"If Olivia thinks you're a couple, then for sure Fletcher has heard about it. He must be pressed." Remington pointed out.

"Why would Fletcher be pressed?" Quinn asked.

"Because... you know. Because?" Remington tried to answer without saying any of the words himself.

Junior faltered. A sick, panicky feeling pooled in her stomach. "You know about me and Fletcher?"

Quinn said, "No!" At the same time, AJ said, "Yes?" and Remington shrugged, "Maybe."

Disbelief made her voice a hoarse whisper. "How?"

What? Since when?

What?!

Junior's mind, capable of complex mathematical equations and verb conjugation in four languages, stuttered to a halt. She would have hyperventilated if her brain hadn't completely checked out on her.

"It wasn't a secret you were seeing someone," AJ pointed out. "I figured something must have happened because he started to look at you with anticipation. It was... a lot. But at the bar that night he was back to irritating you and he was cozy with that blonde, so then I wasn't sure."

"Who's Fletcher?" Claire asked, out of the loop.

"Hold on to your ass cheeks," Roxanne warned, greatly enjoying the reveal. "Dickface!" she trumpeted. "Fletcher is Dickface!"

Claire reared back on the stool. "Not the annoying Know-It-All from your work!"

Junior looked up at the ceiling and nodded. She'd bitched for months about the insufferable dickface the studio sent to the show. Her friends had heard, in fantastic detail, about his every grating *Actually* and judgmental furrowed brow. Her plan to skate over the details of being with someone she'd so openly maligned with a simple 'veni vidi vici' was laughable. She should have known better.

"You dirty, dirty girl!" Claire scolded. "Did you have to keep the lights off so you could pretend he was someone else? I mean, I get it—the rationale behind the Hate Fuck is inexplicable." Claire sighed with a shake of her head. "You can't stand them, you can't stand yourself for doing it, yet you can't stay away."

"Sometimes we put our self-respect aside—" AJ started.

"I didn't put my self-respect aside!" Junior balked.

"There's no judgement here," AJ insisted. "All I'm saying is the heart, the mind, and the vag aren't always in agreement on what's best. Once in a while, you gotta follow your vag and it's okay when you do."

Claire nodded her agreement. "Case in point: you ditching that lickable Spin Hottie for a hate fuck with Dickface. Unless it was more of a concurrent scenario?"

"Spin Hottie?" Roxanne's eyes bored into the side of Junior's face. She dreaded the inevitable fallout of connecting Spin Hottie to Dickface. Because it was coming and there wouldn't be anything she could do to stop it.

Everyone turned to late arrival at the front door. "Seriously, Rocky, how do you live down here? It's mad crowded–there's people and dogs and industrial-sized strollers everywhere–and never anywhere to park!" Ali said, putting his coat and shoes in the closet before joining them.

"Where have you been, Hotspark?" AJ demanded.

"I had some business to handle."

"You missed the big Junior-Fletcher reveal, which I kinda already knew," AJ said a little more smug than appropriate.

"Word? I knew cuz I dropped her at his spot. How'd you know?" Ali asked, to Junior's increased discomfort.

He'd driven her there once, forever ago. She swallowed thickly. He'd known all this time.

AJ swatted at him, annoyed. "You saw them together and didn't say anything? When was that?"

"Yo!" Ali lifted his arms to his face to fend off her attack. "You knew and didn't say shit."

"That's different."

"It most definitely is not!" Ali argued.

"It is because I didn't *know* know–I'm just not surprised now that I do know. The signs were there," AJ reasoned.

"I strongly disagree," Quinn challenged, putting more cheese on her plate.

"Wait, wait!" Claire struggled to get off the chair. "This fucking kid stomps on my bladder all day long. Being pregnant is such bullshit. Don't say any of the good stuff until I get back!"

"God damn!" Ali covered his mouth with his fist at the sight of Claire's distended belly. "You haven't had that baby yet?"

"Believe me, I'm well fucking aware." Claire said, accepting Ali's help getting off the stool.

"Impending motherhood is really mellowing you out," Roxanne teased.

Claire flipped her off and waddled to the bathroom.

"We're getting away from the point," Junior said primly. Ali had known for months and hadn't said a word. Remy and AJ had somehow also figured it out on their own and hadn't mentioned it either.

Junior had been known to indulge in many an ill-advised dalliance. They probably thought this was more of the same. It's how it'd started, after all. And while she'd stopped talking shit about Davis, she certainly hadn't sung them his praises in any way. She needed to recenter herself in this new landscape of people having known about her... affair.

"Which is?" Remington asked.

"The point," Junior shook her whole body to loosen up, "is it's over and I just want to drink and eat and forget about it, okay?"

Quinn squinted at AJ, "There were no signs."

AJ opened her mouth to elaborate when Remington spoke up. "Don't listen to them, Junior. Signs or not, we were waiting for you to tell us." He added, always the voice of reason. "If there was something to tell, we knew you would."

"That's it, Rem—there was something to tell. I was waiting for him to come back from up north but I... I fucked up." Junior lifted her shoulders helplessly. There was no point in getting into it when the end result was the same. Her big Taking Responsibility speech didn't change a thing. "You guys don't have to stop hanging with him or anything. I don't want you to stop being his friend because of me."

Junior didn't know what would happen next. She wasn't even sure how she'd make it through this night. But robbing Davis of these hard-earned friendships–relationships he'd forged completely independent of her–was unthinkable.

"You made it to Acceptance pretty quickly," Roxanne commented. "I thought you were going to languish in Rage a while longer."

"You're being dramatic," Junior deflected.

"Does that count as Denial?" AJ offered.

Claire waddled back into the room. "Denial about what? I told you not to say anything good!"

"Ohhh, you're doing them out of order: Anger *then* Denial. Got it." Roxanne nodded her understanding. Her gentle mockery was oddly comforting.

"The candy wrapper carcasses in the trash certainly tell a story," Claire confirmed, accepting Remington's help back onto the seat. "Plus, the devastation wrought on this poor, defenseless cheese board."

"We helped there." Remington winked at Junior.

"Okay, okay!" Junior waved their silliness away. "I wouldn't have said anything at all, but he doesn't deserve that. So, now you know. I was with Fletcher. I'm not anymore. Everything is as it was, there is nothing to see here." She ended with a deep, cleansing breath. Slowly, they all started to chatter amongst themselves.

AJ complained to Remy that her men's NCAA bracket was in shambles, but the women's bracket was going to cover her wager on both. Ali offered Claire different concoctions from the motherland to convince her baby brute to come out quietly so no one got hurt. Junior kept guessing at potential names, each more outlandish than the last, while keeping one ear on Roxanne and Quinn.

"When did you find out?" Quinn asked Roxanne, trying to be discreet.

"Last night," she said out of the side of her mouth.

"And when did it end?" Quinn continued.

"Unclear." Roxanne admitted, "I'm still processing that they were together at all, y'know?"

"It makes a weird kind of sense, now that I think about it," Quinn mused louder than she'd intended.

"How so?" Claire asked from across the island, ignoring Junior's huffy indignation. Turns out she wasn't the only one eavesdropping. All eyes were on Quinn as she explained.

"I don't know… I've known him for years and there has never, not once, been any indication of his relationship status. Even when we sat around making get-to-know-you noises, having a beer after work, it was a complete nonstarter with him." Quinn thought a moment before continuing. "He's really smart, right? He's laser-focused and single-minded about his career, throwing himself fully into achieving his goals. So… it would take someone pretty dynamic to even get his attention. It would have to be someone like Junior to make him stop and notice."

It was silent as they absorbed her words.

"I didn't… I hadn't considered that," Junior's voice was strangled, "but it… I… what you said, I–"

It was inevitable.

"Oh, Hammer," Roxanne pulled Junior into a hug when the first tear fell. "It's okay, babes."

Junior barely made a sound as she sobbed into Roxanne's shoulder.

She cried for her broken heart and for the part of it she'd unwittingly given to Davis. She cried for the instinct that had prevented her from giving it to him freely. She cried because even after everything, she still sought the centered, grounded feeling of his presence and knew she would never have it again. Finally, Junior cried because deserved consequences or not, this fucking sucked.

AJ and Quinn flanked her, rubbing her arms and back. Once again, Roxanne was right—Junior did not want to be alone when the tears finally came and she was grateful to Roxanne for calling everyone here, for knowing when to push Junior and when to coddle her, so she could be surrounded by her friends when she needed them most.

"Jesus fuck, you guys! I am very goddamn pregnant," Claire grumped as Ali and Remington helped her off the seat and over to Junior. "I can't move that quickly!" Quinn and AJ made room for Claire to hug Junior around her impossible belly. Roxanne let go to find a box of tissues, leaving Remington to take her place comforting Junior.

When she'd calmed down enough to take full, clear breaths again she turned to Ali who said to her in Arabic, "You should only cry happy tears." And then asked, quietly, in English, looking in her eyes, "Are you okay? For real?"

Junior nodded, feeling much better now even though things were way worse. "Yes. I'm good. For real."

Ali kissed her between her eyebrows, where he always kissed her whenever she was upset. "I have to make some moves. Hit me up if anything changes. Okay?"

"Yeah, okay." She smiled at him. It was a weak smile, but it wouldn't be for long.

Ali looked up and said to the group, "Yo, I gotta dip. Holler if you need me to pass through later."

"I should probably go, too," Claire said. "Now that I've started crying, there's no telling what will set me off. I cried the other day because there was only skim milk in the fridge when I wanted cereal." Claire hugged Junior again and called to Ali, "Are you going my way?"

"I am. Let me pull the car around. But Claire, I swear to god, you can't be giving birth in my whip."

"Then you better hurry up!" Claire threatened.

"I'm also taking off," Quinn said. "I'll check in later, yeah?"

"I'm okay Quinn, I swear," Junior insisted. "Please don't–" she stopped and then tried again, "He didn't do anything wrong. I'm mad at him because I'm mad at him but nothing has to change between you two."

"It already has." Quinn hugged her tight. "Don't you see? Now that I know, how can I ever look at him the same way again?" Quinn blew kisses on her way out the door.

Ali honked, then came in to say goodbye and help Claire to the car.

"There you go, Claire," AJ called after her. "No floor births as promised!" Which earned a hearty bit of laughter from everyone.

AJ and Remy stayed to help clean up and then hung around cracking jokes about family members and mutual acquaintances to keep Junior's spirit light. Their work done, Remy promised to touch base in the morning and went on with his evening.

AJ collapsed on the couch, spent. Roxanne turned off the lights in the kitchen and dining room, leaving only the hall light on. She brought over a box of tissues, a large bottle of water, a bottle of red, three glasses, and a bag of fruit-centered chocolates to the couch and said, "Okay, Junior, start at the beginning. Tell us about Davis."

Junior poured them each a glass of wine, settled herself between them, and told them all about the way Davis Fletcher had wholly and completely loved her.

Chapter 27

J UNIOR DROPPED THE KEYS on the counter and immediately went to pour herself a drink and gulped it down. Then another. After her embarrassing ordeal at the restaurant, she needed complete and total obliteration. Junior changed her clothes, removed her makeup and poured herself another drink. On her couch, her head full of liquor, she scrolled through her socials and responded to the birthday wishes while she poured yet another drink.

She'd had a good day. A great day! She'd finished her book about the self-exiled beauty summoned home for her sister's debut determined to ignore the man who'd jilted her, enjoyed a boozy brunch with her friends, which helped make the mandatory Mass more tolerable, and received a video of Ryan's interpretive dance to Stevie Wonder's *Happy Birthday* that she'd already watched over a dozen times. It wasn't until the restaurant that things took a turn.

Junior always spent her birthday dinner with her immediate family. It was an extremely rare occurrence for there to be any additions to the guest list. But she'd made the reservation months ago, while Davis was still in Red Lake, because you needed to book well in advance for Alo, especially if you wanted to secure the circle booth in the corner turret.

It had completely escaped her mind to adjust the reservation after their split. When her family got to their table, the extra place setting mocked her and she'd had to endure her mother's thinly veiled comments on the matter for the rest of the night.

And now she was moping into a bottle of bourbon.

Ridiculous. If there was one thing she could be grateful for, it was that no one was around to witness this sad pity party.

"There isn't even music at this party," she muttered to herself. If she was going to wallow in recrimination and self-pity, she should at least do it in style with silk robes and fur slippers, not in a ratty t-shirt and sweat socks. Junior had officially hit critical levels of pathetic, and this? This whole situation was beneath her.

Which is unfortunate, because I'm trying to be beneath you.

The lock for the place where she kept Davis was loosened by drink. Fragments of mundane and unremarkable moments crashed to the surface, superimposing on themselves until she couldn't discern fact from fiction, memory from nightmare.

Junior examined them like specimens under glass.

Davis was making coffee. He'd watched in horror as she microwaved a cup of coffee and added a heaping tablespoon of sweetened condensed milk to it. From that moment on he'd refused to let her anywhere near his morning brew. Fact.

Davis was making coffee. She was sitting on the counter watching him fiddle with his chemistry equipment. She'd told him that he could have had two cups by now if he'd lower himself to drink out of the press. He refused, insisting that since Junior's coffee was a vessel for sticky milk, she didn't care how the coffee tasted so, no, he would not be drinking what was in the press. Fact.

Davis was making coffee. He stepped away to fill the glass bulb with warm water and then attached the cylinder with the filter to it.

The whole contraption was placed over a burner. She'd joked that her people would be hauled off for cooking meth, no questions asked, if they were caught making coffee this way. Davis kissed her, saying it was lucky that cooking meth didn't generally fall under the purview of her people. Fact.

Davis was making coffee. A breeze was blowing through the curtains. He smiled and told her he loved her. She attempted a reply but nothing came out. He said it again. Her throat worked as she tried to get words out of her mouth. The water in the bulb started to boil, rattling the siphon in its frame. The wind howled through the open window and the curtains obscured their faces. She clawed helplessly at her throat. The dishes in the drying rack shook, the siphon whistled like a kettle. He said it again. She tried to speak over the noise and commotion. When she reached for him, her hands came up empty. The siphon exploded, spraying them with water, bits of glass, and coffee grounds. Davis looked at the destruction in the now silent kitchen. He said it again, the distress unmistakable. Fact?

No. Whether she called it a dream or a nightmare, it was Davis' features contorted with the anguish of fruitlessly loving her that delivered her from the misery of sleep to the torment of wakefulness. No one could accuse her subconscious of subtlety.

The first night, she woke from the dream crying into her pillow. Eventually, the tears subsided but the panicky, trembly feeling remained. In the cold darkness of dawn, the dream always left her feeling hollow and rattled. Tonight, Junior's longing expanded, compromising the structural integrity of the lock, until all the memories broke free.

How was she supposed to know Davis goddamned Fletcher was the one? She never saw him coming. Every single thing about him was unexpected. Maybe if she'd been able to see it sooner, analyze the situation without letting her stupid pride paint her into a corner, she could have made different choices. Instead, she'd thrown up her ridiculous walls and boundaries all to protect herself from a man whose only crime was wanting to share a life with her.

Junior had realized it too late, of course, but she had tried.

She'd stood on his porch and told herself she'd face the music, that whatever came of their conversation, she'd accept it and not make a scene. Come what may she would say her piece and respect Davis' decision like a mature adult. If it was over, she would walk away knowing nothing was unfinished between them.

But then he'd kissed her. He'd kissed her like she was essential to his very existence and all her resolute maturity melted away.

What more could she have done? She'd asked Davis to try again and he refused. The night had turned sour so quickly. One moment she was nervous to see him, the next he'd pressed her ravenously against his house, and then he could barely look at her as he asked her to leave. She had no idea what went wrong and now, it seemed, she never would.

He'd all but shouted that he wasn't interested in communicating with her by blocking her number. Davis went so far as to choose office space on the other side of the city when Junior knew for a fact that the fourth floor of the building she worked in was available. The message could not be any clearer. Davis was gone and he'd taken the safety and stability of his love with him.

The words snagged in her mind with an ugly, discordant clang.

Safety and stability.

Security.

Taking another gulp of bourbon to push down the bile, she let the condemnation wash over her. Davis didn't retreat to protect his heart–he'd repeatedly let her bat it around like a cat toy–he'd retreated because Junior had become a threat to his stability.

Davis was fighting battles on multiple fronts and by forcing his hand, she'd left his flank exposed.

How could she have so completely misread the board? Instead of reciprocating the security he offered so readily, she'd endangered his. She never even told him she loved him. Never told him, out loud, what he meant to her. No wonder he wanted nothing to do with her.

And yet... the last time she saw him, the way he looked at her, his feelings were very much alive. He was hurt, not divested.

Ugh, that ridiculous man, Junior grumped. Didn't he know that you weren't supposed to look at someone that way when you were dumping them? Standard operating procedure dictated that your features be blank and your eyes be coolly detached when you were refusing further contact with a person whose skin still held your secrets–skin that bore witness to your whispered confessions and promises.

Maybe that had changed and time had rid him of those feelings. She certainly wasn't the type of woman who chased after people who didn't want her–never had been, never would be–so this, technically, was all his fault! If she just had a chance to look into his eyes and see that it was over, she could move on.

This equation was missing its term. That was it! She had the constants, the coefficient, and the operation, so all Junior needed to know was if the variable was greater than zero. And if it *was* greater than zero...

A plan began forming in her pickled mind. Plan was probably too strong a word since what Junior had was little more than a disjointed collection of events. Still, she pushed ahead before a sober second thought could shine logic or reason on her actions.

Davis had only ever made her one promise and, standing at the mail chute in her hallway, Junior banked on him keeping it.

"Your move, Fletcher."

Chapter 28

Davis pulled up to the address on the invitation. The location turned out to be a staggering split-level that backed onto the Scarborough Bluffs overlooking Lake Ontario. He wasn't sure what he was walking into or if he should walk in at all. But he'd once told Junior that if she ever invited him to a party he'd show up, so here he was, despite his better judgement.

He hadn't seen Junior in close to two months and he'd managed his misery by allowing himself one single hour a day to think about her. All the memories and feelings and thoughts that threatened to overwhelm him and weaken his resolve were condensed into one scheduled bout of torment so that he could attempt functioning daily.

The plan was working, too. He could almost sit on his couch and not reach for her. Almost watch the news without hearing her voice condemn the inherently biased coverage. Almost forget the silky feel of her hair scarf on his chest as she braided their limbs together while she slept. Almost look through his window without remembering how it felt to hold her, kiss her, for the first time.

When he allowed himself to admit it, he realized there was a definite upside to having kept their relationship a secret–he didn't have to answer questions about her or them and he didn't have to see the pity in anyone's eyes when he was forced to explain that it was over. He'd even gone so far as to convince himself that there was nothing left of her inside and that his anger and disappointment had vanquished the traitorous part of him that still wanted her.

Getting the invitation to her cousin's first birthday–a weird enough proposition on its own–swiftly laid bare that lie.

It seemed impossible that Eduardo was a year old already. Davis remembered Junior going to his baptism. It was the first time she'd spent the entire night. He was so used to her vanishing act, the surprise of finding her there when he woke nearly outweighed the thrill of it. Careful not to disturb her, he had gathered her in his arms and drifted back to sleep. When next he woke, she was ready to leave–she had overslept and needed to go home to get ready for church. He tried to haggle with her, plying her with kisses and even luring her back to bed momentarily, before extracting a promise that she'd return later.

Now, he stood in front of what he guessed was Junior's childhood home.

For her repeated insistence she grew up in a regular house in a regular neighborhood, it occurred to him that his issues with Junior might be due to her fundamental inability to appreciate scale. He knew that she had grown up with an amount of wealth that isolated her, but this was something he simply could not comprehend. Davis half expected a butler to open the door.

Instead, he was met by an older, olive-skinned woman with a long, thick braid hanging over her shoulder, eyeing him suspiciously. "Hello. Can I help you?" She asked in heavily accented English.

Though they shared no other physical characteristics, nothing in their features to indicate any relation at all, Davis had been on the receiving end of that steely-eyed expectation too many times to not recognize this woman as Junior's abuela, Regina Sano. He smiled. "Señora Sano?"

Arching her brow in an all too familiar manner, Mrs. Sano straightened herself to her full five-ish feet waiting for him to state his business and, presumably, leave.

Just then a woman who could only be Junior's mother turned the corner. "Quién está en la puerta? Oh, hello." She smiled Junior's smile. "You must be Davis." She wore her hair cropped close to her skull. Her voice was deeper than Junior's and she wasn't as tall, but that's where the differences ended. "We've been expecting you."

Mrs. Sano looked at her daughter-in-law skeptically. "Este blanquito?"

"Con permiso, Doña. Soy mestizo." Davis said, remembering Junior's long-ago warning that he would be better received by Regina as Indigenous. Regina concluded her evaluation with a decisive nod and returned to the depths of the house. Davis turned to her mother and smiled, "Hi, Dr. Rosales—yes, I'm Davis."

"It's nice to meet you, Davis. Call me Yesenia." Her eyes were glittering as she welcomed him. She opened the door wider, "Please, come in."

"Thank you." Davis didn't know where to begin. Was this the house where Junior grew up? Why was her mother expecting him? He offered the gift bag with the stuffed turtle he'd been clutching. "This is for Eduardo."

"Oh, how thoughtful." She took the bag and appraised him. "You work closely with my daughter, no?"

"Not really. I mean, we did. Work closely together. For a time. .. last season. I'm on another series now," Davis explained haltingly.

There was nothing overtly invasive about the question, but it still felt extremely loaded.

"Mmm." Her gaze was shrewd but kind. Davis wasn't sure how or why, but he felt like he'd admitted something incriminating. "Tell me about yourself, Davis. Besides the fact Junior has coached you on what to say to her grandmother." A soft sound of amusement escaped her as she led him through the house.

"Uh, yeah... she did. I, um, I grew up in a small town in Kenora but have lived here for seven years." He didn't know how much he was supposed to say.

"It must have been beautiful growing up there." She set the gift bag on a table. "Do you get to visit often?"

"Not as often as I like. My parents still live there so I get back for holidays and stuff."

The final piece of a puzzle Davis couldn't see slotted into place in Yesenia's mind. "Oh," she tutted sympathetically. "It must be difficult being so far away from them."

"Yes, ma'am." He imagined that Dr. Rosales extracted all manner of information from her patients without them even knowing it. A battle of wills between mother and daughter must make 1974's Rumble in the Jungle seem like mere sparring practice.

"Yesenia," she corrected. "I think Junior is in the den. Why don't you go say hi and then come get something to eat."

She smiled as she led him past the kitchen and into a large living/dining room with floor-to-ceiling windows allowing for a breathtaking view. The tiered deck and sloped backyard rolled out to the rocky ledge of the bluffs and the lake beyond.

"Go ahead—just down the stairs," Yesenia urged, giving his arm a gentle squeeze.

She's tactile like her daughter. The stray thought bubbled to the surface as he stood taking in the view.

Davis made his way to where she sat—he couldn't confess to her mother that he was stalling, that he was afraid of what would happen when he finally saw Junior again—but there she was and it didn't hurt at all. Or, it did hurt but in the way that relief can hurt, the way you worry at a popcorn kernel stuck in your teeth, the pain and discomfort of it driving you to distraction until it shifts loose and relief washes over you. Seeing Junior again removed the tiny, unreachable splinter of their separation from his skin.

She was sitting on her knees with Eduardo in her lap in a circle of children underneath the demolished remains of a piñata. There were four kids about kindergarten age with a small pile of candy in front of them. Davis smiled. They never talked about the future, he didn't know if she ever wanted a family of her own, but watching her with the baby and a gaggle of preschoolers hanging on to her every word, he felt a crushing pang of What If.

Junior turned her attention to a striking girl who dug through her pile of candy and pulled one up for inspection. Junior nodded and the rest of the kids searched their piles. "Me too, please." She smiled and the little girl crawled over to Junior, found the candy in question, and placed the unwrapped treat in her waiting mouth. "Mmm! What do you think, Noor?"

Ryan noticed him first. "We're having a taste test!" she announced.

Davis couldn't tell if she recognized him or if *obviously* was always strongly implied when she spoke. He figured it was probably the latter.

Junior smiled with the red ball between her teeth to show him. "This one is the best so far!"

"Is that right?" Spectacularly, Davis managed to override his body's reaction and not scandalize the group of preschoolers. He watched as Junior chattered happily with the kids, each loudly making a case for their favorite.

He was in awe of how easily Junior managed the children.

"Go ask Grandma Yossi for some bags and a marker, please," she said to Ryan before turning to Davis. "Give me a minute to put this away."

He nodded.

"Owen, can you please pick up all the wrappers? Langley, you can help." She instructed, rising to her feet with the baby on her hip facing outward so he could watch the revelry.

Ryan skipped back into the room with paper bags and a Sharpie.

Junior had each child write their names on their bags and load up their treasure. "Put your bags on that table. We'll try some more later."

"Is this the man of the hour?" Davis wiggled Eduardo's leg as the children dispersed.

"Yes, he is!" She bounced him a little. "Are you hungry? There's lots of food."

"I'm all right, thanks. Your mom already insisted I come back to eat. I think your abuela thinks I'm here to sell her something."

"Taking and finishing a plate of food will go a long way to getting her onside," Junior confirmed. "The hallway you passed on the way here is where the bedrooms are and this is the living room. The kitchen is up there. That's the deck and backyard, which you can access through there or there." She pointed to the door where the piñata's carcass dangled and to a screened-in porch. "So, the only thing left on the tour is the den."

Davis again marveled at her total disregard for the sheer size and grandeur of the house. He followed her to a door behind the staircase into a paneled room with a kitchenette, three card tables with inlaid Panamanian flags, a large TV mounted on the far wall, and a leather sectional in the opposite corner. There were easily twenty people in this room and still space for plenty more.

"D Fleezy, what it do?" Jamal called from the counter as he opened a beer. Remington and Ali glanced at Junior before saluting Davis in welcome.

"I heard there was a party," Davis called.

"Smart. You do not want to miss out on a Sano joint!" Jamal laughed and offered Davis a beer.

Junior handed off the baby to a woman making eyes at Jamal and brought Davis to the bigger of the three card tables where a loud game of dominoes was underway. One of the men held a domino in his hand and pointed to the other three players. "You pass. You pass. You to play," and slammed his domino on the table, rattling the tiles.

"Tío Mito," the second man who 'passed' shook his head sadly before flinging the slammed domino away and laying his down in its place.

"Carajo!" he hissed, to everyone's laughter.

Junior took the break in gameplay to make introductions. "That's my cousin Diego." She pointed to the disappointed passer who raised a hand from across the table. "That's his dad, my Tío Manuel." She pointed to the first passer who took Davis' hand and shook it heartily. "This is Eddie, Alma's partner and Lalo's dad."

"Lalo?" Davis asked, confused.

"It's short for Eduardo. Just go with it," Eddie said amiably, raising a fist for Davis to bump.

"And this is my Dad, Jaime."

Davis wasn't sure how he thought Junior's father would look, but it certainly wasn't this youthful man trash-talking his family over a game of dominoes. His complexion was more golden compared to Junior and Yesenia's rich, warm brown and his features were all angular, but seeing them together, Davis noticed they had the same doe eyes.

"Hi. Davis. Nice to meet all of you."

"Call me Jefe," her dad said loudly while dramatically puffing out his chest. His voice carried the same hint of an accent as Junior's.

"Do not call him Jefe." Junior rolled her eyes and swatted her dad. "Jaime is fine. Old Man also works."

"Tell me you don't speak to your father this way!" he pleaded. You might believe that Jaime was greatly affronted if it wasn't for the clear adoration in his eyes.

"His father isn't a menace like you!" Junior scolded. "Necesitas algo más?"

"Sí, hielos." Jaime rattled his glass.

"Anyone else?" she asked the table.

Davis had always found it fascinating that Junior maintained individual relationships with her parents. Where Davis spoke with his mother every so often and Deidre acted as a proxy for Charles, Junior spoke to her mother every day, spoke to her father multiple times during the week and, as far as Davis could tell, neither conversation referenced the other.

When she was finished seeing to everyone's drink and ice needs, she turned to Davis. "Come on."

Junior led him from one room to another, introducing him to aunts and uncles and cousins and neighbors. Three of her cousins specifically–Claudia, Alma, and Silvana–eyed him speculatively, but, like everyone else, were friendly and welcoming. Davis got the distinct impression that having fifty people in the house for a child's birthday party was a minor effort for the Sano family. There was certainly no risk of running out of food if the cauldron Junior scooped his rice out of was any indication.

"I need to do a quick lap; will you be alright? You can eat on the deck or in the dining room or downstairs…"

"Yeah, I might go back downstairs. I don't think I've ever seen dominoes played so aggressively before."

"Whatever you do, do not let them goad you into playing," she warned.

He chuckled. "I wouldn't dream of it."

"I won't be long." Turning, she hollered at one of the tween boys to stop doing something before someone caught him—he couldn't follow the rapid-fire Spanglish—and took his plate to the den.

***

"It's time for Lalo to sleep." Junior announced to no one in particular, "I'd better go put him down."

She was being a coward and she knew it. After she'd sent Davis to the den with his food, she'd used every excuse she could think of to avoid spending any real time with him. Flitting from room to room in constant motion—refilling drinks, bringing extra helpings of snacks, corralling children—anything she could think of to avoid facing him. She couldn't bring herself to look in his eyes and see nothing there, so she was hiding behind a baby.

Junior padded out of the room and down the hallway to the nursery.

She lowered the shade and set Lalo on the changing table to remove his adorable white shirt, navy bow tie, brown pants and suspenders like an old-timey paperboy—leaving him in his onesie. For his comfort, and for her desperation to be away from the party, from Davis, a little longer, she also changed his diaper before settling him into the crib.

"What do you think, Lalito?" she murmured to the half-asleep baby. "Will I sleep through the night tonight?"

Junior wasn't sure it was the answer, but she had to hope that she'd eventually make it through the night without seeing the heartbreak on Davis' face. With enough time, they could even be friends. After all, she'd successfully managed to not throw herself at him or press her lips anywhere on his person.

"You're not sleeping?" his voice came from the doorway.

"Dios! Ay, Sapó–why are you creeping around back here?" Her hands clutched her racing heart. She wasn't too startled to forget the embarrassment of using the pet name that still came so easily. "I mean... That's not... I shouldn't–" she trailed off, flustered.

"It's okay." His mouth lifted in a ghost of a smile. "It's grown on me."

"Hmph," she huffed playfully. "It's grown on you? After all that sulking 'Stop calling me a snitch! I'm not a snitch!'"

He gave a small laugh in reply. They could do this, she thought. They could learn to be friends.

Yes. They would look back fondly at this time and shake their heads at how insurmountable it had seemed; how silly it was now that they had the benefit of time.

It was because she stood in that wished-for future, one she could envision so clearly, that she raised a challenging eyebrow and flirted, "I suppose you've taught my replacement how to say it."

As soon as the words left her mouth, she knew it was wrong. This wasn't her rosy future; it was her tense and fraught right fucking now. If she didn't already feel the cringe in the soles of her feet, the storm cloud that crossed Davis' face, knitting his brow and tugging the corners of his mouth downward, was all the confirmation she needed.

"Shit! That was a joke. A bad, inappropriate joke. Seriously. I swear, I didn't mean it. It's none of my business and you do not have to dignify that with an answer."

She couldn't look at him with her humiliation crawling all over her face, so she turned and fussed with Lalo's blankets, shifting him this way and that. Finally, when she could stall no longer, she leaned into the crib and kissed the bottom of Lalo's foot. She whispered a small benediction, ending it with, "Sleep now, Lalo. When you wake up it will be time for cake."

Turning on the baby monitor, Junior straightened herself and headed for the door. "Were you looking for somewhere quiet to make a call or something? You passed two washrooms on the way back here." She led him down the hall.

"Aren't you going to close the door?" Davis looked back at the nursery.

"What for?"

"Because the baby is trying to sleep?"

Junior paused, waiting for him to make a compelling argument for closing the door. Realizing 'the baby is trying to sleep' was the sum total of that argument, she continued towards the kitchen.

"We don't do that," she said simply. "How else will he learn to sleep when he's sleepy if we eliminate all the distractions?"

"Right. Latine problems need Latine solutions. How could I forget?" he replied drily.

"You mock, but that kid has a Panamanian mom and a Peruvian dad. This is as quiet as it gets."

"Will you please talk to me?" Davis stopped walking, forcing her to stand in the junction of the hallways. "What am I doing here, Junior?"

"That's what I asked you," she hedged. She was not prepared to have any version of this conversation. Not anymore.

Davis' nostrils flared as he pressed his lips together in frustration.

Deciding not to press her luck, Junior explained, "I invited you because..." She turned towards the sounds of the party. Why did she invite him? This plan made perfect sense when she'd formed it, half-cocked in a drunken bout of longing.

It all seemed so simple: invite him to the party, dazzle him with her cool and collected demeanor, and remind him of how it was between them–how it could be again–and fall into his waiting arms. Now? She just felt foolish. He came because he'd told her he'd show up to any party she ever invited him to. This was nothing more than him keeping a promise, rubbing her nose in the fact that he'd managed what she had not.

Junior decided on a different truth and took a deep breath before looking at him. "I wanted to show you it doesn't have to be weird between us. I'm sorry about the way things ended. I should have trusted you to know what was best for you and not left you open to that kind of risk. I didn't need to include you when I'd already made my point to Olivia. I think... I think I wanted to hurt her for being loyal to someone so heinous." Junior shrugged feebly. "But that doesn't mean you have to stop hanging around those guys. We're okay." She smiled at him, "We can be friends."

Davis gave a small shake of his head. "I don't think we can."

"Oh." She nodded her understanding. "Okay." Junior let out a soft breath and forced her lips to smile. "Well, I'd better get back before Tía Lovie tries to make a move on Jamal. Again."

She left him in the hall, desperate to get away before her thin veneer of poise cracked for good. How could she have been so stupid? Wasn't it enough, she wondered, that she had accumulated all of those teeny, tiny stupids along the way? Did she need to add this one enormous stupid to the pile, too?

She had her answer and now she needed to move on.

Junior cleared her head, put on her game face, and proceeded to divert her aunt's attention from an entirely too into it Jamal. She'd get through this party and get through this heartache.

Chapter 29

DAVIS STARED AT THE spot Junior vacated.

In one breath she'd said the words he'd been desperate to hear, followed immediately by words that landed like an uppercut, rattling his teeth and making his head spin.

The seven months between their first kiss against the window and their last kiss against his house were filled with such vexing, teeth-pulling efforts to get Junior to let him in, to commit. They were also filled with laughter, dancing, exuberance, and a passion he didn't think possible.

Davis had thought that nothing could be worse than her complete disregard for his existence while he yearned futilely, but this was way, way worse. He was a fool. He hadn't achieved any balance! Nothing had changed–he loved her and she merely liked him well enough.

And now she wanted to talk about hanging out together? About being friends? Did she think he could survive being around her without touching her again? As if there was some type of valve for all the built-up touches that could not be expressed? He laughed to himself bitterly, already chiding himself for this exercise in masochism. Even if the valve existed, who could understand what suddenly drove him to seek the desperate relief of his palm on her neck or his finger run along her wrist? No, they were not okay. He was not okay. It was time to go. Davis would wait out this agitation and then say his goodbyes.

He took in the wall of photos. They were in matching frames in three rows on the long, uninterrupted wall. Some of the frames held a single eight by ten picture while others held two or four smaller images. There was a certain chronology to the spacing. Junior and her family got older as you moved down the hall.

"Davis," Yesenia said warmly, turning the corner to find him staring at the pictures. "Are you enjoying yourself?"

"Yes, thank you," he answered politely.

"Ah, the Gallery." Yesenia looked at the framed pictures. "I guess we went a bit overboard." She chuckled to herself.

"No, it's great!"

"I couldn't take it down even if I wanted to. Her father would sooner build another house." Her tone was one of mild annoyance, but it was clear Yesenia Rosales wouldn't put up any kind of resistance if it came to that.

"That's my mother, Paolina Garza, the great beauty." Yessenia pointed with pride and adoration at a black and white headshot of the beauty queen turned soap star. "Her priorities might have leaned more toward the superficial, but I learned everything I know about drive and ambition from her."

She slowly led him down the hall. There were pictures of parents and siblings and a column of wedding photos–Regina and Ernesto, Paolina and Javier, and Yessenia and Jaime. Davis wondered what it was like for Ernesto, Javier, and Jaime to have married such vivacious women that would always attract a certain kind of attention. Did they enjoy it or did they endure it? For the flickering moment he held her, Davis only ever cared that he had

Junior's attention—that she chose him. Looking at the pride and love on those men's faces, he understood they likely felt the same way.

"That was taken when she was ten, maybe?" Yesenia guessed. "Her abuela had that pollera shipped from Panama City just so Junior could participate in an International Day Parade."

Davis smiled at a picture of her in a green and white ruffled dress with a large gold pompom on the center of the neckline, her hair filled with clips and barrettes and her tiny body draped in layers of gold necklaces. She'd told him that she was a fat kid, not at all recognizable as the woman she was today, but that adorably chubby little girl had the same dazzling smile that bowled him over the first time he'd been graced with it.

"And this," Yesenia said, pointing out another favorite, "was at her Quinceañera." It was a picture of Junior in a ball gown, slow dancing with her abuela and an older gentleman not quite facing the camera while her parents looked on lovingly.

"Is this—" Davis started.

"My father, Javier. Yes," she answered, wistful. He looked closer at Junior's beloved grandfather, the man whose loss still haunted her, a hole she tried to fill with acts of service.

"Ugh, this stupid tree," Yesenia huffed. It was a frame that held four pictures of Junior in a cap and gown, arms wide, in front of her tree. In the top left, she was maybe five years old in a handmade cap and a large white dress shirt for a gown. On the top right, she was graduating from what must have been elementary school in a teal cap and gown. The bottom right was high school in burgundy, and the bottom left was university in black. "She has spent more time spilling her secrets into the bark of that gnarled thing, you cannot imagine."

Yesenia shook her head, confounded by her daughter's loyalty to this plant. He remembered all the afternoons they'd spent under the shade of that tree and his insides clenched. A thought was trying to form, to break through the cloudiness of his jumbled mind, but Yesenia kept going.

"Ah, and this, her thirtieth birthday in Nassau."

Many faces were crowding the shot, all surrounding a laughing Junior. Everyone in the photo had had too much sun and too much drink, but all he could see was how happy Junior looked. Slowly, he took in the other faces in the image. Roxanne, her first friend, had a red flower behind her ear. AJ, the friend Junior said she waited her whole life to meet, was blowing a kiss to the camera. Leigh, her soul mate, had her glass raised. Quinn and Remy were on either side of Junior pressing a kiss to her cheeks. Claire and Ali were throwing up complicated finger poses with playful snarls. And at the bottom of the picture was Jamal, who seemed to have launched himself into the frame at the last moment.

"I know it seems excessive, but after the year we'd had, my father's passing and Junior taking it so hard—we were so worried about her for so long—seeing her this way..." Yesenia smiled at the photo. "We have operated on a strict Don't Ask Don't Tell policy for all aspects regarding this party. To this day, all I know is that everyone returned in one piece, I got my rental deposit back in full, and no authorities were involved."

It occurred to him that he recognized everyone in the picture. When the penny dropped, Davis felt the realization, cold and sharp, like an ice cube rolling down his back. This was a record of the most important people in Junior's life, her very best friends, the loves of her life, celebrating her birthday in the Bahamas and Junior had made sure he spent time with all of them in one way or anoth-er. The evenings being test subjects at Leigh's bakery. Spin classes with Claire that ended in the richest, most high-calorie breakfasts he'd ever ingested. Even the brief introduction to Roxanne when she'd swung by the production office to drop something off that, at the time, he didn't recognize for what it was, but now understood as the opportunity to see them, their sisterhood, together.

Was there a clearer indication of what he meant to her than this? She had quietly shared her innermost self with him, but again, because she didn't use the words he wanted, he hadn't recognized her offering. He hadn't heard her.

"How is your father? Dr. Redwood is an excellent physician. Your family will be safe in her hands."

Davis struggled to find the breath to form words but under Yesenia's kind and expectant gaze all he could do was stammer, "You know Dr. Redwood?"

"Mostly by reputation, though she gave an impressive talk on holistic geriatric care that I attended a few years ago. Very well researched."

Davis searched his memory for the kind of doctor Junior's mother was. Orthopedic surgeon, he thought. How would she know anything about his dad or Dr. Redwood? "I... um, I mean—yes, we're very lucky."

"Membership does have its privileges, doesn't it?" She smiled and tapped her nose. "Would you mind helping me get some ice from the garage?"

He nodded and mutely followed her down the hall and through the mudroom that led to the garage. In the corner was a large deep freezer. She lifted the lid and indicated the solid block of ice for Davis to handle. "I couldn't vote on your parent's case—conflict of interests, and all—but once the board accepted them into the program, it was no longer an ethics violation for me to put my thumb on the scale."

"Your thumb on the scale?" Davis, who prided himself on his ability to carry a conversation, was reduced to a babbling simpleton. What was it about Rosales women specifically that threw him so wildly off balance? He cleared his throat and tried to regain control of himself. "I'm sorry. I'm a bit overwhelmed with all of it. I'm not following."

"I know it can be a lot. I warned Junior not to get your hopes up and that sometimes spaces in these facilities can take years to become available. But you know my daughter–rare is the 'no' that stops her. She's stubborn like her father." Yesenia rolled her eyes and Davis had to blink to clear the image of Junior standing there. "Anyway, we reached out to Dr. Redwood and she agreed that while your parents were a bit young for the community she's building, they would benefit from the atmosphere. It might take another six-to-eight months, but the home visits should help until then." She spoke so nonchalantly, as if she hadn't tilted his world's whole axis. "Ready?" she smiled again, indicating the block of ice.

"Yes, I–my parents have only had a consult with Dr. Redwood. The follow-up is scheduled for next month. I didn't... we didn't know they were eligible to join her community."

"Really? Junior's harangued me for weeks about it, I was sure she would have said." Yesenia's hand flew to her mouth "Oh, have I ruined something? Was it supposed to be a surprise?"

Had she ruined something? Only the last hold of his increasingly unsure footing. Davis reeled. It was the final blow in a series of body shots that he'd absorbed in the last hour.

At every crossroad in his life there was a woman, smarter and braver than he, guiding him toward betterment: his mother, Deidre Fletcher, advocating for his education from the very beginning; Arlene Cassidy, the librarian who quietly plied him with sandwiches while helping navigate the grant application process; Suneetha Mohammed, who steered him away from derailment and toward the finish line of higher education; Tara Legault who held his hand through the unfathomable step of homeownership; Olivia Young who had seen something in him and given him the opportunity, mentoring him to the realization of his dreams; and now he would add Jaime Sano, Jr. who, in her quiet understated way, set in motion the steps to remove the burden of his father's long-term care.

AJs words came back to him. *There is no one better to have in your corner in a crisis.* Even after he'd refused her, Junior had been there for him. The truth of it almost buried him. "No, it's okay. Thank you, Dr. Rosales–"

"Yesenia," she insisted.

"Thank you, Yesenia. I'm sure you haven't ruined anything." He tried to say something else–anything else–but his thoughts were so jumbled that he couldn't hold any single idea in his head long enough to make sense of his feelings. "Shall we?"

***

"Well?" AJ asked when Junior joined them in the solarium.

"Well, what?" Junior fussed around the room, clearing discarded plates and cups.

"Did you talk to Fletcher?" AJ pressed.

Junior wheeled on Roxanne, "Really, Rocky?"

"Whatever. It wouldn't take a rocket scientist to guess you were making a play for Fletcher." She blew a raspberry at Junior.

"Doesn't matter now anyway. It's too late. He's moved on," Junior admitted, defeated.

"You goofy motherfuckers." Jamal heaved a dramatic sigh. "He can barely breathe he wants you so bad. Do I have to do everything?"

"Here we go," Remington said to himself.

"What are you bitching about?" Junior asked, confused.

"That man has been in love with you from time. Everyone knew it except you, Junior," Jamal explained.

"I didn't!" AJ cried. The look on Ali and Remington's faces told Junior that Jamal was grossly exaggerating, which gave her a small amount of relief.

"I couldn't stand it anymore! Watching him follow you around hoping you'd notice him was wearing on my spirit. I had to do something. I vetted him. I invited him out. I made sure he saw you in action so he'd understand what he was getting himself into. I got you to scope out his place. I put him in your way again and again. I did everything but wrap him in a bow and leave him on your doorstep! How is it I gotta fix this, too? My mans is pining and I already told you, I can't have that."

Junior plopped herself in a chair and then sprung back up again.

"Wait, so… Jamal was behind everything this whole time?" AJ stage-whispered to Remy.

"So he'd have us believe."

AJ's eyes bugged out. "This is even bigger than finding out Spinelli was an Ashley!"

"I am a *superior* wingman. I Inceptioned the shit outta that shit." Jamal straightened his imaginary cuffs. "Keyser Soze ain't got nothing on me."

"Why are you worried about Davis pining?" Roxanne admonished Jamal's misplaced loyalties.

"I'm not. I'm worried about that man's pining." He jerked his thumb at Junior.

Junior was speechless. She looked around the room and was met with varying degrees of sympathy and understanding. She was slowly getting her head around the truth of Jamal's confession when AJ piped up, "It's not like you can do anything about it now. It's been over for, like, a month already!"

"Actually," Davis cleared his throat in the doorway, "it's been over for fifty-seven days."

When all the knowing eyes turned on him, Junior thought distantly, *I warned you. You wanted to stand in a room full of people eagerly anticipating your next move*–noting Roxanne's posture screamed she knew where to hide a body if it became necessary–*have at it.*

"You're still here," Junior murmured.

"I was helping your mom haul a giant block of ice from the garage. Then your grandmother had me reaching things from high shelves." He rubbed his neck self-consciously.

"The raspados," Junior said, mostly to herself.

"That's the icies, right?" She heard Jamal whisper to Remington who nodded.

"Um, Junior, may I speak with you for a minute, please?" Davis asked.

"Whatever it is, you can say it here. They all knew apparently," her trademark eye-roll on full display.

"Not the whole time," AJ muttered.

"Don't sulk, AJ," Rocky tried and failed to speak for AJs ears only.

"I'm not sulking," AJ sulked under her breath.

The clamor of stampeding kindergarteners approached. "Mom! Abuela was giving us a raspado but Grandma Yossi said we have to ask if we're allowed first." Ryan burst into the room, red-faced and out of breath with Noor and Owen in tow. "So, can we?"

"Yes, but remind her that Owen can't have any milk on his," Junior said to the hyper, over-sugared kids before Roxanne had a chance to instill any lame Mom regulations on the proceedings. The sugar fiends cheered loudly.

"Come on," Roxanne said. "We'd better go supervise."

"Supervise?" Jamal scoffed. "I'm tryna have dat ice!"

The rest of the group took their cue and started to file out of the room.

On her way past Davis, Roxanne asked in her too genial voice, the one that signaled danger to the highly trained ear, "Have you ever had a raspado? Shaved ice with chopped fruit and syrup topped with condensed milk? They're very good. Refreshing. You might even say they are fun and easy, yet made with real ingredients." She gave him a hard, pointed look. "You should try it."

By his choked, wide-eyed reaction, Junior was sure Davis recognized his words being thrown back at him. Roxanne narrowed her eyes before turning on her heel toward the kitchen.

"You wanted to talk?" Junior asked, unsure of how long she could maintain her composure.

"Junior," he said, standing in front of her now. "Why did you invite me here?"

She looked at him with a mix of confusion and suspicion. They'd literally just had this conversation. It took all of her grace and tact to not ask him if he was losing his marbles.

"Your mom mentioned her board and my parents... that's what I applied to? Those were the forms you sent me?" They couldn't meet each other's eyes at the memory of that night and how it ended.

"I told you, I wanted to help."

"Two weeks later we were screaming at each other. Two weeks after that, it was truly over. Why didn't you pull the application? One word to your mom would have done it," he pressed.

"There was no reason to pull the application because there was no guarantee that your parents' case would have been accepted by the board. The whole thing was a Hail Mary."

"But it was accepted," Davis continued. "Their case was accepted by the board."

Junior was in no mood to play Davis Asks A Million Questions. There were too many feelings coming at her too quickly. She lashed out defensively, "So I should have fucked them over because I was no longer fucking you?"

He winced but didn't take the bait. Davis grabbed her shoulders, "Why did you keep fighting for me?"

"What do you want from me, Fletcher? You want me to apologize for meddling in your affairs?" she mocked, throwing more of his words back at him.

"I want you to tell me why."

"Why? Because!" Junior's arms flew out at her sides, flustered and frustrated. "I don't know, okay? Just because we aren't together anymore doesn't mean I don't love y–"

Davis was on her before she finished her sentence.

Junior put her hands on his chest and pushed him away. "You said we couldn't be friends."

"We can't. I want all of you, Junior. I've always wanted all of you."

"You had all of me and it wasn't enough." She stepped away, putting more space between them. "You said I wasn't enough." Her words were dazed.

"No," he corrected her, "I said I wanted more."

"Semantics." She held out a hand to stop his rebuttal. This infuriating man! She hadn't even had a chance to come to terms with the colossal failure of her big plan or the subsequent rejection of her offer of even a peripheral place in his life and here he was kissing her? "You wanted more. I said there was no more. Ergo I wasn't enough."

"There was more. There was this, you and me, in the open."

"We were on our way to this! And, fine, I messed up but it's not like you accepted my apology, either," she charged on mulishly.

"No, I didn't." Davis pulled her close and said low in her ear. "I was having a Big Feeling."

Looking up at him, she chuckled and the sound was soft, tender.

"Junior..." He hesitated, as though afraid of giving voice to his hopes, "Why am I here?"

In that moment, she understood: Davis was daring her, pleading with her, to tell him the truth. If she wanted him, she was going to have to swallow her pride and say so. "You're here because I needed to see you," her head spun but she continued through the mortification. Junior had never been here before—what did she know about expressing feelings?

Be brave, she reminded herself, and started again with a deep breath, "I needed to show you it wasn't a mistake to love me and to ask... if maybe you could love me again."

Davis' face slackened. "C'mere," he pulled her into his arms, "Of course I love you, Junior—I don't know how to stop."

The riot of emotions was catching up to her and her nerves were frayed. Junior didn't think she could handle the turmoil. Her eyes lowered and she looked away. "Is it enough?"

Davis followed her gaze to the yard where Ali stood with Jamal, Remington, Diego, and Eddie tossing squealing kindergarteners between them like hot potatoes. "Sometimes it's not enough," she added almost to herself.

That was the closest Junior and Davis had ever got to acknowledging her relationship with Ali. They needed to discuss that particular devilishly handsome elephant.

He took both of her hands in his, "I'm sorry that I allowed my insecurities about us to turn into resentment of you and Ali. I was frustrated because he seemed to have access to a part of you that I couldn't reach."

"He doesn't magically go away—you understand that, right? If I call, if he calls... that doesn't change."

"I know," he said sincerely.

"We have other problems," she insisted. "Bigger problems."

"We do," Davis said simply.

"We do." Junior nodded, barely a whisper, as that small truth sent her into a tailspin. "Oh, god, what am I doing?" Junior pulled her hands free of his grasp and stepped back. "I'm so sorry, I know this is all my fault. I know I ruined everything." Junior paced and babbled through huge, gasping breaths.

She'd vowed that she wouldn't ever be here again. The back-and-forth rollercoaster was too dizzying. Once a relationship was over it was over, which is how things had to be. How had she forgot? "If I'd remembered to change the reservation for my birthday dinner, my mother wouldn't have been at me all night with her thinly veiled comments." Davis' sharp intake of breath at the implication earned him a baleful glance as she continued muttering, "Then I wouldn't have gone home and made exciting new advances in drunken wallowing."

Junior's best worst mistakes were made with bourbon. It would appear her streak remained unbroken.

"I just missed you so much and I'd wasted all that time." Her voice broke but still, she wouldn't let Davis touch her. "I thought I could do this. I invited you here because I thought I could. I'm sorry, okay? I wanted to go back to what we had, but that's over and I know that now."

She hunched her shoulders over and pressed her hands on her ribs, trying to contain the feelings ricocheting through her body. "I can't go through that again. Do you understand me? I won't."

"Junior, please –"

She dodged his grasp. "No!"

He pulled her firmly against his body, "Stop running from me."

His words snapped her out of her spiral.

Davis closed his eyes, inhaled, and said without malice or judgement, "You're worried about history repeating, but whatever you guys had? This is not that. I'm not him." When she stilled in his embrace he added, "I'm asking you to be with me. Now." Davis kissed her softly and whispered, "I am hopelessly, immeasurably, in love with you."

Junior looked at him fully, squarely in the eye, for the first time since he walked in the door. The certainty she found there gave her the strength to be brave, to face some truths of her own. And the truth was she had to stop ignoring thoughtful, Caring Davis and finally let him in. The idea of opening herself up, fully and completely, filled her with abject terror.

But wasn't it thoughtful, Caring Davis who knew, right from the start, that she was a fragile, delicate thing? Hadn't he seen through all the bravado and the thunder to the very secret heart of her? Who better to trust with her most nerve-racking fear? The answer was another truth she had to face.

"I love you," she admitted and kissed him with everything she had.

Davis wrapped an arm around her waist to pull her to his chest, kissing her thoroughly in the alcove of the sunroom. When her tongue found his, he pressed his body even closer to hers.

Junior pulled back to catch her breath. Davis' mouth trailed kisses along her jaw and throat. "Davis," she started, but he clamped his lips against hers. "Ay, Sapó, stop—we need to figure out what happens now." She broke free of him.

"I like the way you say my name," he said into her hair.

"You should, for all the times I say it!" she scoffed.

"That was only the second time," he said throatily, kissing her neck.

Her disbelief made her obstinate. "I say your name all the time!"

He smirked into her doubting face. "You've preferred variations of 'snitch'. Sometimes you even get as close as 'Fletcher'." He watched as she considered this evidence and kissed her to stop himself from laughing.

"Well then, *Davis*, what do we do now?" She loved him and he loved her. There was nothing left to say, but they still had so much to talk about.

"We talk about our feelings, of course!" he teased.

"Ugh–what else is new?" she rolled her eyes dramatically. "I guess that means I need to mentally prepare to talk all night."

"Well, not all night."

The look in his eye no longer signaled an intention to talk for any portion of the evening. "Maybe we should do this on the phone."

"No. No more nights apart. In fact, you should move in with me."

"What? We can't. I don't want to give up my apartment and you can't sell your house." Junior argued.

"I can sell my house. Who says I can't sell my house? I'll sell mine and we'll live in yours. Whatever. We'll figure it out. I don't care. One hundred and two nights, Junior. That's how many nights I've spent without you. Move in with me."

"There are easier ways to get in my pants," she teased with a raised eyebrow. "The sauna is soundproof and has very sturdy benches."

"I want us to start a life together," Davis insisted.

"A 'life' with me comes with a lot of baggage."

"I want all of you, Junior. Always."

Junior smiled up at Davis, the panicked, jittery feeling in the pit of her stomach settled for the first time in fifty-seven days. "You have all of me. I was too scared to face what was happening so I lied to myself and everybody else. But the truth is, Davis Fletcher, yours is the last kiss I'm ever gonna want."

"Yeah?" The sweet, bashful look on his face was its own reward.

She nodded and kissed him, "Yeah."

It crossed her mind, for a brief second, that she and Davis could slip out through the garage and be back at her place in twelve minutes. The last romantic partner she'd introduced to her extended family was in the backyard smoking with her cousin and uncle. She wasn't looking forward to answering the avalanche of questions, especially since Junior had no doubt Claudia had engaged in some pendejismo, giving every consenting adult the full timeline of her relationship with Davis and the implications of their current absence.

But Junior was tired of hiding and Davis deserved to be loved out loud. "Okay," she exhaled, "Are you ready?"

When he nodded, she grabbed his hand and led him through the solarium and out to the lawn. There were way more people milling around outside since the last time she'd looked. The bigger kids were playing soccer with some of the adults and the little kids were chasing bubbles and balloons. Junior noticed that Hodan had arrived. As had Leigh, with the birthday cake, and Claire with the baby.

"Oye, familia!" Junior called, still holding Davis' hand. Her voice didn't carry over the music and merriment. Davis let out a loud, sharp whistle which got everyone's attention. Junior looked up at him in surprise. "And here I thought I knew everything your tongue was capable of!"

"Behave." Davis squeezed her hand and smiled a secret smile.

Junior looked around at her family–found and genetic, chosen and inherited–who knew all of her quirks and flaws and idiosyncrasies and accepted her, loved her, anyway. "I'd like to introduce you to my boyfriend, Davis Fletcher. He has asked me to move in with him and I am going to seriously think about considering it!" she announced to cheers and laughter.

"Davis *Fletcher*." Leigh and Claire said to each other, putting the pieces together.

"Spin Hottie is Dickface?" Claire almost screeched.

"I know!" Roxanne had still not got over it.

"Dickface?" Davis looked at Junior, waiting for her to elaborate.

"Oh, absolutely," she answered. "You're an insufferable pedant. I wanted nothing to do with you!"

Davis threw his head back and laughed. "I'll show you insufferable!" He grabbed her face and kissed her senseless.

"What did I tell you? Get 'em on your turf, surrounded by your people and your things–the kickback works every time!" Jamal overstated. "It's undefeated!"

"You owe me a hundred dollars!" Hodan gloated.

"What? No way!" AJ defended. "I said he was with Junior and I was right!"

"Nuh-uh. I bet you one hundred dollars that Fletcher got his lady and you said no because he was with Junior. That Junior happened to be his lady is irrelevant," Hodan insisted.

"Good point," Remy agreed at the same time Ali nodded and said, "True, true."

"What lady?" Leigh demanded.

"Oh, it was a whole thing," Roxanne answered, daring them to believe it. AJ and Hodan proceeded to explain to Leigh and Claire about Davis and the quest for his mythical lady.

Junior looked up at Davis, indicating their group of bickering, squabbling friends and asked "Happy now?"

"Indescribably," he said, smiling brighter than the sun.

THE END

Do you want a little more of Junior and Davis? Click here to sign up for my mailing list or copy/paste https://bookhip.com/TAVQJHH in your browser to get a bonus extended epilogue straight in your inbox! And, if you enjoyed this book, please consider leaving a review online via Goodreads, Storygraph, or wherever you purchased this novel.

Thank you!

Author's Note

When I first started outlining this story, I needed a job for Junior that would give her enough autonomy to highlight her savvy but still be something feasible for a Toronto based production. After a bit of back and forth, the totally made up yet plausible title of "Design Tracker" was born. Turns out, a version of this role exists in Montreal! And why shouldn't it? Toronto doesn't have Unit Managers like Montreal does so why wouldn't they have an Art Department Accountant when Toronto doesn't?

To that end, I still don't know if anyone performs the exact role I've given Junior. She, her job, and the TV show she works on are pure fiction pulled from the depths of my addled mind. But if you're out there, you are gods amongst mortals and I am in awe!!

Further to that, if you've ever wanted to tell off a Production Designer (and, honestly, whom among us – am I right?) I hope you were able to live vicariously through Junior.

On a more serious note, the enfranchising of Indigenous peoples is just one of the very real, very shameful practises of the Canadian Government. From 1867 until 1985, the Indian Act stripped 'Status Indians' of their legal treaty rights and ancestral identities for a variety of reasons. The British colonists imposed a truly heinous set of regulations that, in ways large and small, denied Indigenous peoples agency and opportunity, disproportionately effecting women. [1]

While I do not share this identity, I am keenly aware of the barriers imposed by structural inequality and wholeheartedly support their efforts toward reconciliation and equity. Being Canadian means many things to many people and as such, we cannot afford to ignore the injustices of our own history.

I hope you've received my fictional tale about the diversity of the Canadian experience with the grace and respect intended.

---

1. Encyclopedia, The Canadian. "Indian Act". *The Canadian Encyclopedia*, 23 September 2022, *Historica Canada*.

Junior's Bookshelf

In order of appearance*:

The Devil Comes Courting, Courtney Milan
Night Hawk, Beverly Jenkins
Reluctant/Runaway Royals series, Alyssa Cole
A Caribbean Heiress in Paris, Adriana Herrera
The Duke, the Lady and a Baby, Vanessa Riley
Hell's Belles series, Sarah MacLean
Ravishing the Heiress, Sherry Thomas
The Governess Game, Tessa Dare
The Siren of Sussex, Mimi Matthews
Aphrodite and the Duke, J.J. McAvoy

(*All books listed are either written by or feature BIPOC/LGBTQIA+ persons. Junior wouldn't have it any other way.)

Acknowledgements

Thank you, gorgeous reader, for making it to the end of my debut novel. This wild ride that I couldn't possibly have prepared for all started during lockdown. I was reading romance novels as one of the few tethers to my sanity at a time of great tumult and upheaval, and wondered *"Can I do that?"*. My eternal thanks to Amy who answered loudly *"You sure can!"*. Then, as if it weren't enough, proceeded to cheer and guide and encourage me every step of the way. Thanks, AC – this book literally would not exist without you and your willingness to answer my innumerable contextless questions.

Thank you to my earliest readers Hockey-Name, Le God-damned Situation, J Bird, D, and The Boss – you mean the world to me.

For all the struggles I had crafting this novel – and believe me when I say there were many – filling these pages with fully realised people wasn't one of them. Each and every passing character in these pages is real to me. I feel like if you picked any solitary one, I could give you a thousand-word essay on their backstory and fill you in on what they're doing right now. So, thank you Adrian,

Amy, Candice, Cheryl, Chloe, Chrissy, Deanna, Francine, Jennifer, Jill, Jordana, Karla, Leah, Lianne, Loffieann, Marie-Noëlle, Marr (and Martha!), Michelle, Nicole, Patty, Rachel, and Ryan for allowing me to shamelessly steal everything up to and including your names and family histories, hobbies, nationalities, social media handles, and your wonderful quirks and habits. (I realise "allow" is doing a lot of work, but… can we agree that getting a shout out here is fairly badass way of seeking forgiveness for the permission I didn't get in advance?)

Thank you to Faridah Àbíké-Íyímídé, for creating the Avengers of Colour Mentorship Program and to Priyanka Taslim for choosing me out of all possible candidates (#TeamMantis!) – your kindness, generosity, wealth of knowledge, and all-around brilliance have been a blessing. Please check out her YA debut The Love Match – it's phenomenal and I'm not just being biased. Shout out to my fellow Class of 2021 Mentees: Busayo Matuluko, Dawn Elize, Haroun Mansaur, Hien Fox, Keshe Chow, Lilian Lai, Nadia Bhatti, Shantal Small, Sulagna Hati, Trinity Nguyen, and Vanessa Uy who have taught me so much – I can't wait to fill my shelves with your books!

Thank you to the boundless generosity of the collective known as Romancelandia. Whether it was authors, agents, or editors sharing their experiences and resources, giving tips, or readers gushing about the myriad ways to celebrate Happily Ever After, I have been blown away by the depths of kindness of this group. To wit, I have benefitted from this group's fundraising efforts for: an author trying to escape housing insecurity, combatting voter suppression, reproductive justice, autism awareness, and aid for Maui. Thank you to Laura Wally Johnson, Jacie Floyd, Phyllis Laatsch, Susannah Nix, Jen Prokop, and Sherry Thomas for donating your time and expertise; and the Trigger Warning Romance and Buzzing About Romance podcasts, Bookmarked.Indie, and Paola Mancera, for the promotional opportunities. I can't ever thank you enough for being so very gracious with me and my abject newness to it all.

Thank you to Toronto Romance Writers for welcoming me and providing valuable resources and community. Thanks to Happily Ever After Books, Canada's first Romance Only bookstore, and North 49 Books, Canada's only trade books wholesaler, for your support.

I want to thank my family. Specifically my father, who has waited a long time for this moment; my mother, who doesn't think there's a thing I can't accomplish once I set my mind to it; my brother, who has always been my biggest fan; and to my big, loud, supportive, Latino-Caribbean family for filling my life with love, inspiration, and endless laughter.

To my real-life Ryan(s) – Auntie loves you so, so much!

And, finally, to my husband. You're not Davis and I'm not Junior but still… yours is the last kiss I'm ever gonna want.

See you all on the next one!

xx

About the Author

L INDO FORBES IS A first gen Canadian who lives in Toronto where you can find her at her day job or procrastinating on social media – sometimes both, simultaneously. She speaks enough French to not disgrace herself when she visits Montreal but not enough Spanish to please her abuela. She's also been known to spend her free time working on her works-in-progress, battling with the Libby App, thinking of varied ways to corrupt her nieces and nephews, holding grudges against fictional characters and celebrities she's never met, and/or searching for the world's best street food with her husband.

Join her mailing list to get updates on these very noble endeavors.